"You make me feel things I haven't in a long time. I'm sorry, Jase. I can't—"

He didn't wait for her to finish. There was no way he was going to listen to the word *can't* coming from her, not when she'd basically told him she wanted him. In one quick movement, he leaned down and brushed his lips over hers.

The moment was cut short when a dog barked—the sound coming from his house—and Emily pulled back. "You have a dog?"

"A puppy," he said, scrubbing a hand over his jaw and trying to get a handle on the lust raging through him. "Ruby—my pup—was the runt. She was weaker than the rest and her brothers and sister tended to pick on her."

"You rescue puppies, too? Unbelievable."

"It's not a big deal."

"Tell that to Ruby." She reached up on tiptoe, touched her lips to the corner of his mouth and then moved away. "You're damn near perfect, Jase Crenshaw."

"I'm not—"

"You are." She shook her head. "It's too bad for both of us that I gave up on perfect."

ALWAYS THE BEST MAN

BY
MICHELLE MAJOR

First Published in Great Britain 2016
By Mills & Boon, an imprint of HarperCollins*Publishers*
1 London Bridge Street, London, SE1 9GF

© 2016 Michelle Major

ISBN: 978-0-263-92009-3

23-0816

Our policy is to use papers that are natural, renewable and recyclable products and made from wood grown in sustainable forests. The logging and manufacturing processes conform to the legal environmental regulations of the country of origin.

Michelle Major grew up in Ohio but dreamed of living in the mountains. Soon after graduating with a degree in journalism, she pointed her car west and settled in Colorado. Her life and house are filled with one great husband, two beautiful kids, a few furry pets and several well-behaved reptiles. She's grateful to have found her passion writing stories with happy endings. Michelle loves to hear from her readers at www.michellemajor.com.

For Stephanie.
You have the strongest, bravest spirit of
any mother I know and you inspire me every day.

Chapter One

Some women were meant to be a bride. Emily Whitaker had been one of those women. For years she'd fantasized her walk down the aisle, imagining the lacy gown, the scent of her bouquet and the admiring eyes of family and friends as she entered the church.

When the day had finally arrived, there was no doubt she'd been beautiful, her shiny blond hair piled high on her head, perfect makeup and the dress—oh, her dress. She'd felt like a princess enveloped in so much tulle and lace, the sweetheart neckline both feminine and a little flirty.

Guests had whispered at her resemblance to Grace Kelly, and Emily had been foolish enough to believe that image was the same thing as reality. Her fairy tale had come true as her powerful white knight swooped her away from Crimson, the tiny Colorado mountain town where she'd grown up, to the sophisticated social circles of old-money Boston.

Too soon she discovered that a fantasy wedding was not the same thing as real marriage and a beautiful dress did not equate to a wonderful life. Emily lost her taste for both daydreams and weddings, so she wasn't sure how she'd found herself outside the swanky bridal boutique in downtown Aspen seven years after her own doomed vows.

"You can't want me as your maid of honor."

Katie Garrity, Emily's soon-to-be sister-in-law smiled. "Of course I do. I asked you, Em. I'd be honored to have you stand up with me." Katie's sweet smile faltered. "I mean, if you'll do it. I know it's short notice and there's a lot to coordinate in the next few weeks so…"

"It's not that I don't want to…"

Katie was as sweet as any of the cakes and cookies sold in the bakery she owned in downtown Crimson. She'd been a steadfast best friend to Emily's brother, Noah Crawford, for years before Noah realized that his perfect match had been right in front of him all along.

Emily was happy for the two of them, really she was. But if Katie was pure sugar, Emily was saccharine. She knew she was pretty to look at but after that first bite there was an artificial sweetness that left a cloying taste on the tongue. Emily didn't want her own bitterness to corrupt Katie's happy day.

"You have a lot of girlfriends. Surely there's a better candidate than me?"

"None of them are going to be my sister-in-law." Katie pressed her fingers to the glass of the shop's display window. "I remember the photos of your wedding that ran in *Town & Country* magazine. Noah and I don't want anything fancy, but I'd like our wedding to be beautiful."

"It will be more than beautiful." Emily swallowed back the anger that now accompanied thoughts of her marriage. "You two love each other, for better or worse." She took a breath as her throat clogged with emotion she'd thought had been stripped away during her divorce. She waved her hand in front of her face and made her voice light. "Plus all the other promises you'll make in the vows. But I'm not—"

"I'm a pregnant bride," Katie said suddenly, resting a hand on her still-flat stomach. She smiled but her eyes were shining. "I love your brother, Emily, and I know we'll have a good life together. But this isn't the order I planned things to happen, you know?"

"You and Noah were meant to be," Emily assured her. "Everyone knows that."

"Crimson is a small town with a long memory. People also know that I've had a crush on him for years and until I got pregnant, he had no interest in me."

Emily shook her head. "That's not how it happened." It had taken Katie walking away for Noah to realize how much she meant to him, but Emily knew his love for his fiancée was deep and true.

"It doesn't stop the talk. If I hear one more person whisper *shotgun wedding*—"

"Who?" Emily demanded. "Give me names and I'll take care of them for you." Since Emily had returned to Colorado at the beginning of the summer, she'd spent most of her time tucked away at her mother's farm outside town. She needed a do-over on her life, yet it was easier to hide out and lick her emotional wounds. But it wouldn't be difficult to ferret out the town's biggest gossips and grown-up mean girls. After all, Emily had been their ringleader once upon a time.

"What I need is for you to help me take care of the wedding," Katie answered softly. "To stand by my side and support me as I deal with the details. You may not care about the people in Crimson anymore, but I do. I want my big day to be perfect—as perfect as it can be under the circumstances. I don't want anyone to think I tried to force Noah or rush the wedding." She smoothed her fingers over her flowery shirt. "But I've only got a few weeks. Invitations have already gone out, and I haven't even started planning. Josh and Sara had one free weekend at Crimson Ranch this fall, and I couldn't wait any longer. I don't want to be waddling down the aisle."

"None of that matters to Noah. He'd marry you tomorrow or in the delivery room or whenever and wherever you say the word."

"It matters to me." Katie grimaced. "My parents are coming for the wedding. They haven't been to Crimson in years. I need it to be…" She broke off, bit down on her lip. "You're right. It doesn't matter. I love Noah, and I should just forget the rest of this. Why is a wedding such a big deal anyway?"

But Emily understood why, and she appreciated Katie's need for validation even if she didn't agree with it. So what if Emily no longer believed in marriage? She'd picked a husband for all the wrong reasons, but Katie and Noah were the real deal. If the perfect wedding would make Katie happy, then Emily would give her a day no one would forget.

"I could be the wedding planner, and you can ask one of your friends to—"

"I want *you*," Katie interrupted. "I'm an only child and now I'll have a sister. My family's messed up, but that makes me value the one I'm marrying into even more."

"I haven't valued them in the past few years." Emily felt her face redden, embarrassment over her behavior rushing through her, sharp and hot. "Until Davey was born I didn't realize how important family was to me."

"When your dad got sick, you helped every step of the way."

That much was true. Her father died when Emily was in high school. She'd taken over the care of the farm so her mom could devote time to Dad. Meg Crawford had driven him to appointments, cooked, cleaned and sat by his bedside in the last few weeks of home hospice care when the pancreatic cancer had ravaged his body.

It had been the last unselfish thing Emily had done in her life until she'd left her marriage, her so-called friends and the security of her life in Boston. As broken as she felt, she'd endure the pain and humiliation of those last six months again in a heartbeat for her son.

"You're a better person than you give yourself credit for," Katie said and opened the door of the store. The scent of roses drifted out, mingling with the crisp mountain air.

"I know exactly who I am." Emily removed her Prada sunglasses and tipped her face to the bright blue August sky. She'd missed the dry climate of Colorado during her time on the East Coast. It was refreshing to feel the warmth of the sun without miserable humidity making it feel like she'd stepped into an oven.

"Does that include being my maid of honor?" Katie asked over her shoulder, taking a step into the boutique.

"Shouldn't it be matron of honor?" Emily followed Katie, watching as she gingerly fingered the white gowns on the racks of the small shop. The saleswoman, an older lady with a pinched face, stepped forward. Emily waved her away for now. Shopping was one thing she could do with supreme confidence. Not much of a skill but today she'd put it to good use. "What's the protocol for having a divorcée as part of the bridal party?"

"I'm sticking with maid. There's nothing matronly about you." Katie pulled out a simple sheath dress, then frowned when Emily shook her head. "I think it's pretty."

"You have curves," Emily answered and pointed to Katie's full chest. "Especially with a baby on board. We want something that enhances them, not makes you look like a sausage."

Katie winced. "Don't sugarcoat it."

"We've got a couple of weeks to pull off the most amazing wedding Crimson has ever seen. You can be sweet. I don't have time to mess around."

"It doesn't have to be—"

Emily held up a hand, then stepped around Katie to pull a dress off the rack. "It's going to be. This is a good place to start."

Katie let out a soft gasp. "It's perfect. How did you do that?"

The dress was pale ivory, an empire waist chiffon gown with a lace overlay. It was classic but the tiny flowers stitched into the lace gave a hint of whimsy. The princess neckline would look beautiful against Katie's dark hair and creamy skin and the cut would be forgiving if she "popped" in the next few weeks. Emily smiled a little as she imagined Noah's reaction to seeing his bride for the first time.

"You're beautiful, Katie, and we're going to find the right dress." She motioned to the saleswoman. "We'll start with this one," she said, gently handing over the gown.

The woman nodded. "When is the big day?"

"Two weeks," Emily answered for Katie. "So we'll need something that doesn't have to be special ordered."

"Anything along this wall is in stock." The woman turned to Katie. "The fitting room is in the back. I'll hang the dress."

"Do I have to plan a cheesy bachelorette party, too?" Emily selected another dress and held it up for Katie's approval.

Katie ignored the dress, focusing her gaze on Emily "Is that your way of saying you'll be my maid of honor?"

Emily swallowed and nodded. This was not a big deal, two weeks of support and planning. So why did she feel like Katie was doing her the favor by asking instead of the other way around? "If you're sure?"

"Thank you," Katie shouted and gave Emily a huge hug.

This was why, she realized, as tears pricked the backs of her eyes. Emily hadn't had a real friend in years. The women who were part of her social circle in Boston had quickly turned on her when her marriage imploded, making her an outcast in their community. She'd burned most of her bridges with her Colorado friends when she'd dropped out of college to follow her ex-husband as he started his law career. Other than her mom and Noah, she had no one in her life she could count on. Until now.

She shrugged out of Katie's grasp and drew in a calming breath. "Who else is in the bridal party?"

"We're not having any other attendants," Katie told her. "I'll try on this one, too." She scooped up the dress and took a step toward the back of the store. "Just you and Jase. He's Noah's best man."

Emily stifled a groan and muttered, "Great." Jase Crenshaw had been her brother's best friend for years so she should have expected he'd be part of the wedding. Still, Crimson's favorite son was the last person she wanted to spend time with. He was the exact opposite of Emily—warm, friendly, easy-to-like. Around him her skin itched, her stomach clenched and she was generally made more aware of her long list of shortcomings. A real prince among men.

Katie turned suddenly and hugged Emily again. "I feel so much better knowing you're with me on this. For the first time I believe my wedding is going to be perfect."

Emily took another breath and returned the hug. She could do this, even with Jase working alongside her. Katie and Noah deserved it. "Perfect is my specialty," she told her friend with confidence. Behind her back, she kept her fingers crossed.

"What the hell was that?" Noah Crawford held out a hand to Jason Crenshaw, who was sprawled across the Crimson High School football field, head pounding and ears ringing.

Jase hadn't seen the hit coming until he was flat on his back in the grass. He should have been paying more attention, but in the moment before the ball was snapped, Emily Whitaker appeared in the stands. Jase had done his best to ignore the tall, willowy blond with the sad eyes and acid tongue since she'd returned to town.

Easier said than done since she was his best friend's sister and…well, since he'd had a crush on her for as long as he could remember. Since the first time she'd come after Jase and Noah for ripping the head from her favorite Barbie.

Emily'd packed quite a wallop back in the day.

Just not as much as Aaron Thompson, the opposing team's player who'd sacked Jase before running the ball downfield. Jase brushed away Noah's outstretched hand and stood, rubbing his aching ribs as he did. "I thought this was flag football," he muttered as he turned to watch Aaron do an elaborate victory dance in the end zone.

"Looks like Thompson forgot," Noah said, pulling off his own flag belt, then Jase's as they walked toward the sidelines.

"We'll get 'em next time." Liam Donovan, another teammate and good friend, gave Jase's shoulder a friendly shove. "If our quarterback can stay on his feet."

"This is a preseason game anyway," Logan Travers added. "Doesn't count."

"It counts that we whipped your butts," Aaron yelled, sprinting back up the field. He launched the game ball at Jase's head before Logan stepped forward and caught it.

"Back off, Thompson," Logan said softly, but it was hard to miss the steel in his tone. Logan was as tall as Jase's own six feet three inches but had the muscled build befitting the construction work he did. Jase was in shape, he ran and rock climbed in his free time. He also spent hours in front of his computer and in the courtroom for his law practice, so he couldn't compete with Logan's bulk.

He also wasn't much for physical intimidation. Not that Aaron would be intimidated by Jase. The Thompson family held a long-standing grudge against the Crenshaws, and hotheaded Aaron hadn't missed a chance to poke at him since they'd been in high school. Aaron's father, Charles, had been the town's sheriff back when Jase's dad was doing most of his hell raising and had made it clear he was waiting for Jase to carry on his family's reputation in Crimson.

Jase took a good measure of both pride and comfort in living in his hometown, but there were times he wished for some anonymity. They weren't kids anymore, and Jase had long ago given up his identity as the studious band geek who'd let bullies push him around to keep the peace.

He stepped forward, crossing his arms over his chest as he looked down his nose at the brutish deputy. "Talk is cheap, Aaron," he said. "And so are your potshots at me. We'll see you back on the field next month."

"Can't wait," Aaron said with a smirk Jase wanted to smack right off his face.

The feeling only intensified when Aaron jogged over to talk to Emily, who was standing with Katie and the other team wives and girlfriends on the sidelines.

"Let it go." Noah hung back as their friends approached the group of women. "She wouldn't give him the time of day in high school, and now is no different."

"Nice," Jase mumbled under his breath. "Aaron and I actually have something in common."

Noah laughed. "Katie's asked Emily to be the maid of honor. You'll have plenty of excuses to moon over her in the next few weeks."

Jase stiffened. "I *don't* moon."

"You keep telling yourself that," Noah said as he gave him a shove. "It doesn't matter anyway. Emily has her hands too full with Davey and starting over even if she wanted a man." He gave Jase a pointed, big-brother look. "Which she doesn't."

"I'm no threat," Jase said, holding up his hands. "Nothing has changed from when we were twelve. Your sister can't stand me."

"I get that but you'll both have to make an effort for the wedding. Katie doesn't need any extra stress right now."

"Got it," Jase agreed and glanced at his watch. "I've got to check in at the office before I head home."

"How's the campaign going?"

"Not much to report. It seems anticlimactic to run for mayor unopposed. Not much work to do except getting out the vote."

"You're more qualified for the position than anyone else in Crimson," Noah told him, "although I'm still not sure why city council and all the other volunteer work you do isn't enough?"

"I love this town, and I think I can help it move forward."

Noah smiled. "Emily calls you Saint Jase."

Jase felt his jaw tighten. "How flattering."

"She might have a point. What are your plans for the weekend? Katie and I are going out to Mom's place for a barbecue tomorrow night. Want to join us?"

Jase rarely had plans for the weekend. Juggling both

his law practice and taking care of his dad left little free time. But Emily would be there and while the rational part of him knew he shouldn't go out of his way to see her, the rest of him didn't seem to care. If he could get his father settled early tomorrow…

"Sounds good. What can I bring?"

"Really?" Noah's brows lifted. "You're venturing out on a Saturday night? Big time. We've got it covered. Come out around six."

"See you tomorrow," he said and headed over to his gym bag at the far side of the stands. He stripped off his sweaty T-shirt and pulled a clean one from the bag. As he straightened, Emily walked around the side of the metal bleachers, eyes glued to her cell phone screen as her thumbs tapped away. He didn't have time to voice a warning before she bumped into him.

As the tip of her nose brushed his bare chest, she yelped and stumbled back. The inadvertent touch lasted seconds but it reverberated through every inch of his body.

His heart lurched as he breathed her in—a mix of expensive perfume and citrus-scented shampoo. Delicate and tangy, the perfect combination for Emily. Noah had accused him of mooning but what he felt was more. He wanted her with an intensity that shook him to his core after all these years.

He'd thought he had his feelings for Emily under control, but this was emotional chaos. He was smart enough to understand it was dangerous as hell to the plans he had for his future. At this moment he'd give up every last thing to pull her close.

Instead he ignored the instinct to reach for her. When she was steady on her feet, he stepped away, clenching his T-shirt in his fists so hard his fingers went numb. "Looks like texting and walking might be as ill-advised as texting and driving."

"Thanks for the tip," she snapped, tucking her phone into the purse slung over her shoulder. Was it his imagination or was she flushed? Her breathing seemed as irregular as his felt. Then her pale blue eyes met his, cool and impassive. Of course he'd imagined Emily having any reaction to him beyond distaste. "My mom sent a photo of Davey."

"Building something?" he guessed.

"How do you know?"

"I was at the hospital the day of your mom's surgery. I made Lego sets with him while everyone was in the waiting room."

She gave the barest nod. Emily's mother, Meg, had been diagnosed with a meningioma, a type of brain tumor, at the beginning of the summer, prompting both Emily and Noah to return to Crimson to care for her. Luckily, the tumor had been benign and Meg was back to her normal, energetic self.

The Crawford family had already endured enough with the death of Emily and Noah's father over a decade ago. Having been raised by a single dad who was drunk more often than he was sober, Jase had spent many afternoons, weekends and dinners with the Crawfords. Meg was the mother he wished he'd had. Hell, he would have settled for an aunt or family friend who had a quarter of her loving nature.

But she'd been it, and lucky for Jase, Noah had been happy to share his mom and her affection. With neither of her kids living in town until recently and Meg never remarrying, Jase had become the stand-in when she had a leaky faucet that needed fixing or simply wanted company out at the family farm. He'd taken the news of her illness almost as hard as her real son.

"I remember," she whispered, not meeting his gaze.

"Every time I've been out to the farm this summer, Davey was building something. Your boy loves his Lego sets. He's—"

"Don't say obsessed," she interrupted, eyes flashing.

"I was going to say he has a great future as an engineer."

"Oh, right." She crossed her arms over her chest, her gaze dropping to the ground.

"I know five is young to commit to a profession," he added with a smile, "but Davey is pretty amazing." Something in her posture, a vulnerability he wouldn't normally associate with Emily made him add, "You're doing a great job with him."

Her rosy lips pressed together as a shudder passed through her. He'd meant the compliment and couldn't understand her reaction to his words. But she'd been different since her return to Crimson—fragile in a way she never was when they were younger.

"Emily." He touched a finger to the delicate bone of her wrist, the lightest touch but her gaze slammed into his. The emotion swirling through her eyes made him suck in a breath. "I mean it," he said, shifting so his body blocked her from view of the group of people still standing a few feet away on the sidelines. "You're a good mom."

She stared at him a moment longer, as if searching for the truth in his words. "Thanks," she whispered finally and blinked, breaking the connection between them. He should step away again, give her space to collect herself, but he didn't. He couldn't.

She did instead, backing up a few steps and tucking a lock of her thick, pale blond hair behind one ear. Her gaze dropped from his, roamed his body in a way that made him warm all over again. Finally she looked past him to their friends. "Katie told me you're the best man."

He nodded.

"I've got some ideas for the wedding weekend. I want it to be special for both of them."

"Let me know what you need from me. Happy to help in any way."

"I will." She straightened her shoulders and when she looked at him again, it was pure Emily. A mix of condescension and ice. "A good place to start would be putting on some clothes," she said, pointing to the shirt still balled in his fist. "No one needs a prolonged view of your bony bod."

It was meant as an insult and a reminder of their history. She'd nicknamed him Bones when he'd grown almost a foot the year of seventh grade. No matter what he'd eaten, he couldn't keep up with his height and had been a beanpole, all awkward adolescent arms and legs. From what he remembered, Emily hadn't experienced one ungainly moment in all of her teenage years. She'd always been perfect.

And out of his league.

He pulled the shirt over his head and grabbed his gym bag. "I'll remember that," he told her and walked past her off the field.

Chapter Two

Emily lifted the lip gloss to her mouth just as the doorbell to her mother's house rang Saturday night. She dropped the tube onto the dresser, chiding herself for making an effort with her appearance before a casual family dinner. Particularly silly when the guest was Jase Crenshaw, who meant nothing to her. Who probably didn't want to be in the same room with her.

Not when she'd been so rude to him after the football game with her reference to his body. He had to know the insult was absurd. He might have been a tall skinny teen but now he'd grown into his body in a way that made her feel weak in the knees.

That weakness accounted for her criticism. Emily had spent the last year of her marriage feeling fragile and unsettled. Jase made her feel flustered in a different way, but she couldn't allow herself be affected by any man when she was working so hard to be strong.

Of course she'd known Jase liked her when they were younger, but she hadn't been interested in her brother's best friend or anyone from small-town Crimson. Emily'd had her sights set on bigger things, like getting out of Colorado. Henry Whitaker and his powerful family had provided the perfect escape at the time.

Sometimes she wished she could ignore the changes in herself. She glanced at the mirror again. The basics were the same—blond hair flowing past her shoulders, blue eyes and symmetrical features. People would still look at her and see a beautiful woman, but she wondered if anyone saw beyond the surface.

Did they notice the shadows under her eyes, the result of months of restless nights when she woke and tiptoed to Davey's doorway to watch him sleeping? Could they tell she couldn't stop the corners of her lips from perpetually pulling down, as if the worry over her son was an actual weight tugging at their edges?

No. People saw what they wanted, like she'd wanted to see her ex-husband as the white knight that would sweep her off to the charmed life she craved. Only now did she realize perfection was a dangerous illusion.

She heard Jase's laughter drift upstairs and felt herself swaying toward the open door of the bedroom that had been hers since childhood. Her mom had taken the canopy off the four-poster bed and stripped the posters from the walls, but a fresh coat of paint and new linens couldn't change reality.

Emily was a twenty-eight year old woman reduced to crawling back to the financial and emotional safety of her mother's home. She dipped her head, her gaze catching on a tiny patch of pink nail polish staining the corner of the dresser. It must have been there for at least ten years, back when a bright coat of polish could lift her spirits. She'd had so many dreams growing up, but now all she wanted was to make things right for her son.

"Em, dinner is almost ready," her mom called from the bottom of the stairs.

"Be right there," she answered. She scraped her thumbnail against the polish, watching as it flaked and fell to the floor. Something about peeling a bit of her girlhood from the dresser made her breathe easier and she turned for the door. She took a step, then whirled back and picked up the lip gloss, dabbing a little on the center of her mouth and pressing her lips together. Maybe she couldn't erase the shadows under her eyes, but Emily wasn't totally defeated yet.

Before heading through the back of the house to the patio where Noah was grilling burgers, she turned at the bottom of the stairs toward her father's old study. Since she and Davey had returned, her mom had converted the wood-paneled room to building block headquarters. It had been strange, even ten years after her father's death, to see his beloved history books removed from the shelves to make room for the intricate building sets her son spent hours creating. Her mother had taken the change easier than Emily, having had years alone in the house to come to terms with her husband's death. That sense of peace still eluded Emily, but she liked to think her warmhearted, gregarious father would be happy that his office was now a safe place for Davey.

Tonight Davey wasn't alone on the thick Oriental rug in front of the desk. Jase sat on the floor next to her son, long legs sprawled in front of him. He looked younger than normal, carefree without the burden of taking care of the town weighing down his shoulders. Both of their heads were bent to study something Jase held, and Emily's breath caught as she noticed her son's hand resting on Jase's leg, their arms brushing as Davey leaned forward to hand Jase another Lego piece.

She must have made a sound because Jase glanced up, an almost apologetic smile flashing across his face. "You found us," he said and handed Davey the pieces before standing. Davey didn't look at her but turned toward his current model, carefully adding the new section to it.

"Dinner's ready," she said, swallowing to hide the emotion that threatened to spill over into her voice.

Jase had known her too long to be fooled. "Hope it's okay I'm in here with him." He gestured to the bookshelves that held neat rows of building sets. "He's got an impressive collection."

"He touched you," she whispered, taking a step back into the hall. Not that it mattered. Her son wasn't listening. When Davey was focused on finishing one of his creations, the house could fall down around him and he wouldn't notice.

"Is that bad?" Jase's thick brows drew down, and he ran a hand through his hair, as if it would help him understand her words. His dark hair was in need of a cut and his fingers tousled it, making her want to brush it off his forehead the way she did for Davey as he slept.

"It's not...it's remarkable. He was diagnosed with Asperger's this summer. It was early for a formal diagnosis, but I'd known something was different with him for a while." Emily couldn't help herself from reaching out to comb her fingers through the soft strands around Jase's temples. It was something to distract herself from the fresh pain she felt when talking about

Davey. "Building Lego sets relaxes him. He doesn't like to be touched and will only tolerate a hug from me sometimes. To see him touching you so casually, as if it were normal..."

Jase lifted his hand and took hold of hers, pulling it away from his head but not letting go. He cradled it in his palm, tracing his thumb along the tips of her fingers. She felt the subtle pressure reverberate through her body. Davey wasn't the only one uncomfortable being touched.

Since her son's symptoms had first started and her ex-husband's extreme reaction to them had launched the destruction of their family, Emily felt like she was made of glass.

Now as she watched Jase's tanned fingers gently squeeze hers, she wanted more. She wanted to step into this tall, strong, good man who could break through her son's walls without even realizing it and find some comfort for herself.

"I'm glad for it," he said softly, bringing her back to the present moment. "What about his dad?"

She snatched away her hand, closed her fist tight enough that her nails dug small half-moons into her palm. "My ex-husband wanted a son who could bond with him tossing a ball or sailing. The Whitakers are a competitive family, and even the grandkids are expected to demonstrate their athletic prowess. It's a point of pride and bragging rights for Henry and his brothers—whose kid can hit a ball off the tee the farthest or catch a long pass, even if it's with a Nerf football."

Jase glanced back at her son. "Davey's five, right? It seems a little young to be concerned whether or not he's athletic."

"That didn't matter to my in-laws, and it drove Henry crazy. He couldn't understand it. As Davey's symptoms became more pronounced, his father pushed him harder to be the *right* kind of boy."

She pressed her mouth into a thin line to keep from screaming the next words. "He forbade me from taking him to the doctor to be tested. His solution was to punish him, take away the toys he liked and force him into activities that ended up making us all more stressed. Davey started having tantrums and fits, which only infuriated Henry. He was getting ready to run for congress." She rolled her eyes. "The first step in the illustrious political campaign his family has planned."

"Following in his father's footsteps," Jase murmured.

It was true. Emily had married into one of the most well-known political families in the country since the Kennedys. The Whitakers had produced at least one US senator in each of the past five generations of men, and one of Henry's great-uncles had been vice president. "I didn't just marry a man, I took on a legacy. The worst part was I went in with my eyes open. I practically interviewed for the job of political wife, and I was ready to be a good one." She snapped her fingers. "I could throw a party fit for the First Lady with an hour's notice."

Jase cleared his throat. "I'm sure your husband appreciated that."

She gave a harsh laugh. "He didn't appreciate it. He expected it. There's a big difference." She shrugged. "None of it mattered once Davey was born. I knew from the time he was a baby he was different and I tried to hide...tried to protect him from Henry as long as possible. But once I couldn't anymore, there was no doubt about my loyalty." She plastered a falsely bright smile on her face. "So here I am back in Crimson."

Davey looked up from his building set. "I'm finished, Mommy."

She stepped around Jase and sat on the carpet to admire the intricate structure Davey had created. "Tell me about it, sweetie."

"It's a landing pod with a rocket launcher. It's like the ones they have on *The Clone Wars*, only this one has an invisible force field around it so no one can destroy it."

If only she could put a force field around her son to protect him from the curiosity and potential ridicule that could come due to his differences from other kids. "I love it, Wavy-Davey."

One side of his mouth curved at the nickname before he glanced at Jase. "He helped. He's good at building. Better than Uncle Noah or Grammy."

"High praise," Jase said, moving toward the bookshelves. "If you make a bridge connecting it to this one, you'd have the start of an intergalactic space station."

Emily darted a glance at Davey as Jase moved one of the sets a few inches to make room for this new one. Her boy didn't like anyone else making decisions about the placement of his precious building sets. To her surprise, Davey only nodded. "I'll need to add a hospital and mechanic's workshop 'cause if there's a battle they'll need those."

"Maybe a cafeteria and bunk room?" Jase suggested.

"You can help me with those if you want." Leaving Emily speechless where she sat, Davey gently lifted the new addition and carried it to the bookshelf. With Jase's help, he slid it into place with a satisfied nod. "I'm hungry. Can we eat?" he asked, turning to Emily.

"Sure thing," she agreed. "Grammy, Uncle Noah and Aunt Katie are waiting." Her family was used to waiting as transitions were one of Davey's biggest challenges. Sometimes it took long minutes to disengage him from a project.

Her son stepped forward, his arms ramrod straight at his sides. "It's time, Mommy. I'm ready."

She almost laughed at the confusion clouding Jase's gaze. People went in front of a firing squad with more enthusiasm than Davey displayed right now. It would have been funny if this ritual didn't break her heart the tiniest bit. Embarrassment flooded through her at what Jase might think, but the reward was too high to worry about a little humiliation.

She rose to her knees and opened her arms. Davey stepped forward and she pulled him close, burying her nose in his neck to breathe him in as she gave him a gentle hug. A few moments were all he could handle before he squirmed in her embrace. "I love you," she whispered before letting him go.

He met her gaze. "I know," he answered simply, then turned and walked out of the room.

She stood, wiping her cheeks. Why bother to hide the tears? She'd left the lion's share of her pride, along with most of her other possessions, back in Boston.

"Sorry," she said to Jase, knowing her smile was watery at best. Emily might be considered beautiful, but she was an ugly crier. "It's a deal he and I have. Every time he finishes a set, I get a hug. A real one."

"Emily," he whispered.

"Don't say anything about it, please. I can't afford to lose it now. It's dinnertime, and I don't need to give my family one more reason to worry about me."

A muscle ticked in his jaw, but he nodded. "In case no one has said it lately," he said as she moved past, "your ex-husband may be political royalty, but he's also a royal ass. You deserve to be loved better." The deep timbre of his voice rumbled through her like a cool waterfall, both refreshing and fierce in its power.

She shivered but didn't stop walking out of the room. Reality kept her moving forward. Davey was her full reason for being now. There was no use considering what she did or didn't deserve.

Chapter Three

"Is that you, Jase?"

"Yeah, Dad." Jase slipped into the darkened trailer and flipped on the light. "I'm here. How's it going?"

"I could use a beer," Declan Crenshaw said with a raspy laugh. "Or a bottle of whiskey. Any chance you brought whiskey?"

His father was sprawled on the threadbare couch that had rested against the thin wall of the mobile home since Jase could remember. Nothing in the cramped space had changed from the time they'd first moved in. The trailer's main room was tiny, barely larger than the dorm room Jase had lived in his first year at the University of Denver. From the front door he could see back to the bedroom on one side and through the efficiency kitchen with its scratched Formica counters and grainy wood cabinets to the family room on the other.

"No alcohol." He was used to denying his dad's requests for liquor. Declan had been two years sober and Jase was hopeful this one was going to stick. He was doing everything in his power to make sure it did. Checking on his dad every night was just part of it. "How about water or a cup of tea?"

"Do I look like the queen of England?" Declan picked up the potato chip bag resting next to him on the couch and placed it on the scuffed coffee table, then brushed off his shirt, chip crumbs flying everywhere.

"No one's going to mistake you for royalty." Jase's dad looked like a man who'd lived a hard life, the vices that had consumed him for years made him appear decades older than his sixty years. If the alcohol and smoking weren't enough, Declan had spent most of his adult life working in the active mines around Crimson, first the Smuggler silver mine outside of Aspen and then later the basalt-gypsum mine high on Crimson Mountain.

Between the dust particles, the constant heavy lifting, operating jackhammers and other heavy equipment, the work took a physical toll on the men and women employed by the mines. Jase had tried to get his father to quit for years, but it was only after a heart attack three years ago that Declan had been forced to retire. Unfortunately, having so much time on his hands had led him to a six-month drunken binge that had almost killed him. Jase needed to believe he wasn't going to have to watch his father self-destruct ever again.

"Maybe they should since you're a royal pain in my butt," Declan growled.

"Good one, Dad." Jase didn't take offense. Insults were like terms of endearment to his father. "Why are you sitting here in the dark?" He picked up the chip bag and dropped it in the trash can in the kitchenette, then started washing the dishes piled in the sink.

"Damn cable is out again. I called but they can't get here until tomorrow. If I lose my DVRed shows, there's gonna be hell to pay. *The Real Housewives* finale was on tonight. I wanted to see some rich-lady hair pulling."

Jase smiled. Since his dad stopped drinking, he'd become addicted to reality TV. Dance moms, little people, bush people, swamp people, housewives. Declan watched them all. "Maybe you should get a hobby besides television. Take a walk or volunteer."

His dad let out a colorful string of curses. "My only other hobby involves walking into a bar, so I'm safer holed up out here. And I'm not spending my golden years working for free. Hell, I barely made enough to pay the bills with my regular job. There's only room for one do-gooder in this family, and that's you."

It was true. The Crenshaws had a long history of living on the wrong side of the law in Crimson. There was even a sepia-stained photo hanging in the courthouse that showed his great-great-grandfather sitting in the old town jail. Jase had consciously set out to change his family's reputation. Most of his life decisions had been influenced by wanting to be something different...something more than the Crenshaw legacy of troublemaking.

"I read in the paper that you're sponsoring a pancake breakfast next week."

Jase placed the last mug onto the dish drainer, then turned. "It's part of my campaign."

"Campaigning against yourself?" his dad asked with a chuckle.

"It's a chance for people to get to know me."

Declan stood, brushed off his shirt again. "Name one person who doesn't know you."

"They don't know me as a candidate. I want to hear what voters think about how the town is doing, ideas for the future—where Crimson is going to be in five or ten years."

His dad yawned. "Same place it's been for the last hundred years. Right here."

"You know what I mean."

"Yeah, I know." Declan patted Jase on the back. "You're a good boy, Jason Damien Crenshaw. Better than I deserve as a son. It's got to be killing Charles Thompson and his boys that a Crenshaw is going to be running this town." His dad let out a soft chuckle. "I may give ex–Sheriff Thompson a call and see what he thinks."

"Don't, Dad. Leave the history between us and the Thompsons in the past where it belongs." Jase didn't mention the hit Aaron had put on him during the football game, which would only make his father angry.

"You're too nice for your own good. Why don't you pick me up before the breakfast?" Declan had lost his license during his last fall from the wagon and hadn't bothered to get it reinstated. Jase took him to doctor's appointments, delivered groceries and ran errands—an inconvenience, but it also helped him keep track of Declan. Something that hadn't always been easy during the heaviest periods of drinking. "I'll campaign for you. Call it volunteer work and turn my image around in town."

Jase swallowed. He'd encouraged his father to volunteer almost as a joke, knowing Declan never would. But campaigning… Jase loved his dad but he'd done his best to distance himself from the reputation that followed his family like a plague. "We'll see, Dad. Thanks for the offer. Are you heading to bed?"

"Got nothing else to do with no channels working."

"I'll call the cable company in the morning and make sure you're on the schedule," Jase promised. "Lock up behind me, okay?"

"Who's going to rob me?" Declan swept an arm around the trailer's shabby interior. "I've got nothing worth stealing."

"Just lock up. Please."

When his father eventually nodded, Jase let himself out of the trailer and headed home. Although he'd driven the route between the trailer park and his historic bungalow on the edge of downtown countless times, he forced himself to stay focused.

Three miles down the county highway leading into town. Two blocks until a right turn onto his street. Four hundred yards before he saw his mailbox. Keeping his mind on the driving was less complicated than giving the thoughts and worries crowding his head room to breathe and grow.

He parked his silver Jeep in the driveway, since his dad's ancient truck was housed in the garage. It needed transmission work that Jase didn't have time for before it would run again, and Declan had no use for it without a license. But Jase couldn't bring himself to sell it. It represented something he couldn't name…a giving in to the permanence of caring for an aging parent that he wasn't ready to acknowledge.

He locked the Jeep and lifted his head to the clear night. The stars were out in full force, making familiar designs across the sky. He hadn't used his old telescope in years, but Jase never tired of stargazing.

Something caught his eye, and when he looked around the front of his truck everything in the world fell away except the woman standing in his front yard.

Emily.

He wasn't sure where she'd come from or how he hadn't noticed her when he pulled up. Out of the corner of his eye he saw her mom's 4Runner parked across the street.

She didn't say anything as he approached, only watched him, her hands clasped tight together in front of her waist. Her fingers were long and elegant like the rest of her. As much as he would never wish her pain, the fact that she wore no wedding ring made him perversely glad.

"Hi," he said when he was in front of her, then silently cursed himself. He was an attorney and a town council member, used to giving speeches and closing arguments to courtrooms and crowded meetings. The best he could come up with now was *Hi*? Lame.

"I owe you an apology," she whispered. "And I didn't want to wait. I hate waiting."

He remembered that about her and felt one side of his mouth curve. Her mother, Meg, had been an expert baker when they were kids and Emily had forever been burning her mouth on a too-hot cookie after school.

"You don't owe me anything."

She shook her head. "No, it's true. You were good with Davey tonight. Before bed he told me he wants to invite you for a playdate."

He chuckled. "I told you we bonded over plastic bricks."

"His father never bonded with him," she said with a

strangled sigh. "Despite my brother's best efforts, Noah has trouble engaging him." She shrugged, a helpless lift of her shoulders that made his heart ache. "Even I have trouble connecting with him sometimes. I understand it's the Asperger's, and I love him the way he is. But you're the first…friend he's ever had."

"He'll do fine at school."

"What if he doesn't? He's so special, but he's not like other boys his age."

"He's different in some ways, but kids manage through those things. I didn't have the greatest childhood or any real friends until I met your brother. I was too tall, too skinny and too poor. My dad was the town drunk and everyone knew it. But it made me stronger. I swear. Once I met Noah and your family took me in—"

"I didn't."

"No. You hated me being in your house."

"It wasn't about… I'm sorry, Jase. For how I treated you."

"Em, you don't have to—"

"I do." She stepped forward, so close that even in the pale streetlight he could see the brush of freckles across her nose. "I haven't been kind to you even since I've come back. It's like the nice part of my brain short-circuits when you're around."

"Good to know."

"What I said to you the other day on the football field about putting on your shirt."

He winced. "My bony bod…"

"Had nothing to do with it. You're not a skinny kid anymore. You must know…" She stopped, looked away, tugged her bottom lip between her teeth, then met his gaze again.

Something shifted between them; a current of awareness different than anything he'd experienced surged to life in the quiet night air.

"The women of this town would probably pay you to keep your shirt off." She jabbed one finger into his chest. "All. The. Time."

He laughed, because this was Emily trying to be nice and still she ended up poking him. "I'm popular at the annual car wash, but I figure it's because most of the other men on the council are so old no one wants them to have a heart attack while bending to soap up a front fender."

She didn't return his smile but eased the tiniest bit closer. "I didn't want you standing bare chested in front of me because I wanted to kiss you."

Jase sucked in a breath.

"I wanted to put my mouth on you, right there on the sidelines of the high school field with half of our friends watching." She said the words calmly, although he could see her chest rising and falling. He wasn't the only one having trouble breathing right now. "That's something different than when we were young. You make me feel things I haven't in a long time, and I don't know what to do about it. But it doesn't give me the right to be rude. I'm sorry, Jase. I can't—"

He didn't wait for her to finish. There was no way he was going to listen to the word *can't* coming from her, not when she'd basically told him she wanted him. In one quick movement, he leaned down and brushed his lips over hers.

So this was where she hid her softness, he thought. The taste of her, the feel of her mouth against his. All of it was so achingly sweet.

Then she opened her mouth to him and he deepened the kiss, threading his fingers through her hair as their tongues glided together. It was every perfect kiss he'd imagined and like nothing he'd experienced before. He wanted to stay linked with her forever, letting all of his responsibilities and the rest of the damn world melt away.

The moment was cut short when a dog barked—the sound coming from his house, and Emily pulled back. Her fingers lifted to her mouth and he wasn't sure whether it was to press his kiss closer or wipe it away. Right now it didn't matter.

"You have a dog?" she asked, glancing at his darkened front porch.

"A puppy," he said, scrubbing a hand over his jaw and trying to get a handle on the lust raging through him. "My former secretary Donna had a female Australian shepherd that got loose while in heat. They ended up with a litter of puppies, part shepherd and part who knows what?"

The barking turned into a keening howl, making him cringe. "Maybe elephant based on the size of their paws. But Ruby—my pup—was the runt. She was weaker than the rest and her brothers and sister tended to pick on her. They kept her, but it wasn't working with their other dogs. I went for dinner last week and…" The barking started again. "I need to let her out to do her business. Do you want to meet her?"

Emily shook her head and a foolish wave of disappointment surged through him.

"I need to get back to the farm. Mom thinks I was running to the store for…" She broke off, gave an embarrassed laugh, then looked at him again. "You rescue puppies, too? Unbelievable."

"It's not a big deal."

"Tell that to Ruby." She reached up on tiptoe, touched her lips to the corner of his mouth and then moved away. "You're damn near perfect, Jase Crenshaw."

"I'm not—"

"You are." She shook her head. "It's too bad for both of us that I gave up on perfect."

Before he could answer, she walked away. He waited, watching until she'd gotten in the SUV and pulled down his street. Until her taillights were swallowed in the darkness. Then the silence enveloped him once more, and he wondered if he'd dreamed the past few minutes.

An increasingly insistent bark snapped him back to the land of the wide-awake. He jogged to the front door and unlocked it, moving quickly to the crate in his family room. Her fluffy tail wagged and she greeted him with happy nips and yelps. He led her to the back door and she darted out, tumbling down the patio steps to find her perfect spot in-yard.

He sank down to the worn wood and waited for her to finish, lavishing praise when she wiggled her way back to him.

"I've got a story for you," he told the puppy as she covered him in dog slobber. "It's been quite a night, Ruby-girl."

Early Tuesday morning, Emily pasted a bright smile on her face before opening the door to Life Is Sweet, the bakery Katie owned in downtown Crimson. The soothing scent of sugar and warm dough washed over her as she automatically moved toward the large display case at the front of the shop.

The ambiance of the cozy bakery cheered her, even with the hellish morning of job interviews and application submissions she'd had. No surprise that businesses weren't lining up to hire an overqualified, single-mom college dropout who could only work part-time hours and needed to be able to take off when her son had a bad day. Yet it felt personal, as if the town she'd so easily left behind wasn't exactly opening its arms to welcome her back.

Life Is Sweet was different. With the warm yellow walls and wood beams stretching the length of the ceiling, the shop immediately welcomed customers both new and familiar. A grouping of café tables sat in one corner of the small space and the two women working the counter and coffee bar waved to her.

Katie pushed through the door to the back kitchen a moment later, carrying a large metal tray of croissants that she set on the counter.

"Should you be carrying pastries in your condition?" Emily asked with a laugh. Last weekend during dinner, Noah hadn't let Katie bring any of the serving bowls out to the table on the patio or clear the dishes. In fact, he'd all but insisted she sit the whole time they were at their mother's house. No matter what any of the women had told him about Katie and the baby remaining healthy despite normal activities, he couldn't seem to stop fawning over his wife-to-be.

Katie rolled her eyes. "I would have never guessed your brother had such an overprotective streak. He wants me to cut back even more on my hours at the bakery." She waved to one of the customers sitting at a café table, then looked at Emily. "I've hired a manager to run the front, but I'm still in charge of most of the baking. As long as my doctor says it's okay, I want to keep working."

"He'll get over it. I'll talk to him. Dad's death made him funny about keeping everyone he loves healthy." Her whole family had felt helpless when the pancreatic cancer claimed her father, and it had taken years for Noah to get over the guilt of not being around to help those last months.

When their mom had her health scare, Noah had returned to Crimson right away and remained at Meg's side for the duration of her recovery. But losing one parent and being scared for the other had taken a toll on him, and Emily understood his reasons for wanting Katie to be so careful.

"I know, and I love him for it." Katie sighed. "The morning sickness is done, so I feel great." She put all but two of the croissants in the case. "I'm just hungry all the time. Can I interest you in a coffee-and-croissant break? They're chocolate."

"How did you know I need chocolate?"

"Everyone needs chocolate." Katie set the remaining pastries on a plate, then poured Emily a cup of coffee and handed it to her. "You look like you've been through the job search gauntlet today." She got the attention of one of the women working the counter and mouthed "Five minutes." There was a line forming at the cash register so the worker gave her a harried nod. "Let's go to the kitchen. More privacy."

"You're swamped right now. I'm fine."

"Never too swamped for a snack," Katie answered and picked up the plate. She led Emily through a heavy swinging door into the commercial kitchen. "I'm going to sit on a stool while you take my picture and text it to Noah. You're the witness that I'm not working too hard."

Emily snapped the photo, sent it to her brother and then pulled off a piece of the flaky dough. "Fresh from the oven?" she asked as she popped the bite into her mouth. She climbed onto a stool next to Katie, trailing her fingers across the cool stainless steel counter.

"The best kind."

"If my brother becomes too much of a pain, I'll marry you," Emily said when she finished chewing. The croissant melted in her mouth, buttery and soft with the perfect amount of chocolate in the middle.

"Don't distract me with flattery," Katie answered but moaned as she took a bite. "What happened today?"

"No one feels a burning desire to hire the woman who publicly ridiculed the town on her way out."

Katie made a face. "It was a well-known fact that you had no plans to stay in Crimson any longer than necessary."

"Or maybe I got drunk one night and announced to a bar full of locals that I was too good to waste away in this…"

"*Hellhole mountain slum*, I think you called it."

"Right. Classy."

"And endearing," Katie agreed, clearly having trouble keeping a straight face.

"I'm stupid." Emily pressed her forehead to the smooth stainless steel, let it soothe the massive headache she could feel starting behind her eyes.

"You can make this better," Katie said, placing a hand on Emily's back. "Crimson has a long history of forgiving mistakes."

"And an even longer one of punishing people for them." She tipped her head to the side. "Look at how hard Jase has worked to make amends for trouble he didn't even cause."

"But people love him."

"Because he's perfect."

"Why are you so hard on him, Em?"

Emily shook her head, unable to put into words her odd and tumbling emotions around Jase.

"You could work for him," Katie said with a laugh.

"For Jase?" Emily asked, lifting her head. "What do you mean?"

"I'm joking," Katie said quickly. "From what I can tell it bothers you to be in the same room with him."

"That's not exactly true." Emily had really liked Jase kissing her. It had been easy to lose herself in the gentle pressure of his mouth. His hands cradling her face made her feel cherished. She'd wanted to plaster herself against him and forget she was alone, at least for a few minutes. She was definitely bothered by Jase, but not in the way Katie believed. "Is he hiring for his campaign?"

"No," Katie answered slowly, as if reluctant to share what she knew. "His secretary retired a few months ago."

"The one with the litter of puppies?"

"How did you know about that?"

Emily ignored the question. "Why hasn't he hired someone?"

"He won't say, but as far as I know he hasn't even interviewed anyone for the position." Katie took another bite of pastry. "There are plenty of people who would love to work with him."

"Plenty of single women," Emily clarified.

"He's pretty hot," Katie said, her smile returning. "Not as handsome as Noah, of course. He makes me—"

"I'm working on being a good friend." Emily held up a hand. "But I draw the line on listening to you ruminate on the hotness of my brother." She hopped off her stool and took a final drink of coffee. "Break's over, friend. I just got a tip on a job opening." She picked up the plate and walked it over to the sink.

"Are you sure that's a good idea?"

"Clearing my plate?"

"Asking Jase for a job."

Emily straightened her suit jacket and smiled, pretending the nervous butterflies zipping through her belly didn't exist. "I'm not sure, but when has that ever stopped me?"

She gave Katie a short hug. "Thanks for listening. You're a pro at this whole supportive girlfriend thing."

Katie returned her smile. "Good luck, Em."

"I've got this," Emily answered with more confidence than she felt. But bluffing was second nature to her, so she squared her shoulders and marched out of the bakery to get herself a job.

Chapter Four

Jase reached for the file folder on the far side of his desk just as he heard Emily call his name. His hand jerked, knocking over the cup of leftover coffee that sat on another stack of papers, dark liquid spilling across the messy top of his desk.

"Damn," he muttered, grabbing the old towel he'd stuffed under the credenza behind him. This wasn't the first time most of his work papers had been dyed coffee brown. The mug had been half-empty so this cleanup wasn't the worst he'd seen. He quickly wiped up the spill, then moved the wet files to the row of cabinets shoved along the far wall.

By the time he turned around, Emily stood inside the door to his office. Her blue gaze surveyed the disorder of his office before flicking back to him. "Is it always this bad?"

He kicked the dirty towel out of sight behind his

desk. "I've got things under control. It only looks like chaos."

She arched a brow. "Right."

Jase hadn't seen Emily since she'd walked away from him Saturday night. Letting her go had been one of the hardest things he'd ever done, but Emily wasn't the same proud, confident girl she'd been in high school. Whatever had happened when her marriage fell apart had left her bruised and tender. Jase had always been a patient man, and if she needed him to go slow he could force himself to honor that.

She didn't appear fragile now. This morning Emily wore a tailored skirt suit that looked like it cost more than the monthly rent on his office space. It was dark blue and the hem stopped just at her knee. Combined with low heels, a tight bun and a strand of pearls around her neck, Jase could imagine her on the stage next to her ex-husband, the perfect accessory for a successful politician.

He wanted to pull her hair loose, rip off the necklace that was more like a collar and kiss her until her skin glowed and her mouth turned pliant under his. Until he could make her believe she was more than the mask she wore like a coat of armor.

"Why haven't you hired a new secretary?"

He blinked, the question as much of a surprise as her appearance in his office. "I don't need one."

"Even you can't believe that." She nudged a precariously balanced pile of manila folders with one toe, then bent forward to right it when the stack threatened to topple.

"I haven't had time," he said, running a hand through his hair and finding it longer than he remembered. A haircut was also on his to-do list. "I did some interviewing when Donna first retired. She took a medical leave when her husband had a heart attack, and then they decided to simplify their lives and working here got cut. But she'd been with the practice when I took it over and ran this place and my life with no trouble at all. If I hire someone new, I'll have to train them and figure out if we can work together and…" He paused, not sure how to explain the rest.

"Let me guess." She arched a brow. "The women applying for the job think they're also interviewing for the role of your wife?"

"Maybe," he admitted, grabbing the empty coffee cup from his desk and walking toward her. There were plenty of single men in Crimson, so it was an irritating mystery how he'd ended up on the top of the eligible bachelor list. He didn't have time for dating, and even if he did…

"It would have been easier if Donna had helped screen the applicants."

One side of her mouth curved even as she rolled her crystal-blue eyes. "Because you have trouble hurting their feelings."

"You think you've got me all figured out."

She shrugged. "You're nice, Jase. Not complicated."

He touched the tip of one finger to her strand of pearls. "Unlike you?"

She sucked in a breath and stepped back so he could pass. There was a small utility sink in the kitchenette off the hallway, and he added the cup to the growing pile of dirty dishes. When he turned around, Emily was standing behind him, holding four more mugs by their handles.

"You forgot these."

He sighed and reached for them. Add washing dishes to the list.

"I appreciate the social call, but was there a reason you stopped by?" He turned and moved closer, into her space. "Unless you want to continue what we started Saturday night. That kind of work break I can use."

"No break and Saturday night was a mistake." She frowned. "You and I both know it."

He wanted to kiss the tension right off her face. "Then why can't I stop thinking about how you felt pressed against me?" He dropped his voice. "The way you taste…"

Color rose to her cheeks.

"I'm not the only one, am I? You walked away but you came back." His fingers itched to touch her. "You're here now."

"This isn't a social call." Emily straightened the hem of her jacket, looking almost nervous. "I think you should hire me."

Jase almost laughed, then realized she was serious. "No." He shook his head. "No way."

"Don't I at least get an interview?" Now her gaze turned mutinous. "That's not fair. I can do it." She spun on her heel and marched toward the front of his office. The space had a tiny lobby, two interior offices and a conference room. Jase loved the location just off Main Street in downtown Crimson.

The receptionist desk had become another place to stack papers since Donna'd left, and as he followed Emily toward the front door he realized how cluttered the area had become. Damn.

She picked up a thin messenger bag from one of the

lobby chairs and pulled out a single sheet of paper. "My résumé," she said, handing it to him. He stared at it, but didn't take it from her. Her mouth thinned. "During college I was an academic assistant for two law school faculty members. I managed calendars, helped with grant proposals and assisted in the preparation of teaching materials. I'm organized and will work hard. I can come in two days this week, and then make my hours closer to full-time once Davey starts school. I'd like to be able to pick him up, but my mom can help out if you need me later in the afternoons."

She kept pushing the résumé toward him, the corners of the paper crumpling against his stomach, so he finally plucked it out of her fingers.

"Emily," he said softly. "I need a legal secretary."

"Right now," she shot back, "you need a warm body that can do dishes."

She had a point, but he wasn't about to admit it.

"I can do this. I can help you." She kept her hands fisted at her sides, her chin notched up. It must have cost her to come to him like this, but Emily still made it seem like she was doing him a favor by demanding he hire her.

"This isn't a job you want." He folded the resume and placed it on the desk. "You're smart and talented—"

"Talented at what?" she asked, breathing out a sad laugh. "Shopping? Planning parties? Not exactly useful skills in Crimson. Or maybe I'm good enough to kiss but not to work for you."

He pointed at the sheet of paper. "You just told me why you're qualified. If you can work for me, you can find another job."

"Don't you think I've tried? I spent this entire morning knocking on doors. I'm a single mom with a son who has special needs, which is a hard sell even if someone did want to hire me." She bit down on her lip. "By the way, they don't. Because I wasn't nice when I was younger and that's what people remember. That's what they see when they look at me."

"I don't."

"You're too nice for your own good," she said, jabbing a finger at him. "That's why I'm here begging." A strangled sound escaped her when she said the word begging. He studied her for crying, but her eyes remained dry. *Thank God.* He couldn't take it if she started crying. "I'm begging, Jase, because I need to know I can support my son. When I left Henry, I wanted out fast so I took nothing. Hell, I'm borrowing my mom's car like I'm a teenager again. I have to start somewhere, but I'm scared I won't be able to take care of Davey on my own. He's about to start kindergarten, but what if something happens? What if he—"

"He's going to be fine, Em." He could see her knuckles turning white even as color rose to her cheeks.

"This was a horrible idea," she muttered, turning her head to stare out onto Main Street as if she couldn't stand to meet his gaze another second. "I'm sorry. I'm a mess."

Jase took a step toward her. It was stupid and self-destructive and a bad idea for both of them, but the truth was he didn't care if Emily was a mess. He wanted her to be his mess.

Emily felt the tips of Jase's fingers on the back of her hand. She couldn't look at him after everything she'd said. All of the shattered pieces of herself she'd just revealed.

But her fingers loosened at his touch, and she wanted to sway into him. Somehow he grounded her and just maybe...

The front door to the office opened, a rush of fresh mountain air breezing over her heated skin. "Jase, you're late."

Emily whirled around to see a short, curvy woman in an ill-fitting silk blouse and shapeless skirt staring at her.

"Sorry," the woman said quickly, glancing between Emily and Jase as she adjusted the bulky purse on her arm. "I didn't realize you had a meeting or..."

"It's fine," Jase told her, stepping away from Emily. "I'll grab my keys, and I'm ready. The Crimson Valley Hiker's Club today, right?"

The woman nodded. "If you're busy—"

He shook his head. "Mari, this is Emily Whitaker. She's Noah's sister and just got back to town. Em, Mari Simpson. Mari works at the library in town but has been kind enough to help keep me on track with my campaign." He gave Mari a warm smile, and Emily's throat tightened. Jase could smile at whomever he wanted. It didn't matter only...

"He'll be a great mayor," Mari chirped with a bright smile of her own. While the woman wasn't classically pretty, the smile softened her features in a way that made her beautiful. "I'm happy to do whatever I can." Her face was sweet and hopeful. The face of a woman who would make a perfect wife. Emily forced herself not to growl in response.

"Keys," Jase said again and disappeared into his office.

Mari continued to smile but it looked forced. "So you're Noah's sister?"

"I am."

"You moved back from Boston, right?"

A simple question but Emily knew it meant that although Mari Simpson wasn't a Crimson native, she'd been downloaded on Emily's past and reputation in town. "Yes," she answered, forcing herself to stay cordial. This was new Emily.

Emily 2.0. Nice Emily.

"It's good to be close to my family and friends again."

Mari tapped a finger to her cheek. "I think I saw your name on the application list for our reference desk opening."

Emily nodded. "I applied at the library."

"Too bad we filled the position already," Mari said a little too sweetly. "Lots of talented people want a chance to live in such a great little town. We only hire people with at least an undergraduate degree. I'm sure you'll find something."

Emily 2.0.

"Thanks for the vote of confidence," she said through clenched teeth. "I think—"

"Emily's going to work for me," Jase said, pocketing his phone and keys as he came back into the room. He kept his gaze trained on Mari.

Her jaw dropped and Emily was pretty sure her own reaction was the same.

"Here? But I've heard… I thought…she's—"

"Organized and hardworking," Jase said, repeating

Emily's words from earlier. "Just what I need to get the office back on track." He patted the tiny woman on the shoulder. "It'll be easier for you, too, Mari. You won't have to keep tabs on me all the time."

She gave a small nod but muttered, "I don't mind."

Finally Jase turned to Emily. "Does tomorrow work for an official start date? I can be here by eight. We'll keep your hours flexible until Davey starts school." For once his eyes didn't reveal any of his feelings. It was as if he hadn't said no and she hadn't broken down in an emotional rant. As if he wasn't offering her this job out of pity.

He held out his hand, palm up. On it sat a shiny gold key. "Just in case you're here before me." He flashed a self-deprecating smile. "Punctuality isn't one of my best qualities."

No, Emily thought, he didn't need to be on time. Jase had more important traits—like the ability to rescue distressed women with a single key.

She should walk away. He knew too much about her now. If there was one thing Emily hated, it was appearing weak. She'd learned to be strong watching her father lose his battle with cancer. She'd married a man who valued power over everything else in his life.

During her divorce she hadn't revealed how scared she'd felt. She'd been strong for Davey. Even when she'd been nothing more than a puddle of uncertainty balled up on the cool tile of the bathroom floor. Every time she got dressed, Emily put her mask into place the same way she pulled on a T-shirt.

But she'd kissed Jase like she wanted to crawl inside his body, then pleaded for a job as if he was her only hope in the world.

When she'd left behind her life in Boston, she'd promised herself she would never depend on a man again. She'd create a life standing on her own two feet, strong and sure.

But maybe strong and sure came after the first wobbly baby step. Maybe...

Forget the self-reflection. Right now she needed a job.

Her pause had been too long, and Jase pulled back his hand, his brown eyes shuttering. She snatched the key at the last moment and squeezed her fingers around it. The metal was warm from his skin and she clutched it to her stomach. "I'll be here in the morning," she told him and with a quick nod to Mari, ducked out of the office before he could change his mind.

A job. She had a job.

She took a deep breath of the sweet pine air. The smell of the forest surrounding Crimson always made her think of her childhood. But now as she walked down the sidewalk crowded with tourists, the town seemed a little brighter than it had been when she'd first returned.

A text came through from her mother, telling her Davey had fallen asleep on the couch so Emily should take her time returning home. What would she do without her mom? She hated asking for help when Meg had recently come through her own health scare, but her mother insisted she loved spending time with her grandson.

Baby steps. A job. Davey starting kindergarten. After things were settled, Emily could think about finding a place of her own. Jase hadn't mentioned a salary, and she didn't care. The job was enough.

The weather was perfect, brilliant blue skies, bright sun and a warm breeze blowing wisps of hair across her cheek. She shrugged out of the suit jacket and folded it over her arm. Just as she walked by a small café, her stomach grumbled.

When was the last time she'd eaten at a restaurant? Not since leaving Boston and then it was always for some law firm party or campaign event. She and Henry hadn't gone on a proper date since their honeymoon. Here in Crimson, Davey liked the quiet and routine of her mother's house.

She sent a quick text to her mom and walked into the restaurant. It was new in town, which she hoped meant unfamiliar people. This space had been a small clothing store the last time she'd been in Crimson. The inside was packed, and she wondered if she'd even get a table in the crowded dining room. It was a disappointment, but not a surprise, when the hostess told her there was nothing available. Just as she turned to leave, someone called her name.

A woman with flaming red hair was waving at her from a booth near the front window.

"You're Emily, right?" the woman asked as she stepped closer. "You must think I'm a crazy stalker, but I recognize you from the Fourth of July Festival. I'm April Sanders, a friend of Katie's."

"The yoga teacher out at Crimson Ranch?"

April nodded. "I got the last empty booth. No pressure, but you're welcome to join me."

Emily thought about declining. She knew Katie had a big group of friends. Hell, everyone in town loved her future sister-in-law. But even though she'd grown up in Crimson, Emily had no one. That's the way she'd wanted it since she got back to town. It was simpler, less mess.

But now the thought of a full meal with adult conversation actually appealed to her. So did spending time with April. The woman was a few years older than Emily but with her gorgeous copper hair and bright green eyes, she looked like she just stepped off the pages of a mountain resort catalog. "Are you sure you don't mind?"

"I'd love it," April said, gesturing to the empty banquette across from her. "It feels strange to be eating alone when there's a crowd waiting for tables."

Emily slid into the booth. "Thank you."

A waitress came by the table almost immediately with a glass of water and another menu. Thankfully, the young woman was a stranger to Emily.

"Are you interested in staying incognito?" April asked when they were alone again. "You looked terrified the waitress might recognize you."

Emily blew out a breath. "I don't have the best reputation in town."

"A sordid past?" April leaned forward and lifted her delicate brows. "Do tell."

"Nothing exciting," Emily answered with a laugh. "Simple story of me thinking I was better than I should have as a girl. Life has a way of slapping you down if you get too big for your britches." She shrugged. "People in small towns like to bear witness to it."

"Life throws out curveballs whether you're big or small," April agreed.

The waitress returned to the table and, as she took

April's order, Emily studied the other woman. April wore no makeup but her fair skin was smooth, and her body fit under a soft pink T-shirt. She looked natural and fresh—perfect for Crimson. After Emily ordered, April smiled. "I met your mom a couple of times at Katie's bakery. She's lovely."

Emily nodded. "One of the most amazing women I know."

"How is she feeling?"

"She gets tired more quickly, but otherwise is back to her normal self. We were lucky the tumor was benign and they could remove it without damaging any other part of her brain."

"She was lucky to have you and Noah come back to help her."

"I wouldn't have been any other place but by her side. That's what family is for, you know?"

"I've heard," April answered softly. "My friend Sara is the closest thing I have to family."

Sara Travers, who ran the guest ranch outside town with her husband, Josh, had moved to Crimson a couple years ago from Los Angeles. Sara had been a famous child star and still acted when the right project came along. Otherwise, she and Josh—a Crimson native and one of Noah's good friends—spent their time managing Crimson Ranch. "Did you come to Crimson with Sara?"

April nodded. "We didn't plan on staying, but then she met Josh and..."

"The rest is history?"

"She had a tough couple of years and deserves this happiness."

"If my brother is any indication, Crimson is *the* place

for happy endings." She smiled. "Have you found your happy-ever-after here?"

"It's a good place to build a life," April said and Emily realized the words weren't an answer to the question.

"Or rebuild a life." The waitress brought their orders, a club sandwich for Emily and a salad for April. Emily leaned across the table. "I like you and I appreciate the invitation to lunch, but after seeing what you eat I'm not sure we can be friends." She pointed to the bowl of dark greens. "Your salad is so healthy I feel guilty picking up a fry from my plate. You don't even have dressing."

The willowy redhead stared at her a long moment and Emily did a mental eye roll. She had the uncanny ability to offend without meaning to by tossing off comments before she thought about them. Her family was used to it and she'd managed to tame the impulse during her marriage but now...

April burst out laughing. "You remind me of Sara. She gives me grief about how I eat, too. I've always been healthy but became more diligent about what I put in my body when I was diagnosed with breast cancer a few years ago."

Emily thumped her palm against her forehead. "Now I feel like an even bigger jerk."

"Don't," April said, still smiling. "I've been cancer-free for over five years."

"My dad died when I was in high school. Pancreatic cancer." She took a bite of sandwich, swallowing around the emotions that always bubbled to the surface when she thought about her father. "I still miss him."

"It's difficult for you being back in Crimson."

"I thought I'd made a life beyond this little town. Returning to Colorado has been an adjustment."

April snagged a fry and popped it in her mouth. "So is divorce."

"Are you…"

"My ex-husband left me during my cancer treatments," April answered. She shrugged. "He couldn't handle me being sick."

"Jerk," Emily muttered.

"And yours?"

"Another jerk." Emily pushed her plate closer to the center of the table, a silent invitation for April to take another fry. When she did, Emily figured this friendship might stand a chance. "I was the one who did the leaving, but it was because my ex couldn't handle that our son wasn't the child he expected or wanted. Henry needed everything to appear perfect, and I bought into the lie."

"And lost yourself in the process?" April's voice was gentle, as if she'd had experience in that area.

Emily bit down on her lip, then nodded.

"I don't have the same history with this town as you, but I can tell you it's a good place to rediscover who you are." April nabbed another fry. "Also to reinvent yourself."

"Is that what you've done?"

"I'm working on it. In addition to Crimson Ranch, I also teach yoga at a studio on the south side of town. You should come in for a class." April leaned closer. "I like you, but I'm not sure I can be friends with someone whose shoulders are so stiff they look like they could crack in half."

Emily laughed, feeling lighter than she had in months. "I may," she told April. "If only to support a friend."

April held up her water glass. "Here's to new friends and new beginnings."

Chapter Five

Jase walked toward the front door of his office at 8:05 the following morning. His tie was slung over his shoulder, his hair still damp from the quick shower he'd taken, but he'd made it almost on time.

Downtown was quiet this early in the morning, one shopkeeper sweeping the sidewalk in front of his store as another arranged a rack of sale clothes. Life Is Sweet bakery would be crowded, so Jase hadn't bothered to stop for his daily dose of caffeine.

He'd been second-, third- and fourth-guessing his decision to offer Emily a job since the words had left his mouth yesterday. He wasn't sure how he was going to handle being so close to her every day, especially when she'd told him their kiss had been a mistake. But he'd also woken up with a sense of anticipation he hadn't felt in years. Not much else could ensure that he was *almost* on time.

He opened the door, then stopped short, checking his watch to make sure he hadn't lost a full day somewhere. The entire space had been transformed. The reception desk was clear other than the papers stacked neatly to one side. The wood furniture in the waiting area had been polished, and the top of the coffee table held a selection of magazines. There was even a plant—one that was green and healthy—on the end table next to the row of chairs where clients waited.

He caught the faint scent of lemon mixed with the richer smell of fresh coffee. His office hadn't looked this good in all the years he'd been here. There was a freshness to the space, as if it had been aired out like a favorite quilt.

He was still taking it all in when Emily appeared from the hallway.

"I hope you don't mind," she said, almost shyly. "I started cleaning up before we talked about how you wanted it done."

He rubbed a hand over his jaw, realizing in his haste to be on time he'd forgotten to shave this morning. "I didn't even know it needed to be done. Are you some kind of a witch who can wiggle her nose and make things happen?" He shook his head. "Because I'm five minutes late and what you've done here looks like it took hours." He glanced at the closed door to his office.

"I didn't touch anything in there. Yet." She reached behind her and shook out her loose bun, blond hair falling over her shoulders. Jase was momentarily mesmerized, but then she gathered the strands and refastened the bun. "I came in early," she told him, moving to stand behind the receptionist's desk.

"How early?"

She moved the stack of papers from one side of the desk to the other before meeting his gaze. "Around five thirty."

"In the morning?" he choked out. "Why were you awake at that time?"

"I don't sleep much," she said with a shrug. "I've gone through the filing system Donna set up and think I understand how it works. We need to talk about how you record billable hours."

He stepped close enough to the desk that his thighs brushed the dark wood. "We need to talk about you not sleeping. How often does that happen?"

"A few times a week," she said quietly. "It's no big deal."

"How many times is a few?"

Her mouth pressed into a thin line. "Why do you care, Jase?"

"How many?"

"Most nights," she answered through clenched teeth. "My doctor in Boston gave me a prescription for pills to help, but I haven't refilled it since I've been back. Davey had trouble adjusting when we first got here, and I wanted to hear him if he needed me."

"And now?"

She shrugged. "I watch him sleep. He's so peaceful, and it makes me happy. This morning my mom's schedule allowed her to watch him for me when he woke up, so I came into the office to get a few things done." She looked up at him, her gaze wary. He noticed something more now, the shadows under her eyes and the tension bracketing her mouth. It didn't lessen her beauty or her effect on him, but he kicked himself that he hadn't seen it before. This woman was exhausted.

"You didn't have to do this," he said, gesturing to the shiny clean space. "But I'm glad you did."

She rewarded him with a small smile. "It was a pit in here, Jase. It's like you don't even care."

"I do care," he argued. "I care about my clients and this town. So what if the office isn't spotless?"

"You're a business owner and you're running for mayor. People have expectations."

He choked out a laugh. "Tell me about it." He didn't mind taking grief from her because the brightness had returned to her gaze. The Emily he remembered from high school had been so sure of herself and her place in this world. She'd held on to that pretense since returning to Crimson, but the more time he spent with her the more he could see the fragile space between the cracks in her armor. A part of him wanted to rip away all of her defenses because they were guarding things that held her heart captive. But he hated seeing her troubled and knew she hated revealing any weakness.

"Thank you for this job. I know you didn't want to hire me."

No. He wanted to kiss her and hold her and take care of her. The kissing and holding weren't going to be helped by working with her, but he could take care of her and that was a start.

"You were right," he admitted. "I needed help. There are too many things on my plate right now, so I've been ignoring the office. It's starting to show in my work, and that's not going to help anyone."

"The town loves you. They'll cut you some slack."

"They love what I do for them."

"You do too much."

He shook his head. "There's no such thing. Not for someone with my history."

"The Crenshaw family history isn't yours, Jase. The weight of a generations-old reputation shouldn't rest on one man's shoulders."

If only that were true. "My dad isn't going to help carry the load." He didn't want to talk about this. Emily was here so he could help her, not the other way around. "I have to be at the courthouse at nine, so we should talk about what else needs to be done. I'm going to get a cup of coffee first, and you're an angel for making it. For all of this. Thank you, Em."

She tapped one finger on the screen of the desktop computer. "Eight thirty."

"Already?" He glanced at his watch.

"No, you have to be at the courthouse at eight thirty." She moved around the desk, her hips swaying under the fitted cropped pants she wore. She'd paired them with a thin cotton sweater in a pale yellow along with black heels. It was more casual than yesterday but still professional. "I'll get your coffee."

"You don't have to—"

"I want to." She tipped up her chin, as if daring him to contradict her. "So you can get ready to go."

Before he could argue, she disappeared around the corner.

This place wasn't good enough for someone like Emily. His office, even though it was clean, was too shabby for her crisp elegance. He imagined that she'd fit perfectly into the upper echelons of Boston society. Emily looked like a lady who lunched, a fancy wife who could chair events and fund-raisers and never have a hair out of place. Yet as he followed her, he watched wisps of blond hair try to escape from the knot at the back of her head.

She poured coffee into a travel mug, and Jase was momentarily distracted by the fact that the clean dishes and coffee mugs were put away on the shelf above the utility sink.

Emily turned, thrusting the stainless steel mug toward him. Her fingers were pink from the water and had several paper cuts on the tips. Not as delicate as she looked, his Emily.

No. Not his. Not even for a minute.

But she was here. Although he'd done her a favor, he needed her. He wanted her. Any way he could have her.

"You're welcome in my office while I'm gone." He brushed a lock of hair behind her ear and felt a small amount of satisfaction when she sucked a breath. "I should be back by noon."

"You have a meeting with Toby Jenkins here at one thirty."

He nodded, thankful he'd set up the calendars on his cell phone and office computers to sync automatically. He was in the habit of entering meetings in his calendar, but that didn't mean he remembered to check it every day.

"I told my mom I'd be home by two today. Davey still naps in the afternoons, and I like to be there when he wakes up."

"I can pick up lunch on my way back. Any requests?"

"You don't need to—"

"It's the least I can do, Emily. The way you transformed the office went beyond anything Donna could have done. It feels good not to be surrounded by my usual mess."

One side of her mouth curved. "I'm glad to be useful."

What had her ex-husband done to beat down the spirited girl he'd known into this brittle, unsure woman? Jase wasn't a fighter, but he would have liked to punch Henry Whitaker.

Instead, he gave Emily a reassuring smile. "You're the best."

Her smile dimmed, but before he could figure out why, she tapped her watch. "You need to go or you're going to be late."

"They're used to me being late."

"Not with me running the show." She pointed to the door. "Now go. I've got your inner sanctum to tackle."

He laughed, then wished her luck and headed back out into the bright sunshine. It was the best start to a morning he'd had in ages.

By the time he parked in front of his father's trailer a few minutes before noon, Jase's mood had disintegrated into a black hole of frustration. Even though he expected it from Emily's text, seeing the Crawfords' 4Runner at the side of the mobile home only made it worse.

He didn't want Emily here. This part of his life was private, protected. Most people in town knew his father, or knew of him if they'd lived in Crimson long enough. But even as a kid, Jase had never let anyone visit the run-down home where he'd lived. Not even Noah.

He stood on the crumbling front step for a moment trying to rein in his clamoring emotions. Then he heard Emily's laughter spill out from the open window and pushed through the door.

Her back was to him as she faced the tiny counter

in the kitchen. "Canned spaghetti is not real food," she said with another laugh.

"It's real food if I eat it and like it," his dad growled in response, but there was humor in his tone. His father sat in one of the rickety wooden chairs at the table. He watched Emily like she was some sort of mystical being come to life inside his tumbledown home.

"I'm not a great cook," she shot back, "but even I can make homemade meatballs. I'll teach you." He could see she was dumping the can of bright red sauce and pasta into a ceramic bowl.

"If we're having Italian night," his dad said, pronouncing Italian with a long I, "you'd best bring a bottle of wine with you."

Jase let the door slam shut at that moment. Emily whirled to face him, her smile fading as she took in his expression. Declan shifted in the chair, his own smile growing wider.

"Just in time for lunch," his dad said, even though he knew how much Jase hated any food that came from a can.

"How was the courthouse?" Emily covered the bowl with a paper towel and put it in the microwave shoved in the corner of the counter.

Taking a breath, he caught Emily's scent overlaid with the stale smell of the trailer. The combination was an assault on his senses. The hold he had on his emotions unleashed as he stalked forward, shouldering Emily out of the way to punch in a minute on the microwave timer. "What the hell are you doing here?" he asked, crowding her against the kitchen sink.

"My fault," his father said from behind him. "I forgot I had a doctor's appointment this morning. When you didn't answer your cell phone, I called the office. Emily explained you were unavailable but was nice enough to drive me."

Jase looked over his shoulder. "You should have rescheduled the appointment."

"It wasn't a problem," Emily said. "Your office was organized and I—"

"I offered you a job as a legal secretary," he bit out. "That's work with professional boundaries. Inserting yourself into my personal life isn't part of the job description."

Those blue eyes that had been so warm and full of life iced over in a second. He expected her to argue but instead her lips pressed together and a moment later she whispered, "My bad. Won't happen again."

"Jase, what's crawled up your butt?" his dad asked, his voice booming in the tense silence that had descended between him and Emily.

She lifted one eyebrow. "I'm not going to stick around to find out." Skirting around him, she gave Declan a quick hug. "Enjoy your spaghetti. I'm going to hold you to that cooking lesson. But grape juice, no wine."

"Thank you, darlin'." His dad's voice softened. "You're a good girl. I'm sorry about this."

"It's not on you," she whispered.

Jase didn't turn around, his hands pressed hard to the scarred Formica. He heard the creak of the door as it opened and shut, not the angry bang he expected but a soft click that tore a hole in his gut. Still he didn't move.

The chair scraped as his father stood. He moved behind Jase to take the bowl out of the microwave. For several minutes the only sound was the spoon clinking and the rustle of a newspaper.

"She doesn't belong here," Jase said finally, rubbing his hand over his face as he turned. "Emily works for me now. That's all, Dad. She isn't part of this."

"That girl has been a part of you for years," Declan answered, setting down the spoon in the empty bowl.

Jase felt his eyes widen before he could stop the reaction. He'd never talked to anyone, especially his father, about his feelings for Emily. He understood Noah knew but had never spoken it aloud.

"I'm a bad drunk," Declan said with a shrug. "But I was never blind, and you're my son. I know you better than you think."

"Emily's in a rough place now. I'm helping her get back on her feet. That's all."

"You're embarrassed about me and how you grew up."

Another bit of unspoken knowledge better left in the shadows. "You're in a better place, Dad. I'm proud of you for staying sober."

Declan choked out a laugh. "I'm the one who's proud, Jase. But you take on too much that isn't yours. My reputation and our family history. The way you were raised. You've overcome a lot, and you don't need to be ashamed of it. You don't have to make it all better."

Jase thought about his ancestor's picture in the town jail and how he wanted his family legacy to be something more than it was. "If you won't let me move you to a better house, I respect that decision. But I don't want her here. You need to respect that."

"From what I can tell, Emily Crawford is plenty capable of making her own decisions."

But she was *working* for him now. It was what she'd wanted, and it changed things. Not his need or desire, but his inclination to act on it. "Her name is Emily *Whitaker*, Dad. She was married. She has a son. Neither one of us is who we were before."

His father smiled. "I think that's the point."

Chapter Six

Emily looked up from the old rocker on her mother's front porch at the sound of a car coming down the gravel driveway. It was almost nine at night, and Davey had been asleep close to an hour.

She hadn't expected her mother to return from her date with Max Moore so soon. But when Emily recognized Jase's Jeep, her first inclination was to run to the house and shut the door.

He'd hurt her today, and she hated that anyone—any man—had the power to do that. While she understood that Jase's reaction had been about his own issues, a part of her still took the blame he'd placed on her. Her faults sometimes felt so obvious it was easy to hold herself accountable for any perceived slight. Flawed as she might be, Emily had never been a coward.

So she remained on the rocker, her legs curled under

the thin blanket she'd brought out to ward off the evening chill of the high mountains. Although she couldn't concentrate on the actual words, she kept her eyes trained on the e-reader in her lap as a door slammed shut and the heavy footfall of boots sounded on the steps.

"What are you reading?"

She ran one finger over the screen of the e-reader but didn't answer.

"You can ignore me," he said as he sank into the chair next to her, "but I won't go away."

"There's always hope," she quipped, her fingers gripping the leather cover of the e-reader tighter at his soft chuckle.

They sat in silence for a minute, and Emily's grasp began to relax. As if sensing it he said, "I'm sorry, Em."

"It's fine," she lied. "Point taken. I overstepped the bounds." There she went, instinctively making his mistake her fault.

"My reaction wasn't about you. What you did for my dad today was kind. It made him happier than I've seen him in a long time to have a beautiful woman caring for him."

"No big deal."

"Don't do that." His hand was around her wrist, warmth seeping through the fleece sweatshirt she'd pulled on when the sun disappeared behind the mountain. "It was special to him, and it should have been to me, as well." He stood, releasing her, and paced to the edge of the porch. "I love my father, but I hate the man he was when I was younger. He was mean and embarrassing. Everyone knew the problems he had, but that didn't stop me from being humiliated when I'd have to get him home after a night at the bars."

She could see the tension in his shoulders as he gazed out into the darkening night. "He showed up one year for a parent-teacher conference so drunk he ended up puking all over the first-floor bathroom. I never let him come to another school function."

She flipped closed the cover of her e-reader, her heart already melting for this man's pain. "Jase—"

He turned to her, folded his arms across his chest. "It killed me to live in that trailer growing up. The only saving grace was that no one but me had to see him at his worst. Even Noah, all the times he picked me up, has never been inside. That place represents my greatest shame, and my dad refuses to move. To see you there with all of the memories that seem to seep out of the walls to choke me... I couldn't stand it. It felt like you'd be contaminated by it."

Emily stood, placed the blanket and e-reader on the chair and walked toward him.

Jase shook his head. "You're too good for that, Em. Too good for him. I'm sorry I lashed out, but I still hate that you—that anyone—has seen that piece of who I am."

"No." She stepped into his space until she could feel his breath whispering over the top of her head. "You're too good to give in to that shame. Where you came from doesn't change who you are now."

"Are you kidding?" He didn't move away from her but leaned back against the porch rail as if he needed space. "That trailer and what it represents *made* me who I am. The night in my front yard, you said I was perfect, and I know what my reputation is around town. Nice Jase. Sweet Jase. Perfect Jase. No one sees anything else because I don't let them. Everyone thinks I work so damn hard despite my family's reputation in Crimson. I work hard *because* of where I came from. Because I'm scared to death if I don't, the poison that has crushed the self-respect of so many people in my family will take me down, too."

Something dark and dangerous flashed in his eyes and she saw who he was under the Mr. Perfect veneer he'd spent years polishing to a bright shine. He was a man at the edge of his control and a part of her wanted him to shuck off his restraint. With her. Yes. She could handle it. She would welcome whatever he had to offer.

He blinked, and the moment was gone. His chest rose and fell like he'd sprinted up Crimson Mountain. She placed her hand on it, fingers splayed, and felt his heartbeat thrumming under her touch. "You aren't your father." She said the words softly and felt his breath hitch. "I know what it's like to want to prove something so badly it makes you into someone you're not. Someone fake and false. You're real, Jase. Not perfect. Real."

"I'm sorry," he said again, lifting his palm to press it over her hand. "For what I said and how I treated you."

She let a small smile curve her lips. "I think this makes us even."

"You did good today. In my office and with my dad. Thank you."

This was the part where she should step away. If they were even, it was a fresh start. But she couldn't force herself to move. Emily might not believe in perfect, but she had learned to appreciate real. The knowledge that Jase was different than she'd assumed both humbled and excited her. Of all people, she should have known not to judge a person by who they were on the outside.

She'd built an entire life on outward impressions only to watch it crumble around her.

The connection she felt with Jase, her awareness of him, suddenly flared to life stronger than it had before. She moved her hand up his chest and around to the back of his neck. At the same time she lifted onto her tiptoes so she could press her mouth to his. He tasted like night air and mint gum, and she loved how much he could communicate simply through the pressure of his mouth on hers.

He angled his head and ran his tongue across her bottom lip. His hands came to rest on her hips, pulling her closer until the front of her was plastered against him. Unlike other men she'd known, he didn't rush the kiss. It was as if learning her bit by bit was enough for him. He savored every taste, trailing kisses along her jaw before nipping at her earlobe.

"Your ears are sensitive," he whispered when she moaned softly. His breath feathered against her skin. "You touch them when you're nervous."

"I don't," she started to argue, then he bit down on the lobe again and she squirmed. "You're observant," she amended.

"I want more. I want to know everything about you," he said and claimed her mouth again.

Her brain was fuzzy but the meaning of his words penetrated the fog of desire after a few moments. "No." She lifted her head and tried to step away but he held her steady.

"Why?" A kiss against her jaw.

"I can't think when you do that."

"Then I'll do it more."

She opened her mouth to argue, and he took the opportunity to deepen the kiss. One thing she'd say for Jase Crenshaw—the man was persistent. Even though she knew she should stop it, she gave in to the need building inside her. Her body sang with desire, tremors skittering over her skin. Jase ran his fingers up under the hem of her sweatshirt and across her spine. Everywhere he touched her Emily burned. Her breasts were heavy and sensitive where they rubbed against his T-shirt and she wanted more.

So much more.

So much it scared her into action. As Jase's hands moved to the front of her waist and brushed the swell of her breasts, she wrenched away from him. With unsteady hands, she grabbed on to the front porch rail to prevent herself from moving back to the warmth she already missed.

"We've determined I'm not perfect," Jase said, his tone a mix of amusement and frustration. "So what's the problem now?"

"I work for you."

"Are you asking to be fired?"

She glanced at him and saw he was teasing. Her shoulders relaxed. "I don't want to complicate things, Jase. I know you gave me the job because you felt sorry for me and this…" She pointed between the two of them. "Would only muddy the waters more."

"I don't feel sorry for you." He came closer and she didn't resist when he cupped her face in his hands. "I respect you, and I want you. But neither of those emotions involves pity."

"Why are you running for mayor?"

His hands dropped to his sides. "I think I can help

the town move forward. I've been on city council long enough to understand what needs to be done and—"

"You have a responsibility," she finished for him.

"You say that like it's a bad thing."

"It's not, but your life is filled with obligations. I don't want to be another one."

"You're—"

"I'd like to be your friend."

He stared at her for several seconds, then blew out a breath. "I'd like that, too, but it doesn't have to mean—"

"Yes, it does," she interrupted, not bothering to hide her smile at the crushed puppy-dog look of disappointment he gave her.

With a small nod, he moved around her. "Good night, Emily."

"Good night, Jase." She watched his taillights disappear into the darkness, then turned for the house. For the first time in forever, she fell asleep within minutes of her head hitting the pillow.

Friday morning, Jase walked the three blocks from his office to the Crimson Community Center and thought about how nice it was not to be rushing through town. He was speaking to the downtown business coalition and probably would have been late for the meeting if Emily hadn't shoved him out the door.

She was a stickler for punctuality, something that had never been a strength of his. He cared about being on time, but he often got so lost in whatever he was doing that he stopped paying attention to anything else. She hadn't been in the office yesterday, and despite how organized she'd left things on Wednesday, he'd found he missed knowing she was sharing his space.

She was a distraction but the best kind possible, and now he spent the minutes going over what he planned to say to the group of business owners. Ever since Emily had asked the question, Jase had been pondering the answer to why he was running for mayor. It wasn't as if he didn't have enough to keep him busy with his law practice.

He came around the corner and noticed Mari pacing in front of the entrance to the community center. Automatically he checked his watch, since his one campaign worker tended to pace when she was anxious.

"We have a problem," she said, adjusting her heavy-rimmed glasses as she strode toward him.

He held up his hands. "I'm not scheduled to speak for another ten minutes. It's good."

"Your opponent got here first," she answered, shaking her head. "It's *really* bad, Jase."

"What opponent?"

"Charles Thompson."

Jase's stomach dropped to the pavement like a cement brick. "Charles Thompson isn't running for mayor. I'm unopposed in the election."

"Not anymore. He has the signatures he needs to put his name on the ballot and filed as a candidate with the courthouse before yesterday's deadline. I don't understand why he's doing this."

"Because it's me." Jase rubbed a hand over his eyes. "Charles has been at loose ends since he retired as sheriff. I bet my dad called and rubbed the election in his face. If there's anything the Thompsons can't stand, it's a Crenshaw getting ahead."

"That's plain spiteful."

Spiteful and stupid and why was he doing this again?

Because he owed it to the town? Because he had some-thing to prove?

"You have to get in there and prove you're a better candidate." Mari tugged on his arm, but Jase stood his ground. He didn't want to face Charles and everything the older man knew about his childhood. If there was one person who knew where all the Crenshaw skeletons were hidden, it was Charles Thompson. "Jase, let's go."

He could walk away right now, withdraw his can-didacy. Charles would be a fine mayor, maybe even better than Jase. The older man had nothing but time to devote to the job. But if Jase won, maybe he could stop trying so hard to make amends for a past he didn't own. Perhaps it would finally be enough—he would be enough—to excise the ghosts of his past.

Jase wasn't his father or any of the infamous men in his family. He'd paid more than his dues; he'd tried to atone for every sin committed by someone with the last name Crenshaw. Now was his time to bury the past for good. He couldn't walk away.

Taking a deep breath, he straightened his tie and smoothed his fingers over the hair curling at the nape of his neck. A haircut was still on the to-do list, right after fighting for his right to lead this town.

He followed Mari into the crowded meeting room where Charles Thompson stood at the podium. A ruth-less light snapped in his eyes as he met Jase's gaze over the heads of the members of the coalition. Jase knew he had friends in this room, but facing Sheriff Thomp-son turned him into the scared, cowering boy he'd been years ago. He'd dreaded seeing the patrol car parked in front of his dad's trailer and knowing what it meant.

Those days were a distant memory for most people,

Declan Crenshaw having faded into the background of the Crimson community. But for Jase they were like a razor across an open wound—raw and painful.

"My esteemed opponent has arrived," Charles announced into the microphone, his deep voice booming through the room.

People in the audience turned to where Jase stood at the back and he forced a neutral look on his face. He made eye contact with a couple of friends, Katie Garrity, who was representing her bakery, and Josh Travers from Crimson Ranch. Katie gave him a sympathetic smile and Josh looked almost as angry as Jase felt.

Their support bolstered his confidence but his courage took a nosedive at Thompson's next words. "Come on up here, boy," Charles said, his gaze boring in Jase's taught nerves. "I want to talk to you about the future of this town and family values."

Jase banged through the front door of his office an hour after he'd left, holding on to his temper by the thinnest thread. Emily jumped in her chair, glancing up from the computer screen.

"How did it go?"

"Fine," he bit out, not stopping. He could feel the mask he wore beginning to crumble and needed the safety of being behind a closed door when it did. "I have a meeting with Morris Anderson at eleven. Let me know when he gets here."

He dropped his briefcase on the floor, slammed his office door shut behind him and stalked to the window behind his desk, trying to get his breathing under control as he stared out to the parking lot in back of the building.

"All those slamming doors don't sound like *fine* to me."

He didn't bother turning at Emily's cool voice behind him. "Do you understand what a closed door means?" he asked.

"Better than you'd imagine," she answered with a small laugh. "But in this case, I don't care. Either you tell me what happened at the meeting, or I can call Katie. Which do you prefer?"

Jase closed his eyes and concentrated on making his lungs move air in and out. He knew there were no secrets in Crimson, at least not for long. His phone had started ringing and beeping with incoming calls and texts as soon as he walked out of the community center.

"Charles Thompson is running against me for mayor. He announced his candidacy to the downtown coalition this morning."

She didn't say anything, and Jase finally turned. Emily stood just inside the doorway to his office. After his secretary retired, Jase convinced himself that he preferred running the entire office on his own. So much of his life was filled with people and responsibility. This space had become a sanctuary of sorts, a place where he was in total control. He answered to no one.

In only a few days, Emily's presence had become the answer to a secret need he didn't know how to voice. Not only was she organized and efficient, but she breathed new life into an existence that had become so predictable Jase couldn't seem to force its path out of the familiar ruts.

This morning she wore a simple cotton dress with a light sweater thrown over her shoulders and strappy sandals. Her hair was held back with a clip but the length of it tumbled over her shoulders. The scent of her shampoo mixed with perfume tangled in the air, and Jase had noticed on Wednesday the hint of it lingered even after she left for the day.

"So what?" she asked when he finally met her gaze. "You've done more for this town than Charles Thompson. People love you."

He shook his head. "He was sheriff," he told her, as if that explained everything. The word *sheriff* captured the past Jase had worked so hard to bury under the duty and responsibility he shouldered in town.

"You've been the de facto leader on town council for several years. Noah told me you were instrumental in convincing Liam Donovan to move his company's headquarters to Crimson."

She stepped farther into the room and, like he was magnetized, Jase moved around the desk toward her. Toward the certainty of her unmistakable beauty and the sound of her voice. Maybe if he listened to her long enough, he could believe in himself the way she seemed to.

"From what I remember, Thompson was a decent sheriff, but this town has never had a big problem with crime. Business and keeping things moving forward have been a struggle for some of the older generation. Things are different now than when I left, and people say you're the reason."

If only it were that simple. "He knows everything about me."

Her delicate brows came down, as if she couldn't understand the significance of what he was saying.

"Charles ran the department when we were kids," he explained. "During the time when my grandpa died and Mom left with Sierra. My dad was still working at the mine, and he was at his lowest. It was worse than anyone knows." He paused, cleared his throat to expel the emotions threatening his airways. "Except Charles. He knows every sordid detail."

"That past has nothing to do with you."

"That past *is* me," he argued.

She shook her head. "Charles can't use anything he knows because of his position as sheriff in this election."

"He already has. Most of what he talked about at today's meeting was family values. He had his wife of thirty-four years and his two sons sitting in the front row. Hell, Miriam brought muffins to hand out."

"You want muffins? Katie will make you dozens of them. We can hand out baked goods to every voter in this town."

"That's not the point. You know how perception plays into politics. He's sowed the seeds of doubt about me. Now people will start talking…about me and my family and our history in Crimson."

"They'll understand he's running a smear campaign."

"No, they won't." He ran his hands through his hair, squeezed shut his eyes. "He was so smooth. Charles actually talked about how much he admired me, how much I'd overcome. He claimed he'd always felt protective of mc because my mother abandoned me and my dad was so messed up. Would you believe he even compared me to his own sons?"

"Aaron and Todd?" Emily snorted. "Those two caused more trouble as teens than anyone else in the school. I haven't seen Todd, but from what I can tell, Aaron hasn't changed a bit. He's still a big bully. I don't know how many times I have to say no to a date before he quits calling me."

"He's calling you?" As angry as Jase was about Charles, temper of a different sort flared to the surface of his skin, hot and prickly. It was almost a relief to channel his frustration toward something outside himself. Something he could control. Above all else, Jase understood the value of control. "I'll take care of it."

"Hold on there, Hero-man. I don't need you to handle Aaron for me. I can take care of annoying jerks all on my own."

"You can handle everything, right?"

He regretted the rude question as soon as it was out of his mouth. Emily should snap back at him because he was lashing out at her with no cause. Instead, she flashed him a saucy grin. "Takes one to know one."

The smile, so unexpected and undeserved, diffused most of his anger, leaving him with a heaping pile of steaming self-doubt. He sat on the edge of his desk and leaned forward, hands on his knees.

"I'm sorry. I know you can take care of yourself." His chin dropped to his chest and he stared at the small stain peeking out from under one of the chairs in front of the desk. "But it's a lot easier to worry about other people than think of how quickly my own life is derailing."

A moment later he felt cool fingers brush away the hair from his forehead. He wanted to lean into her touch but forced himself to remain still. "Did you ever meet Andrew Meyer who used to run this office? I took over his practice four years ago, and I haven't changed a thing." He pushed the toe of his leather loafer against the chair leg until the stain was covered. "Not one piece of furniture or painting on the wall. You can still see the frame marks from where he took down his law school diploma and I never bothered to replace it with mine. I inherited his secretary and his clients, and I haven't lifted a finger to make this place my own. Hell, I think the magazines in the lobby are probably four years old. Maybe even older."

"I switched them for current issues," she said softly.

Her fingers continued to caress him and it felt so damn good to take a small amount of comfort from her. Too good. He lifted his head, and she dropped her hand.

"Why haven't you changed anything?" She didn't move away, and it was the hardest thing Jase had ever done not to pull her closer.

"Because this place isn't mine."

"It is," she said, her tone confused. "It's your office. Your clients. Your reputation." She laughed. "Your mortgage."

"This is the oldest law practice in the town. It was founded in the early 1900s and passed down through the Meyer family for generations. Andrew didn't have kids, so he offered a partnership position to me when I was still in law school. He wanted a Crimson native to take over the firm. This is his legacy. Not mine."

"Jase, you are the poster child for the town's favorite son. Charles Thompson can't hold a candle to the man you've become. Whether it was despite where you came from or because of it, the truth doesn't change."

"What if who people see isn't the truth? What if I've become too good at playing the part people expect of me?"

"You don't have to reflect the town's image of you back at them. You're more than a two-dimensional projection of yourself. Show everyone who you really are."

Staring into Emily's crystal-blue eyes, it was tempting. The urge to throw it all away, create the life he wanted, curled around his senses until the freedom of it was all he could see, hear and taste. Right behind the whisper of release came a pounding, driving fear that cut him off at the knees.

Who he was, who he'd been before he'd started down the path to redeeming his family name was a lost, lonely, scared boy. The memories he'd secreted away in the parts of his soul where he didn't dare look threatened to overtake him.

He stood abruptly, sending Emily stumbling back a few steps. "I'm going to win this election. I need people to see the best version of me, not the grubby kid Charles remembers."

Her eyes were soft. "Jase."

"I've worked toward this for years. It's what people expect…" He paused, took a breath. "It's what I want."

"Are you sure?"

"Charles isn't right for this. I'm going to be mayor."

She placed a light hand on his arm. "I'm going to help you."

He looked at her elegant fingers wrapped around his shirtsleeve. "Because you work for me."

"Because we're friends."

His eyes drifted shut for a moment. "Right. I forgot."

He felt a poke at his ribs. "Liar."

She had no idea. "I saw Katie at the meeting," he told her, needing to lighten the mood. He was too raw to go down that road with Emily. As much as he craved her kiss, he couldn't touch her again and not reveal the depth of his feelings. He thought he could control how much he needed her, but not when he was carrying his heart in his hands, ready to offer it to her if she asked. "She asked about plans for the bachelor and bachelorette parties."

Emily pulled a face. "No strippers."

He laughed in earnest. "I wasn't even thinking that."

"All men think that."

"You've got the whole male population figured out?"

"Like I said before, you're not complicated."

When it came to Emily, he wished it were true. His feelings for the woman standing in front of him had been simple for years. He wanted her. An unattainable crush. Unrequited love. End of story.

But a new chapter had started since she'd returned to town, and it was tangled in ways Jase couldn't take the time to unravel. Not if he was going to stay the course to his duty to Crimson.

"Then we're talking beer and poker night?"

Emily opened her mouth, then glanced over her shoulder as the door to the outer office opened. "Your appointment's here."

"Admit it, you like beer and poker."

She shook her head. "Come over for dinner tonight and we'll brainstorm better options." Her hand flew to cover her mouth as if she was shocked she'd extended the invitation.

"Yes," he said before she could retract the offer. "What time?"

Emily blinked. "Six."

"I'll be there."

"Jason, are you here?" a frail voice yelled from the front office.

"In my office, Mr. Anderson," Jase called. "Come on back."

"I should go...um..."

"Finish editing the brief I gave you?" Jase suggested, keeping his expression solemn.

"Exactly," she agreed.

As Morris Anderson tottered into the room, Emily said hello to the older man and disappeared.

"That Meg Crawford's girl?" Morris asked after she'd gone. Morris was here to revise the terms of his will, which he did on a monthly basis just to keep his four children on their toes.

Jase nodded, taking a seat behind his desk.

"I went to school with her grandmother back in the day. Spunky little thing."

"Good to know where Emily gets it." Jase pulled out Morris's bulging file. "Who made you angry this month?"

"Who didn't make me angry?" Morris asked through a coughing fit. "My kids are ungrateful wretches, but I love them." He pointed to the door, then to Jase. "The spunky ones are trouble," he said after a moment.

"Do you think so?" Jase felt his hackles rise. His protective inclination toward Emily was a palpable force surrounding him.

"I know so," Morris answered with a nod. "Trouble of the best kind. A man needs a little spunk to keep things interesting."

"I'd have to agree, Mr. Anderson," he said with a smile. "I'd definitely have to agree."

Chapter Seven

Emily wasn't sure how long she'd been sitting on the hallway floor when a pair of jeans and cowboy boots filled her line of sight.

"Emily?" Jase crouched down in front of her, placed a gentle hand on her knee. "What's wrong, sweetheart?"

"Nothing," she whispered. "Except dinner might be a little delayed. Sorry. I didn't realize you were here."

"I could see you through the screen door. I knocked but…"

"Hi, Jase." Davey's voice was sweet. Her boy didn't seem the least concerned to see his mother having a meltdown on the hardwood floor. "I built the space station hospital. Want to see it?"

"In a minute, buddy," Jase told him. "I'm going to hang out here with your mom first."

She tried to offer her son a smile but her face felt brittle. "Are you getting hungry, Davey?"

"Not yet." Small arms wrapped around her shoulders. "It's alright, Mama." The hug lasted only a few seconds but it was enough to send her already tattered emotions into overdrive. If her son was voluntarily giving her a hug, she must be in really bad shape.

She expelled a breath as Davey went back into the office. The tremors started along her spine but quickly spread until it felt like her whole body shook.

"Let's get you off the floor." Jase didn't wait for an answer. He scooped her into his arms and carried her toward the family room. Jase was strong and steady, the ends of his hair damp like he'd showered before coming over. She breathed in the scent of his shampoo mixed with the clean, woodsy smell she now associated with him alone. How appropriate that the man who was the poster child for Crimson would smell like the forest. As much as she wanted to sink into his embrace, Emily remained stiff against him. If she let go now, she might really lose it. "Where's your mom?"

"Book club," she managed between clenched teeth. "We should probably reschedule dinner for another night."

"I'm not leaving you like this." He deposited her onto the couch. "Not until you tell me what's going on."

Emily fought to pull herself together. She was so close to the edge it was as if she could feel the tiny spikes of hysteria pricking at the backs of her eyes. The cushions of the couch were soft and worn from years of movie nights and Sundays watching football. She wanted to curl up in a ball and ignore the constant pounding life seemed determined to serve up to her.

She couldn't look at Jase and risk him seeing the humiliation she knew was reflected in her eyes. She stood, moving around the couch in the opposite direction. The kitchen opened to the family room, separated by a half wall and the dining room table. "I'd planned to make steaks," she said quickly, ignoring the trembling in her fingers. "But I didn't get them out of the freezer, so we may be stuck with hot dogs. Do you mind turning on the grill?"

He let himself out onto the flagstone patio as she opened the pantry door and scanned the contents of the cupboard. She heard him return a few minutes later but kept her attention on the cupboard. "How do you feel about boxed mac and cheese? I don't know how Mom managed to make a home-cooked meal every night when we were younger. She worked part-time, drove us around to after-school activities, and still we had family dinners most evenings. You remember, right? She loved cooking for you and Noah."

He was standing directly behind her when she turned, close enough she was afraid he might reach for her. And if he did, she might shatter into a million tiny fragments of disappointment and regret. "I know I'm babbling. It's a coping mechanism. Give me a pass on this one, Jase."

His dark eyes never wavered. "What happened?"

Her fingers tightened on the small cardboard box so hard the corners bent. "An overreaction to some news. My meltdown is over. I'm fine."

"What news?"

"Does it matter?" She shook her head. "I lost the privilege of a major freak-out when I became a mother. Moms don't have a lot of time for wallowing when dinner is late."

"Tell me anyway."

She slammed the box of mac and cheese on the counter, then bent to grab a pot out of a lower cabinet. "I liked you better when you were nice and easygoing and not all up in my business."

Elbowing him out of the way she turned on the faucet and filled the pot with water. "Apparently, my ex-husband got remarried last weekend. One of my former friends in Boston was nice enough to text me a photo from the wedding."

She set the pot of water on the stove and turned on the burner. The poof of sound as it ignited felt like the dreams she'd had for her life. There one minute and then up in flames. "It was small—nothing like the extravaganza I planned—only family and close friends."

She laughed. "My friends are now her friends. She was a campaign worker. What a cliché." She glanced over her shoulder, unable to stop speaking once she'd started. "You know the best part? She's pregnant. A shotgun wedding for Henry Whitaker III. It's like Davey and I never existed. We're gone and he's remaking our life with someone else. Our exact damn life."

"I'm sorry."

"Don't be sorry." She ripped off the top of the box with so much force that an explosion of dried macaroni noodles spilled across the counter. "I'm not."

"You don't have to pretend with me."

"I'm not sorry, Jase. I'm mad. It's mostly self-directed. I let myself be sucked into that life. I was so busy pretending I couldn't even see Henry for who he was." She scooped up the stray noodles, dropped them in the water and then dumped the rest of the box's contents in with them. "My son has to pay the price."

"Your ex-husband is an idiot."

"To put it mildly."

"There are other words going through my mind," Jase said, his tone steely. "But I'm not going to waste my energy on a man so stupid he would let you go and give up his son because of a political image."

Emily took a deep breath and released it along with much of her tension. "I don't miss him." It had been a shock to get the text about Henry but she hadn't been lying to Jase when she told him she was most angry at herself. "How did I marry a man who I can feel nothing but revulsion for five months after leaving him?"

"He hurt you," Jase answered simply.

"I should have seen him for who he was. My parents had a good marriage. There was so much love in this house."

He reached out, traced a fingertip along her jaw. "There was also a lot of pain when your dad died."

"Yes, and it left scars on all of us. But Noah managed to fall in love with an amazing woman. Mom is now dating someone who makes her happy. I seem to be the one with horrible taste."

Jase smiled. "Did you meet any of the women your brother dated before Katie?"

"From what I've heard, *date* is a fairly formal term for Noah's pre-Katie relationships."

"Exactly."

"He's one of the lucky ones." She sighed and stepped away from Jase. Staring into his dark eyes made her forget he wasn't for her. Jase Crenshaw was all about duty and responsibility. Whether he was willing to admit it or not, his image was a big part of his identity. He wasn't motivated by the hunger for power and prestige that had influenced her ex-husband. But it didn't change the fact he would eventually want more than Emily was willing to give.

She opened the refrigerator and grabbed a pack of hot dogs from the shelf. "Man the grill, Mr. Perfect. We're eating like kids tonight."

Jase watched her for a long, heavy moment before his lips curved into a grin. "The only thing perfect about me is my grilling skills."

She smiled in return, knowing he'd given her a pass. Maybe he'd sensed her frazzled emotions couldn't take any more deep conversation. "Let's see if your hot dogs can beat my mac and cheese."

"I'm up for the challenge," he said and let himself out onto the patio.

Alone in the kitchen, Emily went to check on her son. He was still busy with his Lego structures and she watched him for a few minutes before giving him a fifteen-minute warning for dinner. Davey's difficulty with rapid transitions had driven Henry crazy. Her ex-husband had loved spontaneity when he wasn't working or campaigning. A game of pick up football with the neighbors, a bike ride into town for dinner or an impromptu weekend at the shore. Henry had to be moving at all times, his energy overpowering and bordering on manic.

She'd kept up with him when Davey was a baby but as the boy grew into a toddler, he liked notice if things were going to change. Henry had never been willing to accept the difficulty of swooping in and changing Davey's schedule without warning. Davey's difficulty with change only got worse over time, and it had become a huge source of tension with Henry.

Since returning to Crimson, Emily had done her best

to keep her son on a regular schedule. Her mother and Noah had quickly adapted, making her understand the issues her ex-husband had were his own and not her or Davey's fault.

She filled a plastic cup with milk for Davey, then pulled out two beers for her and Jase. As she was setting the table, Jase let himself back into the house. "Perfect dogs," he said, holding up a plate.

"Do you know Tater?"

Emily turned to find Davey standing behind her, looking at Jase.

"She's my uncle Noah's dog," the boy explained. "Her fur is really soft, but she has stinky breath and she likes to lick me."

"Tater is a great dog," Jase answered, setting the hot dogs on the kitchen table.

"Let's wash hands," she said to her son. "Mac and cheese and hot dogs for dinner."

He climbed on the stool in front of the sink, washed his hands, then went to sit next to Jase at the table. "Tater used to live here with Uncle Noah. Now they both live with Aunt Katie. Do you have a dog?"

Jase nodded. "I have a puppy. Her name is Ruby."

"Does she have soft fur?"

"She sure does and I bet she'd like you. She's six months old and has lots of energy. She loves to play."

"I could play with her," Davey offered, taking a big bite of mac and cheese.

"Would you like to meet her sometime?"

Davey nodded. "We can drive to where you live after dinner."

"If that's okay with your mom," Jase told him.

"A short visit," Emily said, trying not to make Davey's

suggestion into something bigger than it was. Which was difficult, because her son never volunteered to go anywhere. She planned outings to local parks and different shops downtown, and Davey tolerated the excursions. But there was no place he'd ever asked to go. Until now. She wondered if Jase understood the significance of the request.

He tipped back his beer bottle for a drink and then smiled at her. "I love mac and cheese."

She rolled her eyes but Davey nodded. "Me, too. And hot dogs. Mommy makes good cheese quesadillas."

"I'll have to try for an invitation to quesadilla night."

"You can come to dinner again." Davey kept his gaze on his plate, the words tumbling out of his mouth with little inflection. "Right, Mommy?"

"Of course," she whispered.

Jase asked Davey a question about his latest Lego creation. Once again, her son was talking more with Jase than he normally would to his family. Henry had a habit of demanding Davey make eye contact and enunciate when he spoke, both of which were difficult for her quiet boy. The last six months of her marriage had been fraught with tension as she and her ex-husband had waged a devastating battle over how to raise their son. The arguments and tirades had made Davey shrink into himself even more, and she'd worried the damage Henry was unwittingly doing might leave permanent scars on Davey's sensitive personality.

The way he acted toward Jase was a revelation. When Jase smiled at her again, his eyes warm and tender, Emily's heart began to race. How could she resist this man who saw her at her worst—angry or in the middle of an emotional meltdown—and still remained at her side, constant and true?

The answer was she didn't want to fight the spark between them. For the first time since returning to Crimson, Emily wondered if she hadn't squandered her chance at happiness after all.

"She needs to go out and do her business, and then you can play with her." Jase unlocked the front door of his house as he spoke to Davey.

The young boy stayed behind Emily's legs but nodded.

Emily gave him an apologetic smile. "He always takes a few minutes to acclimate to new places."

"Take all the time you need, buddy." As soon as the door began to open, Ruby started yelping. "She's usually pretty excited when I first get home."

"Davey, let's go," Emily said, her voice tense.

Jase looked over his shoulder to see the boy still standing in front of the door, eyes on the floor of the porch.

She crouched down next to her son. "It's okay, sweetie. You wanted to meet the puppy. Remember?"

"Take your time," Jase called. "I'm going to bring her to the backyard because it's fenced. Come on out whenever you're ready." The yelping got more insistent, a sure sign Ruby needed to get to the grass quickly. He lifted the blanket off the crate in the corner and flipped open the door, grabbing the puppy in his arms as she tried to dart out. She wriggled in his arms and licked his chin, but as soon as he opened the back door she darted for her favorite potty spot near a tree in the corner. He followed her into the grass with a glance back to the house. Emily and Davey hadn't emerged yet.

Ruby ran back to him and head-butted his shin before circling his legs. He didn't bother to hide his smile. Even after the worst day, it was hard not to feel better as the recipient of so much unconditional love. It didn't matter how long he'd been gone. She greeted him with off-the-charts enthusiasm every time.

After a few minutes, Ruby stopped, her whole body going rigid as her focus shifted to the back of the house. Jase went to grab her but she dodged his grasp and took off for the porch. He called for her but she ignored him as a six-month-old puppy was apt to do.

To his surprise, she slowed down at the top of the patio steps and didn't bark once at Emily or Davey. His puppy normally gave a vocal greeting at every new person or animal she encountered. She trotted toward Emily, stopping long enough to be petted before moving closer to Davey.

The boy was standing ramrod stiff against the house's brick exterior, his gaze staring straight ahead. Jase could almost feel Emily holding her breath. Ruby sniffed at Davey's legs, then nudged his fingers with her nose. When he didn't pet her, she bumped him again, then sat a few feet in front of him as if content to wait. After a moment, Davey's chin dipped and he glanced at the puppy. She rewarded him by prancing in a circle, then sitting again. He slowly eased himself away from the house and took a hesitant step toward her.

Ruby whined softly and ran to the edge of the porch and returned to Davey with a tennis ball in her mouth, dropping it at his feet. The ball rolled a few inches.

"She's learning to play fetch," Jase called. "Do you want to throw the ball for her?"

Davey didn't give any indication he'd heard the question other than picking up the ball gingerly between his fingers and tossing it down the steps. Ruby tumbled after it, and in her excitement to retrieve the ball, she lost her balance and did a somersault across the grass. With a small laugh, Davey made his way down the steps toward the grass.

Ruby returned the ball to him and the boy threw it again.

"She'll go after the ball all night long," he told the boy. "Let me know when you get tired of throwing it."

Davey walked farther into the yard.

Jase turned for the patio to find Emily standing on the top step, tears shining in her blue eyes. "What's wrong?" he asked, jogging up the stairs to her side.

She shook her head. "Davey laughed. Did you hear him laugh?"

"Puppies have that effect on people."

"I can't remember the last time he laughed out loud," she whispered, swiping under her eyes. "It's the most beautiful sound."

"I'm glad I got to hear it."

Ruby flipped over again as she dived for the ball and this time when Davey giggled, Emily let out her own quiet laugh. She clapped a hand over her mouth.

Jase wrapped an arm around her shoulder. "It's been a while since I've heard his mother laugh, too."

"I don't know whether to laugh or cry." She sank down to the top step and Jase followed, his heart expanding as she leaned against him. "He used to laugh when he was a baby. Then things went sideways... He became so disconnected."

"You're a good mom, Em. You'll get him through this."

She turned to look at him. "Do you really believe that? You don't think I messed him up by leaving Henry and moving him across the country?"

"You protected him. That's what a mom is supposed to do." He tried not to let decades-old bitterness creep into his voice but must have failed because Emily laced her fingers with his.

"How old were you when your mother left town?"

"Nine. My sister was seven. I haven't seen either of them since the day Mom packed up the car and drove away."

"Have you ever looked?"

"My mother made it clear any man with the last name Crenshaw was bound for trouble."

"She was wrong. You've changed what people in this town think of your family. She needs to know who you've become."

"It's too late."

"What about your sister?"

"I don't blame her. Who knows how my mother poisoned her against my dad and me. I'm sure Sierra has a good life. She doesn't need me."

Emily squeezed his hand. "I didn't think I needed my family when I left Crimson. I was stupid."

He glanced down at their entwined fingers and ran his thumb along the half-moons of her nails. "You used to wear polish."

"You're changing the subject." She waved to Davey

with her free hand when he turned. The boy gave her a slight nod and went back to throwing the ball.

"I don't want to talk about my family tonight." He threw her a sideways glance. "My turn for a pass?"

"Fine. Let's go back to my former beauty routine, which is a fascinating topic. I had my signature nail color and perfume. I was determined to be someone people remembered."

"You were."

"For the wrong reasons," she said with a laugh. "It's pretty sad if the thing I'm recognized for is a top-notch manicure and a cloud of expensive perfume."

"Now they'll recognize you as a strong woman and an amazing mother." He leaned closer to her until his nose touched the soft skin of her neck. "Although you still smell good."

Her breath hitched. "I wish I hadn't been so mean to you when we were younger."

"I suppose you'll have to make it up to me."

She turned, and he was unnerved by her serious expression. "I'm not the right woman for you, Jase."

The certainty of her tone made his gut clench. "Shouldn't I be the one making that decision?"

"I'm doing you a favor by making it for you."

"I don't want favors from you." He narrowed his eyes. "Unless they involve your mouth on me. Isn't that what you told me you wanted?"

Color rose to her cheeks and she dropped her gaze. "Wanting and needing are two different things."

He *wanted* to haul her into his lap and kiss that lie off her mouth. It was becoming more difficult to be patient when she was sitting so close that the warmth of her thigh seeped into his skin.

"We should talk about plans for the prewedding parties." She tugged her fingers out his and inched away from him until the cool evening breeze whispered in the space between their bodies. Jase hated that space. "Since so many of Noah's and Katie's friends overlap, I think the bachelorette and bachelor parties should be combined."

"Makes sense. Party planning is not exactly my strong suit."

"You're lucky I'm here."

There were many more reasons, but she was already spooked, so he didn't mention any of them. "I can tell you have an idea."

She flashed him a superior grin. "A scavenger hunt."

"Like we did as kids?"

"Sort of. We'll put together groups and give everyone clues to search for items important to Noah and Katie. They both grew up here so there's plenty of things to choose from."

"I like it," Jase admitted.

"Because it's brilliant."

"That's the Emily I know and…" He paused, watched her eyes widen, then added, "like as a friend."

She bumped him with her shoulder. "Mr. Perfect and a comedian—quite a combination."

"We've already established I'm not perfect."

"I like you better as a real person." She nudged him again. "And a friend."

As the sun began to fade, they watched Davey throw the ball over and over to the puppy.

"I wonder who will give up first," Jase muttered. The answer came a few minutes later when Ruby dropped the ball on the grass in front of Davey, then flopped down next to it.

"Wavy-Davey, it's time to head home," Emily called to him. "Bedtime for puppies and little boys."

The boy ignored her and sat next to Ruby, buried his face in the puppy's fur and began to gently rock back and forth.

Emily sighed. "Too much stimulation," she said, a sudden weariness in her eyes. "You might want to go inside. Chances are likely he'll have a tantrum."

"How do you know?"

"The rocking is one of his tells." She pressed her hand to her forehead. "I should have monitored him more closely but…" She gave Jase a watery smile. "I was having fun."

"Me, too," he told her and lifted his fingers to the back of her neck, massaging gently. "I'm not going to leave you. He's a kid and if he has a tantrum, so be it."

"I don't want the night to end like this." She walked down the steps slowly, approaching her son the way she might a wounded animal. Jase followed a few paces behind.

"Davey, we're going back to Grandma's now."

The rocking became more vigorous.

"Do you want to walk to the car or should I carry you?"

"No."

"You can decide or I'll decide for you, sweetheart." Emily's tone was gentle but firm. "Either way we're going home. You can visit Ruby again."

Davey's movement slowed. "When?"

"Maybe this weekend."

He shook his head and Jase stepped forward. "Hey,

buddy, you did an awesome job tiring out Ruby. I bet she's going to sleep the whole night through."

"She likes the ball," the boy mumbled.

"She likes you throwing the ball," Jase told him. "But even as tired as she is, I bet she'll wake up tomorrow morning with a ton of energy."

Davey gave him a short nod.

"Do you think it would be okay if I brought her out to your grandma's farm in the morning? You can puppy-sit while I go to a meeting."

The boy glanced up at him, then back at Ruby. He nodded again.

Jase crouched down next to Davey. "I'll ask your mom if it's okay with her, but you have to get a good night's sleep, too. That means heading home now and going to bed without a fuss. Do you think you can do that?"

Davey got to his feet and lifted his face to look at Emily before lowering his gaze again. "Can Ruby come over in the morning, Mommy?"

Emily reached out as if to ruffle her son's hair, then pulled her hand tight to her chest. "You'll have to eat breakfast early."

"Okay."

"Then it's fine with me. Your grammy will love to meet Ruby."

"She can walk with us." Without another word, he turned for the house. "Let's go home, Mommy."

Jase bent and scooped the sleeping puppy into his arms. Ruby snuggled against him.

Emily ran her hand through the dog's fur, then cupped Jase's cheek. "Thank you," she whispered and pressed a soft kiss to his mouth.

"A better way to end the night?" he asked against her lips.

"Much better. Good luck at the breakfast tomorrow." She kissed him again, then ran up the back steps.

Jase followed with the dog in his arms, watching as Emily buckled her son into his booster seat. He waved to Davey as they drove away.

"You did good," he whispered to the puppy sleeping in his arms and walked back to his house.

Chapter Eight

"You're looking at those pancakes like they're topped with motor oil instead of syrup."

Emily smiled as Jase spun toward her, almost spilling his cup of coffee in the process.

"You came," he said.

She glanced around at the basement reception room of one of Crimson's oldest churches. The last time she'd been here was after her father's funeral, but she tried to ignore the memories that seemed to bounce from the walls. Instead she waved a hand at the display of Sunday school artwork. "Where else would I be on a beautiful Saturday morning?"

"I don't really need to answer that, do I?"

"No, but I would like to know why the candidate who sponsored this breakfast is hiding out in the corner? Are you familiar with the term *glad-handing*?"

"I'm eating breakfast," he mumbled, pointing to the paper plate stacked with pancakes that sat on the small folding table shoved against the wall. "They're actually quite good." He set down his coffee cup and picked up the plate, lifting a forkful of pancake toward her mouth.

"I had oatmeal earlier."

"Edna Sharpe is watching. You don't want her to think you're too good for her pancakes."

Emily rolled her eyes at the glint of challenge in his gaze. But she allowed him to feed her a bite. "Yum," she murmured as she chewed. Her breath caught as Jase used his thumb to wipe a drop of syrup from the corner of her mouth.

"Jase," she whispered, "why aren't you talking to everyone?"

He dropped the plate back to the table and folded his arms across his chest. "I hate how they look at me."

"Like you're Crimson's favorite son?"

"Like I'm the poor, pathetic kid with the mother who abandoned him to his drunken dad." He held up a hand when she started to speak. "I understand most people in town know my family's history. But I've worked hard to make sure they see me and not the Crenshaw legacy. Now Charles Thompson is leaking small details about my childhood—dirty laundry I don't want aired—to anyone who will listen. You know how fast those bits of information travel through the town grapevine."

"So you're going to let him have the last word? Give up on everything you've done for Crimson?"

"Of course not."

She pointed toward the crowded tables. "Then go visit with these people. Shake hands. Kiss babies."

"Kiss babies," he repeated, one side of his mouth curving. "Really?"

"You know what I mean. I understand what happens when you let someone else's perceived image guide your actions. That's not who you are."

"They expect—"

"You're not perfect. Neither is your history. People can deal with that. But you have to put yourself out there."

"Is that what you're doing?"

"I'm supporting a friend," she said and straightened his tie.

His warm hands covered hers. "I'm glad you're here, Em. I could use a friend right now."

"What you could use is a kick in the pants."

His smile widened. "Are you offering to be the kicker?"

She nodded. "Katie and Noah are stopping by in a bit and I left a message for Natalie."

"You didn't need to. It's a Saturday morning and they have lives."

"Support goes both ways, and you've given plenty to your friends. They're happy to return the favor."

He took a deep, shuddering breath. "There wasn't supposed to be this much scrutiny."

"Welcome to the joys of a political campaign."

"And part of a life you left behind." He bent his knees until they were at eye level. "This isn't the plan for rebuilding your life." His fingers brushed a strand of hair away from her face. A flicker of longing skittered across her skin, one that was becoming all too familiar with this man.

"I can help," she said with a shrug. "It's what I know how to do."

He glanced over her shoulder and cursed. "My father is here," he said on a harsh breath.

Emily could feel the change in Jase, the walls shooting up around him. "You mingle with the voters," she said quickly. "I'll talk to your dad."

"You don't have to—"

"Too late," she called over her shoulder. She hurried to the entrance of the reception hall, where Jase's father stood by himself. A few of the groups at tables nearby threw him questioning looks. Emily knew Declan Crenshaw's history as well as anyone. The man had been on and off the wagon more times than anyone could count.

Once Jase and Noah had become friends, Emily's whole family had been pulled into the strange orbit circling Declan and his demons. Jase had slept over at her parents' farm most weekends, and she remembered several times being woken in the dead of night to Declan standing in their front yard, screaming for Jase to come home and make him something to eat.

As a stupid, spoiled teenage girl, Emily had hated being associated with the town drunk. She'd unfairly taken her resentment out on Jase, treating him like he was beneath her. Shame at the memory rose like bile in her throat. She'd been such a fool.

Now Declan's gaze flicked to her, wary and unsure behind the fake smile he'd plastered across his face. Without hesitating, Emily wrapped him in a tight hug.

"Jase is so glad you could make it," she said, loud enough so the people sitting nearby were sure to hear.

"You're a beautiful liar," Declan murmured in her ear, "and I know you hate these events as much as I do."

She pulled back, adjusted the collar on his worn dress shirt much as she'd straightened his son's tie. Declan would have been a distinguished man if the years hadn't been so hard on him. "Maybe not quite as much. I wasn't very nice, but at least I never embarrassed the people who loved me."

"Good point," he admitted with a frown, his shaggy eyebrows pulling low. "But things are different now. I'm sober for good. Am I ever going to live down the past?"

"I'm more concerned Jase feels the need to live it down for you." She led him toward the line at the pancake table.

"I know what Charles Thompson is trying to do." Declan picked up a paper plate and stabbed a stack of pancakes with a plastic fork. "It's my fault and it's not fair."

"Life rarely is." Emily took one pancake for herself. "We both know that."

"You're good for him."

She shook her head. "I'm not. As small of a community as Crimson is, the life Jase has here is still more public than I'm willing to handle."

Declan greeted the older man standing behind the table wiping a bottle of syrup. "Morning, Phil."

The other man's eyes narrowed. "Surprised to see you out of bed so early, Crenshaw."

Emily braced herself for Declan's retort, but he only smiled. "I'm full of surprises. How are Margie and the kids?"

Phil blinked several times before clearing his throat. "They're fine."

"I heard you have a grandbaby on the way." Declan poured syrup over his pancakes.

"My daughter-in-law is due around Thanksgiving," the other man answered, his face relaxing.

"I can't wait for Jase to find the right girl," Declan said. He nudged Emily's plate with his, which she ignored. "But until then, he's giving everything he has to this town. Do you know how many times he's taken payment for his services as a lawyer with casseroles or muffins?"

"I don't," Phil admitted. Several other volunteers had gathered around him.

Declan leaned over the table and lowered his voice, as if he was imparting a great secret. "More than I can count. He shares the food with me, and while I appreciate it, blueberry muffins don't pay the bills. But Jase wants to help people. There's his work on city council and getting Liam Donovan to move his company headquarters here." Declan glanced toward the doors leading into the hall. "There's Liam now, along with Noah Crawford. My son is good for this town, you know?"

The group on the other side of the table nodded in unison. "We know," Phil said.

With a satisfied nod, Declan turned to Emily, his dark eyes sparkling. "Shall we sit down and have breakfast, darlin'?"

She nodded, stunned, and followed him to a table, waving Noah and Liam over toward them. "You were amazing."

He threw back his head and laughed. "That's the first time I've ever heard that adjective used to describe me."

"I thought you'd get angry when Phil made the comment about you getting out of bed early."

"I don't get mad about hearing the truth. Phil and I go way back. It may have taken me a whole morning to climb out of bed in my hangover days, but at least I wasn't wearing my wife's undies when I did."

Emily felt her mouth drop. "What are you talking about?" she asked in a hushed whisper.

He winked at her. "I know plenty about the people in this town. For years, there was only one bar the locals liked. My butt was glued to one of the vinyl stools more nights than I care to admit. Most folks like to talk and they figure a drunk isn't going to remember their secrets." He tapped the side of his head with one finger. "But I got a mind like a steel trap. Even three sheets to the wind, I don't forget what I hear."

"There's more to you than anyone knows," Emily murmured with a small smile. She wouldn't forget what this man had put Jase through because of his drunken antics, but she could tell Declan was sincere in his desire to support his son.

"I think we have that in common," Declan told her.

A moment later Noah put an arm around her shoulder. "Hey there, sis. Trading one politician for another?"

She shoved him away, panic slicing up her spine.

"I'm joking, Em," Noah said quickly. "Didn't mean to strike a nerve."

"You should let Katie do the talking while you stick to looking the part of a handsome forest ranger." Emily tried to play off her reaction, but the way Noah watched her said he wasn't fooled.

He smiled anyway, smoothing a hand over his uniform. "I *am* a handsome forest ranger." His expression sobered as he looked over her shoulder. "Hello, Mr. Crenshaw."

"Noah." Declan nodded. "Congratulations on your upcoming wedding."

"Thanks. I owe a debt of thanks to Jase for helping me realize the love of my life had been by my side for years." He moved back a step to include Liam in the conversation. "Have you met Liam Donovan?"

Declan stuck out his hand. "I haven't but I've heard you're rich enough to buy the whole damn mountain if you wanted it."

Noah looked mortified but Liam only smiled and shook Declan's hand. "Maybe half the mountain," he answered.

As she greeted Liam, Emily could feel her brother studying her. She and Noah hadn't been close after their father's death, especially since they'd each been wrestling with their own private grief, and neither very successfully. They'd begun to forge a new bond since returning to Crimson, but Emily wasn't ready to hear his thoughts on her being a part of Jase's life.

Pushing back from the table, she grabbed her plate and stood. "You two keep Declan company. I see an old high school friend." She leaned down to give Jase's father a quick hug. "Thanks for breakfast," she said with a wink.

"Best date I've had in years."

Noah looked like he wanted to stop her, but she ducked around him and headed for the trash can in the corner. She waved to a couple of her mother's friends, then searched for Jase amid the people mingling at the sides of the reception hall.

Of course he was in the middle of the largest group, gesturing as he spoke and making eye contact with each person. They all stood riveted by whatever he was saying, nodding and offering up encouraging smiles.

A momentary flash of jealousy stabbed at her heart.

She understood what it was like to be on the receiving end of Jase's attention, sincere and unguarded. He was the only man she knew who could make his gaze feel like a caress against her skin, and this morning was proof of why that was so dangerous to her.

Even when he was living up to other peoples' expectations, Jase was comfortable in the role. He belonged in the spotlight and in the hearts of this town. Emily had left behind her willingness to trade her private life for public favor. Davey had changed her. She'd never put anyone else's needs before his. Even her own.

She slipped out the door leading to the back of the church, needing a moment away from the curious eyes of the town. The midmorning sun was warm on her skin. She closed her eyes and tipped up her face, leaning back against the building's brick wall.

A moment later the door opened and shut again.

"What happened to catching up with old friends?" Noah asked, coming to stand in front of her.

"You're blocking my sun," she told him.

"Because from what I remember of how you left this town, you don't have many friends here."

She opened her eyes to glare at him. "Don't be mean."

He sighed. "I don't understand what you're doing. For years you couldn't stand Jase—"

"That's not true." The protest sounded weak even to her own ears.

"You certainly gave him a hard time. I stopped out at the farm this morning and saw Mom and Davey with his puppy."

"Davey bonded with Ruby right away, so Jase was nice enough to bring her by so they could play."

"Of course. Jase is a nice guy."

"Too nice for someone like me?"

Noah stepped out of her line of sight, turning so he stood next to her against the wall. "You know he's had a crush on you for years."

"It's different now. I'm working for him."

"Which means you two are spending a lot of time together. He'd moved on until you came back. Jase has a lot of responsibility in this town. Between his practice, his father and now dealing with a real campaign—"

"I understand, Noah." She hated being put on the spot and the fact her brother was doing it. "Are you telling me to stay away from him?"

Noah shook his head. "You're coming off a bad divorce. I'm saying don't use Jase as a rebound fling. Both of you could end up hurt."

Pushing off the wall, she spun toward him. "It's Jase you're worried about, not me."

"Emily—"

"No. You don't know anything about my marriage."

"Why is that?" He ran a hand through his hair. "How the hell am I supposed to understand anything about your life? You cut me out after Dad died."

"That was mutual and you know it."

"I thought we were doing better since Mom's illness?"

"We are, Noah. But it might be too soon for brotherly lectures on my private life."

"Nothing is private in Crimson. You know that. Besides, I thought you came back to here to heal?"

"Maybe Jase is a part of me healing." Until she said the words out loud, she hadn't realized how true they were. Tears sprang to the backs of her eyes and she swiped at her cheek, refusing to allow herself to break down. She'd promised herself she was finished with crying after she'd left Henry.

Noah cursed under his breath. "I'm sorry. Don't cry."

"I'm not crying," she whispered and her voice cracked.

"You really care about him."

"We're friends. It's not a fling. Not a rebound. I don't know what is going on between us, but I'm not going to hurt him. I think…" She paused, forced herself to meet Noah's worried gaze. "I think I'm good for him. It goes both ways, Noah. I know it does."

"Okay, honey." Noah pulled her in for a tight hug. She resisted at first, holding on to her anger like an old friend. But her brother didn't let go, and after a few moments she sagged against him, understanding that even if he made her crazy, Noah was far better comfort than her temper could ever be.

"I'm sorry," he whispered into her hair.

"You're a good friend to Jase."

"But I need to be a better brother to you. You're important to me. You and Davey both."

"You have to say that because I helped your bride pick out a wedding dress that will bring tears to your eyes."

"I can't wait," he said with a lopsided grin and a dopey look in his eyes that made her smile. "But I'm *choosing* to tell you the truth about supporting you more. I mean every word."

"Then will you help me find my own place to live?"

"Mom loves having you at the farm." He frowned. "She loves helping with Davey and having you close."

"I'll still be close, but I want a home of my own, even

if it's a tiny apartment somewhere. After the wedding will you help me look?"

"Of course."

"Do you have any prewedding nerves?" she asked, stepping out of his embrace. "You spent a long time avoiding commitment."

"I was a master," he agreed.

"Marriage is a big deal, especially when there's a baby on the way."

"I felt the baby kick the other night."

"Oh, Noah."

"It made this whole thing feel real. I mean, I know it's real but…yes, I'm nervous." He looked over her shoulder toward the mountains in the distance. "Not about marrying Katie. I can't believe I was blind for so long, but now I've got her and I'm never letting go." He took a breath, then said, "Even if I don't deserve her."

"You do." She nudged him with her hip. "You're a pain in my butt, but you deserve happiness."

"What if I mess up? What if I can't be as good as Dad?"

"Don't compare yourself." She gave a small laugh. "Do you think I could ever hold a candle to Mom?"

"You're an amazing mother."

"You'll be an amazing dad." She held up her hand, fist closed. "We've got this, bro."

"Are you trying to be cool?"

She shrugged and lifted her hand higher. "Don't leave me hanging."

With a laugh, Noah fist-bumped her, then pulled her in for another hug. "We'd better head back inside. I have a feeling Declan and Liam together are a dangerous combination."

* * *

Jase's lungs burned as he ran the final stretch to the lookout point halfway up the main Crimson Mountain trail. At the top, he bent forward, sucking in the thin mountain air.

The late-afternoon trail run was supposed to clear his head, but his mind refused to slow down. Images of Emily and his dad swirled inside him, mixing with thoughts of the questions he'd answered at this morning's campaign breakfast.

How do you feel about Charles Thompson running against you?

Do you have too much going on to add mayor to your list of responsibilities?

When are you going to settle down and start a family?

Are you worried about not having time to take care of your dad?

What if Declan starts to drink again?

He'd answered each of the inquiries with a nod and an understanding smile, but he'd wanted to turn and run from the crowded church hall. Those questions brought up too many emotions inside him. Too much turmoil he couldn't control. Jase's greatest fear was losing control and it seemed he had less of a grasp on it with each passing day.

He sank down to one of the rock formations and watched as Liam Donovan came over the final ridge, a few minutes behind Jase. Liam's dark hair was stuck to his forehead and his athletic T-shirt plastered to his chest. The run up to the lookout point was almost three miles of vertical switchbacks. Jase had been running this trail since high school but today even the beauty of the forest hadn't settled him.

"Are you crazy?" Liam asked, panting even harder than Jase. "You were running like a mountain lion was chasing you."

Jase wiped the back of one arm across his forehead. "A mountain lion would have caught you instead of me. I thought you wanted a challenge."

"A challenge is different than a heart attack. You'd have a tough time explaining to Natalie that you left me on the side of the mountain."

"I wouldn't have left you." Jase grinned. "I'm too afraid of your wife."

"The strange thing is she'd take that as a compliment." He sat on a rock across from Jase. "You had a good turnout at the breakfast this morning."

"I appreciate you stopping by."

"Always happy to do my part with a plate of pancakes. Your dad is a character."

Jase laughed. "That's one word for him."

"He's really proud of you." Liam used the hem of his shirt to wipe the sweat off his face. "My dad never gave a damn about anything I did. Not as long as I stayed out of his way."

Liam's father owned one of the most successful tech companies in the world. It had been big news in the technology world when Liam broke off to start his own GPS software company and chose Crimson as the headquarters for it.

"I couldn't exactly stay out of Declan's way. I was too busy cleaning up behind him."

"A fact your new opponent in the mayor's race is exploiting?"

Jase blew out a breath. "Sheriff Thompson has seen me at my lowest. He and my dad grew up together in town and the Thompsons and Crenshaws have always been rivals—sports, women, you name it." He stood and paced to the edge of the ridge, taking in the view of the town below. "Anytime a situation involved my dad, Thompson made sure he was on the scene. Didn't matter if it was the weekend or who was on duty. The sheriff always showed up to personally cuff Dad."

"Declan seems sincere about changing."

"He's always sincere." From up here, Jase could see downtown Crimson and the neighborhoods fanning out around it. The creek ran along the edge of downtown, then meandered through the valley and into the thick forest on the other side.

As a kid, he'd battled the expectations that he'd follow in his father's footsteps. People always seemed to be waiting for him to make a misstep, to become another casualty of the Crenshaw legend. He'd worked so hard to prove them wrong. When would he be released from the responsibility of making up for mistakes he hadn't made?

Liam came to stand next to him. "I know what it's like to have to claw your way out from a father's shadow. Our backgrounds are different, but disappointment and anger don't discriminate based on how much you have in the bank."

"But you've escaped it."

"Maybe," Liam said with a shrug. "Maybe not. My dad is known all over the world. I've created a different future for myself but his legacy follows me. I choose to ignore it and live life on my terms."

Jase wasn't sure if he'd even know how to go about

setting up his own life away from the restrictions of his past. "When I graduated from law school, a firm in Denver offered me a position. I turned it down to come back to Crimson and take over Andrew Meyer's family practice."

"Do you regret the choice you made?"

Jase picked up a flat stone from the trail and hurled it over the edge of the ridge. It arced out, then disappeared into the canopy of trees below. "I don't know. Back then, I was so determined to return to Crimson as a success. Part of it was feeling like I owed something to the people in this town. As much as they judged my family, they also came forward to take care of us when things were rough. After my mom left, we had food in the freezer for months."

"Nothing says love in a small town like a casserole."

"Exactly," Jase agreed with a laugh. "There were a couple of teachers who looked after me at school. Once it became clear I was determined to stay on the straight and narrow, the town was generous with its support. I was given a partial scholarship during undergrad and always had a job waiting for me in the summer. I wanted to pay back that kindness, and dedicating myself to the town seemed like the best way to do it."

"But…" Liam prompted.

"I've started to wonder what it would have been like to go to work, come home and take care of only myself. Maybe that's selfish—"

"It's not selfish." Liam lobbed a rock over the side and it followed the same trajectory as Jase's. "It's also not too late. I was going to ask if you need support with the campaign. Financial support," he clarified.

"But now I'm wondering if becoming mayor is what you really want?"

"Does it matter? I've committed to it."

"You can back out. Charles Thompson isn't a bad man. He would do a decent job."

Jase cocked a brow.

"Not as good as you, of course. But the future of Crimson doesn't rest on your shoulders, Jase."

"I'll think about that." As if he could think about anything else. "We should head back down. I'll take it easy on you."

Liam barked out a laugh. "A true gentleman."

Jase started for the trail, then turned back. "Thanks for the offer, Liam. I appreciate it, but I don't want to owe you. Having you at my back is plenty of support."

"I'd think of it as an investment," Liam answered. "And the offer stands if you change your mind."

"Thank you." Jase started running, the descent more technical than climbing the switchbacks due to the loose rocks and late-afternoon shadows falling over the trail. It was just what he needed, something to concentrate on besides the emotional twists and turns of his current life.

Chapter Nine

Monday morning, Emily jumped at the tap on her shoulder, spinning around in her desk chair to find Jase grinning at her.

She ripped the headphones off her ears. "You scared me half to death," she said, wheezing in a breath.

"You were singing out loud."

"You were supposed to be in court all day." She narrowed her eyes.

"What exactly are you listening to?" He reached for the headphones, but she grabbed them, then spun around to hit the mute button on her keyboard.

"Music," she mumbled. "Why are you back so early? I didn't hear the bells on the door when it opened."

"I came in through the door to the alley out back."

"You snuck up on me," she grumbled.

"What kind of music? I didn't recognize it."

"Broadway show tunes, okay?" She crossed her arms over her chest and glared. "*Evita* to be specific. I like musicals." The words came out like a challenge. "You're a lawyer—sue me."

His grin widened. "Don't cry for me, Emily Whitaker."

"Asking for trouble, Jase Crenshaw."

He held up a brown paper bag. "Here's a peace offering. I brought lunch from the deli around the corner. That's why I came through the back. Have you eaten?"

She held up an empty granola-bar wrapper. "I'm working through lunch since I'm leaving early today." Tomorrow was Davey's first day of kindergarten so tonight they were going to the ice cream social at the elementary school. Her son didn't seem worried about the change, but Emily had been a bundle of nerves since the moment she'd woken up this morning.

She'd had a meeting at the beginning of the week with the kindergarten teacher and the school's interventionist to discuss the Asperger's and how to help Davey have a successful school year. For a small school district, Crimson Elementary School offered many special education services. This would mark the first time he'd been away from her during the day.

She'd enrolled him in preschool in their Boston neighborhood, having added Davey's name to the exclusive program's wait list when he was only a few months old. Despite the expense of the private program, the teachers had been unwilling to work with his personality quirks.

Much like her husband, they'd expected him to manage like the rest of the children, which led to several frustrated tantrums. Davey had lashed out, throwing a toy car across the room. It had hit one of the other students on the side of the head and the girl had stumbled, then fallen, knocking her head on the corner of a bookshelf. There'd been angry calls from both the teacher and the girl's mother and even a parent meeting at the school to allay other families' concerns about Davey continuing in the program.

Henry had been furious, mostly because two of his partners had kids enrolled at the school so he couldn't brush the incident under the rug. In the end, Emily had pulled Davey, opting to work with him herself on the skills he'd needed to be ready for kindergarten.

She couldn't control the way Asperger's affected his personality and his ability to socialize with both adults and other kids. Or how he was treated by people who didn't understand how special he was.

"Come to the conference room and eat a real lunch," Jase said gently, as if he could sense the anxiety tumbling through her like rocks skidding down the side of Crimson Mountain.

"I have work to do."

"Em, you are the most efficient person I've ever met. You've already organized this whole office, updated the billing system, caught up on all my outstanding correspondence and done such a great job of editing the briefs that Judge McIlwain at the courthouse actually commented on it."

Pride, unfamiliar and precious, bloomed in her chest. "He did?"

"Yes, and he's not the only one." Jase rested his hip against the corner of her desk. "Do you remember the contract you drafted for the firm I'm working with over in Aspen?"

She nodded.

"The office manager called to see if I'd used a service to hire my new assistant. She wanted to find someone just like you for their senior partner. He's a stickler for detail and notoriously hard on office staff."

"She called me, too." Emily swallowed.

"Why?" Jase's tone was suspiciously even.

"To offer me a job."

"What was the starting salary?"

She told him the number, almost double what he was paying her.

Jase cursed under his breath. "Why didn't you take it? It's one of the most prestigious firms in the state."

"I know. I researched them."

"They can offer you benefits and an actual career path. You have to consider it, even if it makes me mad as hell hearing someone tried to poach you."

She shook her head. "I don't want to work in Aspen. I like it here with you." She flashed what she hoped was a teasing smile. "You'd be lost without me."

His brown eyes were serious when he replied, "You have no idea."

"Jase…"

"At least let me feed you. I've been thinking of ideas for the prewedding scavenger hunt."

She stood at the same time he did, too shocked to protest any longer. "You have?"

He looked confused. "Wasn't that the plan?"

"Well, yes," she admitted as she followed him to the conference room at the far end of the hall. "But I wasn't sure you'd take it seriously. You have so much going on, and it's a silly party theme."

There was an ancient table in the middle of the conference room, with eight chairs surrounding it. On her second day in the office, Emily had taken wood soap and furniture wax to the dull surface, polishing it until it gleamed a rich mahogany. She liked that she could make a difference here in Jase's small law practice.

He held out a chair for her and she sat, watching as he emptied the contents of the bag. He set a wax-paper-wrapped sandwich in front of her, along with a bag of barbecue potato chips. "Noah is my best friend. Making his wedding weekend special isn't silly, and neither was your idea. You need to give yourself more credit."

She nodded but didn't meet his gaze, running one finger over the seam of the wax paper. "What kind of sandwich?"

"Turkey and avocado on wheat," he answered absently. "Do you want a soda?"

"Diet, please," she said, unable to take her hand off the sandwich.

He left the room and Emily sucked in a breath. He remembered her favorite sandwich.

The small gesture leveled her, and the barriers she'd placed around her heart collapsed. This man who was wrong for her in every way except the one that mattered. He seemed to want her just the way she was. Her ex-husband would have brought her a salad, forever concerned she might not remain a perfect size six.

Perfect.

Her life since returning to her hometown had been anything but perfect, yet she wouldn't trade the journey that had brought her here. She was a better person for her independence and the effort she'd put into protecting Davey from any more suffering and rejection.

* * *

She did her best to gather her strength as she pulled up to the elementary school parking lot later that evening. The playground and grassy field in front of the building were crowded with people, and she wished she'd gotten to the event earlier.

Instead she'd changed clothes several times before she and Davey left her mother's house. Difficult to find an outfit that conveyed all the things she needed.

I'm a good mother. Like me. Like my son. Accept us here so I can make it a true home.

Straightening her simple A-line skirt, she got out of the SUV and helped Davey hop down from his booster seat. The desire to gather him close almost overwhelmed her. She wanted to ground herself to him with touch but knew that would only make him anxious. She dropped the car keys into her purse and gave him a bright smile. "Are you ready to meet your new teacher?"

His eyes shifted to hers, then back to the front of the school. "Okay," he mumbled and emotion knitted her throat closed.

"Okay," she repeated and moved slowly toward the playground. Several women looked over as they approached, and she recognized a couple who'd been in her grade. They waved and she forced herself to breathe. If she panicked, Davey was likely to pick up on her energy. Already she could feel him dragging his feet behind her.

"We've got this," she said, glancing back at him.

He crossed his arms over his chest and stared at the ground.

Emily's heart sank but she kept the smile on her

face. All she wanted was to protect her sweet boy, but so often she didn't know how to help him.

Suddenly she heard a female voice calling her name. She looked up to see a tiny woman with a wavy blond bob coming toward her.

"I hoped you'd be here," Millie Travers said as she wrapped Emily in a tight hug. Millie was a recent addition to the community, having moved to town last year to be close to her sister Olivia. Both sisters were married to Crimson natives. Millie's husband, Jake Travers, was a doctor at the local hospital and Emily knew he had a daughter from a previous relationship who was around Davey's age.

Emily had met Millie, along with Katie's other girlfriends, at a breakfast Katie had coordinated shortly after her engagement. Her future sister-in-law was doing her best to make sure Emily felt included in her circle of friends, which she appreciated even if it was difficult for her to trust the bonds of new friendships after her experience in Boston. But she couldn't deny Millie was an easy person to like. "Katie told me to look out for you," the other woman said with a smile. "Your son is starting kindergarten this year, right?"

Emily swallowed. "Yes." She turned to where Davey stood stiff as a statue behind her. "Davey, this is Mrs. Travers, a friend of mine."

Her son stared at the crack in the sidewalk. Around the dull roar in her head, Emily heard the sound of laughter and happy shouts from the other kids on the playground. She wondered if Davey would ever be able to take part in such carefree fun.

If Millie was bothered by Davey's demeanor, she didn't show it. Instead, she sank down to her knees but kept her gaze on the edge of the sidewalk. "It's nice to meet you. My stepdaughter, Brooke, is starting first grade this year. She can answer any questions you have about kindergarten. Mrs. MacDonald, the kindergarten teacher, is really great."

"Whatcha doin', Mama-llama?" A young girl threw her arms around Millie's neck and leaned over her shoulder. Emily saw Davey's eyes widen. The girl wore a yellow polka-dot T-shirt and a ruffled turquoise skirt with bright pink cowboy boots. Her blond curls were wild around her head.

"I'm talking to my new friend, Davey," Millie said, squeezing the small hands wrapped around her neck. "He's starting kindergarten this year."

Brooke stood up and jabbed a thumb at her own chest. "I'm an expert on kindergarten." She stepped around Millie and held out a hand. "Ms. MacDonald has a gecko in her room."

"I have a question," Davey said quietly.

Brooke waited, reminding Emily a bit of Noah's puppy. Finally she asked, "What's your question?"

"Is it a crested gecko or a leopard gecko?"

"It's a leopard gecko and his name is Speedy," Brooke told him. "Come on. I'll take you to see the classroom."

Millie straightened, placing a gentle hand on Brooke's curls. "We need to make sure it's okay with Davey's mommy."

Emily was about to make an excuse for why Davey should stay with her when he slipped his hand into Brooke's. The girl didn't seem bothered by his rigid shoulders or the fact he continued to stare at the ground.

"I'll go, Mommy," Davey said softly.

Emily opened her mouth, but only a choked sob came

out. Biting down hard on the inside of her cheek, she gave a jerky nod.

"We'll be right behind you," Millie said, moving to Emily's side and placing an arm around her waist. "Go slow, Brookie-cookie. Show Davey the room and we'll meet you there so both Davey and his mommy can meet Ms. MacDonald."

"Okeydokey," Brooke sang out and led Davey through the crowd.

"Do you need a minute?" Millie asked gently.

Emily shook her head but placed a palm to her chest, her heart beating at a furious pace. "He doesn't usually…" She broke off, not sure how to explain what an extraordinary moment that had been for her son.

"Brooke will take care of him." Millie smiled. "He's going to be fine here. I know you don't have any reason to believe me, but something in this town rises up to meet the people who need the most help."

"I've never been great at taking help," Emily said with a shaky laugh. "I'm more a 'spit in your eye' type person."

"That's not what I hear from Katie. She's a very good judge of people. We'll follow them." Millie led her along the edge of the crowd, smiling and waving to a number of people as they went. But she didn't stop so Emily was able to keep Brooke and Davey within her sight. Millie's smile widened as she looked over Emily's shoulder. "And she's not the only one."

Emily turned to see a tall, blond, built man she recognized as Dr. Jake Travers, Millie's husband, walking through the parking lot with Jase at his side. Jase was a couple inches taller than Jake and his crisp button-down shirt and tailored slacks highlighted his broad shoulders and lean waist. Her heart gave a little leap and she smiled before she could stop herself.

"My husband is the hottest guy in town," Millie said, nudging Emily in the ribs. "But soon-to-be Mayor Crenshaw holds his own in the looks department. Wouldn't you agree?"

Emily shifted her gaze to Millie's wide grin and made her expression neutral. "He's my boss," she murmured.

The other woman only laughed. "I was Brooke's nanny when I first came to Crimson. That didn't stop me from noticing my *boss*." She gently knocked into Emily again. "Don't bother to deny it. Your game face isn't that good."

"My game face is flawless," Emily countered but the corners of her mouth lifted. Maybe not flawless when it came to Jase. The two men were almost at the playground. She leaned down to Millie's ear and whispered, "I'll only admit Dr. Travers is the second-hottest guy in town."

Millie hooted with laughter, then grabbed her husband and pulled him in for a quick kiss. "Jake, do you know Noah's sister, Emily?"

Jake Travers held out his hand. "Nice to see you, Emily."

"Your daughter was really nice to my son tonight," Emily told him. "She's a special girl."

He laughed. "A one-child social committee, that's our Brooke."

"She's giving Davey a tour of the kindergarten classroom," Millie told him. "How's the campaign, Jase?"

"Pretty good." Jase inclined his head toward the mass of kids on the playground. "But it's never too early to recruit potential voters." He smiled but Emily could see it was forced. Millie and Jake didn't seem to notice.

"Speaking of recruitment," Millie said, glancing up at Jake, who'd looped an arm around her slender shoulders. "I told the classroom mom you'd help coordinate a field trip to the hospital to see the Flight For Life helicopter." She turned to Emily. "She's working the volunteer table now so I'd like to stop by for a second. We'll see you in the kindergarten room. Brooke's classroom is right next door."

Emily nodded and kept moving toward the building. She saw Davey follow Brooke Travers inside.

"Campaign stop?" she asked Jase. He'd taken up Millie's post at her side and more people waved to him as they approached the school.

"I thought you and Davey might like some moral support." He shrugged, ducked his head, looking suddenly embarrassed. "Clearly, you've got it under control. He's made a friend and you—"

"I'm glad you're here," she said, letting out an unsteady breath. "Davey left my side, which was the whole point of this, and I almost broke down in tears on the spot." She stopped and pressed her open palm to his chest. His heart beat a rapid pace under the crisp cotton of his shirt. "Thank you for coming," she whispered.

He covered her hand with his, and then interlaced their fingers. "Anytime you need me," he said, lifting her hand and placing a tender kiss on the inside of her wrist.

Emily felt color rise to her cheeks, and she glanced around to find a few people staring at them. "Jase, we're…"

"At the elementary school," he said with a husky laugh. "Right." He lowered her hand but didn't release it.

Butterflies swooped and dived around Emily's stomach, and she felt like a girl holding hands with her first boyfriend. It took her mind off the worry of fitting in with the other mothers. Between Millie's exuberant welcome and Jase's gentle support, Emily felt hopeful she could carve out a happy life in the hometown that had once seemed too small to hold all of her dreams.

But the biggest dreams couldn't hold a candle to walking into the bright classroom to see her son solemnly shaking hands with his new kindergarten teacher.

"I'm glad Davey will be joining our class this year," the teacher said to Emily as she and Jase approached. "It's great he has a friend like Brooke to introduce him to the school."

Davey darted a glance at Emily and she saw his lips press together in a small smile when he spotted Jase next to her. "They have a Lego-building club," he mumbled, his eyes trained on Jase's shoes.

Jase crouched low in front of Davey. "That's excellent, buddy. Are you excited about school?"

Davey took several moments to answer. Emily held her breath.

Her son looked from Jase to her and whispered, "I'm excited."

Emily felt a little noise escape her lips. It was the sound of pure happiness.

Chapter Ten

Jase pulled up to his house close to nine that night. He parked his SUV in the driveway, then opened its back door for Ruby to scramble out. After the ice cream social, he'd gone directly to his dad's house with dinner.

Declan had gotten his cable fixed so they watched the season finale of some show about dance competitions, the point of which Jase couldn't begin to fathom. But his dad seemed happy and more relaxed than he'd been in ages. Ruby had curled up between them on the sofa and the quiet evening was the closest thing Jase could remember to a normal visit.

As soon as her legs hit the ground, Ruby took off for the house. Jase quickly locked the car, then came around the front, calling the puppy back to him.

But Ruby ignored him, too busy wriggling at the feet of the woman sitting on the bottom step of his front porch.

Emily.

She'd changed from the outfit she wore to the ice cream social to a bulky sweatshirt and a pair of…were those pajama pants?

"Hey," he called out, moving toward her. "These after-dark visits are becoming a habit with us."

She didn't answer or smile, just stood and stared at him.

Worry edged into his brain, beating down the desire that had roared to life as soon as he'd laid eyes on her.

"What's going on?"

She walked forward, her gaze intent but unreadable. When she was a few paces away, she launched herself at him. Her arms wound around his neck and he caught her, stumbling back a step before righting them both. She kissed him, her mouth demanding and so damn sweet. All of the built-up longing he'd tried to suppress came crashing through, smothering his self-control.

He lifted her off the ground, holding her body against his as he moved them toward the house. Ruby circled around them, nipping at his ankles as if she resented being left out of the fun. Emily's legs clamped around his hips as he fumbled with the house key. She continued to trail hot, openmouthed kisses along his jaw and neck.

"Are you sure?" he managed to ask as he let them in, then slammed shut the front door. "Is this—"

"No talking," she whispered. "Bedroom." She bit down on his lip, then eased the sting by sucking it gently into her mouth. Jase's knees threatened to give way.

He moved through the house with her still wrapped around him, and then grabbed a handful of dog treats from the bag on the dining room table as he passed.

He tossed them into the kitchen and Ruby darted away with a happy yip.

He felt Emily smile against his mouth. "Always taking care of business."

"You're my only business," he told her, moving his hands under the soft cotton of her sweatshirt as he made his way down the hall. He claimed her mouth again. "I want to taste every part of you." He pushed back the covers and lowered her to the bed, loving the feel of her underneath him.

"Later," she told him. "I need you, Jase. Now."

He lifted his head to meet her crystal-blue gaze but found her eyes clouded with passion and need. The same need was clawing at his insides, making him want to rip off her clothes like a madman. To think she was as overcome as he was changed something inside him. His intention of savoring this moment disappeared in an instant.

Straightening, he toed off his shoes, then pulled his fleece and T-shirt over his head in one swift move. Emily sat up, tugging at the hem of her sweatshirt and he was on the bed in an instant.

"Let me." As she lifted her arms, he pulled off the sweatshirt, leaving her in nothing but a pale pink lace bra. Lust wound around his chest, choking off his breath as he gazed at her. He felt like a fumbling teenager again, unable to form a coherent thought as he stared.

Her eyes on his, Emily reached behind her back and unclasped the bra, then let it fall off her shoulders and into her lap.

"Beautiful," Jase murmured as her breasts were exposed. He reached out to touch her and she scooted forward, running her hands over his chest.

"Right back at you," she said.

"Emily—"

"I want this," she told him. "I want you. Please don't make me wait any longer."

He wanted to laugh at her impatience. He'd been waiting for this moment for as long as he could remember. He stood again, shucked off his jeans while she shimmied out of her pajama bottoms and panties.

"Condom?" she asked on a husky breath when he bent over her again.

He started to argue, to insist they take their time but the truth was he didn't know how long he'd last if she continued to touch him. He opened the nightstand drawer and grabbed a condom.

She reached for it but he shook his head. "I better handle this part or the night will really be over before it starts."

Emily smiled and bit down on her lip, as if pleased to know she affected him so strongly. Was there really any question?

A moment later he kissed her again, fitting himself between her legs, capturing her gasp in his mouth as he entered her.

Nothing he'd imagined prepared him for the reality of being with Emily. She drew him closer, trailing her nails lightly down his back as they found a rhythm that was unique to them.

Everything except the moment and the feel of their bodies moving together fell away. All of life's complications and stress disappeared as passion built in the quiet of the room. In between kissing her, he whispered against her ear. Not the truth of his heart. Even in the heat of passion he understood it was too soon for that.

Instead he murmured small truths about her beauty, her strength and the complete perfection of being with her. She moaned against him, as if his words were driving the desire as much as the physical act. Her grasp on him tightened and he felt her tremble at the same time she cried out. She dug her nails into his shoulders and the idea that she might mark him as hers made his control shatter.

He followed her over the edge with a groan and a shudder, and she held him to her, gentling her touch as their movements slowed.

Balancing himself on his elbows, he brushed away loose strands of hair from her face. She looked up at him, the blue of her eyes so deep and her gaze painfully vulnerable. She blinked several times, her mouth thinning but her eyes remained unguarded. It was like the normal screens she used to defend herself wouldn't engage. He understood the feeling, so when she closed her eyes and turned her head to one side, he simply placed a gentle kiss on the soft underside of her jaw.

"No regrets," he murmured, then rose and walked to the bathroom. He glanced back to her from the doorway. Emily Whitaker was in his bed, the sheet tucked around her, her long blond hair fanned across his pillow like a golden sea. Tonight reality was indeed much better than his dreams.

Run, run, run.

The voice in Emily's head wouldn't shut up, and she pressed her fists against her forehead trying to press away the doubts blasting into her mind. She felt the wetness on her cheeks and couldn't stop the sobs that coursed through her body.

She wasn't sure how long she lay there before Jase returned. His fingers were cool around her wrists as he tugged them away from her face.

"No, Em." His voice was hollow. "No tears."

"I don't want to hurt you," she whispered, knowing she already had.

"If you mean hurt me with the best sex of my life, bring on more pain."

His kindness at this moment when he should hate her only made her cry harder. All the pain and sorrow and guilt and anger she'd bottled up during her marriage and before came pouring out. It was like being with Jase had torn away all of her emotional barricades.

"So not your best experience I take it," he said with a strained laugh.

She shook her head. "The best ever."

"Look at me and say that."

After several moments, she did. "It was amazing. You were amazing, Jase. I don't regret tonight, but I'm sorry."

"Remember I'm a simple man," he told her. "You're going to need to be a little clearer."

"I'm a mess." She used the edge of the sheet to wipe the tears from her face.

He nodded. "But a beautiful mess."

She poked at him. "You're not supposed to agree with me," she said but laughed at the fact that he had.

"Then I'm sorry. And we're even."

"We're not even." She didn't know how they ever could be. "You've been nice to me when I didn't deserve it, given me a job and connected to my son in ways not even his father could. I'm so grateful to you."

Jase raised an eyebrow. "So that was thank-you sex?"

She gasped and shifted away from him.

"I'm not complaining," Jase added, pulling her back again. "Just trying to figure out where we are here."

"You make me feel things," she whispered, scooting up so her back was against the headboard. She tucked the sheet more tightly under her arms, wishing she'd put on clothes while Jase was in the bathroom. He was wearing a pair of athletic shorts low on his hips but she still had the surprisingly awesome view of his ripped chest and broad shoulders. "Things I thought I put away to concentrate on the serious business of raising a son with special needs."

"Things like?"

She swallowed, worried her fingers together, traced the empty space on her left hand where she'd worn her wedding ring. She'd been so sure of herself when she'd met Henry. Positive that force of will could make her life perfect. Keep her heart safe. Impenetrable.

"Things like…joy…hope." There were other feelings that terrified her, but she wasn't ready to admit to anything more. She drew in a breath. "I came here tonight because I needed…"

"A release?"

"You."

The silence stretched between them, heavy with all they'd both left unspoken. He turned so he was sitting next to her and stretched his long legs out over the bed. "That's the nicest word I've ever heard."

He gathered her into his arms, sheet and all, his strong arms reminding her there was another kind of safety. The type that came from allowing another person to see her true self.

"I wanted you," she told him, circling one finger

through the sprinkling of dark hair across his chest. "I've wanted you since that day at the football game. Maybe since the morning of my mom's surgery when you came to the hospital."

She could feel his smile against the top of her head. "I've wanted you for as long as I can remember."

"But I'm empty, Jase. On the inside. There are a million broken pieces scattered there. I don't know how to fix them." She slid her hand up to his jaw, running her thumb over the rough stubble. "You deserve someone who is whole. I can't be that person yet, and I may never be the woman who can support you in all you do for this town. All people expect of you."

"You already have." He ran a finger along her back at the edge of the sheet. The simple touch was both soothing and strangely erotic. "You've organized my life, focused my campaign when I needed it and smoothed over the rough edges of having my dad involved. I've learned to rely on only myself, which is a difficult habit to end. But I trust you."

She shook her head. "I'll help with your message, not be part of it. I'm comfortable with a behind-the-scenes role. A friend. It's different."

"It doesn't have to be."

"I came here because you mean something to me, but I can't be the person you need." She reached up, pressed her mouth to his and repeated, "I *don't* want to hurt you." She meant the words but she couldn't admit the bigger truth—that she was terrified of her heart being the one to break. The more she cared, the harder the loss was to bear.

"There's more," Jase said softly. "Tell me why you're afraid."

"*I* don't want to be hurt," she admitted on a harsh breath. "I can't give you my heart because having it break again would kill me, Jase."

"I won't—"

"You can't know that." She tucked her head into the crook of his arm, unable to meet his gaze and say the words she needed him to hear. "My dad certainly didn't plan to die from cancer and leave my mom alone. I never thought I'd marry a man who couldn't accept his own son."

"I'm not your ex-husband." Jase's voice was pitched low.

"Henry isn't a villain. He's someone who needs his life to look perfect." She gave a strangled laugh. "I have no room to judge when it's what attracted me to him in the first place. Having a baby opened my heart in ways I didn't expect. I never wanted to feel that way, to be vulnerable. Davey is everything to me. But there isn't room for anyone else. I want you, and I don't regret coming here. But we can't let it go any further." She tried to pull away, but his arms tightened around her.

"What if this is enough?"

She stilled, risked a glance up to find him smiling at her. "Is that possible?" A piece of hair fell across his forehead, and she pushed it back, loving the feel of his skin under her fingers.

"I know it's not possible that once with you is enough for me." He lowered his mouth to hers, his lips tender. Desire pooled low in Emily's belly and she moved in his arms. The evidence she wasn't the only one affected pressed against her hip. She shifted again.

"Emily," he groaned against her mouth. "You're killing me."

"In a good way, I hope. I like being in your arms, Jase. I want to feel something. I'm tired of the nothingness. I want more. With you."

He moved suddenly and she was on her back again with Jase's body pressed to hers. "Then no worries, regrets or expectations."

"Expectations?"

"Expectations most of all." He pulled the sheet down, then skimmed his teeth over the swell of her breast. "I'm drowning under them, Em. But not with you. With you I can just *be*. And I promise you the same. We can be friends and more. But only as much as feels right. No other promises. No blame. No stress."

Another layer of joy burst to the surface inside her. It felt as if her chest was filled with bubbles, fizzy and light. She felt drunk with the exhilaration of it.

Right now, every part of her life was filled with stress. It was part of being a single mother. Even with her family's support, she could never truly let go. What Jase was offering felt like a lifeline. And the best part was she could give the same thing back to him. Pleasure for the sake of pleasure. No expectations.

It felt like freedom.

She wrapped her arms around his neck. "You've got yourself a deal, counselor."

"Sealed with a kiss," he said and nipped at the edge of her mouth.

"Sealed with a thousand kisses," she whispered and set about adding them up.

Chapter Eleven

The following Friday morning, Emily was busy untangling a strand of tiny twinkle lights being used to decorate the wide patio at Crimson Ranch, where tomorrow's wedding would be held. Sara worked on a separate length of lights while April Sanders arranged mason jars that would be filled with wildflowers on the tables set up around the patio.

Jase had closed the office today so they could both concentrate on wedding plans. Her mother was picking up Davey after school while April led a private yoga class for Katie and her girlfriends. The group would then go for facials and massages at a spa near Aspen before joining the men for the scavenger hunt Emily and Jase had organized. Emily had worked to make sure the activities leading up to the wedding were fun, personal and helped celebrate who Katie and Noah were as a couple.

She understood why they'd selected the ranch as their wedding venue. Located on the outskirts of town, the property had been beautifully restored in the past few years to become one of the area's most popular destinations.

In addition to the rough-hewn-log main house, there was a large red barn and several smaller cabins spread around the property. Clumps of pine and aspen trees dotted the landscape, giving the buildings a sense of privacy. Each time the breeze blew Emily enjoyed the sound of aspen leaves fluttering in the wind. She could see where the property dipped as it got closer to the forest's edge and knew the creek ran along the divide.

"You had sex." Sara grinned at Emily.

Emily spit the bite of muffin she'd picked up from the basket sitting on the table. "Excuse me?" She choked on muffin crumbs.

April patted her on the back. "Don't take offense. The more outlandish Sara's comments, the more she likes you."

Sara laughed and continued to string lights. "For the record, I like you a lot, Emily Whitaker. Not as much as I like your brother. When I first came to town, Noah flirted with me every chance he got."

"Noah flirted with everything with a pulse before Katie," Emily muttered.

"But with me he was trying to make Josh jealous." Sara's smile was devious. "You have points in your favor for being related to Noah, but there are other reasons I like you."

"You barely know me." Emily wiped the back of her hand across her mouth. "You definitely don't know me well enough to comment on my sex life." She heard the pretentiousness in her voice that she'd perfected during her short marriage.

Sara only laughed again. It was a rich, musical sound that projected across the vast pasture spreading out behind the house. Sara was petite with pale blond hair and luminous blue eyes. Her bigger-than-life presence made her hard to ignore. Emily supposed the "it girl" vibe contributed to Sara's fame from the time she'd been a child actor.

"We met at the dinner to celebrate your mom's recovery," Sara told her. "You were there with your son, and it's clear you're devoted to him. Another plus in your favor."

"I remember but—"

"You looked tense and defensive, like you might snap in two at any moment." Sara waved a hand toward Emily. "Now you're relaxed and you can't control the good-sex grin on your face—"

"I can control my smile," Emily argued, then thought of Jase and felt the corners of her mouth tug upward. She pressed her fingers to her mouth and glanced at April.

"Don't look at me. I'm certainly not smiling like that."

"Which is what we're working on next," Sara said, moving to April's side. "You've been alone for too long, my friend."

April shook her head, a tangle of red curls bouncing around her face. "One marriage was quite enough, thank you. I'm perfectly content without a man in my life."

"Don't forget I was married, too." Emily wasn't sure

why she felt compelled to argue this point. The idea that these women she was only beginning to know could read her was scary as hell. "I have a son and he's my priority. I don't have time for anything else."

"But you've been making time," Sara said.

April's voice was gentle. "You do seem happier, which is a good thing."

"Maybe it's the yoga." Emily pointed at April. "I've been coming to your classes. Maybe you should take credit for my newfound calm, if that's what I have."

"It's more than calm," April told her with a smile. "It's a glow. I'd love to believe it was the yoga but—"

"It's sex." Sara winked. "You don't have to admit it for it to be true."

"Don't tell Katie," Emily mumbled after a moment. "She and Noah will want there to be more to it than there is." She bit down on her lip, then grinned. "And it's great the way it is."

It had been more than great and her stomach did a slow, sweet roll at the thought of the time she'd spent with Jase. It was easy to have him come to the farm with Ruby after work under the guise of discussing wedding plans or the mayor's race, and he'd become a fixture at their dinner table. Emily's mother had even insisted he bring Declan to join them for several evening meals.

At first it amazed her how seriously he seemed to value her opinion. Whether on reception details or the more important campaign strategies, he listened to her ideas and often used them as the foundation from which to build his own.

Emily liked being someone's foundation. And she loved the private, stolen moments when Jase would wrap her in his arms and shower her with kisses. She felt the telltale goofy smile tug at her mouth again.

Sara threw an arm around April's shoulder. "Yoga classes are lovely but nothing is better than the restorative powers of great sex." She pointed at Emily. "Are you going to tell us who it is?"

"Do I have to?"

Sara thought about that for a moment. "No, but if you don't I'll be forced to ask your soon-to-be sister-in-law."

April lifted her hand to clamp it over Sara's mouth. "Forgive her. She means well. You don't have to tell us anything." April's voice was gentle, her tone so motherly it made Emily warm inside. "For the record," April added, "I think Jase is great."

"He is…" Emily narrowed her eyes. "Wait. That was sneaky." A gorgeous earth mother with a little edge.

"April's the worst," Sara said when April dropped her hand. "She's gentle and sweet, so people don't realize she's also whip smart and far too observant. The thing that makes it less annoying is she'll protect your secrets to her grave."

"Is Jase a secret?" April asked, her eyes all too perceptive.

"Yes." Emily shook her head. "I mean, no. We're friends."

"April needs a friend like that," Sara said with a laugh.

"Why don't you worry about your own love life and leave mine alone?" April crossed her arms over her chest and did her best to glare at Sara. She still looked sweet.

"No worries in my life." Sara wiggled her brows. "Josh is absolutely perfect. In fact, just last night…"

"Save it," April said quickly. "We're talking about Emily."

"Feel free to move on," Emily told them, then held up a hand to Sara. "I'm not asking for details about your private life."

Sara grabbed a muffin off the table and dropped into a chair. "You don't seem like a sell-it-to-the-tabloids type of person."

"No."

"Of course she's not," April agreed. "So you and Jase are friends." April pointed at Emily. "The kind of friends that have seen each other naked."

"That's one way to put it," Emily answered, making a face.

"You like him?"

Emily nodded.

"A lot?" Sara asked.

"Yes."

"Everyone in town loves him," April offered. "Why just friends and why the secret?"

"Because," Sara added, popping a bite of muffin in her mouth. "You understand this town can't keep a secret? People will find out."

"If they don't already know," April said.

"We want something that belongs to us."

Now Sara's face softened. "Oh, yes. I understand." She glanced at April. "We both do."

Sara stood and came to give Emily a hug. She glanced over her shoulder at April. "Come on. Group embrace."

The willowy redhead, who smelled of vanilla and cloves, wrapped them both in a tight hug. "What is between you and Jase is yours," she whispered. "But don't hold on to it too tight. Love is like a garden, Emily. It needs light and air to breathe, or it will shrivel before it has a chance to grow strong."

Emily gasped. "It's not love," she murmured. "It can't be."

Neither Sara nor April answered. They only tightened their hold on her.

By the time the last team came through the doors of the brewpub in downtown Crimson, Jase's mood was as dark as the mahogany paneling lining the walls.

Luckily his friends didn't seem to notice. Everyone had loved Emily's scavenger hunt. The teams had raced through Crimson collecting mementoes that were special to Noah and Katie.

Now they were sharing stories about the couple, laughing and toasting the impending nuptials as the bride and groom held court at one of the large tables in the center of the bar. The entire evening had been a success if he ignored the fact that Emily was doing her best to avoid him.

With so many of their friends around, it was easy to accomplish. No matter how many times Jase tried to meet her gaze or talk to her alone, she managed to slip away. He knew she'd spent the day working out at Crimson Ranch with Sara and April, but he couldn't imagine how things could have changed between them so quickly.

He watched her step away from the main group to take a call on her cell phone, her brows puckering at whatever was being said on the other line. The conversation only lasted a few minutes, and he moved behind her as she ended the call.

"Everything okay?"

She jumped, pressing a hand to her chest. "Sneak up much?"

"Avoid people much?" he countered.

Color rose to her cheeks and she looked everywhere but into his eyes. The sudden distance between them made him angry. This had been the best week of his whole damn life. Even with the campaign, work and all the other pressures of regular life, Jase had felt happier than he could remember. He wanted more from Emily. He wanted the right to give more *to* her.

Maybe it was excitement around the wedding or so many of his friends in relationships, but he was convinced Emily was meant for him. He'd always made decisions in his life based on what was smart and responsible. Duty had governed his actions for as long as he could remember. Being with Emily was about making himself happy. Making her happy. For the first time, he wanted to commit to something more than this town and restoring his family name.

He wanted something of his own.

He wanted Emily.

"It's been a hectic day," she said, her tone stiff. "I want everything to be perfect for Noah and Katie."

"I thought we agreed perfection is overrated."

She looked at him now, her eyes sad. "Not for the two of them. They deserve it."

"You deserve—"

She held up a hand. "I can't have this conversation now. My mom called. One of Davey's completed sets fell off the shelf and broke. He's having a meltdown." The sound of laughter and music carried to them and she glanced over his shoulder at their friends. She looked so alone it made his gut twist. "I've got to go, but I don't want to worry Noah. Will you cover for me?"

"Let me come with you."

"It's better if you don't," she whispered. "People will talk."

"I don't give a damn what anyone says."

She wrapped her arms tight around her middle. "I do."

Those two words killed him. He'd told her he wouldn't push her, and he had to honor that. When she turned to walk away, it took everything in him not to stop her.

Even more when Aaron Thompson slid off his bar stool as she moved past. The man put a meaty hand on Emily's arm and she flinched. Jase saw red as Aaron leaned closer and Emily's face drew into a stiff mask.

Jase was striding forward by the time she shook free and ran out the pub's front door.

"What the hell did you say to her?" He pushed Aaron's broad chest, and the man stumbled into the empty bar stool, knocking it on its side with a clatter.

Jase felt the gazes of the crowded bar on him, but for once he didn't care. He stepped into Aaron's space as the other man straightened.

Aaron leaned closer and lowered his voice so only Jase could hear. "I told her she'd have a hard enough time raising that weirdo kid of hers in this town without hitching herself to the Crenshaw wagon." His beady eyes narrowed farther. "When she's ready for a real man, she should give me a call. Your dad couldn't keep a woman satisfied, and I doubt you're any different."

It didn't matter that Emily was gone. Jase knew Aaron's words would have prodded at her fears, the same way they slithered into his. "Don't ever," he said on a growl, "speak to her again."

"Oh, yeah?" Aaron smirked. "Whatcha going to do about it?"

Jase hauled back his fist and punched Aaron, his knuckles landing against skin with an audible thud. The burly man staggered a few steps before righting himself. Noah and Liam had already grabbed hold of Jase.

"Dude," Aaron shouted into the sudden quiet of the bar. "I'm sorry. My dad wants what's best for this town. You don't have to threaten our family."

"Settle down, man," Noah said when Jase strained against him.

"He's lying." Jase felt blood pounding against his temples. He glanced around the bar to find himself the center of attention from every corner. He was so used to being universally liked, it took him a minute to recognize the emotions playing in the gazes of the friends and strangers who stared at him.

Anger. Disappointment. Pity.

"He's a liar," Jase yelled and felt a heavy hand clasp on to his shoulder.

"What's the problem?" Cole Bennett, Crimson's sheriff, stepped between Jase and Aaron.

Aaron winced. "I made an offhand comment about the election to Jase," he said, holding a hand to one eye. "You know, *may the best man win* and whatever. He went crazy on me." He looked at the sheriff all righteous indignation. "Must have hit a nerve. My dad can tell you plenty of stories about the Crenshaws going ballistic for no reason."

Anger radiated through every cell in Jase's body. He

shifted, then realized Noah and Liam were still holding him. "I'm fine," he said, shrugging away.

"You sure?" Noah's voice was concerned.

"Yeah." He pointed at Aaron. "That's not what went down and you know it."

Sheriff Bennett stepped closer to him, placing one hand on his chest. "You want to tell me a different side of the story?"

Jase opened his mouth, then snapped it shut again. He caught Aaron's smug gaze over Cole's shoulder and realized tonight was no accident. He'd been set up in this scene and had fallen right into the trap. He couldn't contradict Aaron's story without revealing specifics of the truth, which would humiliate Emily.

"No." He closed his eyes and tamped down his temper. "I've got nothing to say."

Cole heaved out a sigh. "Are you sure?"

Jase met the other man's gaze. "I am."

"What if I want to press charges?" Aaron asked.

Cole gave Jase an apologetic look, then turned to the other man. "Do you?"

"I should. It was a cheap shot." The bartender handed Aaron a bag of ice and he groaned a little as he pressed it to his eye. "But I guess we can't expect anything else from a Crenshaw."

Noah took a step forward, anger blazing in his eyes. "Don't be a—"

"It's okay," Jase interrupted, grabbing hold of his friend. "If he wants to press charges—"

"I don't. My father taught me to be the better man."

"Okay, then. Let's move on. Everybody back to their regularly scheduled evening." Cole turned to Jase. "I assume you're heading out?"

Jase nodded.

"I don't know what he did to deserve that punch," Cole said, "but I can guarantee it wasn't the story he told about the election. You sure you don't want to tell me anything else?"

"Positive."

With a nod, Cole moved away. Liam and Noah took his place.

"What the hell, Jase?" Noah asked. "I don't think I've ever seen you take a swing at somebody."

"I've got to get out of here," Jase muttered. "Sorry about causing a scene during your party."

Liam placed a hand on his shoulder. "You want company?" When Jase shook his head, Liam nodded and walked back toward their group of friends.

"Come back to our table," Noah told him. "Don't let this ruin the night."

"I'm not going to," Jase answered, "but I need to go now. Give Katie a hug for me. I'll pick you up in the morning to head out to Crimson Ranch."

Noah looked like he wanted to argue but only said, "No one expects you to be perfect, Jase."

"I know." But both of them knew it was a lie. People in this town expected perfection, duty and self-sacrifice from Jase, all of it offered with a smile. He understood that in the way of small towns, the news of the punch would spread like dandelion fuzz on the wind. The news, while inconsequential in its retelling, only needed to be nurtured a bit before it took root and grew into the start of a weed that could derail everything he'd worked to create.

At this moment he couldn't bring himself to care.

He left the bar and kept his head down as he walked to his parking space in the alley behind his office building. Driving out of town, he was tempted to take the turnoff toward the Crawfords' farm. Thoughts of Emily and her reaction to Aaron's taunts consumed him, but he'd promised not to ask her for more than she was willing to give. In his current mood he might drive a wedge between them if he pushed her.

Instead he steered his SUV toward the trailer park and pulled into his father's small lot. The blue-tinted glow from the television was the only thing lighting the inside of the trailer.

Declan hit the mute button on the remote when Jase walked in. "I thought the big party for Noah was tonight?"

"It is," Jase said, lowering himself to the sofa. "What happened to our family, Dad? Why are we so messed up? Mom leaving with Sierra, you and Uncle Steve drinking, Grandpa in jail. Why does every generation of our family have a sad story to tell?"

His father leaned back against the recliner's worn cushion. "Not every generation. Not you."

"Not yet," Jase shot back. "It's like there's a curse on us, and I don't know if I'm strong enough to break it."

"You already have."

"I decked Aaron Thompson tonight."

"Hot damn," Declan muttered. "That little jerk has been giving you grief since grade school."

"You noticed?"

"I'm a drunk, not an idiot. Hitting Aaron does not make you cursed. Hell, I've taken a swing or two at Charles over the years."

"And gotten yourself cuffed for the trouble."

"Worth it every time."

"I'm not you."

Declan laughed. "Praise the Lord." He leaned forward, placed his elbows on his knees. "In a town like Crimson, people see what they want. Once a reputation is set, it's hard to change it. I don't know how the trouble with our family started, but I do know it's easier to live down to expectations than to try to change them. At least it was for me. Your grandpa went to jail for the first time when I was ten. My brother and I had our first beers when we were eleven. Working in the mine didn't help. Nothing much good comes from sticking a bunch of ornery men inside a mountain."

Jase asked the question he'd been afraid to discuss with his dad for almost twenty years. "What about Mom?"

"Your mom was right to go. I was a mess back then."

"Yeah, Dad," Jase answered, "I know. I was the one taking care of you."

"You don't remember, do you?"

"Mom leaving?" Jase shrugged. He remembered crying. He remembered being alone at night staring at the empty bed where his sister had slept next to him.

"She wanted you to go with her."

"No. She took Sierra and left me behind."

"Because you told her I needed you more." When Declan met Jase's gaze, his eyes were shining with unshed tears. "She had your little suitcase in the trunk but you refused to get in the car. It killed her but eventually she agreed to let you stay. That's how I know you're not like the rest of us. You've never done a selfish thing in your life. You take care of this town like you've taken care of me all these years. With every ounce of who you are. You're not part of the curse. You're our family's shot at breaking it."

Jase closed his eyes and tried to remember the details of the night his mom had driven away. All he could see was Sierra's face in the car window and the taillights glowing in the darkness. The days after were a blur of tears and anger and his father going on a major bender.

"One punch doesn't make you a troublemaker, Jase."

"Tell that to the people who witnessed it."

"What I should do is talk to the man who's the cause of all your recent stress. This is Charles Thompson's fault. If he—"

"It's fine." Jase stood, ran a hand over his face. "Don't go after Thompson again. You're right. The Crenshaw curse ends with me."

He started to walk past his dad, but Declan reached out with a hand on Jase's arm. "It's what you want, Jase. Right?"

"Sure, Dad." Jase didn't know how else to answer and he was too tired to sort out his muddled emotions, either to his father or himself. "I'm picking up Noah early tomorrow to drive out to the ranch. Call if you need anything, okay?"

"Save me a piece of cake," his dad said, sitting back in the recliner. Declan had been invited to the wedding but since alcohol was being served, he'd decided to forgo the celebration. Jase appreciated his dad's effort to stay sober but hated that it isolated Declan even more than he already was.

"Are you sure you don't want me to get you for the ceremony?"

"Enjoy yourself tomorrow, son. Don't worry about me."

Jase gave the smile he knew his dad wanted to see. "Call if you change your mind."

Chapter Twelve

"Are you nervous?" Emily paced the guest cabin where she and Katie were waiting for the wedding to start. "You don't look nervous." She turned to Katie, who was glowing in the ivory gown they'd chosen at the bridal salon in Aspen. "You look beautiful." The satin gown had a sweetheart neckline and a lace overlay that was both delicate and modern. Katie's dark hair was pulled away from her face in a half-knot, with gentle curls tumbling over her shoulders. "Noah is going to lose his mind when he sees you. But, seriously, shouldn't you be nervous?"

Katie smiled and patted the bed next to her. "I don't need to because you've taken care of everything. It's perfect, Em. My dream day." As Emily sat down on the patchwork quilt, Katie took her hand. "Thank you for everything."

"It was easy." She gave a strangled laugh. "My mother-in-law and I were at the reception hall until two in the morning the night before my wedding redoing seating arrangements. There were so many stupid details to focus on but none of them involved preparing Henry and me to make a life together." She squeezed Katie's fingers. "You and Noah are doing this right."

"Unrequited love, fear of commitment, friendship and a baby after a breakup," Katie said with a laugh. "We might have had the order a little off."

"The love is what counts," Emily answered. She stood when Katie sniffed and Emily grabbed the box of tissues from the dresser, handing Katie a wad of them. "No crying. Your makeup is perfect."

"Then don't say sweet things to me." Katie dabbed at the edge of her eyes with a tissue. "I asked you for my dream wedding, and you've given it to me."

"Not quite yet."

A knock sounded on the door. "Ladies, are you ready?" Sara called.

"Perfect timing," Emily said with a smile.

Katie stood, her eyes widening as she pressed a hand to her stomach. "Wow. Just got nervous. Major butterflies."

"You've got this." Emily opened the door and followed Katie out, smiling as Sara oohed and aahed over the dress. Katie's father was waiting at the edge of the barn, out of sight of the chairs set up in front of the copse of aspens where the ceremony would take place. It was a perfect fall day, cool and sunny with just the slightest breeze.

She knew Katie and her parents weren't close, but her father became visibly emotional at the sight of his daughter. It made Emily's heart ache missing her own dad and all the moments she'd never get to share with him.

But this wasn't a day for sorrow, and she was honored to be Katie's maid of honor. She adjusted Katie's train and then stepped away. When the processional music began, she turned the corner from the barn toward the wedding guests. All Katie's and Noah's closest family and friends were in attendance. Emily's gaze sought Davey first, her son looking so handsome in his suit, standing next to his grandma in the front row. His eyes flicked to hers and she saw the stiffness in his small shoulders ease the tiniest bit.

The knowledge that seeing her gave him some comfort made her heart squeeze. She looked up to her brother standing in front of the grapevine arbor and smiled before her eyes met those of the man standing next to him.

She had to work to control her expression as Jase looked at her, his gaze intense. Her knees went weak and she clutched the bouquet of wildflowers tighter. One foot in front of the other, she reminded herself. Breathing in the warm mountain air, she felt her heart skip as Jase's mouth curved up at one end. As much as she'd tried to avoid him the previous night, now she couldn't break eye contact, even as she took her place in front of the assembled guests.

The music changed and Katie came into view. Emily glanced at the beautiful bride but then watched her brother's face as Katie moved closer. There was so much love in Noah's eyes. It was as if the whole world went still for a moment and there was only her brother and his bride. Emily was suddenly grateful for the tissue she'd stuffed under the ribbon of her bouquet.

She continued to need the tissue as the short ceremony progressed. By the time Noah leaned down to kiss his bride, Emily swore she could hear the whole valley choking back tears. Then there were only smiles and cheers as Noah and Katie walked back down the aisle hand in hand.

Jase offered her his elbow and she tucked her hand in it, blushing as he leaned close to her ear and whispered, "You look beautiful." She sucked in another breath and smoothed one hand over the pale pink cocktail gown she wore. She felt beautiful and happy and lighter than she had in ages. As they started down the aisle together, Emily was proud to meet the approving gazes of the people she'd come to think of as her community.

But Jase paused before the first row. "You two belong with us," he said to her mother and Davey.

Emily's heart, already so full, expanded even more at her mother's watery, grateful smile. Jase tucked Meg's arm into his other elbow and nodded at Davey. "Why don't you lead us down, buddy?"

The boy looked at the ground and Emily wanted to curse her own stupidity. She knew her son didn't like people looking at him and was afraid Jase's sweet gesture would backfire.

Davey chewed on his lower lip for a few seconds and finally muttered, "I'll follow you."

Emily breathed a sigh of relief and saw her mother do the same. Jase nodded and the four of them made their way past the other guests.

Emily didn't have a chance to speak to Jase alone until the dancing started. Meg and her new beau had taken Davey home after the cake was cut. To Emily's surprise, Davey had seemed to actually enjoy himself at the wedding, running around through the field behind the tables with the other kids.

He stuck close to Brooke Travers and didn't yell or play fight the way the other boys at the reception did, but he was definitely a part of the group and she couldn't have been prouder.

As the sky darkened over the mountain, silhouetting the craggy peaks against the deep blue of evening, a three-piece bluegrass band began to play. Noah pulled Katie onto the makeshift dance floor near the edge of the patio and other couples followed. Emily was just about to head inside to see if the caterers needed help packing up when strong arms slipped around her waist.

"Dance with me?" Jase asked but was already turning her to face him.

"I should check on things," she said but didn't protest when he lifted her hands to his shoulders.

"It's fine," he said, beginning to sway with her to the lilting sound of the fiddle drifting toward them. "Better than fine. All of your hard work made this a perfect day."

"We both worked hard," she corrected and rested her head against his chest. "You and I make a pretty good team." She was starting to trust the happiness she felt, to rely on it.

One of Noah's high school friends walked by, then stopped and clapped Jase on the shoulder. "Good to see you've grown a spine, Crenshaw."

Emily felt Jase tense and lifted her head.

He said a few words to the man, then tried to turn her away.

"Makes me want to vote for you all the more," the

man said with a chuckle. "I like a mayor with a strong right hook." With another laugh, he walked away.

Emily pulled back enough to look up at Jase. "What was that about?"

He shook his head. "Nothing."

"A strong right hook isn't nothing," she argued. "Did you hit someone?" She couldn't imagine a circumstance where Jase would throw a punch.

"Let's just dance."

"Tell me."

He blew out a breath. "Aaron Thompson," he muttered.

"What about him?"

"I saw him talking to you at the bar last night. You were upset when you left, so I asked him about it."

The happiness filling her moments earlier evaporated like a drop of water in the desert. Shame took its place, hot and heavy, a familiar weight on her chest. She hated that anyone, especially Jase, knew the awful things Aaron had said to her. But even more…

"You hit him?" she asked and several people nearby turned to look at them. She stepped out of Jase's arms and lowered her voice. "I didn't need you to defend me."

"He was out of line. No one has the right to speak to you that way." He reached for her, but she jerked back, giving herself a mental headshake. What was between her and Jase was supposed to be casual. Emily had let it turn into something more because he made her happy. But the way Aaron had taken advantage of that was the unwelcome reminder she needed. She couldn't let this go any further.

She caught Noah's gaze and flashed her brother a

small smile as she waved. "I'm going to check if the caterers need help."

"Emily," Jase whispered, "don't walk away."

But she hurried into the cabin before Jase could stop her. She told herself it was because she was angry at Jase, although it felt more like fear clawing at her stomach. Panic at the thought of depending on someone and allowing herself to be vulnerable again. Of needing Jase and then having him leave her. It was one thing when they were on equal ground, but if she began to rely on him and truly opened her heart...what was to stop him from breaking it?

April was supervising the last of the cleanup so Emily pitched in where she could. Her hands trembled as she moved vases of flowers to the kitchen's large island but she didn't stop working.

"I think we're almost finished in here," April said eventually. "I don't have a hot guy waiting to dance with me, so I can handle the rest."

"It's fine," Emily muttered. "I'm not in the mood to dance."

"Uh-oh." April stepped in front of her as she turned for the sink. "What's wrong?"

"Nothing."

"What kind of nothing?"

Emily sighed and met the redhead's gentle gaze. "Is it really possible to start over?"

April opened her mouth, then shut it again as if she didn't actually know how to answer the question.

"It seems easy in theory," Emily continued. "Cut out the bad parts from your life and move on. Let go. Tomorrow's a new day. I can spout out greeting-card sentiments until I run out of breath. But is it possible?

How can I leave the past behind? Life isn't simple, you know?"

"I do know," April said with a sad smile. "Maybe it's not about a fresh start as much as it is continuing to try to do better."

"Learn from your mistakes?" Emily laughed. "Another cliché, but I have plenty to choose from."

April picked up a flower and twirled the stem between her fingers. "Play it cool as much as you want, but it's obvious you really care for Jase, and he's crazy about you."

Emily swallowed. "I wasn't looking for…"

"For love?"

"It isn't—"

April tapped Emily on the nose with the wildflower's soft petals. "I have no history in this town, Emily. No expectations of who either of you are supposed to be. You can be honest with me."

"Which may be easier than being honest with myself."

"Start with saying the words out loud."

Emily swallowed then whispered, "I love him."

"I have a feeling he feels the same."

"He can't," Emily said, shaking her head. "We want different things from life. I can't be the woman he needs."

"Maybe what he needs is the woman you are."

Emily felt tears clog the back of her throat. A tiny sliver of hope pushed its way through the dark layers of doubt she'd heaped on top of it. "Are you always this good at giving pep talks?"

"To other people," April told her, "yes."

The catering manager walked back into the kitchen with the final bill.

"I'll take care of this," April said. "You find Jase."

"I can't tell him yet." Emily fisted her hands until her nails left marks on the center of each palm. "It's too soon. I don't know—"

"You might start with showing him how you feel," April said and nudged her toward the patio door.

"Right. Show don't tell. I think I can do that." At the thought of being in Jase's arms again, her stomach buzzed and fluttered like a thousand winged creatures were taking flight inside it. "I think I'd like that very much."

As she stepped back outside, she saw that Jase and the other guests had gathered in the center of the patio to say goodbye to Noah and Katie. The newlyweds were staying in one of the guest cabins at Crimson Ranch overnight before driving to the Denver airport tomorrow to fly out for their honeymoon to a Caribbean island.

"I'm so happy to have a sister," Katie said as Emily hugged her.

"Me, too," Emily whispered, then turned to her brother. "I'd tell you to get busy making me a little niece or nephew," she said, punching him lightly on the arm, "but for once in your life, you're an overachiever."

"Always the clever one." Noah chuckled and pulled her in for a hug. "Call if you need anything."

"I absolutely won't," Emily shot back. "You've earned these two weeks in paradise. Enjoy them."

"I intend to and thanks again, Em." Noah tipped up her chin. "You made my bride very happy."

"Go." Emily made a shooing motion. "I've laid all the groundwork for you to get lucky tonight."

Noah leaned in close and kissed Emily on the cheek. "Maybe I'm not the only one," he whispered with a wink, then turned and scooped Katie off her feet.

Everyone cheered as the couple disappeared down the pathway toward the far cabins. As the music started again, guests drifted back toward the patio. Emily continued to stare into the darkness for several minutes, nerves making her skin tingle as she thought about finding Jase in the crowd.

With a fortifying breath she turned and bumped right into him. She yelped and stumbled back. Jase grabbed hold of her arms to steady her.

"Were you some kind of a cat burglar in another life?" she asked, trying to wrestle her pounding heart under control. "You're far too good at being quiet."

He let go of her, dropping his hands to his sides. "My dad wasn't much fun with a hangover. I learned to be quiet so I wouldn't wake him."

"Oh." Her comment had been meant as a joke. The way he answered made her remember they'd each been shaped by their past. "I'm sorry."

"No need," he said quickly. "It's a fact."

"I meant for earlier. Even if it wasn't necessary, thank you for defending my honor with Aaron."

"Again, no need. You don't deserve to be dragged into the long shadow cast by my family's reputation." The music picked up tempo and Jase turned for the house. "Should we head back?"

Emily didn't move. "What do you mean your *family's reputation*? Aaron told me I might as well be campaigning for his father since I was distracting you from the usual attention you pay to Crimson and its residents. He insinuated that a relationship with a divorced mom of a kid with special needs would work against your bid for mayor."

"I'm going to kill him," Jase muttered. "I wish I would have knocked him out cold." He ran his hands through his hair, leaving it so tousled Emily couldn't resist reaching up to straighten it.

"No," she told him. "You shouldn't have hit him at all."

He pulled her hands away from his hair, clamping his fingers gently around her wrists. "Emily, what is the real problem here?"

Where to start?

Your dreams. My fears.

Falling in love with you.

Definitely don't lead with that one.

She raised up on tiptoe and slid her lips along his, the knot of tension inside her unfurling at the warmth of his mouth and the roughness of his stubble when their cheeks brushed. He smelled like the mountains and tasted of mint and sugary wedding cake. Right now, he was everything she wanted in the world.

Show don't tell.

"The only problem is we're not undressed."

Jase gave a harsh laugh. "You're trying to distract me."

"Is it working?"

"Hell, yes." He glanced over his shoulder toward the lights of the party, which was still going strong even in the absence of the bride and groom. "Think anyone will notice if we sneak away?"

"Let them notice." She would deal with the consequences of her feelings for Jase another time. When he laced his fingers with hers, Emily almost forgot her doubts. She simply let them go.

Giving in to the happiness fizzing through her made her giggle.

Jase glanced down at her but didn't stop moving toward his SUV. "What's so funny?"

She shook her head. "Nothing. I'm glad to be with you."

He opened the passenger door and she slipped in. "You just made me the second-happiest guy on this ranch." He pulled the seat belt around her, using it as an excuse to kiss her senseless.

She took out her phone and punched in a quick text to her mother as Jase came around the front of the SUV. "Everything okay?" he asked, turning the key in the ignition.

Emily waited to speak until her mother's answering text came through. Then she smiled at him. "I've got permission for a sleepover."

"The whole night?" His voice was husky.

"Yep. I mean, I'd like to be home in the morning for breakfast. Davey usually sleeps until about eight on the weekend so that gives us…"

"All night long," Jase finished, taking her hand and lifting it to his mouth. Then he cringed a little. "Unfortunately, the puppy doesn't like to sleep in so late."

"I guess you're going to have to make waking up early worth my while."

Of course, Ruby needed some attention when they got back to the house. "One of my neighbors came over a couple of times today to let her out and play with her." Emily laughed as Ruby exploded out of her crate, yipping and running circles around Jase as he struggled to clip on her leash. "Clearly, she's ready for more. I'm sorry. This isn't exactly a great start to a romantic evening. I need to take her for a short walk so she won't be so wound up."

"I'll come with you." They followed the puppy into the front yard toward the sidewalk.

As Ruby sniffed a tree, Jase shrugged out of his coat and wrapped it around Emily's shoulders. She loved being surrounded by his scent and the warmth of him. They started down the sidewalk with Ruby happily trotting next to them. She seemed in no hurry to do her business tonight, making Jase groan and Emily laugh.

"I'm sor—"

"Don't say it." She took his hand as they walked. "This is nice. I love the quiet of your neighborhood and this time of night, especially after the past week of planning the wedding. It feels normal."

"Normal is underrated," he said with a laugh. "Every birthday wish when I was a kid was for a normal family like yours."

"As I remember, a lot of those birthdays were spent at our house."

"Your mom would bake a red velvet cake and you'd refuse to come out of your room to sing."

Emily pressed her free hand to her face. "I was horrible to you."

"You were pretty mean to Noah, too, so I took it as a compliment."

"Only you, Jase."

Ruby finally found the perfect patch of grass and they turned back toward the house. They walked in silence for a few feet until Emily felt Jase's body tense.

"What is it?"

"I wanted to ask you something, a favor really," he told her. "You know city council is holding a town hall meeting in two weeks. Charles and I are both supposed to be there. People will have a chance to ask us questions about our plans as mayor."

She nodded.

"They'll want us to introduce our families as part of the meeting. I think it was Charles's idea as a way to discredit me. He can stand up there with his wife and sons as proof he's an established family man and I'll just be…alone."

"I'm sure your dad will come if you ask him."

Jase shook his head. "He doesn't like crowds. They make him anxious and that makes him want to drink." He let out a small laugh. "Well, everything makes him want to drink but so far he seems committed to his sobriety this time around. I don't want to mess that up."

"You've supported him in so many ways over the years," Emily argued. "He can do this for you."

"Honestly, I'm not sure if having my dad there would be a help." Jase stopped at the bottom of his porch steps as Ruby nosed around in the bushes in front of the house. "I was hoping you and your mom and Davey would stand up for me."

Emily felt her mouth drop open and quickly snapped it shut at the look of disappointment that flashed in Jase's eyes.

"Never mind. Stupid idea." He let go of her hand to scoop up the puppy. "When you mentioned me celebrating my birthdays at your parents' farm, it made me think the Crawfords were almost more of a family to me than my own." Ruby wriggled in his arms and licked his chin. "But you aren't my family, and I know how you feel about being in the spotlight. I'll bring Ruby." He laughed, but it sounded forced. "Puppies are always crowd pleasers."

He turned for the house, then stopped when she placed a hand on his arm.

Show don't tell.

Emily had assumed April meant those words from a physical standpoint, which was easy enough. She wanted Jase more than she could have imagined—longed to be in his arms. She thought about all the little things he'd done for her, from allowing her full control of his office to letting her take the lead on the wedding plans to showing up at the school ice cream social to check on her and Davey.

Despite her fears and doubts, she wanted to give something back to him. The town hall meeting was big, but she was coming to realize starting over was a mix of baby steps and giant leaps. Not pretending the past didn't happen but moving through the old hurts to create new happiness.

"We'll be there," she said and had the pleasure of watching gratitude and joy wash over his features. It felt so good to give this to him. It felt right.

"You don't have to," he told her. "I mean it. I'll be fine."

"You're not alone," she whispered. She leaned forward to kiss him but stopped when Ruby licked her right on the mouth.

Jase groaned as Emily laughed.

"You should still bring the dog," Emily said as she wiped her mouth. "She's your ace in the hole."

"Right now I want her out of my arms." He nudged

open the front door and deposited the puppy on the hardwood floor. "And you in them." He pulled Emily against his chest.

"I take priority over Ruby?" she asked with a laugh. "I feel so important."

"You take priority over everything," he whispered against the top of her head. His words made sparks dance across her skin. "Thank you, Em. I know what I'm asking is a lot." He tipped up her head, cupping her face between his hands. "If you decide it won't work, I'll understand."

His touch was tender. "I'll make it work," she told him and somehow she would.

Ruby scampered toward her basket of toys, picked up a stuffed bunny with her, teeth then walked into her crate to curl up with it.

"She's tired," Emily said.

"Finally."

Jase went over and locked the crate, then returned to Emily. "So how about a sleepover?"

Emily giggled. "Maybe you shouldn't call it that. It reminds me of being a kid…you know, pillow fights and nail-painting parties."

"Pillow fights, yes." Jase kissed the corner of her mouth. "Nail painting, no." He moved closer and deepened the kiss. She held on to him and he lifted her as if she weighed nothing, moving down the hall toward his bedroom. "Do you want to have a pillow fight?" he asked as he set her down on the bed, then covered her body with his.

"Maybe later."

"I'll hold you to that," he told her. "After I hold you to me."

She laughed again, loving how Jase made everything fun. She'd never thought of the bedroom as a place for laughter until the tall, sweet man watching her from chocolate-brown eyes had come into her life.

She slipped off her shoes and reached behind her back for the zipper of the cocktail gown she wore. Her fingers paused as Jase pulled his tie over his head, then undid the buttons of his tailored shirt. His broad chest made her mouth water.

He moved to the edge of the bed and slid his palms up her bare legs. He grasped the hem of her dress and she lifted up onto her elbows as he tugged it off her. His eyes darkened as they raced over her.

"The lingerie," he said in a half growl, "I like it."

Emily whispered a silent prayer of thanks to her new sister-in-law. Katie had insisted she buy the matching bra and panties during one of their prewedding shopping trips to Aspen. At the time it had seemed like a foolish expense, but now the lavender lace made her feel beautiful. Or maybe it was the way Jase was looking at her. Her whole body grew heavy with need.

She crooked a finger at him. "Come closer, Mr. Almost Mayor, and take it off me," she whispered.

He toed out of his shoes and took off his suit pants, then climbed onto the bed, lowering his weight over her as he claimed her mouth. No more joking or laughter. His kiss was intense and demanding, and she moaned as his fingers skimmed across her breast. Emily arched off the bed as his mouth followed, grazing the sensitive peak with his teeth.

Then they were a tangle of arms and legs, sighs and whispered demands. The demands came mostly from her. She was impatient for him but he insisted on moving slowly, savoring each moment and lavishing attention on every inch of her body.

This man wrote the book on show don't tell. She'd never felt so cherished or been so fully possessed. As much as she longed to say the words *I love you*, Emily still held back. But when they moved together as the pleasure built and built and finally shattered them both, all of her defenses crumbled in a shimmer of light and passion. She knew things could never go back to the way they'd been, at least not for her. Jase Crenshaw well and truly owned her heart.

Chapter Thirteen

Jase could feel Emily's heart beating steady against his chest early the next morning. She was wrapped around him, snuggled in tight and sleeping soundly.

She'd told him sleep was often elusive for her, so he reveled in the fact that she was snoring softly as morning light peeked in between the slats of the wood shutters that covered his bedroom windows.

He'd never allowed a woman to spend the night at his house before Emily. This place was a sanctuary to him, and he hadn't been willing to share it with anyone else. The satisfaction he felt at waking up with her beside him should be terrifying. It proved he was already in far too deep when he still expected her to break his heart.

Yet his smile wouldn't fade. It felt so damn *right* to have her here. He'd put the down payment on the modest bungalow shortly after taking over the law practice.

It had been a rite of passage to buy a home he could call his own. But he wasn't sure how to be a host and the women he dated invariably wanted to take over the role. Minutes in the door and they began rearranging sofa pillows and suggesting wall colors.

So he'd stopped inviting anyone over but his guy friends. They didn't care his walls were bare and he had nothing but leftover carryout and beer in the fridge. To his surprise, Emily hadn't either. He'd even solicited her opinion on what he should do to make it homier. She'd told him to keep it as it was, which had been both refreshing and disconcerting. Especially given the ruthlessness with which she'd taken over his office.

At first he'd thought she was respecting his space but over the past few weeks, when she'd stop by but never stay, he'd wondered if it was more about her keeping what was between them casual. Now she was here, and it seemed like a damn good first step.

"I can hear you thinking," she mumbled sleepily, rolling off him.

"Good morning," he said and kissed her cheek.

She yawned, her eyes still closed. "What's got the wheels turning so hard this early?"

"Paint colors."

"Is that code for kinky morning sex?"

He laughed and pulled her close again. "Would you like it to be?"

"Talk to me about paint colors."

He combed his fingers through her hair, loving its softness and the way the scent of her shampoo drifted up to him. "I need to update the house, make it more mine. I was thinking about what color to use for the family room and kitchen."

She rose onto her elbows. "While we're in bed together? What does that say about me?" She frowned but amusement flickered in her blue eyes.

"It says you inspire me to be a better person. Painting has been on the list for years, but I've ignored it. Even though I bought the house, I couldn't quite believe I deserved it. You make me believe."

Her gaze softened. "You make the most unromantic topics into love poems."

He tapped one finger against her nose. "Again, I give credit to you for inspiring me. Can we get back to kinky morning sex?"

"Dorian Gray."

He thought about that for a moment and then shook his head. "As in *The Picture of…*? The creepy book and movie?"

"Yes and no." She flipped onto her back again. "It's also a paint color, the perfect gray. You should use it for your family room and a shade lighter in the kitchen. It faces north so needs more light."

Jase felt a smile curve his lips. "You've been thinking about colors for my house."

Clearly misunderstanding, she crossed her arms over her chest. "You asked," she said on a huff of breath.

He levered himself over her and kissed the edge of her jaw. "Paint talk as foreplay. Works for me. What do you know about the color wheel?"

"I know you're crazy," she said, rolling her eyes.

"Only for you, Em."

She suddenly turned serious. "This isn't casual anymore."

He thought about lying so he wouldn't chase her away, but he couldn't manage it. "It's not casual for me," he agreed. "It never has been. We can still take it slow and I—"

She pressed her fingers to his mouth. "I like it slow." Her hand curled around to the back of his neck and she drew him down for a hot, demanding kiss. "I like it most ways with you."

"Emily," he said on a groan. "Tell me you're good with where this is going." He lifted his head and stared into her eyes. "I need to know."

She closed her eyes for a moment and took a deep breath. Then she looked at him again. "I'm scared of feeling too much. But I…" She paused, bit down on her lip, then whispered, "I want it to be more than casual. I want to try with you, Jase. For you."

"For us," he said. There was more he wanted to tell her, but she wasn't the only one afraid of being hurt. Jase was used to keeping the things he wanted most locked up tight. It was when he said the words out loud that his life usually went to hell.

Mommy, don't leave. Don't take Sierra.
Dad, stop drinking before it ruins you.

His requests met with disappointment so he didn't make them, and he wasn't going to now. He needed time to believe this precious thing between them wasn't going to be taken away.

He smiled and kissed her again. "We've got approximately not many minutes until the puppy starts whining," he said, glancing at the clock on the nightstand. "We've established slow is good. Now let's see how we do with fast."

The next two weeks flew by for Jase. One of his biggest cases went to trial early at the courthouse in Aspen, so he was out of the office most of the time. He'd never been as grateful for Emily, who managed his practice with so much efficiency he didn't worry about anything falling behind while he was in court.

He was even more grateful for her when he got home at the end of each long day. She'd taken over Ruby's care, picking up his energetic puppy in the morning on her way to the office and keeping her all day. She claimed both Davey and Tater, Noah's dog that was staying at the farm during Noah and Katie's honeymoon, loved having the puppy around.

When he could manage it, Jase drove directly to the farm after work. It was like he was a teenager again, showing up for dinner at Meg's big table, only now Emily greeted him with a kiss each time he arrived.

Everything in his life was exactly where he wanted it. Everything but the mayor's race. Charles was taking full advantage of Jase's busy schedule by planning campaign events all over town. Almost overnight, yard signs with the slogan Charles Thompson, A Family Man You Can Trust had popped up on every corner. Jase got calls from friends and business owners, suggesting he ramp up his efforts with the election date quickly looming.

The problem was he didn't want to take time away from the rest of his life to focus on the campaign. He couldn't stop questioning the reasons he'd decided to run for the position in the first place. Yes, he was dedicated to Crimson, but he didn't need to be mayor to prove that. Or did he?

He was getting pressure to be seen around town when all he wanted was to spend his free time with Emily and Davey. Although the boy was adjusting to school, he still preferred the quiet of home. Jase had set up a Lego construction area in the corner of his family room so Davey was becoming more comfortable at his house. That didn't solve the issue of Emily needing a quiet life with her son, while Jase's obligations to the town pulled him to be more visible with every passing day.

He checked his watch for the fifth time as he waited for the city council meeting to end late on Tuesday, one day before the big town hall event. Monthly council meetings were held in the evenings because so many of the members also had day jobs. Jase had never minded before because his life was the town. But Emily had texted that Davey wanted to show him his latest Lego structure, and he'd hoped to get out early enough to make it to the farm.

The council members continued to debate the date for the lighting of the town Christmas tree in December while Jase's mind raced from thoughts of Emily to the trial to the doctor's appointment he needed to reschedule for his father to the campaign he was pretending didn't exist.

"Jase, do you have anything to add?" One of the longtime council members lifted a thick brow.

Jase blinked and glanced around at his fellow council members, reluctant to admit he had no idea where the thread of the conversation had gone. Liam Donovan met his gaze and gave a subtle shake of his head.

"No," Jase said firmly, as if he knew what the hell they were talking about now. "I agree on this one."

Thankfully, the general comment was enough to satisfy everyone and the meeting adjourned. He checked his phone, disappointment washing through him. He'd missed a text from Emily, telling him Davey was going to bed and they'd keep Ruby overnight at the farm. She'd added an emoji face blowing a kiss at the end, which only made him want to hurl the phone across the room.

Jase didn't want emoji. He wanted Emily in his arms.

He punched in a quick text promising to stop by in the morning before heading to Aspen.

"You realize you can't speed up or slow down time by watching the clock," Liam said from behind his shoulder.

Gathering his things, Jase turned and shook his head. "It's a damn shame, too. Thanks for saving my butt just now."

Liam nodded. "You weren't exactly dialed in for this meeting. I'll walk out with you."

Jase watched a group of council members standing on the far side of the conference table, heads together as they talked. Charles Thompson was in the middle, as if holding court, and the sight made a sick pit open in Jase's gut. One of the men glanced back at Jase, guilt flashing in his gaze before he waved.

"Looks like you weren't the only one to notice." He followed Liam out into the cool autumn night. He should be sitting on his back porch with Emily right now. Instead he was heading over to his office to work a few more hours on the cross-examination he was preparing for tomorrow.

"Also looks like your campaign is in the toilet," Liam said without preamble. "Before you got to the meeting, Charles made a pretty convincing speech about you being pulled in too many directions to give your full attention to the duties of mayor."

"Which is not true—"

"He also hinted that your dad is having problems and you've got too many distractions right now."

Jase cursed under his breath and turned on his heel. The town meetings were open to the public so Charles had every right to be there. But not to spread lies about Jase's father. "My dad is fine," he ground out, moving back toward the courthouse. "I'm going to—"

"Whoa, there." Liam placed a hand on Jase's shoulder. "It's not a coincidence Charles showed up tonight, made the comment and now is hanging out after the meeting. He's playing dirty, Jase."

"Why the hell did you tell me, then?"

"Because *you* have a choice to make."

Jase shrugged away from Liam's grasp and paced several steps before turning and slamming his palm against the side of the brick building. He cursed again and shook out his hand. "I've made my choice."

"I'm new to the council," Liam said, "but from what I've heard, the choice was made for you. When the former mayor took off, Marshall Daley stepped in as mayor pro tem. He was never going to seek another term, so the town council members suggested you run."

"That's the basic gist," Jase admitted. "It wasn't supposed to be this complicated."

"Did you ever really want to be mayor?"

"Of course I did. I can do the job."

"I'm not debating that."

"I love this town."

"Again, you'll get no argument from me there. Hell, you had a major impact on my decision to make Crimson the headquarters for LifeMap. But it felt different. You were on a mission to make a name for yourself. I didn't understand it then..."

"And now you do?" Jase sagged against the building, tired at the thought of rehashing his family history one more time. "Everyone around here thinks they know me."

Liam shrugged. "It's clear you don't want it the way you once did."

"Is it so wrong to also want a life for myself, as well?"

"No."

"I won't let Charles win."

"Even if it means you lose in the long run?"

Jase straightened. "I'm going to make sure that doesn't happen."

"How?"

"Can I make a suggestion?"

Both men turned as Cole Bennett stepped out around the street corner.

"Evening, Sheriff," Jase said. "Out for a stroll downtown or is this official business?"

Cole moved closer. He wore jeans and a T-shirt and held up his hands, palms out. "Off duty tonight. I was hoping to talk to you before the town hall meeting this week." He glanced at Liam. "It's private."

Jase started to argue but Liam held up a hand. "I need to get home anyway. Let me know if I can help. No matter what you decide."

"Thanks, man." Jase shook Liam's hand, then watched him walk across the street to where his truck was parked.

"You have some advice for me?" he asked the sheriff.

"Information," Cole clarified. "Your office is on this block, right?"

Jase nodded.

The sheriff glanced over his shoulder. "Let's go there."

"Why do I have a bad feeling about this?" Jase asked as he led Cole a few storefronts down until they reached his office.

"Because you're not stupid," Cole answered bluntly.

With a sigh, Jase unlocked the door and flipped on the light in the reception area. The scent of vanilla from the candle Emily burned at her desk filled the air, and his heart shifted. The subtle changes she'd made to his life mattered and he hated that his sense of duty to the town was keeping them apart.

It wasn't only his schedule. They'd agreed their relationship wasn't casual, but he could feel Emily holding back. He assumed it was because of his increasing commitments to work and the campaign. While he wanted to tell her it would pass, how could he make that promise if he won the election?

"Since you're not on the clock, how about a drink?" Jase asked, moving toward his office. "I've got scotch or...scotch."

Cole chuckled low. "I'll have a scotch. Thanks."

Jase motioned him into the office, then went to the kitchenette area and poured two squat glasses with the amber-colored liquid. Back in the office, he handed one to Cole, then sat behind his desk.

Cole took a slow sip before placing the glass on Jase's desk. "How bad do you want to win the election?"

The question of the hour. "Not bad enough to do something illegal for it." It was the most honest answer Jase could give without exposing the doubts plaguing him.

"What about exposing something your opponent had

done?" the sheriff asked. "Not exactly illegal but it's definitely borderline. Turns out Thompson had been going easy on his friends and neighbors for years. Anytime there was a problem with someone he knew personally, the issue disappeared."

Jase actually laughed. "Everyone except my father."

Cole shrugged. "There's a lot of politics involved in small-town law enforcement. I'm overhauling the department, but I do have records that certain procedures weren't exactly…aboveboard when he was in charge."

"What are you going to do with the information?"

"That's why I'm here. Charles Thompson was supposed to retire and go fishing or whatever the hell else he wanted. I didn't take his bid for mayor too seriously at first." He picked up his glass of scotch and tipped it toward Jake. "You had the blessing of the council, so there was no question you'd be elected."

Jase didn't shy away from Cole's scrutiny. "Now there is?"

The sheriff finished off his scotch before answering. "Thompson is pushing you hard and you're letting him. I don't know if it's because the garbage he's throwing is getting to you or because you've decided you don't care about winning."

"Maybe I'm tired of my whole life revolving around Crimson."

"Fair enough, but I'm asking you to get your head back in the game. We need you, Jase. We need somebody decent in charge of this town." Cole placed his glass back on the desk and stood. "I can leak what I know about Thompson, make him go away, but it won't change how he's trash-talking you or what it means if you don't answer the accusations. You have a chance

to tomorrow night. I hope you take it, but if you need
something more let me know."

"Thank you," Jase said and watched the sheriff walk
out the door. He threw back the rest of his scotch, welcoming the burn in his gut. Maybe he had been ignoring the campaign in the hope the decision would be
taken from him. But that wasn't who he was, and Cole's
visit proved it.

Why couldn't he have Emily and the mayor's position? Yes, she had doubts but he'd worked too hard to
give up now. He needed to prove that she and Davey
fit into his life, every part of it. The town hall meeting
would be the perfect place to do just that.

Emily stopped in front of the entrance to the Crimson Community Center where the town hall meeting
was about to start. She smoothed a hand over the fitted dress she hadn't worn since she'd stood next to her
ex-husband when he'd made partner at his law firm.

"I should have picked something else. This is way
too formal."

Her mother squeezed her hand. "You look lovely and
the sweater softens the look." Meg glanced down at
Davey, who stood a few steps behind Emily, his hands
tightly fisted at his sides. "You are very heroic tonight."

Emily shared a look with her mom, then smiled at
Davey. He'd insisted on changing into his superhero
costume after school today and refused to put on a different outfit for the meeting. She understood that sitting
still in a crowd of strangers was going to be a challenge,
so hoped Jase understood Davey's wardrobe choice. Her
purse was stocked with Davey's favorite snacks, a small
bag of Lego pieces and the fail-safe iPad loaded with a

few new apps. She prayed it would be enough to keep him content during the meeting.

As her mother held open the door, Emily put a hand on Davey's shoulder to guide him, then drew back as he flinched away from her touch.

Breathe, she told herself. Smile.

She'd come back to Crimson for a quiet life, and now she was putting herself on display for the entire town. Her mother led them up the side aisle to the front row of chairs marked Reserved. Emily glanced over her shoulder as she took her seat and saw several of her new friends sitting together a few rows back. April waved and Natalie Donovan gave her a thumbs-up sign. A little bit of the tension knotted in her chest eased.

A tap on her shoulder had her swinging back around.

"It's not Halloween," Miriam Thompson, Charles's wife, said in a disapproving hiss as she made her way into the seat next to Emily, with Aaron's brother, Todd, on her other side. Aaron wasn't with them, a fact for which Emily was grateful. "You should show some respect to the seriousness of this election."

Red-hot anger rushed through Emily. Anger at Miriam for making the comment, at Jase for asking her to do this but mostly at herself for still caring what people thought of her and her son. Before she could respond, her mother whipped around in her seat.

"You should shut your mouth, Miriam," Meg said. "Before I come over there and do it for you. My grandson can be a superhero every day if it makes him happy." She wagged a finger at each of the Thompsons. "We could use more heroes in this town, not people who feel like it's their right to taunt and bully others."

Miriam gasped but turned away, her cheeks coloring bright pink as she made her son shift seats so she wasn't sitting right beside Emily.

Emily tried to hide her shocked smile as she leaned over Davey toward her mother and spoke low. "'Come over there and do it for you'?"

Meg sniffed. "I never liked that woman."

A hush fell over the room as Liam Donovan walked onto the stage, along with Jase and Charles. Liam was moderating the meeting. A few general announcements were made first and then Liam formally introduced Jase and Charles, although Emily couldn't imagine there was anyone in the room who didn't know either man. Crimson had grown in the years since she'd been gone, but it seemed as though everyone in attendance tonight had some history with the town.

The thought made her encouraged for Jase, as so much of Crimson's recent boom could be attributed to work he'd done as part of the city council. No wonder he was torn between making decisions for his own happiness and his duty to the town.

Charles took the mic first, detailing his background as former sheriff. Emily gritted her teeth as he made special mention of his long marriage, and his family's history of service and philanthropy in Crimson.

Jase didn't seem bothered, though, and stepped to the podium after shaking Charles's hand. He smiled as he looked out over the audience.

"It's great to see so many friendly and familiar faces in this crowd," he began. "This town means a lot to me and no matter what our differences, we can all agree that we want the best and brightest future for Crimson." After a ripple of applause, he spoke again. "I'd like to personally thank Charles for his contributions to our town over the years. Families like the Thompsons gave us a strong foundation. As many of you know, my family's history runs in a different direction." He chuckled softly. "Which is why I'm especially grateful for this town and the people in it."

Emily didn't turn around but she could feel the energy building in the crowd as Jase spoke. He was sincere and articulate, not shying away from where he came from but taking the power of his family's troubled history away from Charles by owning it himself. She'd never been prouder. Then she felt Davey shift next to her. It was hard to tell whether he was reacting to the excitement of the crowd or Jase's voice booming through the room or one of any number of things that might disturb his equilibrium.

The reason didn't matter. Something was also building inside Davey. He fidgeted, tugging on the tights of his superhero costume and humming softly under his breath. She reached in her purse and grabbed the bag of Lego pieces.

"Here, sweetie," she said, placing them gently in his lap. Keeping her voice calm and trying to regulate her own energy was key for keeping him from moving any closer to a meltdown.

Her mom shot her a look but Emily shook her head. It didn't matter what anyone thought at the moment. She had to keep Davey calm or everything she'd worked so hard to create would blow up in her face.

Davey opened the bag and methodically pulled out building pieces.

Emily breathed a tentative sigh of relief and focused on Jase. He was looking directly at her.

"With me tonight," he said, "is a family who have

made me a part of their own over the years." His gaze left hers, but she could still feel the warmth of it across her skin. "What makes this town special is that we take care of each other. Meg and Jacob Crawford took care of me when I needed it most. As mayor, I want to make sure we continue to move Crimson forward and, more importantly, that we continue to look out for one another."

"I guess your own father isn't part of your grand plan?" The loud, slurring voice rang out in the quiet of the meeting room. Emily heard the crowd's collective gasp but kept her eyes on Jase. His expression registered shock, confusion and finally a resigned disappointment as he looked out past the audience toward the back of the room. His gaze flicked to hers for a moment. The silent plea in his chocolate-brown eyes registered deep in her heart even as he schooled his features into a carefully controlled mask once again.

"You count, Dad," he said calmly into the microphone. "But we should talk later."

Emily turned to the back of the room to see Declan making his way up the center aisle. The door to the hallway was swinging closed and she caught a glimpse of a figure moving to the side as it shut. Aaron Thompson.

She got up immediately and moved toward Jase's dad.

"Why the hell aren't I up there with your fake family?" Declan yelled. "I'm part of this town, too. Or have you forgotten why you wanted to become such a do-gooder in the first place, Jase?"

"Declan, don't do this," she said as she got closer. The smell of liquor coming off him hit her so hard she took a step back. She had to get him out of this meeting. "This isn't you talking." She tried to make her voice gentle. "It's the alcohol. Jase needs you to get it under control. Now."

His bloodshot eyes tracked to her. "Oh, yeah, sweetheart. My son loves control. He can't tolerate anything less than total perfection." He motioned a shaky finger between himself and Emily. "The two of us are bound to disappoint him."

The words struck a nerve but she smiled and reached for his hand. "Then let's get out of here."

She could see Sheriff Bennett moving around the edge of the room toward them. A glance over her shoulder showed Jase stepping out from behind the podium toward the edge of the stage. She shook her head, hoping to diffuse Declan's alcohol-filled rant before it had a chance to gather steam.

She took his arm just as she heard Davey cry out, "Mommy, my spaceship. It broke." Her son's voice was a keening cry. "It broke!"

"I won't be handled," Declan yelled and tore his hand away from her grasp.

But Emily's attention was on Davey so instead of letting go she stumbled forward, plowing into Declan's chest and sending them both into the edge of the chair at the end of the row.

Edna Sharpe occupied the chair, and as it tipped, the three of them tumbled to the floor. Emily saw stars as her head slammed into the chair.

All hell broke loose.

People from the nearby rows surrounded them. Edna screamed and flailed at the bottom of the pile. "My ankle. You broke my ankle."

Declan moaned. "I think I'm going to be sick."

Emily scrambled to get out from under him but his thigh was pinning her down.

"Mommy!" Davey screeched, his voice carrying over the din of noise to her. "I lost a piece to my spaceship."

She pushed at Declan, recognizing the mounting hysteria in Davey's tone. Cole Bennett was there a second later, but it was too late. Jase's father coughed, then threw up, the vile liquid hitting Emily's shoulder as she tried to turn away.

He was hauled off her then and she stood, the crowd surrounding them parting as she pushed her way through. One bonus to being puked on—it cleared a path quicker than anything else.

Jase was trying to shoulder his way down the aisle, yelling at people as he moved.

Davey had started shrieking now, and she knew a full-blown meltdown could last for several minutes to close to an hour. Meg met her gaze and whispered, "I'm sorry." Meg picked a screaming Davey up and carried him out the side door of the meeting room.

Emily shook her head as she followed. There was nothing her sweet mother could have done to prevent this moment. The responsibility was Emily's. And she failed. Miserably.

Jase was in front of her a second later. She expected understanding. Instead, he glared at her. "What the hell, Em? You tackled my dad. Is Edna really hurt? This is a mess."

She blinked, unable to process the accusation in his tone, let alone to respond. "I've got to get to Davey," she whispered.

His muffled screams echoed from the hall.

Jase ran a hand through his hair. "Can you get control of him? The screaming is only making this disaster worse."

She reeled back as if he'd slapped her. A disaster. That's how Jase saw her attempt at helping him. Her head was ringing from where she'd hit the corner of the chair. Her son was having a public meltdown. And she was covered in vomit.

"We've got to pull out of this," Jase said, searching her gaze as if he expected her to have a magic solution.

"I'm going to my son," she said, pushing at him. "He's not part of a disaster. He's a scared little boy who shouldn't have been put in this situation in the first place."

"The sheriff has your dad out the door," Liam called from where he stood on the stage. "I'm going to get everyone back to their seats."

Jase closed his eyes for a moment and his gaze was gentler when he opened them again. "I didn't mean it like that. Em…"

"No." She pushed away. It was too late. She knew better. Davey was all that mattered, her only priority. "I've got to get him out of here. Take care of your image or your dad. I don't care. I'm not your problem, Jase. We're not yours."

She hurried down the row, bending to pick up a stray Lego piece as she walked. She found Davey and her mother at the end of the hallway, Davey standing stiffly in front of the wooden bench where her mother sat. She crouched in front of him. "I have the missing piece," she said. He continued to scream, his eyes shut tight and his cheeks blotchy pink as he heaved breaths in and out between shrieks. "Davey, sweetie. Look at Mommy. I have the Lego piece. You can finish the spaceship."

His screaming subsided to an anxious whine as he looked at the small yellow brick she held in front of him. Emily held her breath. He hiccuped and reached for it, holding it gently between his first two fingers. "Thank you, Mommy." He wiped at his cheeks with the back of his sleeve. "Can we go home now? You're stinky."

She let out a ragged laugh. Or maybe it was a sob. Hard to tell with the emotions swirling inside her. "Yes, Wavy-Davey, we can go home now."

She straightened, meeting her mother's worried gaze. "I'm so sorry," Meg whispered.

Emily shook her head. "No kind words, Mom. I need to keep it together until we get back to the farm."

Meg's mouth thinned but she nodded. "You might want to take off the sweater."

Emily carefully pulled the nasty sweater over her head, gagging a little as the scent of vomit hit her again. It had been easy enough to ignore when adrenaline was fueling her. But now the reality of everything that had happened—in front of most of the town and everyone who mattered to her—made her want to curl up in a tiny ball. But she still had her son to take care of, which was the only thing keeping her going.

She stuffed the sweater into a nearby trash can. The memories of this horrible evening would prevent her from ever wearing it again.

"Let's go home," she said and her mother took her hand and led them toward the car.

Chapter Fourteen

Jase had returned to the stage after Emily left and Declan had been hauled away. He'd remained calm even though he'd wanted to walk to the front of that room and rip Charles Thompson to shreds. Everything he'd worked for had been destroyed, but he'd seen Aaron Thompson slip into the hallway as the door closed to the back of the meeting room. At that moment he realized how personal the Thompsons felt about his failure and what lengths they were willing to go to make sure he wasn't elected mayor.

None of that really mattered. All he cared about was the hurt in Emily's eyes as he'd demanded she quiet Davey. It had been his shame talking. She didn't deserve the pain he'd caused her. He'd wanted to follow her to the Crawfords' farm right away, but there had been so much fallout to deal with after the scene his dad had caused.

Jase publicly apologized for his dad's behavior. He wanted to call out Charles Thompson, but he wouldn't stoop to Thompson's level or make excuses for Declan. It had been even more difficult to keep his temper in check when Charles complained as Liam officially ended the meeting and sent the crowd home.

Several of Jase's friends had offered words of encouragement and support, but he could barely hear them over the roar in his head. Jake Travers deemed Edna's ankle only a sprain but she insisted on going to the hospital for an X-ray, so Jase stayed with her until her daughter arrived to take her home. Cole offered to let Declan ride out his bender in one of the town's holding cells.

Jase didn't bother to comment on the irony of his father in jail as he was trying to make a bid to lead the town. It was his worst nightmare come to life.

At least he'd thought it was until arriving at the ranch. Meg had come to the door before he'd knocked.

"I need to see her," he said and opened the screen.

Meg crossed her arms over her chest. "No, Jase."

"I only need a minute," he pleaded, letting the emotions he'd tried to tamp down spill into his tone. "I'll wait if she's putting Davey to bed. Maybe I could—"

"No." Meg's normally warm gaze was frigid as she met his. "She was trying to support you tonight even though it wasn't what she wanted. You hurt her when things went bad." She shook her head. "My daughter has been down that road before, and she's only begun to recover from the pain of it. I won't let her be treated that way again. She deserves better."

"I know." He felt desperate in a way he hadn't in years. He could feel the person he loved slipping away from him, only this time it was his own fault. "I let the moment get the best of me. I love her, Meg."

"You want her, Jase. You have for years. I get that, but it isn't the same as love. What happened tonight wasn't love."

"I made a mistake."

"You might not be the right man for her."

"You're wrong."

"I hope I am, and if Emily decides to allow you back into her life, I won't stop her. But for now she doesn't want to see you. You have enough to deal with in your own life. Focus on that."

"I don't care about anything else." The words came out louder than he'd intended and he forced himself to take a calming breath. "At least tell her I was here. Tell her I'm sorry. Please, Meg."

After a moment she nodded. "You're a good man, Jase. You don't have anything to prove to this town but it's time you start believing it." She backed up and shut the door, leaving him alone on the porch.

This house was the one place he'd always felt safe and welcome, and now he'd messed that up along with his relationship with Emily.

It was close to midnight by the time Jase walked into the sheriff's office. He would have been there earlier, but Cole had texted that his dad was sleeping and he'd alert Jase when Declan woke up. Jase had gone home after leaving the Crawfords' and let Ruby into the yard. As the puppy chased shadows around in the porch light, Jase had sat on the top step and left messages for each of the town council members to apologize for the spectacle his father had created at the meeting.

Declan was sitting on the bench in the holding cell when Jase walked into the office.

"It isn't locked," Cole told him, getting up from his chair, "but he said he wouldn't come out until you got here." He patted Jase on the arm. "I'm going to give the two of you some time. I'll be out front. Let me know if you need anything."

Jase walked forward, wrapped his fingers around the cool iron of the holding cell's bars. "You ready, Dad?"

Declan snorted. "That's all you've got to say to me?"

"If you're looking for me to apologize," Jase ground out, his temper sparking even through the numbness of his exhaustion, "forget it. Drying out in this cell was the safest place for you tonight. After the stunt you pulled—"

"You shouldn't be here." His dad stood, paced from one end of the small cell to the other. "You don't owe me anything, least of all an apology. Why the hell aren't you with Emily?"

"Let's go home."

"I puked on her."

"Yep."

Declan rubbed a hand over his face. "I'm sorry."

"Emily is the one who's owed an apology. Maybe she'll talk to you."

"She won't speak to you?"

Jase shook his head. "Come on, Dad. I'm tired and done with this day."

His father lowered himself back down to the metal bench. "You see me here."

"I see you," Jase said quietly, hating the memories the image conjured.

"This is *me* in here, Jase. Not you. I did this to myself, like my dad and his dad before him. Our trouble is not your responsibility."

"It sure as hell felt like it when you barged into the town hall meeting drunk out of your mind."

"I slipped," Declan said. "I let people get to me and I took one drink."

"One drink ended in the bottom of the bottle. I've seen it too many times, Dad. You can't stop at one drink."

"I know, and I didn't want to. I wanted to lose myself. To forget about everything for a little while."

"Aaron Thompson brought you to the meeting."

"It wasn't his fault, even as much as I'd like it to be. I was at the bar when he found me. Yeah," Declan admitted, "he said some things that set me off more."

"They wanted me to be humiliated."

"I brought tonight's shame on you, Jase. Not the Thompsons. I'm the reason you can't have a life of your own."

"I have a life," Jase argued, but his voice sounded flat to his own ears. Because without Emily he had nothing. "I thought we agreed the town hall meeting was too much for you. If I knew—"

"It wasn't the meeting." Declan stood, reached into the back pocket of his jeans and pulled out a small envelope. "Nearly twenty years later and she can still set me off." He handed the envelope to Jase. "It's a letter from your mom, son."

Jase stared at the loopy cursive on the front of the envelope, disbelief ripping through him. "Why didn't she track down my email or cell number? No one sends letters anymore."

"Your mother was always an original." Declan

moved toward the door to the cell. "I don't know what she wrote, but I hope whatever it is gives you some closure."

"Why after all this time?"

"I don't know." He stopped, cupped his rough hand around Jase's cheek. The smell of stale liquor seeped from his skin, both familiar and stomach churning. "What I hope she says is that leaving had nothing to do with you. That she regrets not taking you with her and giving you the life you deserve." His smile was sad as he ruffled Jase's hair. "That's what I hope she says, but I don't want to know. Bennett let me use the phone when I woke up. My AA sponsor is coming by the house in the morning. Whether you believe me or not, this was a one-time mistake."

Jase stood there staring at the envelope for a few more seconds, then turned. "Dad."

Declan turned back, his handle on the door to the outer office. "Yeah?"

"I don't regret staying with you."

"Are you sure you won't stay with Mom?" Noah pulled out from the farm's driveway and started toward town. He and Katie had been home from their honeymoon for a few days so Emily had asked him to go apartment hunting with her.

"I can't keep hiding out there." Emily read the address to the first building, which was in a new development on the far side of town. She watched the midday sun bounce off the snow-dusted peak at the top of Crimson Mountain. The weather was cooler now, and while there hadn't been any snow yet in town, winter would be closing in soon.

"That's not how she thinks of it."

"Doesn't make it less true." She shifted to look at her brother, still tan from his honeymoon on the beach. "I'm staying in Crimson, Noah. I need to start making a life for Davey and me."

"He still likes school?"

She smiled. "He loves it. Since I'm now working in the elementary school front office, I can check in on him during the day." The kindergarten teacher, Erin Mac-Donald, had made a visit to the farm when Emily kept Davey home from school the day after his public melt-down. While Davey had spent the day building Lego sets and baking cupcakes with his grandma, Emily'd barely been able to get out of bed.

The teacher's sensitivity to Davey's outburst had made its way through Emily's fragile defenses and she'd broken down with all the details of her messed-up life. Erin had immediately called the school principal. The new secretary he'd hired had quit after only two weeks. Emily had an interview the following afternoon and started work the next day. "Millie Travers told me Ms. MacDonald was a great teacher, but she's more. She's a great person." She nudged her brother. "Turns out Crimson is full of great people. Davey is getting ac-cess to the resources he needs. He's made a friend—"

"In addition to Brooke?"

"Brooke is his *best* friend," Emily clarified. "But, yes, another boy who loves Lego building. They mainly play side by side, but it's a start."

"Does Henry know how he's doing?"

"I sent him an email," Emily admitted with a shrug. "I don't know what I was hoping for, but he's Davey's father so I thought…" She sighed. "His assistant responded to it."

"The guy is a total idiot."

"Agreed. But we're doing okay without him."

Noah turned onto the road that led into town. The aspen leaves were turning brilliant yellow, shimmering in the sunlight. It gave Emily a bright and shiny glow inside her.

"What about the other idiot in your life?" Noah glanced over at her.

"Jase isn't in my life." She paused, then whispered, "and he's not an idiot."

"You haven't talked to him?"

"You know I haven't, Noah." She'd asked April to go to his office the morning after the meeting to give him Emily's resignation letter. Maybe she should have been brave enough to face him, but the humiliation she'd felt after that night had been too raw.

"Why?"

"There's nothing to say. We want different things." She kept waiting for the pain to ease, the vise around her heart to release. Every time she thought of Jase, her whole body reverberated with the deep ache of missing him. "I hear the election is going well." She'd tried not to hear, not to listen but it was difficult in a small town where people were happy to pass around gossip like it was breaking news.

Noah nodded. "Hard to believe the stunt his dad pulled at the town hall meeting actually helped him in the campaign."

"Not hard with Jase."

"Everyone is talking about how much he's overcome and how he's a self-made success."

"He deserves every bit of his success," Emily said quietly. The Thompsons' plan to discredit Jase in the eyes of voters had backfired. She wasn't the only one who'd seen Aaron as he sent Declan into the town hall meeting. Apparently, Charles had a reputation of bending the rules while he'd been sheriff and no one wanted a man with a twisted moral compass in charge of the town.

"You missed the turn." She straightened in her seat as Noah took a right toward Crimson High School.

"I have a quick stop to make."

"What stop?"

He pulled over to the curb at the edge of the football field. "I'll show you. Hop out."

There were a few teenagers throwing a ball on the field but the stands were empty.

"Do you see it?"

She climbed out of the truck, scanning the bleachers for something familiar. "See what, Noah?"

The truck's engine roared to life and she whirled around. Noah had rolled down the passenger window. "See me making you really angry."

"Have you lost your mind?"

He grimaced. "According to my new wife. I hope you'll forgive me, and I'll be back in ten minutes."

"What are you talking about?"

Noah blew her a kiss and drove off, leaving Emily standing on the sidewalk. She didn't even have her phone. "I'm going to kill him," she muttered.

"It's not his fault," a voice said behind her. She went stock-still even as her knees threatened to sag. "He owed me for something and I called in the favor. He didn't have a choice."

She turned to face Jase, letting anger rise to the top of the mountain of emotions vying for space in her heart. "Of course he had a choice," she said on a hiss of breath. "The same way I have a choice as to which one of you I'm going to murder first."

He took a step toward her and she backed up. "Don't come any closer."

"We need to talk."

She shook her head. What she needed was to get the hell out of there before she gave in to the temptation to plaster herself against him. "No. We don't."

"I need to talk," he clarified.

"Talk to someone who wants to listen to what you have to say."

He ran his hands through his hair, looking as miserable as she felt. "Don't you understand? I only ever cared about you. From the start, Emily."

She closed her eyes and stuck her fingers in her ears, repeating the words *I can't hear you* in a singsong voice.

His hands were on her arms a moment later. She flinched away but secretly wanted to melt into him. She'd missed his warmth. Missed the scent of him, pine and soap and man. Missed everything about him.

"Open your eyes," he said, his tone an irresistible mix of amusement and desperation.

She did, keeping her gaze trained on the football field. Davey would like the symmetry of the lines dissecting the green grass.

"This was where I fell in love with you the first time," Jase whispered, following her gaze. "Every weekend you were at the football games, surrounded by a group of friends. You took great pleasure in ignoring me."

"You were my older brother's best friend. I had no use for you." She glanced back at him and her heart skipped a beat. He was watching her as if it was the first time he'd seen her. As if she really was the only thing he cared about in life.

"And still I was ruined for any other girl." His fingers brushed her hair away from her face. "I remember you on those cool fall nights, bundled up in sweaters and boots, your blond hair like a calling card as you held court in the bleachers. You were the most perfect girl I'd ever seen."

She took a step back, out of his grasp and tried to get a handle on her emotions. "I was a brat."

"I didn't care." His chocolate-brown gaze never wavered as he spoke.

"Why are you telling me this now?"

"Because you need to understand it was always you, Em. You were the first and only thing I ever wanted." He flashed a wry smile and toed his boot against the gravel. "Back then it was because you embodied the perfection that was never a part of my life."

"I wasn't perfect and—"

He pressed his finger to her lips. "Then you returned and *I* got a chance to make you happy. No, you're not perfect. Neither am I. But *real* is better than perfect." He scrubbed a hand over his face and the scratch of his stubble made her melt. Just a little. "I messed up, and I'm sorry. Sorrier than you'll ever know. I let the shame I felt about my own family change me."

"I understand."

"How can you understand when I don't?" He shook his head. "There's no excuse, Emily. I love that boy. Hell, I found myself putting together a Lego town the other night with the bin of blocks you left at the house. I miss him. I miss you."

"I understand life is messy. I wanted it to be put in easy compartments. Even Davey, especially Davey."

"You came here to protect him. I get it."

She shook her head. "I came here to hide. Henry wasn't the only one who failed him. Mothers have dreams for their kids. To-the-moon whoppers like, *Will he grow up to be President?* And the dreams that really mattered. *Will he have friends? Will he be happy?* I felt like I lost control of those the first time I noticed Davey's differences."

He stared at her, patiently waiting as always.

"I want to live life celebrating who he is."

Just when she thought it couldn't get any more painful, Jase ripped open another layer of her heart. "I want that, too, Em. I love you both so much."

And another layer. "I'm pulling out of the mayor's race."

"No," she whispered. "You wouldn't."

"I have a meeting with the council later this afternoon to officially withdraw my name."

"But you're going to win. Charles Thompson—"

"The reasons Charles is running for mayor are as convoluted as mine." The half smile he gave her was weary and strained. A different type of heartache roared through her knowing his distress was her fault. Jase had helped her regain her confidence and spirit, and she'd repaid him by allowing her fears to bring both of them low.

"Your reasons aren't convoluted." She moved to him then, put a hand on his arm. "You are straightforward and selfless. You've done so much already—"

"Trust me, I know what it's like to have fear rule your life. No matter how much I do, I'm scared it isn't enough to make amends for all the mistakes. I worry I'll never be enough."

"Those mistakes weren't yours, but the choice to make a different future for yourself has been." He was standing before her, willing to give up everything he'd built in this town. His whole life. The searing thought that this was exactly what her ex-husband had expected of her almost brought her to her knees.

"My mother contacted me," he said softly. "Her letter is what made Dad drink again."

"Oh, Jase."

He ran a hand through his hair, his jaw tight. "She's sick, and she wants to see me. After so many years, she apologized for leaving."

"You deserve that."

He trailed his fingers over hers, his touch sending shivers of awareness across her skin. "I want to deserve you, Em. We deserve happiness. Together. Give me another chance to prove how much you mean to me. How much I love you."

She pressed a hand to her chest as if she could quell the pounding of her heart. He was willing to give her exactly what she'd wanted from Henry, but it was so wrong. She loved him for his dedication and sense of duty, for the very *rightness* of who he was. She couldn't allow loving her to destroy his dream. "You can't give up the campaign, Jase."

"I will if it means a chance with you."

"It isn't… You don't…" She took a breath, trying to give her words time to catch up with her racing thoughts. "I wanted to make my life manageable again, but love isn't manageable and neither is everything that comes with it. Life is messy. If I hide from the pain, I risk never having the love. So I'm going to stop hiding. I love Davey the way he is—"

"Me, too," he whispered, his voice raw.

"I know." She reached up, cupped his face with her hands. "You must know you're already enough for the people in this town. For me. You're the one who has to believe it now. I want to support you, even when it's a struggle. We'll find a way. I may not be the perfect politician's wife but—"

"I don't want you to be perfect. I want you, all of you. Your bossiness and your skyscraper-tall defensive walls—"

"Hey." She poked him in the chest.

"I want the way you love Davey so fiercely, the way you bullied me into stepping into my own life." He lifted a hand to trail it across her jaw. "I want you when you're fragile and vulnerable, when you're strong and stubborn. I want Davey and a house full of Lego creations." He dipped his head so they were at eye level. "I want you every day for the rest of our lives."

"You're going to win this election, Jase." She felt tears slip down her cheeks. "You are the best thing I never expected to happen in my life." She wrapped her arms around his neck and brushed her lips across his. "How did I miss seeing you for so long?"

"The only thing that matters is we're here now." He lifted her into his embrace. "Tell me you'll give us another chance."

She laughed. "A thousand chances, Jase. Because if you take me on, it's going to be for good."

"For good and forever," he agreed. "Be mine forever."

"Yes," she whispered. "Forever."

He took over the kiss, making it at once tender and fully possessive. Emily lost herself in the moment, in the feel of him and the happiness bubbling up inside her like a newly unearthed spring.

A honking horn had her jerking away a moment later.

"Get a room," Noah called as he slowed the truck. He grinned at her. "I hope this means you're not mad at me."

"I'm not mad," she called. "But you're still in trouble."

His gaze flicked to Jase. "Are you going to help me with her?"

Emily growled as Jase laughed. "I wouldn't be dumb enough to try."

Emily patted him on the shoulder. "Which is why you get a thousand chances." She pointed at her brother. "You get none."

He blew her a kiss and she couldn't stop her smile.

"Are we still going apartment hunting?" Noah asked.

"She's got a home," Jase answered. "With me."

"And I get to pick the paint colors?" Emily asked, raising a brow.

"You get to do whatever you want."

She kissed him again. "What I want is to spend the rest of my life with you." She felt color rise to her cheeks, realizing she'd said too much too soon.

Jase only smiled. "I've only been waiting most of my life," he said, dropping to one knee and pulling a small velvet box out of his jacket pocket. "Emily, will you marry me?"

She swallowed, struggled to take a breath and nodded. He slipped the ring on her finger and stood to take her in his arms once more.

"Katie is going to be so mad she missed this moment," she heard her brother yell. "Good thing I got the whole event on video. Congratulations, you two crazy kids." Noah honked once more, then drove out of the parking lot.

"I love you, Em," Jase whispered. "Forever."

"Forever," she repeated and felt her heart fill with all the happiness it could carry.

* * * * *

Look for
CHRISTMAS ON CRIMSON MOUNTAIN,
the next book in Michelle Major's
CRIMSON, COLORADO series
coming in December 2016

Why on earth had he agreed to host the wedding in the first place?

It was getting more complicated by the day… and bringing back the humiliating memories he had spent the past two years burying.

Yes, he had vaguely agreed to Grace's early arrival—but he hadn't expected her to be so elated about the wedding, or so distractingly beautiful. Her excitement brought home just how much he hated the prospect of this wedding. And, unbelievably, this was her first time abroad on her own. He didn't have the time to babysit her. Having her on the island was a headache he didn't need right now. Unfortunately she had other ideas.

'This view is absolutely stunning.' She didn't turn to him when she spoke, but continued to gaze towards the lights of Naxos in the distance. The sky was a never-ending celestial ocean of stars. Beneath them, far below the cliff-face, the Aegean Sea crashed onto the shore.

She gave a light shiver and rubbed her hands against her bare arms. A silver bracelet jangled at her wrist. He instinctively shrugged off his jacket. When he held it out for her to put it on she jerked back in surprise. In the darkness he could just about see the violet-blue depths of her eyes. Eyes that threatened to swallow his soul.

THE BEST MAN'S
GUARDED HEART

BY
KATRINA CUDMORE

First Published in Great Britain 2016
By Mills & Boon, an imprint of HarperCollins*Publishers*
1 London Bridge Street, London, SE1 9GF

© 2016 Katrina Cudmore

ISBN: 978-0-263-92009-3

23-0816

Our policy is to use papers that are natural, renewable and recyclable products and made from wood grown in sustainable forests. The logging and manufacturing processes conform to the legal environmental regulations of the country of origin.

Printed and bound in Spain
by CPI, Barcelona

A city-loving book addict, peony obsessive **Katrina Cudmore** lives in Cork, Ireland, with her husband, four active children and a very daft dog. A psychology graduate, with a MSc in Human Resources, Katrina spent many years working in multinational companies and can't believe she is lucky enough now to have a job that involves daydreaming about love and handsome men! You can visit Katrina at www.katrinacudmore.com.

To Fin, your unwavering support and love
has made this book possible.
You are my life.

CHAPTER ONE

SOFIA'S VOICEMAIL. AGAIN. Grace Chapman gave her smartphone's contact photo of her best friend a death stare and muttered, 'You can hide, Sofia, but I'll find you.'

Grace loved Sofia to bits; during the madness of the past few years she'd been her rock of cheerful good sense. But every now and again, when life got too intense, Sofia lost the plot big-time. Like today. Yes, Grace might have missed her flight and ended up arriving in Athens seven hours late. But she'd had everything under control. Until Sofia had obviously panicked and called in the big guns: the Petrakis family. Which meant that instead of catching the last ferry of the day at Piraeus port, as she had hoped, Grace was now stuck in the VIP lounge of Athens airport, awaiting the arrival of Sofia's soon-to-be father-in-law. A man who brought the word *intimidating* to a whole new level of meaning.

Sofia would have thought she was helping; but in truth she had totally messed up Grace's already tight schedule. There was no way, now, that she would make it to Sofia's wedding venue, Kasas Island, in time for the flower delivery in the morning.

She wasn't going to panic.

Okay, she *was* panicking.

Less than three days to prepare and organise the flowers for the Greek society wedding of the year.

Three days that would determine the success or failure of her dream to establish her name as a leading wedding floral designer. Three days to prove that she wasn't *'a clueless dreamer'*.

This morning, full of enthusiasm, she had thought she could take on the world. Now she just felt embarrassed and out of her depth.

She pushed the untouched champagne flute the lounge hostess had presented to her further away. Her stomach felt as though it was off doing a moon walk without her.

The lounge door swept open. And her stomach headed into orbit at the prospect of being at the receiving end of Mr Petrakis's surly manner.

But standing at the far end of the airport lounge was *not* the older man she had expected. Instead, penetrating eyes scanned the room and came to a land on her. Long tanned fingers shot upwards. His eyes continued to bore into hers. With a quick tug, he unravelled his bow tie, leaving it to hang lose.

Her smile wavered. She took in the chiselled bone structure, the confidence of his stride as he walked towards her, the perfection of his tuxedo. The tousled disarray of his dark brown hair that made him look as though he had just climbed out of bed.

'Miss Chapman?'

His voice was smooth and refined. If Central Casting was ever looking for a new Bond he would be a shoo-in. Her already racing heart galloped even faster.

Her seat was low and he seemed impossibly tall and menacing as he stood over her.

Clumsily she clambered out of it and tugged down on the hem of her yellow sundress, which suddenly felt too short and casual in the presence of his designer tux and expensive cologne. She was a low-budget package tourist to his first-class sophistication.

His eyes ran leisurely over the length of her body. Her insides melted. A thick dark eyebrow rose as he waited for her to speak, but for the first time in her life no meaningful words jangled in her brain. Instead it was a wasteland of inappropriate thoughts of lust for the man who stood before her.

Just above his left eyebrow a sickle-shaped scar became more prominent as his frown deepened. She balled her hands, worried that she'd give in to temptation and reach out and run her thumb against it.

After another excruciating few seconds of silence she eventually managed to garble out, 'Yes... Yes, I'm Grace Chapman. I was expecting Mr Petrakis. The airport ground staff told me he had asked that I stay here until he arrived.'

With a quick nod he answered, 'Yes I did.'

'Oh.' It slowly dawned on her who he was. '*Oh!* You must be Andreas... Christos's brother. I thought it was your father who had sent the message. He and I met in London last month, at Christos and Sofia's engagement party.' Grace held out her hand. 'You're the best man, I believe?'

He paused for a second before smooth warm skin enclosed her hand. His handshake was firm, the dominant clasp of a powerful man who liked to get his own way.

In her flat sandals she had to arch her neck to meet his stare. Piercing green eyes framed by long dark eyelashes studied her, and his head was thrown back at an arrogant tilt. The apple really hadn't fallen far from the tree. Dark stubble lined smooth golden skin.

'And I believe *you're* to be the chief bridesmaid?'

She ignored the coolness of his tone and let her enthusiasm for the upcoming wedding take over. 'Yes—and also the wedding floral designer. Sofia and I have been best friends for years. It's a shame you missed the engagement party—we had such fun.'

He gave an indifferent shrug and then his mouth curled derisively. 'You missed your flight.'

Her heart leapt at his reproachful tone. About to explain why, she stopped. He really didn't look as if he was in the mood to hear about delayed trains. Instead she said, 'Yes, unfortunately. Now my priority is to get to Kasas as soon as possible.'

'You've missed the last ferry.'

She forced herself not to say something terse and gave a polite smile. 'Yes, I know.' Her smile wobbled. *Don't say anything. Remain calm. I'm sure he doesn't mean to be so arrogant.* Her good intentions lasted all of one second. 'My flight did arrive in time for me to catch the ferry. I had a taxi waiting.'

His mouth thinned. 'And tomorrow the sun will rise in the west…'

Well, really! Frustration hummed in her ears. 'I had an hour.'

He scowled at her, making no effort to conceal his growing irritation. 'Christos realised you would miss the ferry so he called me and asked that I collect you.'

Her frustration gave way to embarrassment. His superior attitude might be rubbing her up the wrong way, but she had to face the fact that his night had obviously ended abruptly because of her.

She gestured to his tux and said, 'I hope I didn't disturb your night out.'

Something flashed in the depths of his eyes. Was it annoyance or some other memory? Had he been with someone? Sofia had said he had a reputation for being a playboy. Maybe she had been right about that tousled hair. It was still relatively early…but then what did *she* know about the bedroom habits of playboys? None of her exes had ever come close to being as dangerously lethal as the man standing before her.

'No doubt Sofia panicked and got Christos to call you. She's worried I'll get lost. It's my first time in Greece. In fact it's my first time being abroad on my own.'

Those dark eyebrows narrowed. He studied her incredulously. An awkward silence followed.

She said the first thing that came into her head. 'I suppose you spend your days travelling…what with your business and everything?'

He tilted his head and gazed at her suspiciously. 'Have you been doing your homework on me?'

'No!' Her cheeks grew hot and she cringed to think he might assume she was blushing out of guilt. 'Of course not. I only know what Sofia told me…that you are Christos's older brother.'

The eldest son of the wealthy and powerful Petrakis family, in fact, who had gone on to amass his own fortune in construction and property.

As he continued to gaze at her sceptically she added, 'I've only met Christos a few times, but from the moment I met him I knew that he and Sofia were perfect for one another. I'm so happy for Sofia. And her dad is equally thrilled that she's marrying a fellow Greek.'

Uncomfortable at the way he studied her, and trying to ignore just how gauche she felt in front of this much too silent and urbane man, she decided to change the subject to something that puzzled her. She gestured towards the other waiting travellers, and frowned when she saw that the other two women in the room, both much more el-

egantly groomed for the VIP lounge than she was, were
staring at Andreas with obvious appreciation.

'How did you know who I was?'

He reached into the inner pocket of his jacket and
took out a phone. After a few quick swipes he handed
it to her. A photo of her and Sofia pulling silly faces at
the camera popped up on the screen. Christos had taken
the photo last weekend, after Sofia's hen party in London…they'd both had one too many mojitos. Grace gave
a squeal of despair.

For the briefest of moments a faint hint of amusement
lifted his mouth upwards, but it faded and he said with
a note of exasperation, 'Christos is flooding my email
with photos of Sofia.'

Confused by his tone, she decided to ignore it and
handed Andreas back his phone. 'That's so cute. They're
so in love. Sofia tells me that Kasas is incredibly romantic. She truly appreciates you hosting the wedding there.'

He deposited the phone back in his pocket and folded
his arms. The side of his upper lip curled upwards. Lord,
he had a beautiful mouth. Wide, with lips that were much
too full. A mouth that promised endless sleepless nights.

She gave herself a mental shake. She had enough on
her plate with the wedding flowers. Getting distracted
by this Greek god standing in front of her was definitely
not a good idea.

He gestured to her chair. 'Please—take a seat. I think
we should discuss your stay on Kasas.'

Puzzled, she sat back down and wished once again
that she had worn a longer dress as her hem rode up the
length of her legs. When she glanced up, Andreas was
sitting opposite her, his eyes trained on her bare legs.
When their eyes met she saw a hint of appreciation. But
then he inhaled a deep breath and moved forward to lean

his elbows on his thighs, the wool of his trousers stretching over hard muscle.

'I had intended taking you to Kasas tonight—'

She could not help but interrupt as relief flooded her veins. 'That would be *fantastic*. The flowers and all the other supplies are being delivered early tomorrow morning, and I need to be there to—'

His hand slashed down through the air to halt her interruption with his own. 'Yes, but considering that you've never been to Greece before why don't I arrange for the wedding planner to organise the flowers? You can spend the next few days travelling. Kasas is isolated. It would be much more enjoyable for you to explore Greece instead. As I'm returning to the island for the rest of the week, you are welcome to use my apartment and the services of my chauffeur here in Athens.'

Her mouth dropped open. Was he being serious?

'But I'm the florist for the wedding.' Through her confusion a horrible thought occurred. 'Christos *did* tell you that I would be arriving early to create all the floral arrangements, didn't he? This has been planned for weeks.'

'He may have mentioned it…amongst all the chaos of the other wedding plans. I hadn't appreciated that you would be staying for so long.'

Heat flared even more brightly on her cheeks. He clearly wasn't keen on her staying on the island. And he obviously had no idea or appreciation for the work and skill involved in flower design.

Memories of her father's sneering comments about her making a living by *'playing with flowers'* had her saying in the politest voice she could muster, 'I appreciate your offer, but tomorrow morning I have over a thousand flowers being delivered to the island. It's essential that I'm there to coordinate their arrival. I take my job very seriously, Mr Petrakis. That's why I've spent the past month planning the designs, sourcing the flowers and organising support florists from nearby islands. I'm not going to walk away from my commitments now to go on *holiday*.'

His jaw tightened and he fixed her with an intense stare. 'My island is secluded. There is only my villa. No shops or bars to entertain you.'

She could not help but give a light laugh. 'I'm not here for shopping or the nightlife.'

'I'm concerned that you will be bored in the evenings, when the wedding planner and her team have left the island. Apart from my married housekeeper and a gardener, who live in a separate villa, there will be no other people around.'

His eyes, filled with a masculine heat, held hers and a surge of tense energy passed between them.

He came a little closer and in a low growl added, 'It will only be you and me.'

For a crazy moment something primal, something beyond comprehension, crackled in the air between them. Heat flared in every cell of her body. Her breath caught as a wave of longing…of desire…rippled through her.

His eyes grew darker as he held her stare, and a slash of heat appeared on his cheeks.

He looked away abruptly, his jaw tightening as he cleared his throat. 'I'll be working late each evening, so I won't be available to entertain you.'

Grace blinked. And blinked again. She felt dizzy with the desire to move towards him, to inhabit his space, to inhale his scent, to feel the heat of his body. What was happening to her?

For the past month she had been so excited about this trip—at the prospect of finally establishing her name as a florist, of finding her freedom. And now her bubble of happiness had truly burst.

Should she take up his offer? The prospect of spending nights alone with him in the seclusion of his island with virtually no one else around was daunting. A strange tug of war of deep attraction and irritation was raging between them…and she wanted to run away from it. And, after years of dealing with her father's unforgiving attitude, did she honestly want to spend time with a man who would be happier if she wasn't there?

But this wedding was about celebrating Sofia and Christos's love. She wasn't going to let Andreas Petrakis stand in the way of her making sure they had the perfect flowers to represent that love and commitment. There was no way he was stopping her from creating Sofia's bouquet—which she intended to do by weaving all her love for her best friend into the design. And she had to remember the importance of this wedding in establishing her career.

So she gave him a brief smile and tried to inject a brusque, no-argument tone to her voice. 'Thank you, but I'm perfectly fine with my own company. I'm here to ensure that the flowers are spectacular on the wedding day, so I'll be extremely busy and certainly won't get in your way. And please don't worry about me missing out. I plan on touring Greece once the wedding is over.'

With that she stood, lifted her weekend bag up and grabbed her heavy pull-along suitcase.

'Now, if it's okay with you, I would like to leave.'

Grace was standing at the edge of the clifftop path that led from the helipad down to Andreas's villa, her weekend bag at her feet. As he neared her the helicopter lifted off to return to Athens, and her hands rushed down to capture the billowing material of her dress as it rose up to expose even more inches of her legs—legs that he had spent the past hour trying not to stare at.

They weren't the longest legs he had ever seen, but there was something about those toned but full thighs and cute dimpled knees that had him fantasising about her in incredibly inappropriate ways. Even as he had stared out into the night sky as they had been flown here images of his fingers trailing along the smooth creamy skin of her thighs had plagued him.

They had barely spoken on the journey, and her quietness surprised him. At the airport she had seemed such an overexcited chatterbox. Had his welcome been too brusque? After all, it wasn't *her* fault that earlier that night at a charity gala ball in the Hotel Grande Bretagne he had been only too aware of the other guests' deliberate avoidance of discussing Christos's upcoming wedding with him. And then Christos had rung to explain that the chief bridesmaid had missed her flight. Asked would he mind rescuing her.

Why on earth had he agreed to host the wedding in the first place? It was getting more complicated by the day…and bringing back humiliating memories he had spent the past two years burying.

Yes, he had vaguely agreed to Grace Chapman's early arrival, but he hadn't expected her to be so elated about the wedding or so distractingly beautiful. Her excitement had brought home just how much he hated the prospect of this wedding. And, unbelievably, this was her first time abroad on her own. He didn't have time to babysit her—not with the serious issues complicating the construction of his new resort on the Cayman Islands. He urgently needed to resolve them to stop further haemorrhaging of the project's finances. Having her on the island was a headache he didn't need right now.

Unfortunately she had other ideas.

'This view is absolutely stunning.'

She didn't turn to him when she spoke, but continued to gaze towards the lights of Naxos in the distance. The sky was a never-ending celestial ocean of stars. Beneath them, far below the cliff-face, the Aegean Sea crashed onto the shore.

She gave a light shiver and rubbed her hands against her bare arms. A silver bracelet jangled at her wrist. He instinctively shrugged off his jacket. When he held it out for her to put on she jerked back in surprise. In the darkness he could just about see the violet-blue depths of her eyes. Eyes that had swallowed his soul for a foolish few seconds at the airport.

Initially she looked as though she would refuse his offer, but then she gave a nod of acceptance. She turned around and pushed her arms into the sleeves. When he pulled it up to her slim shoulders she moved at the same time to sweep up the long length of her golden blonde hair trapped beneath the jacket. Her hair fell against his hands like the gentle weight of silk, her floral scent carried with it. His gut tightened. And when she turned those huge eyes to him they were full of questions, of awareness of the chemistry sizzling between them. He itched to touch the smooth line of her jaw, to run his thumb over the sensual plumpness of her lips.

He took a step away.

She twisted back towards the sea, her shoulders sagging faintly before she went to pick up her weekend bag, but he whipped it up, along with her suitcase.

'The path down to the villa is well lit, but still be careful—it's steep. *Ela*. Come. I will lead the way.'

On the way down the path he paused a number of times, to allow her to catch up and to ensure that she was following him safely. As they rounded the corner that opened up the villa to their view he heard her gasp. He turned in alarm. Grace stood staring at the villa, its walls bathed in the light from the terraces.

'What a stunning building—it's like a stack of sugar cubes perched on the mountainside! How absolutely beautiful.'

Memories of the last woman he had brought here stirred at her words. He pushed them away. 'Thank you. I'll show you to your room as it's getting late. In the morning you can look around the villa and the gardens.'

Instead of following him Grace moved to the furthest reaches of one of the terraces and leaned on the balustrade.

'Now I understand why Christos was so eager to marry here. It's an idyllic wedding location. Sofia showed me some photos, but I had no idea it was so lovely. I can just imagine how incredible it will look on the night of the wedding, when everyone is dancing out here on the terrace, candles lit...'

It was time to move her on. 'As I said, I'll show you to your bedroom and then you can join me for something to eat.'

She stepped more fully into the light of the terrace, as though she didn't want to speak from the shadows. His jacket hung loose on her, almost reaching down to the hem of her dress.

'Thanks, but I'm not hungry.' She wrapped the jacket around her body, folding her arms over it to secure it closed. 'You're not excited about the wedding?'

He paused as he calculated his best response. Time to put his cards on the table. 'I'm concerned that they are rushing into this. They barely know one another. How long have they been together? Four months? The whole thing is unwise.'

'But they are really happy. I've never seen a couple so in love...so right for one another. It truly was love at first sight for them both.'

The gentle wistfulness in her voice had him clenching his fists.

'Really? Love at first sight?'

'Yes—why not?'

Her idealism made him want to be cruel, to shake her out of her romantic bubble. '*Lust* at first sight, maybe.'

Silence followed his words and they stared at each other, the truth of his words, as applied to them, hanging in the space between them.

He forced himself to continue. 'It takes a long time to get to know another person—if you ever can. People aren't what they seem.'

'I'm not sure what you mean.'

'My brother is an exceptionally wealthy man.'

She studied him with a mixed expression of disappointment and hurt. 'That means nothing to Sofia, trust me.'

For a brief moment he hated himself for his cynicism, for causing that wounded expression. But then he remembered how he had been played for a fool before, and he asked with a bitter laugh, 'Do you seriously believe that?'

Hard resolution entered her eyes. 'Yes. Absolutely.' She walked back to him, anger clear in her quick pace, in the way she glared at him.

Well, tough. He would remain convinced that Sofia was marrying Christos for his name and wealth until it was proved otherwise. And as for Grace Chapman... She seemed to know a lot about him. Was she really here just to organise the wedding flowers? Or did she perhaps hope for romance with the best man?

And that wasn't his vanity speaking. He had a constant stream of women eager to date him—to date a Petrakis, date a billionaire. To date him for all the superficial reasons he hated. But it suited him, because no woman was *ever* getting close to knowing the real him again. And no way was he getting entangled with the chief bridesmaid when tradition dictated that they would see each other in the future.

He picked up her suitcase and said once again, 'I'll show you to your room.'

Her phone rang. She checked the screen and turned away. 'Hi, Matt.' A long giggle followed. 'Of *course* I miss you.'

As he took her bags up into the villa he gritted his teeth at how happy she sounded. When was the last time someone had answered *his* call with such warmth and tenderness? And then anger surged through his veins. Was she already in a relationship? If so, why the hell was she allowing the chemistry between them to smoulder on?

'I love you too.'

Grace hung up from Matt and stretched her neck back, easing the tension in her muscles a fraction.

She rolled her shoulders and took in once again the quiet serenity of her surroundings. Then she steeled herself. She walked into the villa and entered a large living room, seeing walls whitewashed in gentle curves, a recessed fireplace. The stillness of the room and its simple refined beauty, from the huge white sofas on white marble floors to the handcrafted teak furniture, were at odds with the sense of injustice raging in her heart.

Andreas had no right to make such horrible assumptions about Sofia. She closed her eyes and inhaled deeply. Was Andreas just like her father? Cold and cynical? A man so obsessed with becoming wealthy he was blind to the magic of love and loyalty?

Whatever the truth, Sofia and Christos could not arrive to find the best man and chief bridesmaid at loggerheads. She and Andreas would have to learn to get on.

She found him in the kitchen, propped against the countertop, peeling an orange. She placed his jacket on the back of a chair. Unconsciously, she let her hand linger for a few moments on the soft wool, until she realised what she was doing.

Long elegant fingers expertly spiralled the peel off the orange, but he didn't glance downwards once to watch his progress—instead he studied her.

She placed a bottle of champagne on the counter. In response to his frown she explained, 'It's a thank-you for having me to stay.'

She had thought it might be an appropriate gift, given the upcoming celebrations, but was rapidly revising *that* idea. She twisted the bracelet at her wrist, her fingers reaching for the two charms that sat at its centre. The tension in her body eased a fraction when she squeezed the silver metal with her thumb and forefinger.

'I think we need to talk.'

He gave a tight nod and walked over to a cupboard. He opened the door on an array of crystal glasses. 'What can I get you to drink? Wine? Beer?'

Not thirsty, she was about to refuse, but then realised that she should accept his offer as a small step forward towards developing some form of *entente cordiale* between them.

'I have a long day tomorrow, so I'd like fruit juice, if that's okay.'

He gestured for her to sit on one of the stools beneath the counter, but instead she leaned against the wall, next to an old-fashioned dresser filled with colourful ceramics which, though at odds with the sleek lines of Andreas's modern kitchen, grounded the room with their reminder of history and other lives lived.

She jumped when her phone rang again. She grabbed it off the dresser. It was Lizzie. She let the call go to her voicemail, but that didn't stop Andreas giving her a critical stare.

The cold apple juice was sharp and refreshing, and thankfully helped her refocus on the task at hand. 'So, can we talk?'

He lifted his own glass of water and took a drink, his eyes never leaving her. 'What about?'

Butterflies fluttered in her stomach at his icy tone. 'Sofia's my best friend. This wedding means the world to her. I don't want anything…or anybody…to upset her.'

'Meaning me?'

She met his gaze and a wave of protectiveness for her friend had her returning his intimidating stare with conviction. 'Yes. Sofia is marrying Christos because she loves him—not for any other reason.'

'So you said before.'

His flippancy irked her and she asked sharply, 'Why have you agreed to host the wedding here, to be best man, if you don't approve?'

He held her gaze with a steady coolness, but his jaw tightened in irritation. 'When Christos asked me to be his best man I told him my concerns. But I believe in family loyalty, so of course I agreed. It would not have been honourable to do otherwise. And as for this island—we spent our childhood summers here, and we always vowed that we would marry in the island chapel one day. I'm not going to deny Christos that wish, no matter what my misgivings are.'

He stared at her hard, as though defying her to ask any more questions. But there was something in his expression that was puzzling her. Was it a hint of wounded pride? Why did she feel as though she was missing some significant point in this conversation? Sofia had mentioned that Andreas had once been briefly married. Was he remembering his own marriage? Or was she just reading this all wrong? Grace had formed the impression from Sofia that he had easily moved on from that marriage to a string of other relationships.

She walked towards him and stopped a little distance away. She forced herself to look into his eyes. Her heart pounded at the hard cynicism she found there. 'I can understand why you might have some concerns. But Sofia is an incredible person and I truly believe they will be extremely happy together. They were made for one another. For their sake I would like us to get on.'

He moved away from the countertop. Beneath his open-necked shirt, golden skin peppered with dark hair was visible. He took a step closer to her. Her breath caught as she inhaled his scent—a sensual muskiness with hints of spice and lemon. She stared at the broadness of his shoulders beneath the slim-fitting white shirt, the narrowness of his hips in the dark tuxedo trousers, the long length of his legs.

He stepped even closer, towering over her, those light green eyes burnished with gold scorching into hers. He leaned down towards her ear and in a low growl asked, 'Tell me...will your boyfriend be joining you for the wedding?'

His voice rumbled through her body. She didn't know

whether to run away from the dark danger that everything about this man screamed or just give in and lean into the heat and invisible pull of his powerful body.

She stepped back. Again he pinned her to the spot with his demanding stare.

'I don't have a boyfriend.'

His eyes narrowed. 'Then who's Matt?'

'Matt? Matt's my brother.'

For a moment he considered her suspiciously, as though searching for the truth. Then abruptly he turned away.

'I understand from Christos that you wish to use the workshops down by the island jetty to prepare the flowers? Tomorrow my gardener Ioannis will show you the way. If you need to travel to any of the other islands Ioannis will take you. My housekeeper Eleni will take care of your meals. Your bedroom is upstairs—the third room to the right. I have left your luggage there.'

Rebelliousness surged through her at his dismissive tone. 'And what about you, Andreas? Will you have a partner at the wedding this weekend?'

He turned and considered her. 'No. I'll be on my own. The way I like it. And, to answer your earlier question, I can see no reason why we cannot get on with one another. I will go along with Christos's wishes…but please don't expect me to embrace this wedding with the same enthusiasm as you. My days of believing in romance and love are long gone.'

He threw the uneaten orange into the bin, muttered, '*Kalinichta*…goodnight…' and walked out of the room.

Grace collapsed against the wall, suddenly exhausted. She closed her eyes and prayed that tomorrow would go more smoothly. That the deliveries would arrive on time.

That in the cold light of the day her senseless attraction to Andreas would diminish.

Because Andreas Petrakis was as far removed from her ideal man as Attila the Hun.

CHAPTER TWO

ANDREAS SLOWED THE pace of his morning swim for the last hundred metres into the shore and trailed his eye up the cliff-face and the numerous terraces built into it.

In only three days' time the island would be overrun with the hundreds of guests who were to be ferried out to the island from Athens. There would be polite avoiding of his eye, curious studying of him to see if he gave any sign of remembering his own vows of commitment, and how his marriage had ended within twelve short months.

He hoped Christos knew what he was doing. That he knew Sofia as well as he said he did. Andreas did not want to see his brother hurt. Or his family humiliated and disappointed again.

He had spent the past month, since Christos had announced his engagement, avoiding any involvement in the wedding preparations. He would respect his brother's decision and play the dutiful best man. Get along with the chief bridesmaid as best he could. But he'd keep his distance from her. To do otherwise, no matter how tempting, would be foolhardy.

There was undoubtedly a spark of attraction between them, but she was an out-and-out romantic and he had no business getting involved with a woman who believed in fairy-tale endings. Not when he knew that love was nothing but a fantasy. Anyway, the best man should *never* get involved with the chief bridesmaid. It was never a good idea in the long run.

On the warm sand at the base of the cliff he grabbed his towel and made his way back up the steep steps to the villa. He had rushed into marriage, like Christos. In the intense whirlwind of infatuation he had thought he had found love. But through her lies and betrayal his ex-wife had hardened his heart for ever. He would never trust again. He had always believed in marriage, in having children. But now those were the long forgotten dreams of an innocent.

Close to the top of his climb, he came to a stop on the final steps. Laden down with files and paperwork, her hair tied up into a high ponytail, bouncing from side to side, Grace rushed down the path towards him. She was dressed in a white lace blouse, pink shorts and trainers, and the sight of her bare legs had his abdominals tensing with frustration.

She spotted him and slowed, her eyes quickly flicking over him. Heat filled her cheeks before she looked away.

'*Kalimera*—good morning, Grace.'

She ventured another quick gaze at him and nodded. This time her eyes held his.

The morning sun highlighted the honey and caramel tones in her hair, emphasising the mesmerising violet colour of her eyes. Eyes that could do funny things to a man's resolve if he wasn't careful.

Invisible strings of mutual attraction tugged tight. He wanted to step closer, to cradle the delicate exposed lines of her neck, draw her mouth up towards his...

The beads of seawater that had been slowly following a lazy path down his body now felt electrified on his unbearably sensitive skin. He felt alive to a world of sensual possibilities.

She made a few attempts to talk, all the while shuffling the files in her arms, her eyes darting to and from him.

Why was she so jumpy? 'Is everything okay?'

Her head moved almost imperceptibly from side to side, as though she was trying to weigh up how she was going to reply. She bit down on her lip, exposing the not quite perfect alignment of her front teeth, with one tooth slightly overlapping the other. Why did he find that imperfection so appealing?

Eventually she said in a rush, 'Ioannis just called. The flowers are already down at the jetty. Apparently they were delivered before dawn. The delivery company were supposed to call me. I was meant to inspect them before they left... And, worse still, they were supposed to carry them as far as the workshops for me.'

The workshops sat on a steep hill overlooking the cove—she would need some help. 'Ask Ioannis to help you.'

'He had to go to Naxos to collect the caterers and the wedding planner and her team. A florist from Naxos was supposed to be coming with them, to assist me today, but she just called to say that she's sick.'

Thee mou! Did Grace know what she was doing? A missed flight, a missed delivery, and now a sick member of staff. 'Get Ioannis and the wedding planner's team to help you when they arrive.'

'I can't leave the flowers out in this heat. I have to get them into the cool of the workshops straight away.'

Why hadn't he opted to stay in Athens for the duration of the wedding preparations? *Because you love your brother. And as his work in London has prevented him from travelling until Thursday you promised to be here in case there were any issues.*

But he had urgent business to deal with too. He didn't have time for this. His instinct about Grace needing baby-sitting hadn't been far off the mark after all.

'Do you usually face so many problems?'

She considered him for a brief moment, her anxiety fading to be replaced by a sharp intelligence. 'There are always unforeseen problems with the flowers for any wedding. It's my job to deal with them as quickly as I can.' She paused, and although her cheeks grew even more enflamed she considered him with a quiet dignity. 'I'm sure *you* must experience unexpected problems all the time in your work…and will therefore understand why I need to ask for your help.'

'*My* help?' He had a mountain of work to do. He didn't have time to act as some florist's assistant.

She inhaled a deep breath and answered, 'I appreci-ate you're probably very busy, but if you could give me half an hour I'd be grateful.'

She awaited his response with a spirited stare of defi-ance, challenging him to say no. Despite himself he ad-mired her feistiness.

Against all logic and his pledges to keep a wide berth around the chief bridesmaid he found himself saying, 'I'll give you half an hour. No more. First I must get changed and reschedule a call.'

Light-headed, Grace turned away as Andreas climbed the path up to the villa, her heart pirouetting with humilia-tion…and something else she didn't want to think about.

He must think she was completely incompetent.

The ground beneath her no longer felt solid. Had she sat in the sun for too long earlier, whilst finalising her plans for the reception flowers out on the terrace? She came to a stop and gulped down some air.

Who was she trying to kid? This had nothing to do with too much sun. Rather too much of Andreas Petrakis. Too much of his near naked body. Too much of seeing the seawater that had fallen in droplets along the hard muscles of his chest, down over a perfectly defined six-pack until they'd reached the turquoise swimming shorts that sat low on his narrow hips.

She had been right last night. He *was* a Greek god. His sleeked back hair had emphasised the prominence of his cheekbones, the arrow-straightness of his nose, the enticing fullness of his mouth. And he had a long-limbed muscular body the likes of which she had only ever seen cast in marble whilst on a school tour to the British Museum. Sofia and she had circled those statues, giddy with teenage fascination.

She would *not* turn around and take one final glimpse. No way.

Oh, what the heck?

His back was a vast golden expanse of taut muscle, from broad powerful shoulders down to those narrow hips. And she could not help but notice the firm muscles of his bottom and the long, athletic shape of his legs as he easily climbed the steep path back towards the villa.

The goofy grin on her mouth faded. Okay, so he was gorgeous, and he did very peculiar things to her heart. But she had to dig one big hole and bury that attraction. She was here to do a job. She had to act professionally. Even if the gods were determinedly working against her right now in a bid to make her appear completely clueless.

Early this morning she had thrown open her balcony doors to dazzling sunshine and the stunning vista of far-away islands floating on the azure Aegean Sea. A light breeze had curled around her like a welcoming hug to the Cyclades Islands. Only the tinkle of goat bells had been carried on the air.

That paradise she had awoken to had given her a renewed determination that she was going to enjoy every second of this trip, which was to be the start of the life of adventure she had craved for so many years. After years of being held hostage to her father's control and manipulation she was determined to be free. Free to love every second of every day, to fill her life with fun and exhilaration. Free to accomplish all her own ambitions and prove that she *did* have worth.

All of which meant that tangling with her arrogant playboy host was the last thing she should be doing. Her priority had to be the flowers. If this project went wrong she could kiss her fledgling career goodbye. And, God forgive her for her pride, she wanted to prove to Andreas that she wasn't a bumbling idiot—contrary to all current evidence.

Set into the cliff-face above the small harbour, the workshops mirrored the sugar cube style of the main house. Inside, the cool double-height rooms with their exposed roof beams and roughly plastered walls would be perfect for storing and assembling the flowers.

Grace quickly moved about the first workshop on the row, sweeping dust off benches and pulling two into the centre of the room for her to work at. Outside again, she raced down to the harbour jetty, grabbed a stack of flower buckets, and ran back up to the workshops. Within minutes her legs were burning because of the steep incline.

Back inside the workshop, she dropped the buckets to the floor and exhaled heavily. What had she taken on? How on earth was she going to strip and trim over a thousand stems of peonies and lisianthus by herself?

She gave herself a shake and scanned the room. There was no tap. What was she going to do about water? She ran into the adjoining room and almost cried in relief when she saw a sink in the far corner. She twisted the tap. The gush of water restored some calm.

Twice more she ran down to the jetty to collect the remaining buckets, and the box she had packed personally, which contained all her essential tools: knives, scissors, pruners and a vast assortment of tapes, wires and cord twine.

By the time Andreas appeared at the workshop door she was not only hot and sweaty but also covered in wet patches from the sloshing water as she carried endless buckets of water from the adjoining room back into her temporary workshop.

He, in contrast, was his usual effortlessly cool and elegant self, wearing faded denim jeans that hung low on his hips and a slim-fitting sea-green polo shirt. Muscular biceps, washboard abs... How good would it be to walk into his arms and feel the athletic strength of his body?

For a few seconds every ounce of energy drained from her and she wondered how she didn't crumble to the workshop floor in a mess of crushing attraction.

Pointedly he glanced at his exquisite platinum watch.

Inwardly she groaned at her lack of focus.

She rushed to the door and pointed down towards the jetty. The pale wooden structure sitting over the teal-blue sea was the perfect romantic setting for the arrival of the wedding guests on Saturday.

'The flowers are all packed in those large rectangular boxes, stacked together. We need to get those inside now. The other boxes can wait until later.'

She was about to pass him when he placed his hand

on her forearm. 'I'll collect the boxes—you stay here and continue with the work you were doing.'

She swallowed hard, her whole body on alert at the pleasurable sensation of his large hand wrapped around her arm. 'We don't have time.'

His eyes moved downwards and lingered on her chest.

Grace followed his gaze. And almost passed out. Her wet blouse was transparent, and clinging to her crimson-trimmed bra.

His lip curled upwards in one corner and for a moment she got a glimpse of how lethal he would be if he decided to seduce her.

'Perhaps it might be better if you stay inside for a while; Ioannis and the wedding team are due to arrive soon.'

Mortified, she twisted away, grabbed some buckets and pointedly turned and nodded in the direction of his watch. 'You'd better get going as your half an hour is ticking away. I reckon you'll struggle to get all of the boxes in by then.'

A smirk grew on his lips. 'I'll try not to break into too much of a sweat...' He paused as his eyes rested on where her wet blouse was sticking to her skin. 'Although it does have its attractions.'

Lightning bolts of lust fired through her body. He noted her wide-eyed reaction and his smirk grew even larger. She twisted around and fled next door. She could have sworn she heard him chuckle.

When she returned with the filled buckets he was gone.

Andreas returned time and time again with the long rectangular flower boxes, and each time Grace heard his footsteps approach she hightailed it into the adjoining room. Only when she realised that he had moved on to carrying in the assortment of different-sized boxes that contained the other essentials did she speak. But despite her assurances that it wasn't necessary for him to bring them in, he continued to do so.

The buckets filled and flower food added, she went about stripping and trimming the stems. With bated breath she opened the first box of peonies and found light pink Sarah Bernhardt, and in the next box the ivory-white Duchesse de Nemours. Both were as big and utterly beautiful as she had hoped, and on track to open to their full blowsy glory for Saturday.

At last *something* was going right for her.

For a moment she leaned down and inhaled the sweet scent of the flowers, closing her eyes in pleasure. She might have to stay up all night to get the prep work done, but she would manage. The flowers had to be perfect for Sofia.

She had the first box completed when Andreas brought the final boxes in. Unfairly, apart from a faint sheen of perspiration on his tanned skin, he didn't appear the least bit ruffled by all the dragging and hauling.

Hitting the timer on her smartphone, she twisted it around to show him the display. 'Thirty-six minutes, fourteen seconds.'

His mouth twitched for a few seconds before he flashed his watch at her and tapped one of the dials. 'Nineteen minutes and forty-three seconds to carry in the flowers, which was all you specified. So I win.'

'I didn't know we were competing.'

Those green eyes flashed with way too much smugness for her liking. 'Why did you time me then?'

'Oh, just curiosity.' Keen to change the subject, she added, 'I'm really grateful for your help—thank you.'

He shrugged in response and turned his attention to

the remaining stack of flower boxes, and then to the already trimmed peonies, sitting in their buckets of water. 'Why so many roses?'

'They're not roses.'

He contemplated the flowers dubiously.

She twisted the stem she was working on and held it out towards him. 'They're peonies. I thought you would have known, being Greek, as apparently they are called after Paean, who healed Hades's wounds. It's thought that they have healing properties. It's also believed that they represent a happy life...and a happy marriage.'

To that he raised a sceptical eyebrow.

With her floral shears, Grace snipped an inch diagonally off the end of the stem. 'Let me guess...you're not the type to buy flowers?'

'On occasion I have.' A grin tugged at the corner of his mouth in reaction to her quizzical glance. 'Okay, I admit that I let my PA organise the details.'

She tried to ignore how good it was to see those eyes sparkle with humour. 'Now, *that's* just cheating... I hope you at least specify what type of flowers you want to send?'

He seemed baffled at the idea. 'No—why should I?'

'Because each flower represents something. When you send a flower you are sending a message with it.'

He looked horrified at that prospect. 'Like what?'

Amused, she decided to make the most of him being on the back foot in this conversation. 'Well, new beginnings are symbolised by daffodils...a secret love is represented by gardenias...' She paused for effect before continuing, 'True love is shown by forget-me-nots, and sensuality by jasmine.'

Their eyes met and tension pulsed in the air. But then

he broke his gaze away. 'How about, *Thanks for a good night, but this is nothing serious*?'

Her heart sank. 'A yellow rose is used for friendship, if that's what you're trying to say. But maybe it would be better not to send anything on those occasions.'

Unable to bear the way his gaze had fastened on her again, she bent her head and trimmed the foliage on the stem with quick cuts, a constant mantra sounding in her brain: *Stay away from him; he's a sure-fire path to heartbreak.*

He eventually spoke. 'Perhaps. But I still don't understand why so many flowers are needed for one wedding.'

So often she had heard the same incredulous question from grooms-to-be, who struggled to understand the volume of flowers needed to create a visual impact and how important flowers were for setting the mood and tone of the wedding day. She was used to talking them through her plans, and always keen to make them comfortable and happy with her designs, but with Andreas she felt even more compelled to spell out the intricacies of wedding floral design and the attention to detail required. She wanted it to be clear to him that she was not *playing with flowers*. That her presence on his island was essential.

'Eight hundred peonies. Two hundred lisianthus, to be precise. Along with the bridal party bouquets, and the flower displays that will be needed outside the chapel and on the terrace, each reception table will have a centrepiece of five vases with five peonies in each, so with twenty tables—'

'That adds up to five hundred flowers.'

'Exactly. Today I have to trim, cut and place all the stems in water. Tomorrow the stems will need to be cut again and placed in fresh water. On Friday fifty potted bay trees and storm lanterns will be delivered, to be placed along the walkway between the jetty and the chapel, and on the main terrace for the reception and the dancing.'

He surveyed the boxes of flowers yet to be opened and then looked over to the large pile of other unopened boxes. His gaze narrowed. 'What's in the other boxes?'

She had gone over her stock list so often she had no problem in recalling all the items she had ordered. 'One hundred glass vases for the centrepieces, two hundred votive candles, fifty lantern candles and thirty pillar candles. Flower foam, more string, wire, ribbon... The list goes on. They all need to be unloaded today, ready to be prepped tomorrow. And I also have to finalise my designs.'

He checked his watch and frowned. 'I have to get back to my conference calls. Is there anyone else who can help you with all this?'

'I'll manage.' Even if it meant she would be working late into the night. 'Two more florists will be joining me tomorrow, but I need to get all the basic prep done today or I'll run out of time.'

His eyes drifted over the now crowded room. 'I have to admit that I hadn't realised the volume of work involved.'

A smile tugged at her lips. 'Perhaps now you understand why I need to be here and not touring the nightclubs of Athens.'

He gave a gracious nod in response, his eyes softening in amusement. 'Yes, but that's not to say that I don't think it's all crazy.'

With that he left the room, and Grace stood stockstill for the longest while, her heart colliding against her chest at being on the receiving end of his beautiful smile.

Six hours later Andreas made his way back down to the workshops. Eleni, although tied up in an argument with the catering team over the use of her beloved pots and pans, had whispered to him that Grace had not appeared for lunch, and gestured in appeal towards a tray of food.

Never able to say no to his indomitable housekeeper, who had him wrapped around her little finger, Andreas approached the workshops now in frustration at yet another disruption to his day. But he had to admit to concern for Grace at the huge amount of work she had to tackle alone, and to a grudging respect for her determination and energy in doing so.

Inside the first workshop the tiled floor was akin to a woodland scene, with green leaves and cuttings scattered everywhere. In the middle, armed with a sweeping brush, Grace was corralling the leaves into one giant pile, her face a cloud of tension.

A quick glance about the room told him she was making slow progress. She needed help. And unfortunately he was the only person available.

'Eleni's concerned that you missed lunch.'

She jerked around at his voice.

He dropped the tray on the edge of a workbench.

'That's very kind of her.' She paused as she grabbed a nearby dustpan and composting bag. 'Please thank her for me but tell her not to worry—I can fend for myself.'

The composting bag full, Grace tied it and placed it in a corner. He, meanwhile, had taken over the scooping of the leaves.

She moved next to him, her bare legs inches from where he crouched down. If he reached out, his fingers could follow a lazy path over her creamy skin. He could learn at what point her eyes would glaze over as his fingers traced her sensitive spots. The desire to pull her down onto the mound of leaves and kiss that beautiful mouth raged inside him.

'There's no need for you to help.'

She sounded weary.

He stood. His gut tightened when he saw the exhaustion in her eyes. 'You need a break. Have some lunch. I'll finish here.'

She hesitated, but then walked over to the tray. The deep aroma of Greek coffee filled the workshop but she immediately went back to work, carrying a fresh box over to the table. In between opening the box and sorting through the flowers she hurriedly gulped down some coffee and took quick, small bites of a triangular-shaped parcel of spinach and feta cheese pie—*spanakopita*.

He gathered up the tray, ignoring her confused expression, and took it to a bench outside. When Grace joined him he said, 'You shouldn't work and eat at the same time.'

'I'm too busy.'

'Let's make a deal. If you agree to take a ten-minute break, I'll stay a while and unpack some of the supplies for you.'

She stared at him suspiciously. 'Are you sure?'

He needed to make clear his reasons for doing this. 'You're my guest—it's my duty to take care of you.'

She paused for a moment and considered his words before giving a faint nod. 'I'd appreciate your help, but I must warn you that it might prove to be a tedious job because the suppliers haven't labelled the boxes. I need you to find the glass vases for me first, as I have to prep them today. There's a box-cutter you can use on the table next to the boxes.'

He went back inside and started opening boxes. She rejoined him within five minutes. A five-minute break that had included her answering a phone call from someone called Lizzie.

A begrudging respect for her work ethic toyed with his annoyance that she hadn't adhered to her side of the bargain. He wasn't used to people going against his orders.

They both worked in silence, but the air was charged with an uncomfortable tension.

Eventually she spoke. 'What were these workshops originally used for?'

Sadness tugged in his chest at her question. He swallowed hard before he spoke. 'My uncle was a ceramicist and he built these workshops for his work.'

She rested her hands on the workbench and leaned forward. 'I noticed some ceramic pieces in your house—are they your uncle's?'

'Yes. He created them in these workshops; there's a kiln in the end room.'

'They're beautiful.'

Thrown by the admiration and excitement in her voice, he pressed his thumb against the sharp blade of the box cutter. 'He died two years ago.'

For a long while the only sound was the whistle of the light sea breeze as it swirled into the workshop.

She walked around the bench to where he was working. 'I'm sorry.'

He glanced away from the tender sincerity in her eyes. It tugged much too painfully at the empty pit in his stomach.

'What was he like?'

The centre of my world.

He went back to work, barely registering the rows of candles inside the box he had just opened.

'He was quiet, thoughtful. He loved this island. When I was a small boy the island belonged to my grandparents. They used it as their summer retreat. My uncle lived here permanently. Christos and I used to spend our summers here, free to explore without anyone telling us what to do and when to be home. That freedom was paradise. We'd swim and climb all day, and at night we'd grill fish on the beach with our uncle. He would tell us stories late into the night, trying his best to scare us with tales of sea monsters.'

'There's a gorgeous ceramic pot in the living room, with images of sea monsters and children...did he create that?'

He was taken aback that she had already noticed his single most treasured possession, and it was a while before he answered. 'Yes, the children are Christos and me.'

'What wonderful memories you both must have.'

He turned away from the beguiling softness in her violet eyes. He closed the lid of the box, still having been unable to locate the vases. It was strange to talk to someone about his uncle. Usually he closed off any conversation about him, but being here, in one of his workshops, with this quietly spoken empathetic woman, had him wanting to speak about him.

'He always encouraged me to follow my dreams, even when they were unconventional or high risk. He even funded my first ever property acquisition when I was nineteen. Thankfully I was able to pay him back with interest within a year. He believed in me, trusted me when others didn't.'

Her thumb rubbed against the corner of a box. He noticed that her nails, cut short, were varnish-free. A plaster was wrapped around her index finger and he had to stop himself from taking it in his hand.

She inhaled before she spoke. 'You were lucky to have someone like that in your life.'

Taken aback by the loneliness in her voice, he could only agree. 'Yes.'

She gave him a sad smile. 'Kasas is a very special place…you're lucky to have a house somewhere so magical.'

Old memories came back with a vengeance. 'Some people would hate it.'

'Hate this island? I think it's the most beautiful place I have ever visited.'

Andreas watched her, disarmed by the passion in her voice. He wanted to believe everything she said was heartfelt and genuine. That he wasn't being manipulated by a woman again. But cold logic told him not to buy any of it.

It was time to move this conversation on. It was getting way too personal.

'The vases aren't here.'

Her mouth dropped open and she visibly paled. 'They *have* to be.'

'I've double-checked each box—they're not.'

She gave a low groan and rushed over to the boxes, while frantically pushing buttons on her phone. As she ransacked the boxes she spoke to someone called Jan.

Andreas walked away and into the adjoining room. Once again he tried to ignore the loneliness crowding his chest at being in these workshops for the first time since his uncle had died.

A few minutes later Grace followed him into the end room, where the kiln was located. She stopped at the doorway and clenched her phone tight in her palm. Her paleness had now been replaced by a slash of red on her cheeks.

She spoke in a low voice, her eyes wary. 'The vases were never despatched by the suppliers in Amsterdam; they won't get here before Saturday.'

He had guessed as much. He gestured to the vast array

of white porcelain pots on the bench beside the kiln. 'You can use these instead.'

Her eyes grew wide and she went and picked one up. And then another. Her fingers traced over the smooth delicate ceramic. 'Are you sure?'

'He had moved back to working predominantly with porcelain in the year before he died. I've never known what to do with all his work, I didn't want to sell it…' Unexpected emotion cut off the rest of what he had been about to say.

Soft violet eyes held his. 'This can't be easy for you.'

He glanced away. 'He would like it that his work is being used for Christos's wedding.'

With that he walked back to the main workshop, wanting to put some distance between him and this woman who kept unbalancing his equilibrium. Frustration rolled through him. What was it about Grace that made him break all his own rules?

He had another ten minutes before he had to leave. There were a few small boxes yet to open.

He unwrapped a small rectangular parcel first, and found inside, wrapped in a soft cloth, a pair of silver sandals. 'These are unusual florist's supplies.'

'My sandals!' She dropped the flowers she was working on and took the slender sexy heels from him.

Imagining Grace's enticing legs in the sandals, he felt his blood pressure skyrocket. In need of distraction, he went back to opening the next box.

'The shop didn't have them in my size so I had them delivered here…' Her voice trailed off and then she said in a low, desperate voice, 'Don't open that box.'

But she was too late. His fingers were already looped around two pale pink silk straps. He lifted the material to reveal a sheer lace bustier.

With an expression of absolute mortification Grace stared at the bustier, and then down at the scrap of erotic pink lace still left in the box, sitting on a bed of black tissue paper. Odds on it was the matching panties. Red-hot blood coursed through his body.

'Yours, I take it?'

For a moment her mouth opened and closed, but then she grabbed the bustier and the box and walked away.

She kept her back to him as she bundled the bustier back into its box. 'It's for the wedding, but I'm not sure I'll wear it.'

Time for him to leave—before he burst a blood vessel. 'I have afternoon calls I have to get back to.' He made it as far as the door before he turned back. 'Grace?'

She turned around towards him.

'Wear it.'

He walked away as her lips parted in surprise. He had never wanted to grab a woman and kiss her senseless more in all his life.

CHAPTER THREE

GRACE REACHED FOR the bell clapper, feeling the ladder wobbling beneath her.

'What in the name of the devil are you doing?'

She jerked at the sound of Andreas's irate voice beneath her and the precarious ladder swayed wildly. A startled yelp from deep within her shot out into the evening air, but mercifully the ladder was steadied before it toppled to the ground.

She dared a quick glance down. A livid Andreas was gripping the side bars, one foot on the bottom rung.

She swallowed hard, uncertain as to what was more daunting: this fury, or the heat in his eyes earlier when he had lifted up her bustier. Heat that had ignited a yearning in her that had left her breathless and just plain exasperated. They didn't even particularly *like* each other. Why, then, did she feel as though she was about to combust any time she came into contact with him?

'I've decided that the chapel needs some extra decoration in addition to what I'd planned, so I'm making a garland that will hang from the bell tower down to the ground. I need to measure the exact length.'

'*Aman!* You are breaking my nerves! You shouldn't be doing this alone; the flagstones are too uneven.'

He was right, but she wasn't going to admit it. 'I'm

fine—it's a quick job.' To prove her point she knotted twine around the bell clapper and then dropped the twine spool to the ground before climbing down the ladder. She avoided looking at him and instead pulled the twine out to the angle she wanted the garland positioned at on the wedding day. Cutting it to the desired length, she ignored his infuriated expression. 'I need to climb back up and untie the other end.'

He gave an exasperated sigh and scaled the ladder himself, dropping the twine when he'd untied it. Back on the ground, he unlocked the extension ladder she had borrowed from Ioannis and collapsed it down.

Then he studied her with incensed eyes, his mouth a thin line. 'Don't try that again.'

Of course she would. But she wasn't going to get into an argument with him. 'Was there something you wanted?'

His gaze narrowed. The uncomfortable sensation that he could see right through her had her grabbing the twine off the ground and asking, 'Is it okay if I use some of the rosemary and bay growing on the terraces for the garland?'

He considered the long length of twine sceptically. 'Is it really necessary? I thought you were under pressure timewise?'

She was, but it was these final touches that would make her work stand apart. 'I'll find the time.' She paused and gestured around her. 'I want the flowers to do justice to this setting.'

Set on a rocky promenade beyond the golden sandy beach, the tiny whitewashed chapel with its blue dome had a dramatic backdrop of endless deep blue seas and skies.

His jaw hardened even more, and she winced to think about the pressure his poor teeth must be under.

'My guess is that Sofia would prefer her bridesmaid *not* to be in a plaster cast on her wedding day for the sake of a few flowers.'

Wow, that was a low blow. 'If you'll excuse me? I need to finalise my plans for the chapel's bespoke floral arrangements—or, as you call them, "a few flowers".'

His mouth twisted at her barbed comment. 'It will be dark soon.'

'I won't be long.' When he didn't move, she added, 'You don't need to wait for me.'

'And have you getting lost on the way back? No, thanks. I don't want to have to spend a second night rescuing you.'

With that he turned and went and sat on the low white-washed wall that surrounded the chapel terrace.

Behind him the deep blue sea met the purple evening sky; it was a postcard-perfect image of the Greek Islands but for the scowling man who dominated the frame.

Grace circled the terrace outside the chapel, all the while taking notes, scribbling into her notebook. Every now and again she would glance in his direction and throw him a dirty glare. Which he was just fine with. Because he was in a pretty dirty mood himself. In every sense.

All afternoon he had been plagued with images of her wearing that sexy lingerie. The bustier hugging her small waist, lifting her breasts to a height and plumpness that demanded a man taste them. Those skimpy panties moulded to her pert bottom... Hell, he couldn't go there again. His call to the Cayman Island planners had been a washout as a result.

She had already put in a twelve-hour day, with less

than five minutes taken for lunch. Did it *really* matter this much what the flowers looked like? Did anyone even *notice* the flowers on a wedding day?

'Why does this wedding mean so much to you?'

She turned to him in surprise, her notebook falling to her side. The long length of her golden ponytail curled over one shoulder and his fingers tingled in remembrance of its softness and her delicate sensual scent last night. His gut tightened. Those legs were once again driving him crazy with images of the chief bridesmaid that he certainly shouldn't be thinking of.

He dated some of the most beautiful women in Athens. Why was he so drawn to this out-of-bounds woman?

Eventually she walked over and sat on the wall beside him. She left a significant gap between them.

'I first met Sofia in our local playground when we were both four. A boy had pushed me off the top of the fire pole. Sofia marched right over and kicked him in the shin before helping me up.' She gave an amused shrug. 'We've never looked back since then. We went to the same primary and secondary school…and we were supposed to go to university together…' She paused and gave a small sigh. 'But that didn't work out for me. After years of coming to school concerts with me, and wet Saturday afternoons standing at the side of a freezing cold soccer pitch, I owe Sofia big-time.'

'I don't understand? Why were you going to school concerts together for years?'

Her lips twisted for a moment before she distractedly rubbed a hand along the smooth skin of her calf. 'My parents weren't always available, so I used to go to Matt's football matches and my younger sister Lizzie's school events. Sofia used to come to keep me company. Even though she could have been off doing something much more entertaining than listening to a school orchestra murdering some piece of music.'

He considered what she'd said. Maybe Christos *was* marrying a good woman.

As though to emphasise that point, Grace studied him coolly. 'Christos is a very lucky man. He's marrying an incredible woman—smart and loving.'

'It sounds like he is.'

A small note of triumph registered in her eyes. 'So, can we agree that we will do everything to make this wedding as special a day as possible for them?'

He wanted to say yes, but the word just wouldn't come. He still feared that Christos might regret his haste in years to come. As he did. So instead he said, 'You're one of life's hopeless romantics, aren't you?'

Those astounding violet eyes narrowed and she leaned away from him as she considered his words. 'Romantic, yes—hopeless, no. I'm not ashamed to admit that I believe in love...in marriage. I see it all the time in my work, and with Sofia and Christos. It's the most wonderful thing that exists.'

'Have *you* ever been in love?'

Her shoulders jerked at his question. 'No.'

'But you want to be?'

An unconscious smile broke on her lips, and her eyes shone with dreams. 'Yes. And I'm greedy... I want it all. I want love at first sight, the whirlwind, the marriage, the children, the growing old together. The perfect man.'

He'd once thought life was that simple. In exasperation, he demanded, 'The perfect man...? What on earth is *that*?'

'A man who will sweep me off my feet, who will make life fun and exciting. A man who believes in love too. In kindness and tenderness.'

For a moment she eyed what must be his appalled expression, given the angry frown that had popped up on her brow. And then, as though his reaction had unlocked something inside of her, she let go with all barrels firing.

'A man who's intelligent, honourable, loyal...and great in bed.'

He tried not to laugh at how disconcerted she seemed by her own last statement. Clearing his throat, he said, 'Wow, that's some guy. But I hate to break it to you... that's not reality. Love is complex and messy and full of disappointment. Not like the fairy tale and the X-rated Prince Charming you've just described. Do you *really* believe someone like that exists?'

Solemn eyes met his. 'I hope so.' Then a hint of fear, maybe doubt, clouded her eyes. For a few moments they sat in silence, until she asked, 'How about you?'

For a while he just stared at her—at the high, slanting cheekbones, the freckle-sized birthmark just below her right ear, surprised by her naivety...by her optimism. In truth, a part of him was wildly envious of that.

'As I said last night, I have no interest in love—in relationships full-stop.'

'Why?'

Even if he'd wanted to, even if he'd trusted Grace he wouldn't be able to find adequate words to describe the mess his marriage had descended into.

'I'd rather not talk about it.'

Disappointment filled her eyes. But then she gave him a sympathetic smile and he instantly realised that she already knew about his marriage. Christos must have said something. Just how much *did* she know? Anger flared inside him. He did not want her sympathy. He did not need the humiliation of her pity.

She shifted on the wall and gazed at him uncertainly. 'Sofia mentioned that you were once married…'

He didn't respond, but raised a questioning eyebrow instead, waiting for her to continue.

She gestured towards the chapel. 'Having the ceremony in the same chapel…' She trailed off.

His heart sank. He really didn't want to talk about this. 'I didn't marry here.'

'Oh.' Clearly flustered by his answer, she muttered, 'Sorry, I assumed you had. After what you said last night about Christos and you always wanting to marry here.'

With an impatient sigh, he answered, 'My ex wanted to get married in Athens.'

She digested this for some time before she asked, 'Did you mind not marrying here?'

At the time he *had* minded. But his ex had been determined from day one that theirs would be *the* society wedding of the year in Athens, and had used his uncle's recent death to persuade him not to marry on the island. She had insisted that he would find it too upsetting to be surrounded by reminders of him on their wedding day.

It had all been lies. In the bitter arguments after he had confronted her with the photos of her with her lover she had admitted as much. His one consolation from the entire debacle was that at least the island wasn't tainted with memories of the worst decision of his life. His biggest failure.

He waited for a few minutes before he spoke, afraid of the anger that might spill out otherwise. 'It doesn't matter; it's in the past.'

'I'm sorry your marriage didn't work out. It must have been a difficult time,' she said quietly.

Disconcerted, Andreas could only stare at her. Was she really the first person who had said such a thing to him? Everyone else had been caught up in outrage at his ex's behaviour, or too embarrassed to say anything. No one—probably in the face of his anger and defiance—had dared to acknowledge just how difficult it had been for him.

His pride demanded that he just shrug off her comments, and he was about to do so when she gave him a glance of understanding that totally disarmed him.

Reluctantly he acknowledged, 'It *was* difficult.'

'You never know—you might find happiness in the future with someone else.'

Not her too. 'Please tell me that you're not one of those women who believe they can change a man…make him fall in love.'

At first she stared at him with a stunned expression, but then her eyes grew hard and cold. 'Andreas, I've had a lifetime's worth of arguments and fights, endless disappointments at failing to get a man to love me. The idea of getting into a relationship with a man who doesn't believe in love or have the capacity to love—for whatever reason—would be my idea of hell. And, trust me, I'm no martyr.'

What was she talking about? Had some guy messed her around?

He tried to remain calm when he spoke again. 'Who were you fighting with?'

Her shoulders dropped and she ran a hand tiredly down over her face. With a heavy sigh, she said, 'How about we get a drink.'

A little while later they sat outside on the main terrace of the villa, with the setting sun disappearing behind the horizon in a blaze of fiery pinks on the purple sky. Along with white wine, Andreas had brought to the table a supper of cheese pie—*tiropita*—freshly baked by Eleni that afternoon, and a bowl of Greek salad.

The filo pastry and salty feta cheese of the *tiropita* melted in her mouth, but she was unable to eat more than a few bites in the silence that had settled between them since returning from the chapel.

Her gaze met his and her stomach clenched at the thought of having to recount her past. She took a sip of wine and pushed back into her chair, squeezing her hands tight in her lap. This trip was supposed to be the start of her new life. She didn't want to remember the past. But she wanted to explain why she would never try to force a man to love her. That despite the attraction between them, and Andreas's obvious thoughts to the contrary, she wanted nothing from him.

'When I was seventeen my mum left us. My brother Matt was twelve, my sister Lizzie fourteen I was due to go to university that year, but I couldn't leave Matt and Lizzie.'

'Why?'

Memories of standing outside her mother's isolated cottage in Scotland, trying to build up the courage to knock, swamped her. The humiliation of begging her mum to allow Matt and Lizzie to go and live with her only for her to refuse.

'My father…'

This was so hard. Should she say nothing? What *could* she say about her father? Would Andreas even understand? After all he was a driven businessman too. Was he as motivated by money and power as her father? Had that ambition caused his marriage to collapse? Despondency washed over her at the thought that that might have been the case. She suddenly had to know if he was like her father.

'What's the most important thing in your life?'

He considered her warily. 'Why do you ask?'

'I'll explain in a little while.'

For a moment she thought he wouldn't give her an answer. Then, 'Without a doubt my family: Christos, my mother.' He paused before he added, 'My father.'

She searched his eyes but he looked away. Though she had only met his father once, at the engagement party, she had quickly formed the impression that he was impatient and brusque—the type of man who would proudly boast that he didn't suffer fools gladly, with no comprehension of just how foolish and shortsighted that comment was.

In a quiet voice she asked, 'Don't you get on? You and your father?'

'It's not the easiest of relationships.'

Why was he so closed? He told her so little about himself. But then maybe he would understand if he too had a difficult relationship with his father.

'With my father, his business is the only thing that matters. Family never features in his priorities. After my mother left, it was down to me to care for Matt and Lizzie. He didn't care. Though we could barely afford it, he wanted to send them away to boarding school. They were both devastated after my mum left. They needed love and comforting, not some impersonal school.'

Apart from Sofia, she had never confided any of this to another person. Vulnerability and embarrassment sat in her throat like a double-vice grip and she studied the terrace table, bewildered by just how upset she felt. Questioning the sense in telling him all of this. Inadequacy washed over her—so ferocious she thought she might drown.

'Are you okay?'

She peeped up and nodded. Her heart slammed to a stop when she saw the gentleness in his eyes.

'You gave up university to stay with your brother and sister; that's very admirable.'

She swallowed against the emotion lodged in her throat and said, 'I thought that I might be able to get my dad to love Matt and Lizzie, to see how much they needed him. But I just couldn't get through to him. I spent years trying to make things perfect, until I realised that there was no point. After that my objective was to get them to university...away from him. Matt started university this year; Lizzie's in her third year. They're both happy and settled.'

'And what about you?'

'I left home last year, at the same time as Matt. I'm hoping I'll be able to buy an apartment soon—one that can be a home for us all. I've always dreamt of being a florist, and for the past few years, while I've studied floristry at night, I've worked with a wedding floral designer at the weekends. Since I left home I've worked as a florist full-time. After this wedding I'm going freelance as a wedding floral designer, and at some point hopefully I'll be able to open my own flower shop too.'

'Why floristry?'

Was that a note of disapproval in his voice? Compared to his success, her dreams must seem so insignificant.

She glanced at him sharply and asked, 'Why do you ask?'

'Out of curiosity...' He considered her for a while, and then with a grin he added, 'And I reckon the best man and the chief bridesmaid should know a little about each other.'

Grace eyed him suspiciously. 'Have we just taken a step forward in peace negotiations?'

He flashed her a wicked grin that almost had her falling off her chair. 'Perhaps. And, for the record, my question wasn't a criticism.'

'Sorry—it's just that you sounded like my dad. He thinks a career in floristry is a dead end.'

'Why would he say that?'

'Because there's little monetary gain to be made in it as a career—certainly not the sort of wealth *he* admires anyway. I worked in my father's business when I left school. He wanted me to stay and take over the logistics department. He even offered to give me a percentage share in the firm to stay.'

'You weren't tempted by his offer?'

'Not for a minute. It was just his way of trying to keep me in his control.'

He looked into the distance and scowled. 'Emotional blackmail.'

She felt something unlock within her at knowing that he understood. 'Yes.'

He gazed at her for a while and an invisible bond stretched between them.

He broke his gaze. 'So, why floristry?'

'I love everything about flowers—their scent, texture, colours. It's challenging to create a beautiful bouquet or a centrepiece, but so much fun too, especially for weddings, which are such happy affairs.'

'I'm impressed that you've taken on *this* wedding. I'm guessing it's a big project for someone relatively new to the business?'

Her doubts and fears about messing up came charging back and she didn't know how to respond as her heart thudded in her chest. She gave a shrug that belied the butterflies soaring in her belly. 'I'm aiming high...

I just hope I don't crash back down to earth in a blaze of bad publicity.'

'That won't happen—not with the amount of prep and planning you've done.'

'I hope so. It's really important to me that my flowers do justice to Sofia and Christos's love and the vows they will be taking.'

'Why did you choose to specialise in weddings? I would have thought they are particularly demanding?'

'They are—but I love pushing myself to design something new and unique for each couple and the time pressures involved. People in love are full of wonder and optimism, and they are usually thrilled with the work you do... What better clients could anyone wish for? I had years of my father's hardness and cynicism. I want to do something that's fun and positive now. I want to live in a world where people care about one another, where there is kindness and respect. Does that sound crazy to you?'

He contemplated her words thoughtfully before eventually saying, 'Perhaps, but it's a nice dream. And to me it sounds like you already show a lot of kindness and care towards your siblings.'

'I try to be there for them as much as I can.'

'Is that why you've never travelled alone before?'

'Up to now I could never go without them. We couldn't afford to travel much, but when we did it was all three of us together—sometimes Sofia came too.'

'They call and text you a lot. Do you still feel responsible for them?'

It wasn't something she had thought about before. 'I suppose I do.'

'Maybe you need to let them go a little in order to focus on your own future.'

Everything in Grace recoiled at what he said. She didn't want to talk about this. She had a duty to them.

She pushed away the uneasy thought that he was possibly right.

'It's not as easy as that.'

Grace stood quickly and began to clear their plates. She kept her eyes low, refusing to look at him.

'I didn't mean to upset you.'

She studied him cautiously. 'It's okay.' She eyed him again for a moment before giving a heavy sigh. 'Anyway, you're not the only one who might say the wrong thing sometimes. I'm sorry if my enthusiasm for the wedding is over the top at times. I should realise not everyone is a wedding freak like I am.'

For a moment he considered challenging her on the fact that what he'd said might not be the wrong thing to point out, but her guarded expression told him to back off. So instead he said, with a smile, 'Wedding freak—that's a new term for me.'

She lowered the dishes in her hands to the table again. 'Thank you for your help today.'

Genuine gratitude shone from her eyes and he was taken aback at how good it felt to be appreciated, to know that he had helped. When had he stopped helping others? Closed himself off from the world?

He was thankfully pulled out of the uncomfortable realisation when she spoke again. 'I realise you must be very busy with your work. I'm sorry if I caused any disruption.'

He tipped back in his chair and scratched the back of his head ruefully. 'I must admit that the contents of that last box affected my concentration all afternoon.'

She gave a nervous smile and hurriedly picked up the

dishes again. 'I'm going in to get a sweater. Is it okay if I get some coffee at the same time?'

'Use the kitchen as you wish.'

'Would you like one too?'

He nodded his acceptance and as she walked away he turned in his chair, his eyes sweeping over the sway of her hips, the pertness of her bottom. She had changed when they'd got back from the chapel, into jeans and a close-fitting baby blue tee shirt that showed the curves of her full, high breasts to perfection.

Damn it, but he was deeply attracted to her. He wanted to hold her and feel those soft lips under his, to touch the plumpness of her bottom, run his thumb along the outline of her breasts.

Aman! This was madness.

Grace wanted love and fairy-tale endings. He couldn't give her either. Being burnt in love, humiliated, was an experience he was never going to repeat. Anyway, this woman who had selflessly raised her siblings and opened up to him so honestly tonight, exposing her tender and honourable nature, deserved more than a short, superficial affair.

He glanced at his watch. She had been gone for well over ten minutes. Was everything okay? Had he upset her more than he'd thought?

He stood and walked out of the alcove in which the terrace table sat, heading towards the kitchen.

In the shadows of the curve of the alcove wall he ran straight into her, their bodies colliding hard. She jerked backwards and he grabbed hold of her as she stumbled. She trembled beneath his fingers.

Disquiet coursed through him. 'Are you okay? Has something happened?'

'I'm fine. I just can't find my sweater. I thought I'd left it in the kitchen this morning.'

She spoke in a low, breathless whisper, and he stepped even closer to her and lowered his head. This close, he could feel the heat of her body. The darkness enveloped them, heightening his awareness of her, of the heat of her body, her sweet floral scent, the smoothness of her skin beneath his fingers, the delicate curve of her arm. He wanted to pull her towards him, to feel her body crushed against his.

His voice was ragged when he spoke. 'Eleni probably moved it...you can borrow one of mine instead.'

She swayed slightly towards him, as though she too was overwhelmed by the need to get closer. He leaned forward in response, their bodies doing a private dance in which neither of them had any say.

He heard her inhale, quickly and deeply. 'No. It's fine. I should just go to bed. I'm feeling tired.'

The thought of Grace and bed had him closing his eyes in despair. He should step away. Now. But with her hair still swept up in that ponytail the delicate column of her neck proved too much of a temptation, and his fingers moved up to caress her soft exposed skin.

She gave a tiny moan and arched her neck. 'I really should go to bed.'

'Yes, you should.'

But neither of them moved.

This couldn't go on. If they didn't say goodnight soon he was going to kiss her.

Desire clogged his brain, but he managed to force out some words. 'We need to be careful.'

'Yes, of course.' She said the right thing, but her low, breathless whisper spoke of nothing but attraction and yearning.

Regret seeped into his bones but he forced himself to say, 'We need to remember that we have years of meeting again because of our ties with Christos and Sofia.'

There was a pause as she registered what he was saying. 'Okay.' She inhaled a shaky breath and took a slight step backwards. 'All the more reason why we need to learn to get on.'

'Yes, and not complicate things between us.'

She cleared her throat and stepped even further back. 'That's sensible.'

He forced himself to be blunt. 'I'm not interested in a relationship; I can't offer you anything.'

She jerked ever so slightly, and for a moment a wounded expression flickered in her eyes, pulled at her mouth. But it was quickly replaced with a proud anger.

'I don't want anything from you.'

He took a step back himself and inhaled a deep breath. '*Kalinichta*. Goodnight, Grace.'

For a few seconds she didn't move, but then she gave a quick nod and turned away.

He leaned back against the alcove wall with a groan. Yes, it was sensible not to complicate things. But sometimes *sensible* hadn't a hope in hell of stopping things getting out of control.

CHAPTER FOUR

THE FOLLOWING AFTERNOON, alone in the workshop, Grace's back ached and her stomach constantly rumbled in protest at not having been fed since dawn. But at least now she was working in the silence of siesta time, which was a welcome reprieve after the frantic pace of the morning.

She plucked up some more rosemary and bay stems and wrapped florist's wire around their base to form a neat and fragrant bundle.

Footsteps approached, at first faint, but then she heard that distinctive stride, with its quick double heel tap on every second step. For a moment they faltered outside, but then quickly climbed the stone steps up to the workshop.

She ducked her head and busied herself with another bundle of herbs, cross with the giddy anticipation that exploded in every cell of her body. She was *not* going to blush. She was *not* going to remember how close they had come to kissing last night and how she had later tossed and turned, tormented with images of beads of seawater dripping down over his taut golden stomach and disappearing beneath his turquoise shorts as they had yesterday morning.

'You're alone.'

Dressed in slim light grey trousers and an open-neck

white shirt, his suit jacket thrown over one shoulder, Andreas stood in the doorway, a hand on his narrow hip.

Why did her heart have to go bananas every time she saw him?

'The other florists have returned to Naxos with the wedding team for siesta. They'll be back later this afternoon.'

This was a detail she stupidly hadn't factored into her plans.

She inhaled a deep breath and decided to change the subject. 'You look like you're going somewhere.'

'I'm returning, in fact. I had a lunch date on Naxos.'

Her head shot up as Sofia's description of Andreas's busy love-life echoed. She gave a wobbly smile, her chest weighed down with disappointment. 'I hope it was enjoyable.'

His gaze narrowed and he walked towards her bench. She wound wire around a new bunch of herbs but almost strangled them in the process. When he didn't speak she eventually looked up at him, frustration now singing in her veins, along with a stomach-clenching sense of dejection.

Dark, serious eyes met hers. 'It was with my lawyer.'

'Oh.' Heat exploded in her cheeks.

She exhaled in relief when he walked away, but tensed when he went to stand in front of her project plans and designs for the wedding day, which she had hung on the wall earlier in order to brief the other florists. She should have taken them down again.

His back still to her, he asked, 'Aren't you having a break? Lunch? A siesta?'

The idea of lying in a darkened room with him had her glancing away from the messy sexiness of his hair, from the mesmerising triangle of the broad width of his shoulders and his narrow hips. 'I can't. I'm already hours behind with my timetable.'

He continued to stare at the plans and her stomach did a nervous roll. What if he didn't like them? Goosebumps of vulnerability popped up on her skin.

When he moved she quickly gazed back at the sad-looking herbs and began to unwind the wire. Maybe she'd be able to rescue them; it wasn't their fault, after all, that she had no sense.

He placed his jacket down on the end of the bench. 'Show me what to do.'

No! He couldn't stay. Her already shot nerves couldn't take it. Nor her pride. 'There's no need.'

'One thing you need to learn about me Grace, is that I don't say things lightly. And I don't make an offer twice.'

'That's two things.'

At first he frowned, but then a grin broke on his lips. His eyes danced mischievously, defying her to say no again to his offer.

Oh, what the heck? She needed all the help she could get.

She gestured to the bench behind her. 'I'm working on the garland for the chapel that I measured out last night. At this bench I'm assembling bunches of herbs, which I will then attach to the twine roping.'

She cut a length of the wire and showed him the required length, to which he nodded.

Then she picked up the herbs and said, 'Take three stems each of rosemary and bay and create a bunch by wrapping the wire around the bottom of the stem.'

He messed up the first bunch, tying the wire too loosely, but within a short few minutes he had picked up on the technique needed.

They worked in silence and she forced herself to

breathe normally. Well, as normally as her adrenaline-soaked body would allow. This was all so strange. Andreas Petrakis, one of the most powerful men in Greece, was standing before her, tying bunches of herbs.

'Why are you so nervous?'

'I'm not!'

He gave her a lazy, incredulous stare.

'I'm not nervous—why should I be?'

He gave a light shrug and went back to work.

'I want this to be right for Sofia.'

For a moment she paused as anxiety steamrollered up through her body, blocking her lungs and throat. She swallowed hard to push the anxiety back down into her tummy, where it nowadays permanently resided.

'But, let's face it, most of Greek society are coming to this wedding—along with various well-connected friends of Sofia and Christos from England. If I mess this up I can kiss my career ambitions goodbye. I'll never be taken seriously as a floral designer.'

He gestured towards the long line of sketches and plans on the wall. 'You have this under control. Of course you're not going to mess up. You're worrying unnecessarily—relax a little.'

Tiredness and frustration rolled through her. 'That's easy for you to say, with *your* success and *your* background.'

Taken aback by her own words, she inhaled deeply. Andreas stared at her, clearly annoyed.

She closed her eyes for a second, abhorring her own behaviour. 'I'm sorry, that was uncalled for.'

'Then why say it?'

His tone said he wasn't about to accept her apology quickly.

Embarrassment and a growing sense of panic that she

didn't have things under control had her saying in a rush, 'Because sometimes I feel so damn inadequate.'

For the longest while they stood in silence. His eyes fixed on hers until humiliation had her glancing away.

'Why inadequate?'

His tone was gentle and she gazed back in surprise. Something unlocked in her at the concern in his eyes, and she spoke in a rush, with all the insecurities tied down inside her for so long launching out of her like heat-seeking missiles.

'I left school early...didn't go to university. I'm not from a particularly wealthy background... I don't understand a lot of the nuances of social behaviour with those who are. I've probably bitten off more than I can chew with this wedding. And as I'm also the chief bridesmaid I'll hear directly any unpleasant comments people make about the flowers.'

For a moment she paused, and then she threw up her hands. A sprig of rosemary from the bundle in her hand worked loose and arced through the air. 'I've no idea why I just told you all of that...but, trust me, I know just how pathetic it sounds. There's no need for you to say anything.'

'You're wrong. There's a lot I need to say.'

She blanched at his grave tone. What had she done? Why couldn't she have kept her mouth shut?

'You're a talented and committed florist, and a good friend determined to give her best friend an incredible wedding day. So what if you didn't go to university? You were caring for your family. And, believe me, coming from a wealthy background doesn't guarantee any advantage for getting through life.'

He leaned forward on the workbench and moved closer to her, his eyes swallowing her up.

'Why do you think you're inadequate? Why do you think people would pass comment on the flowers?'

His voice was low and calm. Its quiet strength made her feel even more vulnerable and exposed. She was used to arguments and threats. Not this gentleness.

With a flippant shrug she said, 'Maybe I've been hanging around my father too long.'

'Meaning…?'

She gritted her teeth. 'My father trusts no one—including me. At work and at home he questioned everything I did, every decision I took. When I was younger I tried to stand up to him, but he would only take it out on Matt and Lizzie…grounding them, dragging them from their beds late at night because we hadn't tidied the house to his satisfaction. Calling them a useless waste of space.'

Andreas picked up a bunch of herbs from the table and plucked at the leaves. The sweetness of rosemary infused the air. His tone was anything but sweet when he spoke, 'Was there nowhere you could go? Why did you stay?'

She winced at his questions. Anger and guilt had her saying bitterly, 'Do you honestly think I would have stayed if I'd had a choice? I was *seventeen*, Andreas. I had no money… Even when I started working there was no way I was going to be able to support myself and Matt and Lizzie. I only took the job with my dad because he offered the best pay. Of course it was his way of controlling me, but I thought I would be able to save enough to move out. But rental costs just kept increasing. We have an aunt who lives in Newcastle, in the North of England, but she has her own family to care for. Anyway, Matt and Lizzie loved their school and their friends. I couldn't take them away from all that.'

He leaned even further over the workbench, resting his hand lightly on hers. When she started his hand enclosed hers, preventing her from jerking away. 'I wasn't blaming you. And you need to realise that you're *not* inadequate.'

She gave him a weak smile and tried to pull away, but his grip tightened.

He scrutinised her with a playful but determined focus. 'Say it for me—that you're not inadequate.'

'Andreas, please…'

'*Say* it.'

Though she squirmed and shook her head in exasperation she eventually gave in. 'Okay, I'll say it. I'm…' She cleared her throat as her chest tightened painfully, thick with emotions she didn't understand. 'I'm not inadequate.'

He gave a satisfied nod. His eyes, deep green pools, flickered with gold, held hers, and her heart thumped frantically.

'Shall I tell you what you *are*? *Ise poli glikos*. You are very sweet, you're loyal, determined and kind, and… very beautiful. A woman with an incredible future in front of her.'

They were the nicest words anyone had ever said to her. And she was totally unable to handle them. Flummoxed, she blushed deeply and said quietly, 'I hope so.'

'And you don't need any man or romance to complete you.'

He was wrong. She *did* need love and romance. Only love would ease the gut-wrenching loneliness that was slowly eating away at her. But she could never explain that to a man so against everything she craved.

'Perhaps, but even you have to admit that it would make life a lot more fun.'

He gave her a light look of warning. 'Be careful what you wish for.'

They worked in silence for the next half an hour, the

pile of bunched herbs between them growing ever larger. Grace tried to maintain a veneer of outward calm, but inside she was a turmoil of emotions: disbelief yet toe-tingling pleasure that he had called her beautiful, regret that he was so against love.

In the end he downed tools with a heavy sigh. 'I can't stand here listening to your stomach rumble any longer. I'm going to get you some food.' He paused to grab his jacket and muttered, almost to himself, 'And then I must tackle my best man's speech.'

Once he had left she carried the completed bunches to the other table and began attaching them to the doubled-up rope twine, creating lush foliage into which she would later place peonies encased in water tubes.

Her hands trembled. He was right. She needed food. And she needed her head examined for saying what she had. So much for staying away from each other. The man was in charge of a multinational empire. He didn't have time to be listening to her.

And yet, even though it had been hard to say what she had, it had felt right. It had been strangely freeing to see his absolute acceptance of what she'd said. None of the doubtful looks or the disinterest that had greeted her in the past when she tried to speak to other family members about her problems with her dad.

Later that evening, Andreas cursed when he reviewed the most recent budget estimates for his Cayman Islands development. The delay in planning was costing them dearly. He would have to bang some heads together to get the outstanding issues resolved. A conference call was scheduled for tonight, with all the key stakeholders. The call would not end until he was satisfied that every single issue was ironed out.

He'd need to have his wits about him for the meeting; the local contractor they were partnering with had a habit of promising the world but delivering very little substantive progress. But this damn wedding was sucking away all his usual focus. For the past few hours he'd had the distraction of the wedding planner and her team outside his window, arguing about the positioning of the reception tables. Then Grace had arrived and she and the planner had locked horns over where the flower displays would be positioned.

Grace. He had to stop thinking about her. Why was she getting under his skin so much? Earlier, she had spoken with such searing honesty he had wanted to take her in his arms and hold her. He was losing his mind.

He propped his elbows on the desk and with his eyes closed massaged his temples. His neck felt like a steel rod.

He made a low groan at the base of his throat when memories of last night returned. Her light floral scent… her skin soft and inviting when he had cradled her neck… What would it be like to trail his hand down further, unbutton her blouse, touch the enticing swell of her high and rounded breasts?

'Are you meditating or asleep?'

He leapt in his seat and let out a curse.

Grace gave a much too sexy giggle in response to his shock.

His disorientation became even more intense when he realised she was freshly showered, her hair still damp, tied up into a messy knot. She had changed into a short-sleeved denim dress that stopped a few inches above her knee and had enticing buttons running the length of it. The top three buttons were undone to reveal the cleavage he had just been fantasising about.

He had allowed physical attraction to override his common sense once before; he wouldn't let it happen again. He would need to keep this conversation short and snappy.

He leaned back in his chair. 'Neither. I was cursing whoever decided that speeches at weddings were a good idea.'

'Have you finished it?'

To that he gave a light laugh, but inside his stomach recoiled. He gestured to the paperwork piled on his desk. 'I need to deal with this first.' He didn't bother to mention his many failed attempts at writing a speech over the past few weeks.

'The wedding is in two days' time—shouldn't you start?'

'I'll get around to it at some point, If I have to, I'll just wing it on the day.'

'You can't *wing it*!'

'Why not?'

'Are you kidding me? With *your* views on love and marriage, you might well say something totally inappropriate.' She paused and shook her head frantically, her hands flying upwards in disbelief. 'Like offering your condolences rather than congratulations. The best man's speech is too important—you can't just *wing it*.'

'Grace, I've presented to thousands at industry conferences worldwide, in a multitude of languages. I think I can handle a wedding speech.'

'Have you given one before?'

'Several times.'

She eyed him for a few seconds. 'Were they before your divorce?'

'What if they were?'

'Well, I'm guessing that your views might be very different now.'

He knew only too well that they were. 'Look, I'm busy now, but I'll pull something together later tonight or tomorrow.'

At that, Grace walked over to his desk and from behind her back brought forward a book, which she dropped onto a set of architectural drawings for a new office block in Melbourne.

He picked it up. She had to be joking. 'Are you being serious? *The Best Man's Survival Manual.*'

She gave him a triumphant smile. 'The wedding planner gave it to me. Apparently she always carries one for emergencies.'

He threw her a disparaging glance. 'The next time I meet with the team at the disaster recovery charity I sponsor, I'll have to check that they carry one at all times.'

She gave him an even brighter smile. 'Hah, very funny. Now, how about I help you pull it together?'

He gestured once again to his desk. 'I'm busy. And I have an urgent conference call in two hours I need to prepare for.'

'Twenty minutes—no more. I promise.'

'Grace, I have to warn you I'm on to you, I overheard your conversation with the wedding planner earlier. I know your technique. You're not going to wear me down by refusing to go away.'

'I'm not!'

She was, but now was not the time to get into that argument. He wanted to get back to his work. 'Why are you doing this?' he asked.

Her laughter died and she sat down on the seat opposite his desk. The indigo denim made her violet eyes shine brighter than ever. 'You helped me with the flow-ers—I'd like to help you in return.'

'I don't need help.'

'Fine. Wing your speech for me now, and if it's up to scratch then I'll leave you alone.'

He knew she wasn't going to leave without a fight—and anyway he never had been able to resist a dare.

He flew through his introduction and then launched into some witty anecdotes about Christos, one of which even had Grace snorting with laughter. But then he dried up. And died spectacularly. He didn't know what else to say. How could he celebrate marriage and love when he didn't believe in either?

He glanced at Grace and then away again—away from the sympathy in her eyes.

'I shouldn't have agreed to be best man.'

'I think it's admirable that you did. It means the world to Christos.'

Guilt churned inside him. He couldn't let Christos down. But right now he wanted to forget the speech, in fact forget the whole wedding.

With a raised eyebrow he deftly changed the subject. 'Christos rang earlier. Sofia and he are delighted we're getting on so well.'

To that she gave a guilty smile. 'Sofia rang me last night. What was I going to say? That you're against the wedding…? That I'm way behind with the flowers? That we disagree on just about everything?'

'Not everything. Apparently you think I'm hot.'

It took a few seconds for Grace to compute what Andreas had just said. 'What? No! Oh, I'm going to kill Sofia when she gets here. We were just messing around on the phone… She kept asking me what I thought of you. I only said it as a joke, to get her off my back. She's always trying to set me up with unsuitable guys.'

He sat back in his chair and folded his arms. 'So I'm unsuitable now?'

'Of course you are. You don't believe in love, commitment, marriage. Need I go on?'

'Hey, but I'm hot—what more do you need?'

Oh, this was excruciating—especially as part of her agreed with him. But if she was going to remain sane for the next few days she couldn't go there.

'It was a joke.' For a second she pressed the palm of her hand against the raging heat on her cheeks. Time to change the subject. 'Back to the speech. Twenty minutes and we'll pull it together. Are you on?'

He considered her for a while and she willed him not to move the conversation back to whether she thought he was hot or not. At first a grin played at the corners of his mouth, but then he cleared his throat, contemplated the messy pile of paper on his desk and shook his head wryly. 'You've been here ten minutes already—you have ten minutes left.'

'Fine. Okay, it was a great start, but now you need to praise Sofia and then finish on your hopes for them as a couple. Let's focus on the last point first: your hopes for them. What *do* you wish for them?'

'I don't know…to be happy-ever-after?'

'Too much of a cliché. Think harder.'

Andreas gave her an exasperated stare and stood up. He walked to the window overlooking the terrace and the Aegean beyond. He rolled his shoulders before he turned to her.

'I spent my lunchtime with my lawyer, agreeing to pay off my ex who's now claiming rights to this island.'

She fidgeted in her seat when his eyes bored into her.

'I could have fought her in the courts, but that would have stopped me giving Christos his wedding present: ownership of half of this island. So forgive me for being a little cynical about marriage. Right now I'm not in the mood to think of anything other than romantic clichés, even knowing that they are unrealistic and unobtainable and the preserve of dreamers.'

Bewildered by the sudden change in his mood, she stood and walked towards him. 'Is that a dig at me?'

Irritation fired in his eyes. 'No, but you can take it as one if you want.'

They stared at each other, angry and frustrated, breathing heavily...and then their anger turned from annoyance to a simmering heat, and the atmosphere in the room grew thick with want and desire.

He crossed the few steps that separated them and yanked her into his arms, muttering words she didn't understand. Her body collided with his and before she could react his mouth was on hers. A hand on the back of her neck held her prisoner, while the other wrapped tight around her waist. For a brief second she tried to pull away, but then she became lost in the heady sensation of his mouth on hers, the intoxicating sweep of his tongue, the pleasure of his hand caressing her back. She wrapped her arms about his neck, deepening the kiss, her body instinctively moving against his hardness.

But then he suddenly pulled away and stepped back, and she stood there, dazed, her lips bruised, her body aching.

He ran a hand through his hair, his jaw flexed tight. 'I'm sorry. That wasn't a good idea.'

No man should be able to kiss like that. Her thoughts

ran in several directions all at once, bringing little sense. Why had he kissed her? What must he be like in bed if his kisses were so scorching? Why? Why? *Why?*

'Are you still in love with your ex?'

'What?'

He glared at her as though it was the most insane question ever, but to her it was the only thing that made sense of his anger and cynical views.

'Is that why you were so upset about the divorce?'

'No, I'm not still in love with my ex. And I'm not upset about my divorce—I'm angry about it.'

'Why?'

'Because I was blind for much too long as to how incompatible my ex and I were.'

'Incompatible in what way?'

'My ex wanted very different things in life to me. She only pretended to want what I did in order to marry me. She was more attracted to what I had than who I was.'

'You mean she married you for your money?'

'Yes. And I was too foolish to see it. Within weeks she was refusing to live here on the island, to spend time with my family. Her social life in Athens was more important.'

'Did you love her when you got married?'

His jaw worked, and he inhaled a deep breath before meeting her eye. 'At the time I thought it was love, but I came to realise that I'd mistaken physical attraction and passion for love.'

'Oh.' Every square inch of her skin was scarlet at this point. She should leave. 'I'm sorry.'

'Don't be sorry. Just learn from it… Love and marriage can be hell on earth.'

'God, Andreas, don't for one second think that I don't know that. I spent my entire childhood witnessing my dad's toxic take on marriage. I know there are bad marriages. But I also know there are wonderful ones. Sofia's parents' marriage, my grandparents'... Now Christos and Sofia's. Marriages that are loving partnerships of trust and respect. Marriages that aren't about judgement and criticism.'

'How can you be so idealistic?'

'Because I believe in love—that the right man is out there for me.'

'Waiting to whisk you away.'

'Yes. And I don't care if you think it's idealistic. To me it's a very real dream. I want a life partner. I want love. I want a man who thinks I'm the coolest thing ever. And I'm not going to settle for anything else.'

She could see a hundred thoughts flickering in the depths of his eyes: puzzlement, incredulity, a hint of tenderness. But then he walked back to his desk, shaking his head. Once he had sat down, he checked his watch.

'Our twenty minutes is up.' The sternness in his voice was matched by the harsh expression on his face; the faint scar above his eyebrow was once again more visible as he frowned. A scar to match the toughness in his soul...

A toughness she would have to feign herself. 'So it is. If you want any further help let me know. And for what it's worth I think you should remember how you felt about love prior to your marriage and include that in your speech.'

When he gave a noncommittal shrug and turned his attention back to his computer screen, she inhaled a deep breath.

'The pre-wedding dinner tomorrow night in Athens...?' she asked.

'My helicopter will collect us at five.'

Grace left the room and walked back towards the

workshops, her heart thumping in her chest. That kiss…
That kiss had been wonderful and sexy…and it had
landed her in a whole heap of trouble.

CHAPTER FIVE

THE FOLLOWING DAY raucous noise spilt through the villa: shouts from the kitchen, the sound of hammering out on the terrace. Andreas sent a final few emails to his office in Athens and shut down his computer; there was little point in trying to get any work done in this mayhem. Anyway, he had worked until three in the morning, resolving the Cayman Islands issues — he needed a break... And, okay, he'd admit it to himself: he wanted to see Grace.

Outside, a crew were fixing lights on to the temporary stage that had been erected on the terrace the day before. He hadn't seen Grace all day, and knew he had no business going in search of her now. It was asking for trouble. But kissing her last night had been unbelievable. For the first time in ages he had lost himself totally in the physical joy of holding a woman, tasting her rather than mentally working out what it was she wanted from him.

He approached the workshops with an eagerness that confounded but exhilarated him. Inside, he felt his enthusiasm waver when two strangers stared back at him. When they finally found their voices one of the women told him that Grace was down on the jetty, helping with the unloading of more supplies. Frustration that she was not alone had him turning abruptly away.

Back outside, he spotted her—lost amongst the potted trees crowding the jetty, which now resembled a small forest. The delivery boat was out in the harbour, sailing back towards Naxos.

As he neared the jetty Grace came towards him unsteadily, carrying one of the potted trees. He went to take it from her but she drew back.

'It's fine—it's not as heavy as it looks; the planter is made from lightweight fibreglass.'

She kept on walking and he called to her. 'Where are you taking it?'

She stopped at the end of the jetty and dropped the white sugar-cube-shaped planter down. 'I want to place the planters and the storm lamps at intervals between here and the chapel.'

Andreas glanced back at the endless planters and storm lamps crowding the jetty. 'Have you any help?'

She rushed back down the jetty and picked up another planter. 'The other florists are finishing off the final prep work and will come and help in a little while.'

She was all business, and barely gave him a glance. He tried not to let it get to him.

'If you take care of the storm lamps, I'll position the planters,' he said.

For a moment she hesitated, as though she was about to refuse his offer, but then she gave a brief nod.

'Thank you.' Picking up the two nearest storm lanterns, she rushed off the jetty, saying, 'The planters were supposed to be delivered this morning but have only just arrived. The other florists have to leave by five as they have to prepare the flowers for another wedding on Naxos tomorrow.'

In silence they worked together: Grace dropping the

storm lamps ten metres apart and he placing the planters in between.

As they moved up onto the path, where it cut along the cliff towards the chapel, her silence and her habit of rushing away from him at every opportunity put him further and further on edge.

They walked back towards the jetty again and he could take no more. He called to her as she walked in front of him. 'Is everything okay?'

She kept on walking, but through the thin material of her pale pink tee shirt he saw her shoulders tense.

'If it's about last night, I apologise.'

She stopped abruptly and swung around to him. 'Apologise?'

'For kissing you. I didn't mean to upset you.'

'You didn't upset me, but it can't happen again.'

She said it with such certainty he was sorely tempted to take her in his arms and test her resolve. But she was right. They were playing with fire.

For the next trip back up the cliff-face Grace insisted on carrying a planter, as she was now way ahead with laying the lanterns. The other florists had joined them, and it had been agreed that he and Grace would carry the planters out as far as the chapel and work backwards from there.

Again silence fell between them. The planter balanced on her hip, she walked before him. He tried hard not to stare at how her cut-off faded denim shorts showed the perfection of her bottom.

He caught up with her when she stopped to move the planter from one hip to the other. Her eyes scanned along the coastline and then she briefly closed her eyes and lifted her face to the afternoon sun.

When she opened her eyes she said quietly, 'Why have

you decided to give Christos half the island? It's incredibly generous.'

'Not generous; just the right thing to do. My uncle should have left it to us both, but he was too stubborn.'

'What happened?'

He gestured for them to continue walking. For a while he didn't speak as an internal argument raged inside him.

Don't answer. You need to distance yourself from her.

But I want to explain. I want her to understand some of the mess that is my life. Why we will never share the same dreams for the future.

'When my grandfather died the family business was left to my father and this island to my uncle. My father has very traditional ideas and he believed that Kasas should also have been left to him as the eldest son. The two brothers fought and didn't speak for years. My father forbade us ever to speak to our uncle again; he wasn't pleased when I disobeyed him. Christos was about to follow my lead, but he gave in when my mother pleaded with him not to do so. For my loyalty, my uncle decided to leave the island to me.'

'But that wasn't fair on Christos.'

'I know. My uncle, usually calm and logical about everything, simply refused to listen to reason. He was a proud man, and in his eyes Christos had chosen my father over him; chosen to side with my father's greed.'

She shifted the planter back to her other hip before asking, 'And now? How do you get on with your father?'

He gave a chortle at the hint of caution in her voice. 'I take it that he left an impression on you when you met him at the engagement party?'

She shrugged uncertainly. 'He likes to speak his mind.'

That was the understatement of the year. His father was opinionated and brash on a good day. His father's angry words about the dishonour brought to the family name echoed in his mind. His grip on the planter tightened as anger and guilt swirled in his chest.

'It's not the easiest of relationships; we're very different. When I was younger I tried to work in the family business, but my father is almost impossible to work with. He'd refuse to delegate authority, question every decision and often reverse them. When all the issues blew up over the inheritance I left.'

'Do you ever regret that?'

'For the upset it caused my mother? Yes. But otherwise, no. I've succeeded on my own terms. Even if at times I've paid the price.'

Grace slowed her pace. 'What do you mean?'

The turmoil and self-doubt of the past few years came back to him in sharp relief. 'The global recession hit my company hard.'

'And succeeding on your own... Was that to prove to him just how capable you are? That you don't need him to be successful?'

'I guess we have that in common...'

She nodded, and for a moment their eyes connected.

'It's not easy, hating a person you love—is it?' he asked.

She came to a stop and readjusted the planter in her hands. At first she frowned, but then she gave a small exhalation of breath. 'I never thought of it like that; but that's exactly how I feel. There's so much I hate about my father's behaviour, but deep down a part of me—reluctant as it is—loves him. I don't understand it, and it would be so much easier if I didn't... Love is such a strange thing, isn't it?'

'Strange, dangerous and unpredictable.'

Her lips pursed and she shook her head crossly. 'Sometimes, but for most it's the one true wonder of being alive.'

Aman! Had she no sense? 'Still dreaming of your prince and happy-ever-after?'

A storm brewed in her violet eyes and her lips drew into a firm line. She glared at him. 'Yes—and when he comes along I'll send you a postcard.'

With that she flounced away and he followed, amusement tugging at his lips even while he tried to ignore the jealousy curling in his stomach at the thought of her with another man.

The chapel was close now, but the planter was starting to weigh heavily in his arms. In a few long strides he caught up with her. 'Do you want to stop for a break?'

Despite the sheen of perspiration on her skin, she shook her head defiantly. 'No.'

'You're persistent, aren't you?'

She stared at him belligerently. 'You sound surprised. Why wouldn't I be?'

He gave a light shrug. 'Most of the women I know aren't too keen on hard physical work.'

'From what I hear, you don't hang around long enough to find out. Maybe those women have a lot more going for them than you give them credit for.' With that she stalked away, and dropped the first planter at the bottom of the chapel terrace.

He dumped his ten metres away. 'So what do you suggest? That I stay and give them all hope of a relationship?'

'No, because you're obviously incapable of having one. I don't want any women getting hurt. But maybe you shouldn't make assumptions about them.'

How sheltered a life had she lived? She'd obviously had the good fortune never to encounter the sycophants he had. 'Are you *really* that innocent, Grace?'

Those violet eyes flared with anger. 'You know what, Andreas? Maybe I am. But I prefer to see the good in human nature.'

Those photographs he had been sent two years ago had shown him the truth about human nature.

With a bitter taste in his mouth, he answered, 'And *that's* where we will always differ.'

Why had someone so beautiful on the outside but so cynical at heart been sent into her life? The gods were truly having a laugh at her expense.

Grace twisted away from him, her blood boiling. She was tired and hungry, stressed about tomorrow, and plagued with an attraction to the six-foot-two, dark and sexy sceptic walking behind her.

If only it was that straightforward.

Though she hated to admit it, and even though Andreas was so disparaging about love and the motives of women, at his core he was a good man. He'd shown care towards her on numerous occasions; he clearly loved his family despite the differences between him and his father. It was as if he wore his scepticism as an armour.

But she had meant it when she'd said that she would never try to change a man. She wanted a man to fall in love with her with no games involved—no persuasion, no pretending she was something she wasn't. More than anything she wanted a relationship based on honesty and respect.

Her phone rang in her pocket and, pulling it out, she answered Matt's call, glad to have a distraction from the pain lancing through at the memory that her mum hadn't even bothered to leave a note when she had walked out on them.

Though Matt professed that nothing was wrong, and

that he'd just called to say hi, she immediately knew he was upset. With Matt she always had to draw him out gradually. They were back at the chapel with the next set of planters when she finally hung up on the call.

She dropped her planter onto the path and was about to pass Andreas when he placed a hand on her arm.

His eyes soft and concerned, he stepped closer. His hand moved up to lie gently on her upper arm. 'Are you okay? You seem tired?'

She wanted to say no, she wasn't okay. That she wanted him to hold her. To tell her everything would be okay. That Matt and Lizzie would do well in life. That tomorrow was going to be okay.

Instead she glanced at the time on her phone and then towards the jetty and the remaining planters. 'I'm not going to be able to go to the pre-wedding reception tonight... I still have so much to do.'

'Ioannis will be back from Naxos soon. He can take over the positioning of the planters.'

'It's not just the planters. I have a lot of other prep work that needs to be completed. Sofia is arriving here at eleven tomorrow, and I want to spend time with her. I need to have all the flowers ready in the workshop by then, for the local florists to position just before the ceremony begins.'

'I'll stay and help.'

'No! Absolutely not.'

But before she knew what was happening Andreas was on his phone. He spoke in Greek, but she understood his greeting to Christos.

Wearing denim jeans and a white polo shirt, now smeared with earth from the planters, he stood watching her as he spoke, his dark hair glistening under the sun, his voice a low and rapid flow of passionate sounds incomprehensible to her.

Her insides melted as his eyes roamed up and down her body. Something dark and dangerous was building in them as the call continued.

When he'd hung up, he gestured for them to start walking again. 'I spoke to Christos and explained that you were tied up with preparations. He told Sofia and she asked him to send her love. They both insisted that I should stay and help. And they agreed that I should take you out to dinner later.'

'They did not!'

'Call them if you don't believe me.'

He was calling her bluff. Well, she'd show him. 'Fine— I will.'

A few minutes later she hung up on her call to Sofia. Though disappointed that Grace would miss tonight, Sofia had been more concerned that Grace was putting herself under too much pressure. And, though Sofia had tried her best to disguise it, Grace had heard the fear in her voice that the flowers mightn't be ready for tomorrow.

After spending an age reassuring Sofia that she had everything under control, Grace hadn't even bothered to get into an argument about Andreas staying on with her.

'Apparently dinner was your idea?'

He didn't even have the decency to look abashed. 'You can't visit the Cyclades and not see some of the other islands.'

Dinner was *so* not going to happen. 'I won't be finished until very late.'

'How late?'

She deliberately adopted a look of grave consideration. 'Oh, at least eleven.'

He gave a smile that was much too smug for her liking.

'That's not a problem—we eat late here in Greece.' With that Andreas picked up his phone again and spoke briefly in Greek.

When they got back to the jetty, he steered her away and back towards the villa.

She gestured to the pots still on the jetty. 'We need to finish the planters.'

'You need a break first.'

He led her down onto one of the lower terraces built into the cliff-face, where a tray of food was awaiting them on a rattan dining table. Despite herself, Grace sank down onto the plump cream cushions of a rattan chair with a sigh, welcoming the shade provided by the raised parasol at the centre of the table.

Andreas poured some homemade lemonade for them both and uncovered a basket of bread and a selection of dips. Another basket held a selection of freshly baked pastries.

Grace greedily gulped the lemonade, only now realising just how thirsty she was.

'Why do you push yourself so hard?'

She lowered her glass to the table. 'I don't think I do…but I grew up with my dad's exacting standards. I suppose I'm still trying to meet those in some way. But, also, I want to deliver the best service that I can. I take my commitments and responsibilities very seriously.'

Andreas leaned forward and broke a bread roll in two. He handed a piece to her. 'Including your responsibilities to your brother and sister?'

'Yes.'

He regarded her thoughtfully. 'Why?'

She busied herself with breaking her roll into smaller pieces. 'When my mum left they had no one else. They were children. They needed someone to care for them.'

'How did it affect them?'

'Matt went quiet and barely spoke for a year…'

Grace stopped for a moment as memories caused her throat to thicken painfully. An unaccountable emotional force shifted around in her chest, as though it was searching for a way out. And suddenly she needed to tell him it all, so that he would understand why her heart had broken every single day in the year after her mum left.

'He used to get up early every morning…' She met Andreas's eye and then gazed away. 'He'd get up to wash his sheets. I used to have to pretend that I didn't notice the load in the tumble drier. I thought Lizzie was coping—she seemed her usual bubbly self—but then one day I was cleaning her bedroom and found that she was hoarding food…which accounted for her clothes not fitting any longer.'

'I'm sorry.'

She forced herself to shrug. 'It was tough, but now we're really close because of having gone through it together—so I guess some good has come from it all.'

'Do you miss them?'

Unexpected tears sprang to her eyes at his question and, perplexed by their suddenness and the powerful loneliness rolling through her, she took a while before she managed to speak. 'I miss them terribly. I miss our little family. I miss being loved.'

'They still love you.'

The gaping hole inside her widened at his words. How would he react if she told him just how desperate she was to be in love? To find companionship and security, fun and exhilaration?

'I know…but it's not the same when we're apart. And Lizzie's dating now. They're both moving on.'

'Do you ever see your mum now?'

Her heart lurched at his question. 'No. At first I was
mad as hell with her and refused to, but after a while I
came to understand why she'd left... After years of putting up with my father, it was kind of understandable. But
by then we had drifted apart from her—to have got back
in contact would have been like opening an old wound.'
She gave him a wobbly smile and stood. 'Anyway, we
don't have time for this now. I'd better get back to work.'

Andreas stood and walked towards her. Next thing
she knew she was in his arms, being given the biggest
bear hug of her life. His arms wrapped around her and
he lowered his chin onto the top of her head. His arm
blocked her eyes so that she was in a cocoon of darkness. She inhaled his scent, a mixture of lemon and fresh
salty perspiration, so earthy and male she felt dizzy with
the desire to lift his tee shirt and press her nose against
his damp skin.

For a moment every worry, every painful memory
disappeared as she was held in his protective embrace.
Her rigid body slowly melted against him and she gave a
little sigh. He drew back and smiled down at her.

Dazed, she hoped her eyes weren't rolling in her head.
'You give a very good hug.'

His thumb ran the length of her cheek. 'I'm here any
time you need one.'

For a moment they both smiled at each other, but then
she pulled away. She was in serious danger of feeling
things she could not afford to for a man intent on never
having love in his life.

As they walked back to the workshops Andreas wondered what was happening to him. He didn't hold women
like that, want to protect them, wipe out every painful
memory for them.

Beside him, Grace gave a contented sigh. 'I haven't travelled to many countries, but Kasas Island has to be the most beautiful place in the world.'

Something dormant in him stirred at her words. When had he stopped enjoying this island? Stopped taking the time to relax in its simple pleasures? For the past two years he had driven himself relentlessly at work, and the island had become a refuge rather than a place he truly enjoyed.

But then a warning bell sounded in his brain. How often had his ex claimed the same?

'You'd tire of it once the novelty wore off.'

She stopped dead and stared at him. 'No, I wouldn't.' She cocked her head to the side. 'You don't believe me, do you?'

Why was he standing here arguing with her? He started to walk away. 'It doesn't matter.'

She caught up with him and pulled him to a stop. 'It might not matter to you, but I'm fed up with the fact that you don't trust me, Andreas. You constantly pull back from telling me about yourself. You'll go so far and then the shutters go down as though you don't trust me. You look at me as though you don't believe what I say. What have I done that makes you think I'm untrustworthy?'

'Come on, Grace, I barely know you.'

'You know me well enough to kiss me senseless.'

She stared at him so indignantly he could not help but smile. 'I kissed you *senseless*?'

Her eyes narrowed and she stamped a foot on the path. 'Wrong phrase—ignore it. Now, are you going to answer my question?'

He took a step closer, his shadow falling over her. He lowered his head and inhaled her scent, his voice automatically turning into a low baritone. 'I have a question for you first: can I kiss you?'

Her violet eyes shadowed and her cheeks flushed deeply. 'I... Not until you promise me that you're going to start trusting me. That you don't think I'm lying to you or that I want anything from you.'

'You drive a hard bargain.'

'You have to mean it. I'm trusting you not to pretend, not to lie to me.'

He drew back, paralysed with indecision. Could he honestly tell her that he trusted her? His stomach was a knot, his heart a time bomb ready to explode. Others might lie, but that was anathema to him. He could just walk away now—go back to the way his life had been a few short days ago. But, gazing deep into her eyes, he realised that he didn't want to this to end—not yet—and that he believed he *could* trust her.

'I trust you.'

She gave him a solemn smile, and when he ran his hand along her cheek she leaned into it.

And then he walked away.

CHAPTER SIX

GRACE STOOD ON the path, dumbstruck. What had happened to their kiss?

She chased after him. 'Did I just miss something?'

He stopped by the steps up to the workshops, his expression sombre. 'You said you wanted to trust in me. Which means that you'll trust me to look out for you, not to hurt you. With that being the case, there's no way that I can kiss you—because, frankly, I don't know where it could lead.'

He was right. Of course he was. She just wished she didn't feel so upset at the prospect of all this being over so quickly. That their kiss last night had been the end of the line for them.

'My helicopter will be here to collect us at eleven. I'll help Ioannis with the remaining planters. What else can we do to help you?'

His businesslike attitude pulled her up short. She needed to start focusing on the wedding.

'The candles need to be placed inside the lanterns…' She paused and gave him a pleading smile. 'And two white ribbons need to be tied to each of the bay trees.'

He inhaled a deep breath. 'If you *dare* tell Christos that I was tying ribbons you'll be in big trouble.'

He looked so hacked off she couldn't help but giggle. And once she started she couldn't stop, because he was studying her so incredulously. But eventually he too laughed, his laughter coming from deep inside him was highly infectious, which only caused Grace to start her 'hiccupping hyena' impression, as Sofia so charmingly called it. He stopped and stared at her, clearly surprised, but then he laughed even harder.

When their laughter eventually petered out he shook his head and eyed her with amusement. 'You do crazy things to me, Grace Chapman.'

With that he walked away, and she stared after him, knowing, despite their differences, that she had never felt so in tune with another person in all her life.

Later that night Grace ran towards the villa. She had fifteen minutes to get ready. Not enough time to wash her hair. *Just great.* She was going out for dinner with the sexiest man she had ever met with unwashed hair and make-up slapped on. But then maybe it was for the best. Maybe he would take one look at her and the attraction between them would wilt.

She took a quick shower and whilst dragging a towel over her body in order to dry herself hopped from one foot to the other in front of the wardrobe, trying to decide what to wear. Would the cocktail dress she had bought especially for the pre-wedding reception tonight be too over the top? Send the wrong message? But all her other clothes were too casual.

She yanked the dress from the wardrobe and pulled it on. Five minutes to go. Quickly she applied some foundation and cream eyeshadow, a rose-pink gloss on her lips. She tied her hair back into a ponytail. A quick spritz of perfume and she was out through the door.

Andreas was waiting for her by the patio doors in the living room, staring out onto the terrace.

She came to an abrupt stop beside him. 'Ready?'

He stood back and his eyes trailed slowly down over her body. He cleared his throat before he spoke. 'You look incredible.'

All evening she had firmly reminded herself that to get involved with Andreas would be a major mistake. Past experience had taught her the awful pain of having someone walk away from her—which undoubtedly *would* happen should she get entangled with this oh-so-gorgeous playboy. This was just a cordial dinner between…

Between what? She had no idea how to define their relationship, but maybe 'friends' was the most suitable description. But how was she supposed to deal with the heat in his eyes and the pull of desire coiling within her?

She gave him a quick smile. 'Thank you…and you don't look half bad yourself.' Which was the understatement of the year. He was freshly showered, and his damp hair was tamer than usual, which emphasised the impossible height of his cheekbones, the green brilliance of his eyes. His dark navy suit fitted him to perfection, the snow-white shirt open at the neck highlighting the golden tones of his skin. She would never get to touch him, to trace her fingers over his skin, to feel the hard muscle underneath…

'Why are you carrying your sandals?'

She tore her eyes away from him and dangled her stiletto heels to swing between them. 'There's no way I'll climb the hill to the helicopter wearing *these* bad boys.'

His gaze travelled downwards and her French polished toes curled when his gaze remained at her feet. When he eventually looked back up there was a new tension to his jaw.

'Your feet will get dirty. Put them on and you can hold my arm—I'll help you to the helicopter.'

Grace sat on the side of a sofa and bent over to place her feet in the sandals. The sandals were new, and she struggled to fasten the strap, the metal bar refusing to go into the tiny eyelet pierced in the dark navy leather strap. She gritted her teeth and pushed as hard as she could, while her hip bone screamed at the awkward position she was leaning over in.

'Sit back and I'll try.'

Before she had time to protest Andreas was crouched down before her. He gently lifted her foot and balanced it on his thigh. She bit down on the dual temptations fighting within her: to pull away—his touch was way too much for a woman already on a knife-edge of temptation—or sigh so loudly she would be heard over on Naxos.

When he was done, he stood up and held his hand out to her. For a moment she hesitated. More than ever this evening seemed like a thoroughly bad idea.

As though reading her mind, Andreas said, 'We're going out for dinner and a little fun—nothing serious.'

Three days ago she had closed the door to her minuscule apartment in Bristol, full of dreams for the future, hoping for excitement. Well, boy, had she got it—in a bucket full. And although she knew she was dancing with danger maybe, just for tonight, she could embrace this crazy scenario and relish being in the company of this utterly gorgeous man.

He was going to have a heart attack. Grace's dress was too much. A mid-thigh-length navy lace wrap dress, embellished with sequins, it was far too short and far too figure-hugging. Way too much flesh was revealed in the deep scoop that ended at the tip of the valley between her breasts. And what was *really* driving his pulse berserk was the knowledge that with a simple tug of the satin ribbon sitting at her waist it would come undone.

How was he supposed to act like a gentleman tonight when she was wearing that?

Next to him in the helicopter, she folded one leg over the other, and he groaned inwardly at the sight of her toned thighs. Thin straps of dark navy leather crisscrossed her foot, which dangled provocatively in front of him, and a jolt of unwanted desire barged through him. Earlier, as he had buckled her sandal, his fingers had trailed against the smooth skin of her slender ankle and he'd had to battle hard against the urge to keep trailing his fingers upwards.

Her words this afternoon that she wanted to trust in him came back to taunt him. He couldn't abuse that trust. He couldn't seduce her as he so desperately wanted to do. Grace believed in love and romance, in happy-ever-after; he had to respect everything she wanted even if the tension of attraction and desire between them was so thick right now he could almost punch it. He had to keep this light and fun—keep the conversation neutral.

'Did you finish all the prep work?'

She gave him a bright grin of relief. 'Yes. All the major displays are finished. I just have to complete the bouquets in the morning.' She puffed out her cheeks. 'I can't believe Sofia's getting married tomorrow; it's all happened so quickly. I need to start getting my head around my chief bridesmaid's duties. Talking of which—have you completed your speech?'

He shifted in his seat. 'Almost.'

She gave him a knowing look. 'Can I help in any way?'

He didn't want to talk about the speech—his ongoing nemesis for reasons he didn't fully understand. 'No, I plan on finishing it tomorrow morning. Christos and my parents aren't arriving until lunchtime.'

For a moment she paused and worried at her lip, doubt clouding her eyes. 'How do you feel about the wedding now?'

Ambivalent was the word that best summed up how he felt about tomorrow…and it was something he didn't want to overthink. Right now he just wanted to pretend it wasn't happening.

'If you're worried that I might object to the vows, or share my views on relationships in my speech, don't worry. I promise to be the perfect best man tomorrow.'

At first she beamed with relief, but then her face clouded with tension. She glanced at him, and then away, and then her eyes darted back to him. 'Do you think the flowers will be okay?'

The fear in her eyes was so sudden and intense his heart jolted. He twisted fully in his seat and placed a hand on hers. 'Grace, I know nothing about flowers. I've been to endless weddings, even my own, and didn't notice them. But even I can see how spectacular yours are. After tomorrow you'll be turning away bookings.'

Her eyes shone with gratitude. 'Thank you.'

The helicopter began to hover down towards the restaurant, which sat high on a clifftop on Santorini Island. Once it had landed Andreas helped Grace out, and as they neared the building the heavy beat of music greeted them.

Friday night was party night at the Ice Cocktail Bar and Restaurant.

He had to lean low, so that Grace could hear him above the music. 'How about we get a cocktail to start and then eat?'

The bar was busy, and as usual the central floor space

had become a dance floor. The music was a fast constant beat, energetic and sensual.

He glanced down when Grace's hand touched against his arm. She reached up to shout in his ear.

'This bar is amazing… I've never seen so many people enjoying themselves so much.'

Her breath tickled his ear. Desire gripped him hard and he had the sudden urge to turn around and lead her somewhere quiet. He bit down on the temptation and taking her hand in his, led her through the throng.

As usual his friend Georgios, Ice's owner, was sitting in the far corner. When Georgios saw him approach he jumped up and the two men embraced. After Andreas had introduced Grace, Georgios insisted they take his seats and promised to return with two of the house specials.

They attempted to have a conversation, but the music was too loud, so they sat sipping their gin and ginger cocktails, watching the dancers out on the dance floor, their movement so carefree and joyful it was addictive. His heartbeat pounded in time with the music, and when Grace moved beside him, her thigh grazing against his, he turned to her.

Her eyes were bright, her skin flushed, and she leaned towards him, a slow smile breaking on her lips. 'Do you want to dance?'

Sense and caution went out of the window at her question, which had been asked in a low voice, whispered against his ear.

He stood and removed his jacket and led her out on to the dance floor, pulling her into the centre of the action.

Her arms reached upwards and her body swayed to the music, her head thrown back. Strobe lights flashed over her tilted face, highlighting the plumpness of her glossy lips, the sultry look in her eyes. The light danced on the sequins of her sexy dress, and the thought of pulling that ribbon and revealing what lay beneath sent firecrackers of desire through his system.

For a few seconds he watched her, trying to resist the inevitable, but then he reached out and pulled her towards him, his hands on her waist, and together their bodies dipped and swayed, their eyes never leaving one another.

Lithe, and with perfect timing, Andreas held her to him, his body lightly controlling her movements. She was on fire. It was all wrong. But right now she didn't care. It felt too good. She felt alive and young and carefree.

Through his shirt her fingers touched against the taut bulk of his biceps. His hips moved against hers and an ache grew in her belly. His hand moved up from her waist and for a brief moment his thumb ran along the side of her breast. She gave him a brief smile and he smiled back, his eyes darkening.

The ache in her belly spread outwards and her breasts grew tight and sensitive. The hard muscles of his thighs pushed against hers, and then he shifted her so that one of her legs was in between his. The ache spread even further, until all her insides felt hollow.

His hands moved around to her back. One held her at the waist while the other splayed downwards, touching the sensitive point at the bottom of her spine. She arched even further into him, her breath catching as his hip bone pushed against her.

She stared at the smooth line of his freshly shaved jaw, fighting the desire to trace her lips against the warm skin. His hard body and his scent of lemons with an undertone of spice tugged her under, into a world where no one but he existed.

Much too quickly the music came to an end. For a brief moment his lips swooped down and he planted a hot kiss on her exposed collarbone. He led her off the dance floor, dazed, and she was unable to wipe the grin from her mouth.

When they reached their seats she sat down, but Andreas remained standing. He took his phone from his back trouser pocket and his brow furrowed when he checked the screen. He pointed at it, and then out to the outside terrace. She nodded and waved towards him, telling him that it was okay for him to go and make a call.

When he was gone an involuntary shiver ran through her body. She was definitely dancing with danger. And she didn't know if she was going to be able to stop.

Andreas sat at a table out on the terrace to return his missed call from Christos. Unlike the other customers, who were all facing outwards towards the spectacle of the night sky, he faced back into the bar, where he had the perfect view of Grace, sitting in front of a low window.

His fear that something was wrong was immediately put to rest when Christos assured him that he was just calling to check that everything was in place for tomorrow. With a jolt Andreas realised that his usually laid-back brother was nervous—*very* nervous, in fact. Guilt pricked against his skin. Yes, he had fulfilled his best man duties so far—including organising a bachelor party last week in Athens—but had he really been there for Christos?

When he thought of the calls Grace shared with Matt and Lizzie, full of warmth and genuine concern and interest, he realised how amiss he had been—both recently and in the past few years. Three days ago he had had no idea that the hopeless romantic he had rescued at the airport would cause him to pause and take stock of his own life.

He deliberately went through a detailed breakdown with Christos, of everything the planner and Grace had done for tomorrow, and then ran through the itinerary for the day again. But as he spoke he got increasingly distracted. A man had approached Grace. He sat down beside her—much too close for Andreas's liking. What was he playing at? And why the hell was she smiling back at him, being so friendly?

Jealous fire raged through his veins. But then Grace turned around and pointed at him. The other man gave him an uncertain smile and backed off. Unbelievably, twice more this happened during the course of his conversation with Christos, before he was able to end the call.

Grace smiled up in relief when Andreas returned. The call had been much longer than she'd expected and she was hungry...for food *and* his company.

His earlier ease was gone, though. His expression was tense, and his eyes barely reached hers.

'Our table is ready in the restaurant.'

She followed him out on to the terrace and then down stone steps to a lower level terrace. Their table was next to a glass balustrade which gave unending views out on to the Aegean and to the lights of the towns to the west. The whole terrace was awash with candles on white tabletops and storm lanterns on the white concrete floors.

Andreas recommended the house special, lobster spaghetti, which they both ordered—along with a bottle of the local *assyrtiko* white wine.

Throughout the ordering process Andreas seemed distracted, and once their waiter had left she asked, 'Is everything okay?'

'Do you usually get so much attention when you're out?'

Perplexed, she sat back into the cushions of her chair. 'What do you mean?'

'When I was on my call several men approached you.'

'So?'

Cold eyes challenged hers. 'Why?'

She recoiled for a moment, at the cynicism in his voice, but then she sat forward and challenged him back. 'Why did they approach me? Oh, come on, Andreas, why are you asking me that? We both know why... They wanted to buy me a drink but I said no, that I was waiting for you.'

He made no response, but kept on staring at her sceptically.

Anger and disappointment collided within her and she said bitterly, 'A few hours ago you said you trusted me. Were you lying?'

He still said nothing, and she knew this night was over.

She placed her napkin on her plate. 'I don't feel hungry any longer. I want to go back to Kasas.'

She went to move, but his hand snapped around her wrist. His eyes were furious, but also shadowed with confusion.

'Why did you refuse their drinks...? It's not as if we are a couple.'

She jerked back in shock. 'Are you angry that I refused? Did you want me to accept?'

He shook his head vigorously. 'Of course not... But there was nothing stopping you, so why didn't you?'

Totally bewildered, she answered, 'Because I'm with *you*. Yes, we might not be a couple, but we *are* out together...why would I accept a drink from another man?'

'To play mind games with me—to make me jealous.'

Frustration surged through her. 'Good God, what do you take me for? I'm not that type of person. I don't play games. I don't hurt other people.'

For a while he stared at her, his jaw flexing. His mouth became a tight grimace. 'I'm sorry. That was uncalled for.'

His remorse looked genuine, but he had some explaining to do and she wasn't going to let him off the hook. 'If you're sorry, prove it to me. Explain what the last fifteen minutes has been about.'

A waiter arrived with their food, but Andreas spoke to him in Greek and the waiter walked away with the plates.

'I told him we weren't ready and that we'd order again when we are.'

She nodded and waited for him to speak.

His hand rubbed against his cheek and then ran up into his hair, messing it up just the way she loved. Oh, why was she so attracted to this man who had *heartbreaker* written all over him?

Andreas felt sick to his stomach. He had behaved abominably. Grace deserved an explanation. But the thought of recounting the past was tearing him apart. His sense of self, his certainty of who he was, felt as unstable as the flickering flames on the candles at the centre of their table.

'Two years ago I received a blackmail threat. A member of the paparazzi had photos of my wife making love to another man on his yacht.'

Grace's hand moved towards his but he pulled away. He didn't want her pity. They sat in silence and eventually he gazed towards her. There wasn't pity in her eyes, but anger. He frowned, and she answered his unspoken question.

'I hope you reported him to the police and told *her* exactly what you thought of her. How could she have done that to you?'

Thrown by her outraged disbelief, he paused, unable to find an answer. Her outrage almost made him want to smile. Grace was a fierce protector; no wonder she'd taken on the task of protecting her siblings.

'How could I have married her, more like.' The exact question his father had shouted at him, accusing him of bringing dishonour into the family.

'What happened between you, Andreas...? Why did she do something so awful?'

'When I confronted her she said she was lonely, that she hated living on Kasos, and the amount of travel I did.'

'It doesn't sound like you believed her.'

'I was away because the recession had taken hold.' Inhaling a deep breath, he arched his neck back and stared briefly up into the night sky; the stars seemed impossibly far away. 'My businesses were struggling in the worldwide property crash, but I knew that, even though it was high risk, it was my opportunity to radically extend my asset base—which would firmly secure the future of the company. I travelled the world, persuading investment firms to finance my property deals. Unfortunately my ex did not agree with my expansion plans, nor the risks involved—and nor the way it curtailed our cash flow. So she had an affair with a man who could provide her with the lifestyle she had expected when we married—a man I had considered a friend.'

Grace considered him nervously and shuffled in her seat before saying, 'You're a shrewd guy...'

'So why didn't I know what she was like when we

married? Because I believed her flattery.' His throat burning, he paused and then admitted, 'I trusted her at a time when I was trying to deal with my uncle's death and the fight with my father that was causing me to lose my family.'

'And you thought *she* could be your new family?'

She spoke so softly and with such emotion he felt the humiliation that had carried him through the conversation to this point evaporate. Only regret remained. 'Yes.'

'And your friend?'

A bitter taste grew in his mouth. 'He knows to stay out of my way.'

Her eyes trailed above his left eyebrow. 'That scar...'

'He came off much worse.'

The flicker of a grimace crossed her face for a moment. 'I'm sorry, Andreas. I'm sorry she caused you so much pain. Your friend too. I can't think of anything worse than being betrayed like that.'

'It taught me a valuable lesson: that I can never again believe I truly know another person.'

She moved forward, passion burning in her eyes. 'No, I don't agree. The timing of your marriage was terrible— you were grieving for your uncle. I think in normal circumstances most of us *can* know another person, even if it's just a gut instinct about them.'

'People wear masks—they tell you what they think you want to hear.'

'Let's put it to the test. How about me? Do you think I would cheat on a partner? On my husband?'

'How would I know?'

'Would I cheat, Andreas? Yes or no?'

Every fibre of his body knew that she wouldn't. But it was hard to admit that his long-held views were wrong—

that in a few short days this woman had turned so many of them upside down.

He inhaled a deep breath and said tersely, 'No.'

'You're right. I wouldn't. Because when I marry it will be for love and because I respect my husband. I want a hundred per cent honesty and trust in a relationship. I will never lie, never play games... My marriage will be too important to me to ever even contemplate compromising it.'

'Your husband will be a very lucky man.'

She gave him a rueful smile. 'I just need to meet him.'

Something hard kicked inside him at the thought of her married to another man. His mind jumped ahead to her leaving Kasas, leaving *him*. 'When are you leaving?'

She tapped a fingernail on the bottom of her fork before she gazed up with a sad smile. 'Monday.'

'Two more days.'

Her smile faded.

His heart began to pound. Could he let her go? Could a brief passionate kiss be all that they ever shared?

CHAPTER SEVEN

LATER THAT NIGHT, back on Kasas, Grace's heart did a funny little jump of delight when Andreas held her hand all the way from the helipad down to the villa.

When they entered the living room, the silence that had been with them for the entire journey home from Santorini continued to bounce between them. It was a silence born from the intensity of the connection they had shared tonight—a connection of emotional honesty.

Andreas opening up about his marriage had changed everything. He had let her into his world, trusted her. He had reached out to her. And she wasn't sure what to do with the emotional chasm that sat in her heart as a result. A chasm full of hunger to connect with him even further. To know him to the depths of his very being. A hunger to express her feelings towards him.

The chasm had her wanting to reach out to him, but she didn't know how. She was scared she would do the wrong thing. Her old self-doubts sat like a cloak on her shoulders.

'Would you like a drink?'

Uncertainty had her dithering for an embarrassing few seconds before she said, 'I think I should go to bed. It's almost two and I have to be up early. Thank you for a lovely night.'

His eyes searched hers for a moment before he nodded. But as she turned away he said, 'Wait. I have something I want to give to you.'

He disappeared upstairs and, intrigued, Grace waited on the edge of the sofa where he had earlier fastened her sandals, a shiver running through her body when she remembered the tender touch of his hands on her ankle.

When he returned, he reached out and said, 'Give me your hand and close your eyes.'

'What are you up to?'

'Just close your eyes. You'll see in a few minutes.'

Grace held out her hand cautiously, and it was just as well that he had told her to close her eyes as she did so anyway, involuntarily, when his fingers held her hand. His thumb stroked down the sensitive skin of her inner wrist. Goosebumps ran the length of her body.

In a low voice that had her jerking forward with a need to close the distance between them he said, 'I was going to give this to you tomorrow, but...'

'But what?'

'We'll probably both be too busy.'

His fingernails lightly grazed against her skin and she giggled. 'That tickles. What *are* you doing?'

'Sit still. You wriggling like that isn't helping.'

Grace inhaled a deep breath and tried to ignore his fingertips stroking her wrist, the way that simple touch was setting her alight, making her yearn for more.

And then her body stilled, although her heart exploded in her chest as a sudden realisation hit home: the empty ache of loneliness that had been her constant companion for so many years was gone. With Andreas she felt whole, somehow. Safe and protected. Understood.

Panic flared inside her. She needed to see him. *Now.* 'I want to open my eyes.'

'In a few seconds.'

His fingers continued to dance on her wrist and she had to squeeze her eyes to stop the burning temptation to fling them open and drink him in. They had so little time left together.

'Now open them.'

On her silver bracelet sat a new charm—an intricate violet flower, its purple-blue design sitting between the miniature flower clippers and the violin that Matt and Lizzie had given her last Christmas. She wore the bracelet as a constant reminder of them; it felt right that Andreas's charm sat with theirs.

She ran a fingertip over the exquisite design. 'It's so pretty…thank you. Why a violet?'

He gazed down at the charm. 'Because it symbolises courage and intelligence.'

She couldn't stifle her giggle. 'You just made that up! And anyway, it symbolises modesty.'

His brows knitted together in consternation. 'Does it?' He gave her a sheepish look. 'I definitely didn't buy it for that reason.'

His expression grew serious and he leaned over to touch the flower charm, his finger briefly brushing against her skin, sending every nerve-ending into a tailspin of desire.

'I bought it to thank you on behalf of my family for everything you've done to make tomorrow special.' His fingers stilled on her wrist. His voice grew deeper. 'And because it's the same incredible colour as your eyes.'

She stood up, her body shaking with the intensity of the emotions surging through her. It couldn't end like this. She couldn't walk away from him without being true to herself.

Her heart raced even faster, and though her stomach

churned she forced herself to speak. 'Stay with me to-night.'

Shock replaced the earlier heat in his eyes. 'What?'

Had she misread this whole situation? But she had seen how he had stared at her all night, felt how he had held her in the bar when they danced.

A deep blush flashed on her cheeks and she went to leave.

He stood in her way. 'Hold on—where are you going?'

She shook her head but kept it dipped down, too mortified to look him in the eye.

'You can't ask a man to stay the night and then run away before he even has the opportunity to reply.'

Humiliation had her answering sharply, 'Your expression was enough of an answer.'

'*Aman*, Grace! The sweetest, sexiest woman I have ever encountered has just asked me to stay the night... and we both know that I should say no.'

He thought she was sweet and sexy... But he was saying no. So she was lacking somehow. Was it the gulf between them career and wealth-wise? Their different backgrounds? Or was it that she simply wasn't attractive enough?

Hurt and humiliation twisted in her chest. 'Let's just forget this conversation ever happened.'

He ran a hand through his hair and a groan came from somewhere deep within him. 'Trust me—I would like nothing more than to spend the night with you. But I can't. I'm not what you're looking for, Grace.'

'Not in the long term, no...'

'You're playing with fire.'

She shook her head vigorously. She knew what she was doing. She had never been more certain of anything in all of her life.

'No, for the first time in many years I'm listening to what I really want.'

She paused, wishing she was brave enough to say everything that needed to be said. That she wanted fun and passion. Wanted to feel as physically close to him as she did emotionally. She searched for words, but everything seemed either too brash or needy.

And before she was able to find the right words Andreas stepped aside, his expression sombre.

'*Kalinichta*...goodnight, Grace.'

Grace's footsteps disappeared along the upstairs corridor and Andreas sank onto the sofa, tiredly dragging his hands over his face.

Turning Grace down had been one of the hardest things he had ever done.

What had he even been *thinking*? A gorgeous woman had invited him into her bed and he had said no!

But there were so many compelling reasons for doing so. The future they would share as part of Christos and Sofia's lives. The future Grace wanted. Her tender, soft heart. So many logical and reasonable arguments for staying the hell away from her.

Why, then, was he sitting here with regret storming through his veins, angry at the recognition that the past two years he had been living a lie, pretending he was content in his life?

Three short days with Grace had shown him just how empty his life really was. Three days in which he had developed a bond with this woman such as he had never had before. A bond of understanding and trust.

He raked his hands through his hair. If he had the energy he would get up and pour himself a brandy. But telling Grace about his failed marriage had hollowed him out. He felt spent. However, it had also brought a lightness, the lifting of a burden he had carried on his own all this time. Her anger and understanding had touched him deeply. It had lifted some of his doubts and guilt. It had shown him that integrity *did* exist.

He respected everything Grace stood for. With her, there were none of the dramatics of his marriage, which had emotionally and physically drained him. Grace instead was intuitive and supportive.

And physically she drove him to despair.

Tonight, when they'd danced, her body had moved against his like a siren call. Her eyes had held a sexy promise, her mouth the whisper of endless pleasure.

They were both adults. Deeply attracted to one another. Why *shouldn't* they act on it if they were both clear on what the future held?

He stood and made for the stairs.

Grace scrubbed at her teeth, her back to the bathroom mirror. She couldn't bear to see the angry blush that still marred her cheeks.

How on earth was she going to face Andreas in the morning?

A knock sounded on her bedroom door and she leapt in surprise. It could only be one person. She turned and stared into the mirror. What was she going to do?

Her pride yelled at her to ignore him. He had made his position clear. She didn't need any further humiliation.

A second knock tapped on the door…slow and patient…like a man confident she would answer.

On the third knock she stalked to the door and yanked it open. 'Andreas, I'm trying to sleep, to—'

He didn't give her an opportunity to finish her sentence. He marched into the room, shutting the door behind him, and forced her back against the wall. Only inches separated them. He reached out an arm and his palm landed on the wall to the side of her head. He loomed over her, his face taut, his body pulsating with frustrated desire.

His dark eyes devoured hers. 'Did you mean it when you asked me to stay the night with you?'

She tried to answer but his gaze moved down her body and her words were swept away.

'Did you mean it?' His words were a low growl.

'Yes.'

'I can't offer you anything, Grace. We have no future together.'

She ignored the way her stomach flinched at his reminder and looked him solidly in the eye. 'I know.'

His hand reached out and sat on her waist. Slowly he drew her forward until their bodies met. She waited for his kiss, but instead he stayed gazing down at her, his hands following a torturously slow path around her body, sending jolts of pleasure to her core.

He lowered his head and kissed the tender spot at the back of her ear. She gave a low groan.

'You're every man's dream…' He paused to trail kisses along her neck. 'Beautiful, sexy, great legs…' His fingers played with the strings of her pajama vest top for a tantalising moment. 'You smell like a summertime garden in the heat of the midday sun…'

His trail of kisses moved upwards, his stubble dragging lightly across her skin, yet another reminder of his forceful maleness. His mouth hovered over hers.

'And you have the most gorgeous kissable lips.'

With that, he began a slow exploration of her lips that had Grace moaning, her fingers digging into the hard muscle of his shoulders, desperate for him to deepen it.

She was close to tears when he did eventually deepen their kiss, and without warning he lifted her up and wrapped her legs around his waist. Still kissing her, he walked to her bed and together they fell down, Grace crying out in pleasure to feel his weight upon her.

The following morning Andreas woke suddenly, when the bed shuddered hard and banged against the wall.

'Oh, that hurts...ouch...my knee...' At the foot of the bed Grace hobbled on the tiled floor, quietly muttering some low expletives.

'Are you okay?'

She jumped when he spoke, and whispered, 'Sorry, I didn't mean to wake you. I couldn't see in the dark and whacked my knee against the bedpost.'

Andreas sat up further in the bed and switched on the bedside lamp. They both turned away from its glare. A hand over his eyes, he asked, 'Why are you dressed? It's still dark.'

'I need to make a start on the bouquets and finish off the other prep work.'

'What time is it?'

'Five.'

'*Five!* We didn't go to bed until two...to sleep before at least four. You can't function on less than an hour's sleep.'

She reached down and massaged her knee. 'I'll be okay. I have to go.'

The anxiety in her eyes told him that she wasn't going to listen to reason. He would have to resort to other tactics.

'Fine. But not until you come here and give me a kiss.'

She pondered his request with a frown, but then walked over and dropped a quick kiss on to his cheek.

She went to move away but he wrapped his arms

around her and pulled her down onto the bed. He rolled her over him and wrapped his legs around hers, holding her prisoner. She glared at him and he gave a small chortle.

'What are you doing?' Her voice was a breathless low whisper. She pushed against him, but already desire was flooding her eyes.

His fingers dipped beneath her sweatshirt and into the waistband of her jeans. Her body jerked against his.

'Grace Chapman, were you just about to leave without even saying goodbye?'

'No!'

'You're not a very convincing liar.'

'I told you—I have to get to the flowers.'

'And *I* say that you need some sleep. So, whether you want to or not, you're staying here with me.'

She pushed hard against him.

He shook his head. 'You'll have to try harder than that.'

For a moment she considered him. But then she nodded her acceptance and he felt her body relax into him. He gave a low groan when her hand reached round and stroked along his spine. Her mouth, hot and warm, trailed kisses on his chest. Every cell in his body stirred.

His eyes closed of their own volition and he murmured into her hair, 'You're not playing fair. We're supposed to sleep.'

Her hand moved to his belly. His eyes popped open. He inhaled deeply when she gave him a dark, sultry look. He untangled himself from her and flipped onto his back, already lost to her touch. But while he was turning Grace flipped around too—and hopped out of the bed.

He caught her just as she was about to make for the door. He pulled her back into the bed beside him and wrapped his arms around her. 'That was a dirty trick if ever I saw one.'

At first she smiled, with a look of guilty conscience, but then the smile faded, to be replaced by a troubled expression. 'Andreas, please.'

His gut tightened. He ran his fingers lightly against her cheek. 'What's the matter?'

'I'm worried the flowers aren't right. That I've forgotten something.'

'The flowers are perfect. And with your military-style planning you can't possibly have forgotten anything. The most important thing now is that you get some sleep.'

Her breath floated against his skin in broken anxious waves. 'When I woke earlier it suddenly hit me that the wedding is *today*. I don't feel ready.'

He held her tighter to him. A hand gently stroking her hair, he whispered, 'Everything's going to be okay. Sleep until seven. Then I'll come and help you with the prep work.'

She arched back and her violet eyes searched his. 'Are you sure?'

'That I want to be a florist's assistant? No. But I'll do it for you.'

To that she gave a small smile. 'Really?'

'Yes, really.'

They stayed locked together in that position for the longest while, staring into each other's eyes. Her lips lifted into a breathtaking grin and she whispered, 'Thank you.'

A surge of protective desire tore through him, so strong he was momentarily stunned. He kissed her, deeply and intensely, and she responded in turn. They kissed as though their lives depended on it. He ripped her clothes from her. His head spun at the feel of her soft round curves again and he inhaled her scent.

He went to flip her onto her back, but she fought against him. She pushed *him* back onto the bed instead, and when they joined together he stared up into those violet eyes and his heart cracked open at the sight of the honest passion and warmth in her endless gaze.

Grace woke later to the sound of her name being called softly, a hand stroking her hair. She opened her eyes lazily and found Andreas crouched down beside her at the side of the bed. Freshly showered, he wore nothing but a towel wrapped around his waist. He was so delicious she gave him a crooked smile. He smiled back, those green eyes flecked with gold and dancing with…contentment?

'It's six-fifty.'

She gave a lazy nod, her body languid.

'Take a shower and I'll get breakfast ready.'

She swallowed against a dry throat. 'Thanks, but I need to go straight down to the workshop. I won't have anything.'

He raised an eyebrow to that. She thought he was about to argue, but then he gave a small shrug. 'Fine, I'll go and get dressed in my room. I'll join you at the workshop in a little while.'

As he walked towards the door she had a sudden impulse to shout out, to tell him not to go. Not to leave her.

On shaky legs she made her way to the bathroom. Soon afterwards she stood under a scalding shower, her mind racing as her body gave up constant reminders of the intensity of her night with Andreas. A night full of passion and tender moments.

Her head dipped when she remembered that she would be leaving in two days. The hot water battered her neck.

She gritted her teeth and clamped down on all thoughts of the future. It was futile. Sofia and the wedding needed her full attention today.

Ten minutes later she hesitated by the terrace door. She should leave immediately for the workshop, but the rich aroma of coffee and the draw of seeing Andreas again pulled her in the direction of the kitchen instead.

Barefoot, he wore navy shorts and a pale pink polo shirt, his back to her. She hovered at the door, weak with sexual attraction. She longed to go and run her hands through his damp hair, to tousle it, kiss that warm mouth, feel the pulse of his body when he pushed against her.

He turned with a lazy grin and beckoned her over to the breakfast counter. Her legs went weak.

'I should go to the workshop.'

'Come here. Now.'

It was lightly said, but the fire in his eyes told her it was an order—not a request.

When she reached him his hands landed on the waistband of her jeans, just above her hip bones.

'*Kalimera*…good morning.'

Her insides melted at the low, sensual tone of his voice. He lifted her up to sit on the countertop.

As weak as water, her resistance was only a low gasp. 'What are you doing?'

He gave her a wicked smile and, with one hand remaining on her knee, stood between her legs and reached along the countertop. He pulled a bowl towards them. He dipped a spoon into the bowl and brought up a spoonful of sinfully creamy Greek yogurt and glistening golden honey.

'I'm going to feed you. You have a busy day ahead of you…' He paused and a mischievous glint danced in his eyes. 'And you just had an exceptionally intense night.'

His eyes stayed glued to her mouth when she opened it, the tip of her tongue nervously running along her upper lip. She opened her mouth even wider and squirmed on the countertop as an explosion of tart yogurt and sweet honey hit her palette, but a groan of pleasure managed to escape.

'That tastes *so* good.'

Andreas dropped the bowl to the countertop. *'Thee mou!'* He pulled her towards him, wrapping her legs around his waist.

His mouth tasted of freshly ground coffee, warm and safe. His kiss, at first light and playful, deepened as his hands reached under her sweater and moved up along her spine, around to dance on her ribcage and then over the lace of her bra.

He broke away and spoke against her hair. 'This is impossible.'

She could only agree. With him, she lost all sense. Forgot everything she'd said she wanted in life.

'I know...'

He pulled back and traced his thumb along her cheek, his eyes sombre but tender. 'We need to be careful today.'

She moved to the side and hopped off the countertop. 'Of course.'

'We don't want anyone jumping to the wrong conclusion about our relationship.'

He was right—but that didn't stop her heart plummeting to the floor. She busied herself pouring a cup of coffee from the cafetière. 'Absolutely. Last night was a one-off. I think we should just leave it at that.'

When he didn't respond she glanced in his direction. His arms crossed on his chest, he asked, 'Are you saying that you don't want anything else to happen between us?'

'Aren't you?'

'When you leave on Monday where are you travelling to?'

Uncertain as to why their conversation had taken this direction, she frowned before she answered. 'I'm taking a ferry to Chania, in Crete. There's a renowned wedding florist based there; I'm taking a two-day course at his school next week.'

'Crete is a beautiful island...you will have a lovely time there.'

She had to act nonchalant, pretend that this conversation was *not* leaving her floundering as to how Andreas felt about her.

'I was planning on returning to England towards the end of next week, in time for Matt finishing his exams, but I've decided to stay a little while longer.'

She had listened to what he had said about not feeling overly responsible for her siblings. It was time that she started to let them go and began building her own life in earnest.

She sipped some coffee and glanced at him. He was staring at her, deep in thought.

She should go, but an innate reluctance to leave him had her struggling for something else to say.

'How do you feel about today?' He frowned, and she tried to ease the tension between them with a joke. 'Are you *nervous*?'

He inhaled deeply. 'What do you think?'

Of course he was. Her joke backfiring, she gave him a tight smile. Could she have been more insensitive? After everything he'd told her last night.

'Sorry...of course you are.'

He nodded and poured himself some more coffee.

'I'd better go and start on the bouquets, or at this rate Sofia will have none.'

He glanced at her briefly. 'I'll join you in a little while to help.'

His tone was distracted, with no hint that they had spent the night in each other's arms, sharing a connection so deep that her heart had felt as if it was going to explode with the need to blurt out everything he meant to her.

CHAPTER EIGHT

WITH SOFIA SURROUNDED by the make-up and hair team, Grace slipped out of the bedroom they had taken over in the villa, telling Sofia's mum that she needed to do one final check on the flowers.

She ran all the way down to the workshop. Inside, the room was empty except for the centrepieces and the displays for the reception. While the wedding ceremony was taking place the local florists would take care of positioning them. The centrepieces were even more of a success than she had hoped. Andreas's uncle's porcelain vases emphasised the delicate beauty of the peonies and lisianthus.

Back outside, Grace ran towards the chapel, passing alongside the bay trees and lanterns elegantly lining the path. She smiled at the ribbons floating in the light breeze, but then a dart of pain shot through her heart. *Their time alone was over.* She pushed that thought away. The wedding guests would be arriving in less than half an hour. She needed to make sure all the flowers looked perfect.

As she approached the chapel her heart sank. The floral displays lined the red-carpeted aisle, sitting at intervals between the rows of white wooden seats. But the florists were still attaching the garland to the frame of the entrance to the chapel, and the garland for the bell tower still sat to one side of the terrace.

She rushed forward to help them and together they finished the door garland. At the same time Grace ran through with them the checklist of all the other jobs that were to be done. When she came to the corsages and boutonnières, the two women studied her blankly.

Grace closed her eyes for a second. *She had forgotten to arrange for them to be delivered to the bride's and groom's parties.* The guests would be here soon, and Christos and Andreas would need to be down at the jetty to greet them.

She raced back to the workshop, praying that the carefully constructed cascading curls the hairdresser had created, twisted into a half-knot at the base of her neck and topped with a spray of lisianthus, wouldn't fall apart.

In the workshop she grabbed the corsages and boutonnières and sprinted back to the villa. She heard loud voices coming from the formal sitting room. She gave a light knock and entered.

Christos was surrounded by at least ten friends, all larking about as Andreas helped him into his tuxedo jacket. They all turned as she entered, smiling at her curiously. She went to turn away, certain she had made a faux pas in her intrusion on this male domain, but Andreas's mother—beautiful and elegant in a powder-blue knee-length dress—suddenly appeared, and with an exclamation of delight gave Grace a warm hug.

'*Kalosìrthes!* Welcome, Grace! How lovely to see you again.'

Over his mother's shoulder she briefly caught Andreas's eye before he resumed buttoning Christos's jacket. Her throat closed over at the sight of the intimacy between the two brothers, and when she pulled away from the floral cloud of his mother's perfume she bent to rearrange the boutonnières, desperate to hide the tears filming her eyes. What on earth would his mother think if she saw them?

There was a lot of good-natured jostling between Christos and his friends. Despite his mum's welcome Grace hovered on the outside of the group, awkward and unsure. She understood why Andreas was staying removed from her, in his desire to hide the truth of their relationship, but part of her longed for him to show some form of acknowledgement, some warmth towards her.

His father approached, pouring champagne into a flute, which he forcibly handed to her. 'You are just in time. I'm about to make a toast.' He twisted around and held his glass up high. 'To Christos and Sofia. May they have a *long* and happy marriage.'

A loud cheer went up from the other men and they all moved in to hug Christos, their affection and friendship for the groom clear. Her eyes darted to Andreas as he stepped out of the friendly jostling. His tight expression told her that he too had heard his father's heavy emphasis on *long*.

'Aren't these flowers so pretty? Grace, you've done a fantastic job.'

His mother fussed around her, and Grace instantly knew that she was accustomed to deflecting any potential arguments.

A laughing Christos extracted himself from the group long enough to draw her into a hug. 'Yes, thank you for all your work.' His eyes glinting, he asked, 'What did Sofia say when she saw the flowers?'

Earlier Grace had taken Sofia to the workshop to show her the flowers. Sofia had burst into tears, and a horrified Grace had thought it was because she didn't like them, but Sofia had assured her it was because they all were so beautiful. The bridal bouquet—a hand-tied spiral cloud of pale pink Sarah Bernhardt and ivory Duchesse de Nemours peonies, finished off with a long length of silver-grey ribbon—now sat in pride of place on the bridal suite's dressing table, along with her own smaller version made with the Sarah Bernhardt.

Grace had never seen Sofia as worked up as she was today. And the last thing an already nervous-looking Christos needed was to know that his albeit deliriously happy bride had been shaking like a leaf all morning.

'She loved them and she can't wait to see you.'

Christos gave a grin of relief which grew into a wide megawatt beam: the gorgeous smile of a man in love. Grace had to walk away for fear that tears would fill her eyes again at witnessing this real-life romantic tale unfolding before her.

She took a sip of champagne and dared a glance at Andreas, who had come to stand next to Christos. Both he and Christos were wearing beautifully tailored tuxedos, crisp white dress shirts and black silk ties. They both looked gorgeous…but when she glanced at Andreas memories of last night had her weak-kneed with desire.

He was staring in the direction of the other men, who had moved over to a table of food at the opposite side of the room. But her instinct told her he was attuned to everything she was doing—as though he was on tenterhooks about her letting slip the truth about what they had shared over the past few days.

Flustered, and feeling too hot, she placed her champagne flute next to the flowers on the coffee table. 'I'd better get back to Sofia.'

'Stay and help us fix the boutonnières,' his mother

said, picking up one of the sprays. 'When Andreas got married I couldn't get them to sit properly.'

Then, as though realising what she had said, his mother glanced towards Andreas and then his father in alarm. Christos threw a worried glance at Andreas, who stood rigid, still, tight-lipped.

His father bristled and in a low voice said irritably, 'I thought we'd agreed not to discuss that wedding?'

Grace picked up his mother's corsage and turned her back to the men. Much taller than Mrs Petrakis, she fixed the single ivory-white peony backed with two sprigs of lisianthus to her powder-blue dress and gave her a sympathetic smile. She smiled back at Grace gratefully, blinking hard at the tears in her eyes. Eyes the same green burnished with gold as Andreas's... Though finished, Grace deliberately fussed with the corsage a while longer, until Mrs Petrakis touched her arm gently and nodded that she was okay.

Next Grace attached a boutonnière to Christos's lapel. She gave him a cheeky smile. 'You look incredibly handsome today.'

Christos smiled back in delight. And then he lowered his head and said, for her ears only, 'I'll take good care of her.'

Tears instantly filled Grace's eyes at his tender but heartfelt promise, and for a few seconds she wondered if she would ever meet a man who would be so keen and happy to marry *her*.

She busied herself with selecting the next boutonnière, and then steeled herself to approach Andreas's dad. He glanced down at her briefly, and then looked away. Though not quite as tall as Andreas, Mr Petrakis exuded the same power and strength as his oldest son.

Her fingers fumbled with the catch of the pin and she could feel his impatience growing.

To distract him, but also in a bid not to allow herself to be intimidated by him, she stood up tall and looked him in the eye. She pretended to speak to the four of them as a group, but her gaze remained on his father. 'I'm afraid that I've been a nuisance to Andreas over the past few days, but to his credit he has been courteous and generous at all times. You should be incredibly proud of him.'

Mr Petrakis glared at her impatiently. 'Of *course* we're proud of him.'

Behind her she heard Andreas give a disbelieving laugh. And as she picked up the final boutonniere, Christos chortled and said, 'My brother? Courteous? Who knew? You're mellowing in your old age, Andreas!' Christos threw an arm around Andreas's shoulder. 'But you're right, Grace, about him being generous—he always has been.' Christos looked directly at Andreas. 'Thanks for hosting the wedding.'

Behind her, Mr Petrakis cleared his throat noisily. 'I still don't understand why you wanted it *here*. It would have been so much easier in Athens, rather than dragging everyone out into the middle of the Aegean.'

Andreas's jaw tightened. In an instant Grace wanted to stand up for him. 'I think the majority of people would *love* to marry on this island—it has to be the most romantic place I've ever been. I'd happily stay here for the rest of my life.'

Flustered at the eyebrows rising around her, and the prospect of placing a boutonnière on Andreas's lapel, Grace walked towards him and, thoroughly distracted, said to Christos as she passed him by, 'You must be pleased with Andreas's wedding present?'

Christos stared at her, confused. 'What present?'

Panic soared through her veins and she looked at Andreas in alarm. His jaw had tightened even more, and irritation flared in his eyes.

'I'll tell you later. It was to be a surprise.'

Grace hesitated in front of him. She swallowed hard as a deep blush fired on her cheeks. She gazed up at him and mouthed, *I'm sorry.*

He gave an almost imperceptible shake of his head before looking away. The double lilac lisianthus was perfect against the black of his suit, but her fingers trembled so much she was worried that she'd never actually manage to pin it on. Her head spun from embarrassment, and the effect of standing so close to him. It reminded her of how good it had been to have those arms around her, being free to inhale his scent all night long, the way his body had dominated hers, the sensuality of his lips, his mouth...

Behind her, his father said, 'Well, if Grace knows about the present, then I think there can be no reason why *we* shouldn't.'

Grace froze. Beneath her fingers Andreas's chest swelled as he inhaled a deep breath. She pulled away just as he spoke, his tone sharp.

'Later.' He checked his watch and turned to Christos. 'We should go down to the jetty—the first boats will be arriving soon.' As though to punctuate his words, the sound of a helicopter overhead reverberated through the air.

His father walked towards the door. 'I'll go and greet the guests coming by helicopter.'

All the men disappeared from the room. Grace tried to ignore the way his mother was studying her and quickly made her excuses and left the room too.

She climbed the stairs and stood outside the bridal

suite for a while, inhaling some deep breaths. How could the man who had looked at her with such impersonal detachment just now be the same man who had made passionate love to her last night? Had whispered private words of endearment.

He had made her feel as though she was the centre of his universe, but right now she felt as if she had been cast out of his world.

Beside him Christos jigged nervously as they waited for Sofia to arrive. The late-afternoon sun was dipping low behind them, casting shadows on the terrace. In front of them Grace's flowers looked like giant balls of marsh-mallow—the perfect romantic finishing touch to what even *he* had to admit was an incredible wedding venue.

His skin itched even at the thought.

He took a glance backwards to check for Sofia's ar-rival and caught his father's eye. Since he had arrived a few hours earlier his father had once again managed to push his every button. The same old grievances about how overworked he was and how lucky his friends were to have sons who gladly took over the family business. A none-too-subtle reminder of how this island should have been his all those years ago. And several digs as to how he hoped *this* marriage would last.

Andreas gave Christos a quick, encouraging clasp of the shoulder. 'She'll be here soon. She can't change her mind and run away too easily on an island.'

He had to forget his father, forget his past, and con-centrate on making this day special for Christos.

'Cheers, brother, that's really reassuring.'

The two brothers grinned at each other and then Christos ducked his head down so that no one else could hear their conversation. 'So what's this about a wedding present?'

Emotion thickened Andreas's throat and it was a while before he managed to speak. 'The paperwork is in my office... I'm giving you half of this island.'

Christos studied him, speechless. 'Seriously?' he said at last.

'Yeah, seriously.'

The two men embraced and then stood side by side in silence. Eventually Christos spoke, 'We had great times here as boys, didn't we?'

Andreas nodded. 'And we'll have them again.'

Christos looked as though he was about to say something, but just then the sound of traditional music reached them. The trio of musicians, playing violin, bouzouki and the *toumbi* drum, would have led the bridal party all the way from the villa to the chapel.

Sofia was the first to appear behind the musicians, on the arm of her father, her dark hair covered in a lace veil. Beside him Christos inhaled a deep breath, and Andreas couldn't blame him. Sofia was radiating elegant beauty and happiness, her eyes dancing, her mouth a wide beam. And when her eyes met Christos's a single tear trickled down her cheek and Andreas had to turn away. He felt as though he'd been punched in the gut.

He tried not to look back but was unable to resist doing so. When he did, he knew he should look away, but he couldn't. His breath had been knocked out of his lungs. Her head slightly bowed, a smile playing on her lips, Grace followed Sofia. Her silver-grey dress was made of fine lace on the bodice, and a full-length tulle skirt. Silver sandals were on her feet. Was she wearing the underwear he had unpacked? And was it truly only twelve hours ago that they had lain together, their bodies entwined and damp with perspiration?

He forced himself to turn. Already he had seen his

parents' curiosity as to what was going on between them. His mother constantly searched for any sign that he was in a relationship again, hoping against hope that one day he would have a family of his own. It would be unjust and cruel to mislead her.

He stared at the peonies cascading down from the garland around the chapel bell. He had helped Grace place the peonies in flower tubes this morning. He had thought then that he could trust her. Had thought so last night. But within minutes of meeting his family she had hinted at the personal nature of their relationship by revealing that she knew about his wedding present to Christos. Was she playing him? Trying to back him into a corner?

His stomach twisted at the thought that he might have been duped once again.

When Sofia reached Christos she raised her hands to his and they stared at each other for long moments, before they drew into each other, their noses touching. Together they grinned and turned to the congregation, who broke into spontaneous applause at how infectious their joy was.

The priest eventually managed to draw the wedding party into a semicircle, so that he and Grace were practically facing each other as they flanked Sofia and Christos. While their eyes would briefly meet, and then fly away from one another, in contrast Christos and Sofia never stopped gazing into each other's eyes, lost in one another.

What was Grace thinking? Was she dreaming of her own wedding? When her eyes landed on him did she imagine *him* in the role of her groom? Panic surged through him. Surely not? He had made his thoughts on marriage clear. But last night they had shared an extraordinary intimacy. One that in truth had rocked him to his core. What if she had felt that intensity too? What if he had given her false hope?

When it came to the time for exchanging the rings, he heard Christos's words of reassurance to Sofia, whose fingers were trembling so much he found it hard to slip the ring on her finger. Immediately Sofia stilled, and the couple shared a look intense with understanding and care. Andreas's gaze moved to Grace. She was staring at Sofia and Christos with tears glistening in her eyes. And then she was looking at him, as though asking him a question.

He glanced away. His heart sank. He had no answers for her.

The whoops of joy from the other guests when the newly married couple kissed for the first time transported him back to three years ago, when a similar whoop had echoed in an Athens cathedral. He had been so blind.

He looked back into the congregation. So many of those faces had witnessed his own marriage. How many still speculated as to why his marriage had gone bad so quickly? Why he no longer spoke to one of his closest friends.

His gaze met his mother's. She gave him a sympathetic smile of reassurance. He glanced away and pulled at the collar of his shirt. He needed a drink.

When they followed the bride and groom down the aisle Grace's hand barely touched his arm. They both smiled, but tension kept their bodies rigid as the crowd shouted, *'Na zisetel!'*—Live happily!—while showering the procession with a mixture of confetti and rice.

Before them, Christos and Sofia stopped at the edge of the terrace, where they would greet each of their guests before moving on to the reception. The couple were tied in an intimate embrace and Grace's footsteps faltered.

'I'm sorry about earlier.'

Andreas turned around to see if anyone was close by before he replied. 'I said that we needed to keep our relationship private.'

The volume of the voices around them increased, and Sofia's soft laughter ran through the air at something Christos had whispered to her while in their embrace.

Grace moved closer to him. 'I know. I wasn't thinking.'

It would be so easy to believe her—especially when her eyes pleaded with him to do so. He stepped back. They were standing way too close together. 'My parents are now speculating as to why I told *you* something so personal.'

Grace peered up at him with hurt in her eyes, but didn't respond. He led her over to stand next to the bride and groom, so that they too could greet the guests and be on hand in case they were needed. He felt torn in two.

Unable to stop himself, he leaned down briefly and whispered in her ear, 'You look beautiful.'

She studied him, confounded, and then looked away into the distance, tears in her eyes.

Andreas began to exchange hugs and handshakes. The happiness of everyone else was pulling him apart—along with the guilt of knowing that last night with Grace had been a major mistake.

Out on the Aegean the sun had long disappeared in a spectacular sunset of fiery pinks when the main courses of grilled swordfish and mouthwatering lamb *kleftiko* were finally cleared away. The wedding reception was proving to be a loud and fun affair, with numerous toasts and shouts for the wedding couple to kiss.

In other circumstances Grace would have been able to relax at this point, knowing that the flowers had proved to be a huge success, with many favourable comments. But not only did she have Andreas's father sitting next to her at the top table, as the day progressed she was feeling more and more alienated from Andreas.

The tapping of a knife-edge on a glass had her glancing along the table. Andreas stood and the terrace grew silent. He threw the crowd a devastating smile, but she could see tension in the corners of his eyes. She held her breath as her heart pounded. *Please let this go well for him.*

He spoke first in Greek, and then after a few sentences stopped and translated into English for the guests from England. At first he spoke about the tricks he had played on his younger brother when they were children, with Christos eager to believe everything his older brother and idol said. And then of what Kasas had meant to them both growing up. He told them about their joint adventures, including a failed entrepreneurial attempt to start breeding goats, in which the stubborn animals had proved much too temperamental for the young teenagers. And then, his voice thick with emotion, he said how happy he was to see Christos marry here today.

Beside her, Grace could feel Andreas's father tense.

He went on to compliment Sofia on how radiant she looked today, which drew a large applause from the crowd. And then he faltered. For the longest while he stared down at his notes.

Grace shifted in her seat, her stomach clenching, her heart thundering as she willed him on.

He pushed his notes away. 'I was told that I shouldn't wing my speech, which was probably good advice—but as my father will tell you I'm pretty stubborn when it comes to taking guidance.'

This drew knowing laughter from some of the crowd

and friendly heckling. At first Mr Petrakis sat frozen, but then he gave a nod of acknowledgement and said, 'Whoever hurries stumbles.'

Andreas and Christos shared a look that said they had often heard that expression before, and then Andreas continued. 'Firstly I must compliment Sofia's chief bridesmaid, Grace, who is also the florist for today. Having seen first-hand the work involved, I must admit to a whole new appreciation for the skill and dedication required.' He raised his glass and said, 'To Grace.'

His eyes met hers for the briefest of moments before he turned away. Grace smiled in acknowledgement of the guests toasting her and shared a hug with Sofia. Inside she felt as if she was going to die. She hadn't expected him to say anything about her, and that would have been preferable to the impersonal way he had just done so. As though they were nothing but mere acquaintances. Where had the fun and the friendship between them gone?

'Passion can spark a relationship, but it can't sustain it. Aristotle described love as being a single soul inhabiting two bodies. Christos and Sofia—that is my wish for you: that you share the same dreams, the same values, have a common life vision. These are the things that keep a couple together.'

Grace bent her head and closed her eyes on the emotion in his voice, swallowing against a huge lump in her throat.

'May you for ever be a single soul, living a life of shared dreams that allows your love to take root and blossom with each passing year.' Then, raising his wine glass, he invited the guests to join him in a toast. 'May your love blossom.'

For the rest of the speeches Grace sat trying to listen,

forcing herself to smile and laugh when others did, but feeling numb inside.

As soon as the speeches were over she made her excuses, while the terrace was being cleared of tables for the dancing, and went to check that all the lanterns were lit on the lower terraces and on the path down to the jetty. She tried to stay focused on her work, refusing to think about Andreas's speech and the obvious implications for them as a couple when they didn't share a single dream.

When she eventually returned to the terrace the music had started.

Sofia rushed over to her. 'I was searching for you! It's time to dance the Kalamatiano.'

Sofia pulled her out on to the dance floor, along with her mum and Andreas's mum. They all held hands and were soon encircled by a large group of female wedding guests. The music started and they began circling the dance floor, using small side-steps. The music was infectious, as was Sofia's happiness, and for a while Grace lost herself in the joy of the dancing, in the endless smiles of the women facing her.

But then she spotted Andreas where he stood beside Christos, watching the women dance. The two brothers couldn't have appeared more different in their expressions. Christos was laughing, his eyes glued to Sofia, while Andreas just stared at her for a moment, his expression devoid of any emotion, before he turned away to talk to a group beside him.

He said something to a striking dark-haired woman and stepped closer when she laughed. Something pierced Grace's heart. She felt like doubling over as jealousy and pain punched her stomach with force.

Memories of her father's voice taunted her. *'You need*

to toughen up, Grace. Your looks are fading as quickly as your mother's did.'

As they twisted and circled around the terrace, the high spirits of everyone around her, the beauty of the candlelit terrace bathed in the scent of jasmine, mocked everything in her.

What had she expected? She had known what she was getting into. One night of fun—nothing else. But as she watched his dark head bend, saw him talking to the woman whose eyes were shining at being on the receiving end of his attention, she knew it had never been that simple.

CHAPTER NINE

'COME AND TALK to Giannis.'

Andreas gritted his teeth and turned at his father's call. He reached out to shake Giannis's hand, but was pulled into an enthusiastic hug instead.

'Good to see you, Andreas. I haven't seen you since…' Giannis's voice trailed off.

His father tensed beside him and Andreas answered deliberately, in a casual drawl, 'Since my wedding.'

Giannis gave him an uncomfortable smile and obviously decided to change the subject. 'I've been following your successes in the business pages.' He paused and glanced to Andreas's father. 'You must be enormously proud of Andreas and everything he has achieved.'

His father frowned, as though he wasn't certain either of the comment or how to respond. He eventually brushed off the comment with a dismissive wave of his hand. 'Of course, of course…but now it's time for Andreas to come back to the family business. Like all good sons would do.'

Andreas didn't want to hear any more. He made his excuses and walked away. Out on the dance floor, the party was in full swing. He should be enjoying himself. But in truth he just felt frustrated. Frustrated and angry. He had sat through Christos's speech with pain and regret burning in his gut, knowing he would never have the same dream for the future, the vision of having a partner for life, children, a family of his own.

This wedding was a constant reminder of his own failings. And now his eyes fixed on his greatest frustration of all. *Grace*.

She was out on the dance floor with his cousin Orestis. They were standing much too close to one another. A cut-out section in her dress exposed her upper back. It was the sexiest thing he had ever seen, and images of his mouth running the length of her spine last night almost knocked him sideways.

They had shared so much last night—physically and emotionally. At the time it had felt right, but now he was questioning everything about it. It had left him feeling exposed, and with emotions so conflicting that he couldn't even begin to process them in the madness of the wedding.

His cousin was a charmer and a heartbreaker. He marched right over.

'Whatever Orestis is telling you, don't believe a word of what he's saying.'

Orestis stood back from Grace and raised an eyebrow. 'Well, I *did* learn everything I know from you, cousin.'

Beside him Grace's lips twitched. Andreas didn't like the feeling that it was him against the two of them. Grace was supposed to be on *his* side.

'Not everything Orestis… I'm not a heartbreaker.'

His cousin squared up to him, Greek male pride refusing to back down. 'True, but from what I hear you don't hang around long enough to be one. You don't break hearts—you just steal them.'

Grace looked from Orestis to him and back again.

'Two peas in a pod, I would say.' She walked away into the crowd.

He caught up with her in the centre of the dance floor as the band moved to a slower tempo. 'I've been neglecting my best man's duty to dance with the chief bridesmaid.'

Angry violet eyes damned him. 'Thanks, but I'm not in the mood.'

She went to walk away but he pulled her around and into his arms. His frustration with the whole damn day boiled over and he lowered his head to her ear. 'You weren't so reluctant last night.'

Her foot stamped on his. He held back a groan and tightened his grip. Her body squirmed against him, her heat and scent sending thunderbolts of desire to every sensitive point in his.

He glanced up in time to see some speculative gazes been thrown in their direction. He took a step back but kept a firm grip on her, in case she decided to bolt. With a false smile he warned, 'If we don't dance, people will be even more suspicious of us.'

She gave him a frustrated glare and said through clenched teeth, 'I don't care what people think of us.'

'Really? So the next time we meet you don't care if everyone is wondering about us? Hoping that we get together?'

She hesitated for a moment. 'They won't.'

'Look around you, Grace.'

She gave an indifferent shrug. 'I just see women staring at you and looking as though they would love for *me* to disappear off the face of the earth.'

'And beyond them are my aunts and uncles, my parents, hoping that one day I will marry again.'

'Would that be such a bad thing?'

It was a question he didn't even want to entertain. 'We're not going over that again, are we? You know how I feel.'

The anger in her eyes disappeared. 'I know. I just hate the thought of you going through life on your own.'

Her comment hit a raw nerve and he tried to bite down on the anger coiling in his stomach. 'Not everyone needs a fairy-tale ending to be happy.'

She gave him a long, hard stare. 'As long as you *are* actually happy.'

He wasn't going there.

Inch by inch they moved towards one another. His hand touched the bare skin of her back. He had to swallow a groan as he felt the smoothness of her skin, the delicate ribbon of her spine, the slender span of her waist.

'I haven't seen much of you today.'

He glanced down in order to understand the true meaning of her comment. Her wounded expression had him looking away quickly. A surge of defensiveness followed. 'I've been busy talking to all the guests. I haven't seen many of them in a number of years.'

She didn't respond, which only upped his frustration a notch. Was he messing up *everything* today? He needed to get them back on neutral ground. Grounds of friendship. If that was possible.

'Many guests have spoken to me about how incredible the flowers are; you must be pleased.'

She threw him a dirty glare and said with a note of sarcasm, 'So you said in your speech.'

He'd felt all day as though he was under attack—from memories, from others' expectations, from his own stupid pride. He was sick of it, and his defensiveness surged back at her comment. 'You didn't like my speech?'

For a while she glared at him, and then the fight

seemed to leak out of her. 'No, it was a perfect speech. Funny, heartfelt, kind...just like you.'

He gave a disbelieving laugh. 'That's not how many people would describe me.'

'If you let them into your life they would.'

'Maybe I don't *want* to let them in.'

A small shrug was her only response. Her breasts moved against his shirt and he pulled her a little closer. He was unable to hold back a low groan at the feel of her body pushed against his.

Her voice was unsteady when she spoke. 'Are you enjoying the day?'

He could take no more.

In a low growl he answered, 'Not as much as last night.' His pulse went wild when he pulled back to see the heat in her eyes. 'Let's go somewhere private.'

Grace followed him into the villa, wondering if she was losing her mind. It was as though she was addicted to him and to what he could do to her body.

The villa was empty, and at the bottom of the stairs he took her hand. Upstairs, he pulled her down the corridor and into a dark room. In the moonlight she could see a bed in the far corner.

'Where are we?'

'My bedroom.'

'Is this a good idea?'

'Of course not, but you started it.'

And she had—last night, when she'd asked him to stay the night with her.

In the near darkness his eyes blistered with need, pinning her to the spot. Her body was already on high alert to him, tense with building desire. His head lowered even closer…his hand lightly touched against her neck. She gave an involuntary shiver and a small cry of frustration.

His mouth hovered over hers. 'You do crazy things to me… Do you realise just how beautiful, how sexy you look today?'

She shook her head, unable to speak as her body cried out for his mouth, for the pressure of his weight.

'Are you wearing that lingerie I unpacked?'

He spoke in a low, demanding whisper, his lips agonisingly close to hers, pulling every nerve in her body exquisitely tight.

She was incapable of doing anything other than giving a simple nod.

He gave a primal groan and his mouth landed heavily on hers. His hands clutched the sides of her head, so that he could deepen the kiss even more. His mouth was familiar, but wondrous, hot, seeking, relentless. Her hands ran down the hard thick muscle of his outer chest, over the indentations of his ribs.

She gasped when his hands dropped to work on the buttons of her dress.

She should pull away. But she didn't care. She wanted him. *Now*.

Her dress fell in a puddle to the floor and he stepped back. His eyes devoured her. A powerful jolt of desire rocked her body as she saw his hunger, his ravenous appreciation of her almost naked body. His head dipped to her breasts, his lips running along the curve of exposed flesh cupped by the bustier. His hands trailed along the delicate flesh of her inner legs. With a groan he twisted her around to face the wall and ran his hands over her bottom. The weight of his body pushed against her.

He dropped his head down to her ear. 'I can't get enough of you.'

A tremor went through her at his low tone and suddenly, for some unfathomable reason, she was unable to stop shivering.

Behind her, he stilled. And before she knew what was happening her dress was being pulled back up and he was closing the buttons.

Too confused to speak, she waited, her body a mess of desire and unstoppable tremors. Buttons finished, he twisted her back towards him. He said nothing, but ran a hand through his hair, frustration clear in his expression.

'What's wrong?'

His mouth was a tight grimace. 'We can't do this again. I was wrong to bring you here.'

Just like that, he was shutting her out again. She had no idea what he was really thinking. Why had he suddenly decided to push her away?

Humiliation clawed in her chest. 'Tell me the truth, Andreas. What's going on?'

He gave a frustrated sigh. 'The truth? The truth is we should be downstairs with the others…and I like you too much to hurt you again.'

Confusion built thick and fast in her chest until it ached. His words were bittersweet. She didn't know how to respond. All she knew was that a ball of rejection had been growing inside her all day. For the past little while it had shrunk, whilst they had danced and kissed, but now it was a giant boulder inside her, weighing her down, consuming her.

The last time she had felt so rejected had been when her mum had told her that there was no hope of them ever being a family again.

Feeling lonelier than she had in a long time, Grace walked away, terrified that she was about to start crying in front of him. Downstairs, before she walked back out to the terrace, she glanced backwards to see Andreas following her, his head bent as though in defeat.

Andreas stared out onto the dance floor, knowing he had two choices. He could either walk away from the celebrations now, in an attempt to try to pull his head together. Or he could forget about everything and embrace the wild momentum of the party.

It was an easy choice.

He walked onto the dance floor and was pulled into the dancing.

The pace and communal elation, the sheer goodwill, numbed him to the emptiness inside him. He joined Christos and their mutual male friends. Wasn't this camaraderie and friendship enough?

And then the floor cleared and he was pushed forward to perform the *zembekiko*. He resisted the pushes from the other men. It was a hot-blooded dance that demanded that all emotions, all weaknesses be expressed. To dance the *zembekiko*, the manly dance of improvisation, you had to be unafraid of expressing the true you...and right now he didn't know who he was.

The guests were crowding around the dance floor, some kneeling, others standing, all urging him forward. He still resisted. To do this dance right he would need to expose his feelings of pain, of unfulfilled dreams. The crowd would think of his failed marriage. He would think of the future that had been wiped out the moment he had opened the blackmail letter and seen those photos of his wife.

Sofia was moving through the crowds, pulling Grace behind her, and they dropped to the floor in front of all of the other guests.

The band began the low plaintive music. He glanced

towards Grace. She returned his gaze with eyes heavy with sadness.

He moved to the centre of the room. He would dance for her. It was the only way he could reveal what was in his soul.

Andreas stood in the middle of the dance floor, proud and dignified. He stared into the distance, his broad shoulders tense, his arms flexed. His tux jacket had long disappeared and his shirtsleeves were rolled up.

He started the dance with slow, deliberate movements, his leg bending in a fluid movement upwards so that his hand tapped his heel. He circled the dance floor, assured and noble, ignoring the crowd who were calling out his name and clapping to the beat of the music.

Grace clapped blindly, her heart beating heavily in her chest.

His movements intensified, growing ever quicker, and he dipped and twirled, lost to the rhythm of the music. His movements were strong, but they held sadness, loneliness. He was all alone out on the dance floor, with the world looking in.

Suddenly she wanted to go to him. Wanted to comfort him as his body stamped out a message of despair. But she sat there, her hands clenched, her heart aching, as he spun around, his hand whirling down to slap the floor. The crowd shouted out whoops of approval. Tears filled her eyes. Sofia reached for her hand. Together the best friends watched this powerful man dance with passion, his focus only on expressing the emotions within him. His aloneness.

The dance ended abruptly. Andreas walked straight off the dance floor towards Christos, his gaze never meeting hers. The crowd erupted into loud applause.

Beside her Sofia gave a soft chuckle and exhaled loudly, wiping her eyes. 'Wow, I feel worn out! That was incredibly moving. I've seen the *zembekiko* danced many times before, but never with such raw emotion.'

Grace could only nod, her throat much too tight to utter even a few meaningless words. She stared at Andreas's back as he stood silently amongst a group of friends, wanting to go to him, to place a hand on his arm, on his back. To be with him. To be part of his life. And in that moment she knew that she was in love with him.

She closed her eyes and winced. She couldn't be. He wasn't what she wanted. He didn't want a relationship, or romance in his life.

Beside her Sofia stood and held out her hand to Grace. As Grace stood, Sofia whispered, 'Are you okay?'

She could not burden Sofia with her problems. Anyway, what had happened between her and Andreas was too personal, too private. She doubted she would ever tell another person about what they'd shared. *Ever.* It was a secret she would hold in her heart for the rest of her life.

She forced herself to smile. 'I think it's just culture shock—weddings in England are so much more tame in comparison to this… I hadn't realised Greek weddings were so passionate.' She paused and gestured around her at the dancers back out on the floor, the large groups laughing and hugging, dancing with abandon as though there was no tomorrow. 'And so much fun.'

Sofia tugged her out onto the dance floor, where they joined Sofia's beaming dad. He twisted and twirled them around the floor and Grace tried to forget about the man standing in the crowd behind her, who had stolen her heart.

It was well after midnight when the band leader called Sofia and Christos to the stage. With the encouragement of the crowd Christos knelt down and helped Sofia step out of her shoes. He lifted them up to Sofia and together they inspected the soles.

Earlier that morning Grace had watched Sofia write the names of all the single woman attending the wedding onto the soles, as was tradition. Now it was time to reveal the names that were still visible on the soles—the women whose names still showed would be the next to marry.

Sitting with a group of Andreas's family, Grace watched, bemused, smiling at the hopeful girls and women eagerly waiting for their names to be called out. It seemed she wasn't the only romantic in the world.

A dart of pain shot into her heart and she glanced towards Andreas, who was seated at a table with a group of fellow young and beautiful Athenians. He was engrossed in conversation with another man, oblivious to her. The group seemed so effortlessly chic and full of vitality. Inadequacy crept along her bones. She touched a hand to her hair, fixed her dress, wishing she had taken the time to check her make-up.

Sofia gave a squeal that echoed into the microphone. It hooked everyone's attention and conversations died as they all focused on the stage.

Christos stepped closer to the microphone and spoke first in Greek and then in English. 'There's only one name remaining.' He chuckled when Sofia gave another squeal of excitement, and stepped back to allow her to speak.

Sofia scanned the terrace. When her gaze landed on her, Grace stared back, fearing her heart was about to give way. *Oh, please, would someone tell her that Sofia hadn't included her name. She didn't want attention... this number of eyes on her.*

Sofia held up the shoe. 'The only name remaining is… my bridesmaid, Grace!'

All two hundred guests turned to study her. Her heart leapt with joy for a few insane seconds, but then she pushed it away. Heat fired through her body. What was she supposed to do? Stand up and wave? Make a speech? Protest and say that it had to be a mistake…that she was the most unlikely woman to marry…that she had just fallen in love with a man who didn't want to be in a relationship, never mind marry?

She grimaced at Sofia, silently warning her best friend that she would get her back for this. Sofia responded with a defiant grin. Grace squirmed, and wished that people would stop staring in her direction. Her cheeks burnt brightly. Vulnerability swept through her and she wished she was anywhere but here. She forced herself to smile; to do otherwise would be churlish. She didn't dare peek in Andreas's direction.

His aunts made cooing noises of appreciation around the table, and his mother translated for her. They were saying that it would soon be Grace walking down the aisle, as hers was the only name remaining. His mother watched her curiously and she squirmed even more into her chair.

'That's very unlikely.'

His mother translated her response back to his aunts but it was greeted with frowns and shakes of their heads. His mother didn't need to translate their words contradicting her disbelief and she sat there, dumbfounded, wondering how she had ended up in this surreal mess.

The dancing resumed and she exhaled in relief when her five minutes of attention faded. She took a sip of her white wine and glanced towards Andreas. He was staring directly at her. His expression was impossible to pin down...thoughtful...frustrated...hacked off.

He needed to know that she gave no significance to the shoe tradition. That she thought it was a silly bit of fun.

She approached his table and threw her eyes to heaven. 'Well, *that* was embarrassing.'

'Was it?'

'Lord, yes...your aunts are predicting a wedding before Christmas.' She shrugged and laughed, but clearly Andreas wasn't finding it funny.

He gave her a brief, impersonal smile—the kind of smile that passed between strangers. Then he stood and gestured for her to sit on his chair. He introduced her to the others at the table and said, 'I need to go and speak to some of the other guests.'

He walked away.

Grace sat there, randomly smiling at the people around her, trying to pretend that she didn't feel as if she had just been punched in the chest...trying to convince herself that he hadn't just blown her off.

CHAPTER TEN

GRACE ADJUSTED HER sunglasses against the glare of the afternoon sun as it bounced off the body of the helicopter and forced herself to smile and wave enthusiastically, saying goodbye to Sofia and Christos. Her throat felt as raw as sandpaper and her eyes burnt with tears.

A sharp wind whipped around her as the helicopter blades picked up speed and she backed away, glad to have an excuse to move away from Andreas who had also come to the helipad to say goodbye to the honeymoon couple.

As soon as the helicopter was in the air she gave one final wave and walked away. Andreas caught up with her on the main terrace, now restored to its original state after yesterday's wedding reception. The terrace, as with the rest of the island, both so full of chatter and merriment yesterday, now felt empty and forlorn. All the guests had left over the course of the night and this morning. Only she and Andreas remained.

'Come and have some lunch.'

She turned at the brusque nature of his invitation. Was this the same man she had slept with, shared so much intimacy with, less than two days ago? Not trusting her own voice, she shook her head and went to follow the path back down to the workshops.

In an instant he was at her side and pulling her to a stop. He regarded her curiously. 'Are you okay?'

Even the brief touch of his fingers on her arm made her resolve to stay away from him waver dangerously. 'I'm fine…'

'You obviously aren't. What's the matter?'

'I'm just upset that Sofia's gone. Yesterday went too fast, and this morning…' Grace paused and willed herself not to blush. 'I didn't get to speak to her for more than five minutes.'

They both knew that the reason this had been the case was because the honeymoon couple had been holed up in their bedroom all morning.

Andreas looked unconvinced by her answer. But before he could ask any further questions she turned again for the workshops, where she had already spent the morning tidying away all the floral displays from yesterday, glad to have a reason to avoid Andreas.

Not once had he spoken to her again after the 'name on the sole' debacle last night. In fact he had barely even glanced in her direction.

She had gone to bed long before the party had ended, heart-sore and mentally shattered. At first she had fallen into an exhausted sleep, but had woken with a start to hear a female giggle as the dawn light had crept between the shutter slats. She hadn't dared move when she had heard Andreas's voice. *Was he with another woman?* The voices had quickly moved on and she had resisted the urge to peek out of her window. She was humiliated enough without adding the role of jealous lover to her repertoire.

Back at the workshop, she busied herself removing the peonies from the long length of garlands. She hesitated when Andreas appeared at the door, but forced herself not to react.

'Did you clear away all these flowers yourself?'

She glanced up at the astonished tone of his voice. He gestured to the peonies Grace had brought back to the workshop during the course of the morning, and then pointed down to the jetty.

'And the pots and lanterns? Who brought all of those back to the jetty?'

'I did.'

He glared at her incredulously. 'By yourself? What time did you start working this morning?'

'At seven.'

'The wedding didn't end until sunrise. What's the rush? I could have helped you if you had asked.'

She stared at him pointedly. 'I went to bed at two. I had plenty of sleep until I was woken by voices at dawn.'

His mouth twisted and he folded his arms on his chest.

Memories of last night felt like a red-hot poker sticking into her heart. Hurt swelled inside her. 'I've decided to leave Kasas today, so I needed to start the clean-up early. Ioannis says he can take me over to Naxos for the five o'clock ferry.'

For a moment he looked stunned, but then his eyes narrowed as though he didn't quite believe her. 'You're leaving today? Why?'

'Do you *really* need me to answer that, Andreas?'

He moved closer to the workbench and bent down to meet her eyes, his eyes boring into hers, his jaw working. 'I wouldn't ask unless I needed to.'

She turned to throw some peonies that were shedding their petals into a composting bin. Her chest ached; she could barely draw in enough breath. The composting bin was starting to fill up and she studied the dying peonies with regret. Their time of beauty was much too short.

She turned and faced him with her head held high, determined she would maintain her dignity. 'I'll be blunt. We slept together Friday night and you ignored me all day yesterday.'

'No. I didn't ignore you. I told you we had to be careful that people didn't get the wrong impression.'

'And what other people might believe is more important than hurting me?'

He gave a disbelieving shake of his head. 'I hurt you? How?'

'You shut me out completely.'

He threw his head back and stared down at her with that arrogant expression he sometimes used. 'You're exaggerating.'

His tone reminded her of her father's belittling attitude. Fire burnt through her veins. 'Really? You barely looked at me all day, never mind actually *talked* to me. I thought I meant a little more to you than that... And I deserve a little respect.'

'Maybe if you hadn't blurted out about knowing what my wedding present to Christos was we wouldn't have had my mother watching us like a hawk all day, wondering what was going on between us.'

Grace marched over and grabbed a cardboard box from the floor. At the bench she began to pack her floristry equipment into it. Without glancing up, she said angrily, 'It seems to me like you were looking for an excuse to push me away.'

'Why would I want to do that?'

She knew she should stop—that she was only hurting herself. But a force inside her—an emotional force she didn't fully understand—pushed her to lash out, even though the rational side of her yelled at her to stop, that she was going too far.

'I don't know. Maybe you regretted Friday night? Perhaps revised your opinion of me because I was the one who suggested it? Maybe, facing your family and friends, you suddenly realised that I was lacking? After all, I'm just a florist—which is pitiful compared to your career. And I certainly don't stack up against the women who were only too keen to grab your attention yesterday. Like the dark-haired woman in the white trouser suit. Was it *her* you were with this morning out on the terrace?'

Andreas moved forward and pushed the cardboard box away, so that nothing stood between them other than the table, which he leaned on in order to eyeball her at a closer range. His eyes were dark with fury.

'Yes, it was. Her name is Zeta and she's my cousin. Orestis's sister, in fact.'

'Oh.'

His lips twisted and he growled, 'And I do *not* regret Friday night. Do you?'

She could barely breathe. In a small whisper she admitted, 'No…'

'What do you want from me, Grace?'

She wanted to go back to what they'd had on Friday night, as they had lain in bed together. That emotional and physical connection. A connection so deep and right and secure. She wondered now if it had all been a dream. How could they have gone from that to this so quickly?

'I thought we were friends.'

He exhaled loudly in irritation. 'Friends don't sleep together.'

'Yes, they do…married couples are best friends to one another.'

He stared up towards the ceiling and rubbed a hand

down over his face. 'I forgot what a romantic you are. All of this was such a bad idea. What were we *thinking*?'

He sounded worn out. She should stop. But the force deep inside her was driving her on, wanting to test him. Wanting him to admit what was in his heart. That, yes, he *was* pushing her away. Closing himself off from her and everything that they'd shared.

'I don't know…what were *you* thinking? Was I just another conquest for playboy Andreas Petrakis?'

He walked away from her and stood at the door. His body was rigid, his hands balled at his sides.

It was a while before he turned and said coolly, 'I am not going to dignify that with a response. Why do I feel you're trying to back me into a corner, here? I have always been honest with you. I told you that I could never give you the type of relationship you wanted.'

He was right, in a way. She *was* trying to back him into a corner—but not to try to manipulate him into a relationship with her. No, what she wanted was him to tell her out loud that it was over, that the connection they had shared had been of no consequence to him. That without a backward glance he would walk away from her.

'I know… I just wish I hadn't fallen in love with you.'

He felt as though someone had punched him. Every fibre of muscle in his chest constricted painfully. His ears rang. Nothing made sense.

He looked away from the pain in her eyes. He had to get away before he did something stupid. Something he would regret for ever. Like taking her in his arms and making her promises he could never fulfil.

He sucked in some air. 'I wish you hadn't said that.'

She flinched, but said nothing.

His chest felt as if it was about to explode. He walked closer, his eyes never leaving hers. 'Why did you?'

Her eyes held his for a few moments. She was clearly bewildered by his question. And then they grew wide with shock. 'You think that I'm *lying*?'

'Are you?'

She stood stock-still, only her eyelids blinking, a thousand thoughts flashing in her violet eyes. Eventually he saw a grim determination take hold and she stared at him coldly. 'No, I wasn't lying. But if you can think that I'm capable of doing so, maybe I was wrong.' She paused, her hands gripping the side of the workbench. 'No, I'll rephrase that. Not *maybe*. I *was* wrong. I can't possibly be in love with a man who can think that I would lie about something so important.'

He didn't want her to be in love with him—and yet her words twisted in his gut. 'Your love seems pretty fickle if you can change your mind so rapidly.'

'Maybe you've just revealed your true self to me... Don't blame me for falling for your pretences.'

'What pretences?'

'That you trusted me, respected me enough to show me kindness and consideration. Yesterday just proved that you never truly did trust or respect me.'

'Oh, come on! That's utter rubbish. Yesterday I had responsibilities that needed my attention. I was the host and the best man. I had to speak to the other guests. I'm sorry if that made you feel neglected. Added to that, I had my family breathing down my neck. Why on earth are you blaming me for trying to protect you from years of my family wondering what happened between us and if anything will happen again? Do you honestly want that speculation? That pressure? You heard Christos. He wants us all to meet here in August for a family get-together. Christos sees you as *family* now, Grace.'

Her shoulders sagged. 'I know. And somehow we need to try and get on. Put these days behind us.'

Her voice now held sad resignation. Her anger he could handle; this pain was unbearable to witness.

She reached for some floristry wire and twisted it in her hands. 'We have to put some distance between us. That's why I must go today.'

'I do respect you…and I've always been honest with you.'

'But you're not even honest with *yourself*, Andreas. How can you possibly be honest with me? You've put a barrier up against the world because you were hurt before. You put on this mask of being hard-headed and cynical. But deep inside you are kind and lovely. Or at least I thought you were. Right now I don't know who you really are. Maybe even *you* don't know.'

'Are you suggesting that I *don't* learn from my past? From my mistakes? If you take that path, Grace, you'll be hurt time and time again. Maybe being cynical and tough is the only way to survive this world. Maybe those barriers will help me thrive. And are they any different to the romantic dreams you hold…? Aren't they a barrier in themselves? Will you ever meet your ideal man? Or will you realise we are all made with feet of clay?'

About to drop a spool of wire into the box, Grace paused and peered at him with a distracted expression, deep in thought. Any remaining fight in her seeped away.

'Maybe you're right.'

She went into the adjoining room, returned with a sweeping brush and began to clean the floor. Exasperated, he walked out of the workshop, his fear of ever really trusting a woman battling with the desire in his heart to turn around and take her in his arms and make this mess go away.

Later that afternoon Grace sat on the side of her bed and stared down at the blank page of her notebook. She wanted to write him a note but didn't know where to start. She didn't even know if it was the right thing to do. Maybe she should go and speak to him. But her heart plummeted to her feet even at the thought.

She was in love with him. And it was so wrong. She wasn't supposed to fall in love with a man who was cynical about love, who could shut her out with such ease, with such indifference as he had shown yesterday. Unfortunately she knew that there was another side to him—a man who was fun and attentive, kind-hearted and tender. A seductive, powerful man who made her melt just by looking at her.

But he didn't love her.

In truth she had no idea what he *did* feel for her. Friday night, when they had made love, she'd thought he felt the same strength of connection. In the moonlight he had lain with her, his eyes holding hers, filled with the same happiness and amazement that had flowed through her. She had thought his feelings for her were as deep and profound as hers for him.

How could she have got it so wrong? And why were a hundred different emotions chasing her down? One minute she was in shock, the next close to tears, the next wanting to yell at Andreas and demand to know what those tender words he had whispered to her in Greek when they made love had meant. Because to her they had sounded like declarations of love.

What was she going to do about August? Sofia was

moving to Athens with Christos next month, and had been so excited about inviting Grace to join them here on the island for holidays. Sofia would be hurt if Grace said no. Perhaps she should promise to come next year instead. But then would she just be putting off the inevitable? Would it be even harder to face Andreas next year?

A small voice in her head mocked her, goading her weak resolve, pointing out that she couldn't possibly bear not to see him for another year.

'Ioannis is waiting for you out on the terrace.'

Her head shot up to find Andreas standing at her bedroom doorway, his sombre expression only adding to his unfair good looks. He propped a hand against the door frame, his burnt-orange polo shirt riding up to expose an inch of muscled torso above the band of his faded jeans. Her pulse thundered even faster.

She shut her notebook and stood. 'I'm ready to go.'

His eyes moved to her suitcase and to the weekend bag beside the dressing table. He nodded, but didn't say anything.

She gripped the notebook. So much adrenaline was coursing through her body that despite her legs feeling weak and shaky she was possessed with a burning need to run. To run out of the room, to run away from the gut-wrenching desire to touch him again, to feel his lips on hers.

She placed the notebook and pen into her weekend case. 'I have already told Ioannis, but just so that you know, the florists from Naxos are coming tomorrow to take away the floral supplies, and they will reuse the peonies for a church.'

Again he nodded, but didn't say anything. She grabbed her suitcase and walked towards him. He didn't move. She forced herself to give him a tight smile, her eyes darting over his face quickly, instinctively knowing that to linger would spell trouble.

Tension crackled in the room. Even a few feet away from him she felt the tug of his body. Her eyes blinked rapidly as she tried to ignore the pull of memories: the weight of his body, the overwhelming power and strength of his hold.

In a low voice he said, 'I meant what I said last night. I do like you. A lot. And I never meant to hurt you.'

Distress coiled in her chest, in her throat, blocking off her airways. He went to place a hand on her arm but she stepped back. If he touched her she wouldn't leave here with a shred of self-respect intact.

Though she had never wanted more to run away, she forced herself to speak. 'Thank you for everything you did to make yesterday so special for Sofia.'

'Will you tell Sofia?'

How could he ask her that? Did he know her at *all*? 'Of course not.'

'Why not?'

Now she definitely wanted to yell at him. Yell at him that she wouldn't betray his trust, that she couldn't possibly reveal what they had shared, the awful soul-wrenching beauty of it, even to her best friend. Disappointment invaded every cell in her body.

'Why? Are you going to tell Christos?'

'Of course not…but women like to share these things.'

'Why *wouldn't* you tell Christos? Maybe then he would understand if we were tense when we're together. In fact, maybe we should tell them. And then they might do the sensible thing and keep us apart as much as possible.'

Grace was staring at him with wild eyes, a slash of anger on her cheeks. What was he *doing*? Why did he have such a burning need to prove that he couldn't trust her? It was like a monster inside him, consuming him. He hated himself for it. But it was out of control.

'I'm hoping the next time we meet the heat will be gone out of our relationship.'

She jerked back. The blood drained from her face. 'The heat?' She grabbed her suitcase and made for the door.

If he hadn't stepped out of the way he was certain she would have shoulder-charged him. As it was, the wheels of her suitcase rolled over his toes.

He cursed and ran after her. He yanked the suitcase out of her hand. 'I'll carry it downstairs for you.'

She grabbed it back. 'No. Just back off, Andreas. *I don't need you.*'

Her biting words felt like fingernails clawing into his heart. He followed her down the stairs.

She walked out to Ioannis on the terrace and called to him in a happy voice. Then she turned to him. He'd expected a scowl, but she gave him a bright smile. Only the tremble in her hand when she reached it out to him told of her pretence.

'Thank you…' For a moment she paused, as though uncertain as to how to continue. 'For your help with the flowers.' Affecting a breezy air, she added, 'I'll see you again in August. It will be lovely to spend some time with Sofia.' Her tone was cool and distant.

He needed to let go of her hand, yet he held on to it. He felt her trying to tug it away but his fingers clasped tighter. 'Enjoy your time in Crete.'

Tears shone in her eyes and her smile quivered for a moment. 'I can't wait.'

CHAPTER ELEVEN

FOUR DAYS LATER Grace sat at a waterfront bar on the horseshoe-shaped historic harbour of Chania city. Around her tourists ambled in the early-evening sun, soaking in the architecture and beauty of the Venetian harbour, stopping to inspect the menus at the vibrant restaurants or to step into the craft shops that lined the waterfront. Behind the harbour, on one of the criss-crossing narrow lanes, lay her hotel, one of many boutique hotels located in the restored town houses of the Venetian quarter.

Her floristry workshop had finished an hour earlier, and while part of her had wanted nothing more than to go back to her room and collapse onto her bed, she had forced herself instead to make the most of her time in this pretty city. To ignore how her heart bent in two every time a couple passed her.

This city seemed to do something to people. It was as if its romantic laid-back atmosphere insinuated itself into everyone's mood. Couples held hands and whispered intimacies to one another. Families sat at café tables and chatted for hours on end. And Grace was so lonely she felt physically ill with the pain tearing at her heart, the empty pit in her stomach.

But she could not let it defeat her. For the past few days she had stared that loneliness in the face, and as small chunks of realisation had formed into a larger under-standing she had slowly begun to make sense of her past. And why Andreas pushing her away had hurt so much.

A couple passed in front of the bar, bent into one an-other, laughing and teasing, hands tucked into each oth-er's sides as they tickled one another. She glanced away and grabbed her wine glass. She lifted it to her mouth but put it back down untouched. Blindly, she pulled out some coins from her purse and left them on the table.

On the cobbled street of the waterfront and in the side laneways she kept her head down, navigating the crowds, racing away from memories of how Andreas had pulled her back into bed that Saturday morning and held her hos-tage with teasing and tickles—a prelude that had quickly led to the most shattering of lovemaking.

Her hotel was tucked along a narrow lane in the middle of a stacked terrace of four-storey town houses. The re-ception was a simple hallway that daylight only touched early in the morning. In the evenings the owner—Ada, warm and generous—lit a row of candles that beckoned her guests in.

Grace climbed the wooden stairs to her bedroom on the top floor, hearing the now familiar sound of her own footsteps on the worn threads and smelling the scent of furniture polish. The higher she climbed the more sun-light penetrated the windows as the town house crept out of the hold of the neighbouring properties.

On the landing turn of the top floor her eyes met the sight of familiar polished tan shoes. She stumbled against the banister. Shoes she suspected were handmade. Es-pecially for him.

Her heart started. Was she seeing things in her sleep-deprived state?

She saw dark navy trousers, tanned hands gripped

tightly between bent legs as he sat on the top step of the
stairs, a pale blue shirt and then his broad shoulders, muscled neck, sharp jawline, the hint of an evening shadow.
Her eyes lingered on his mouth and she was assailed by
memories of intimate moments, but also afraid to move
them upwards. What would she find there?

She gripped the banister and peeked up. Her heart
stopped. Deep shadows filled his green-eyed gaze; lines
of tension crinkled the corners of his eyes.

'Hi.'

Such a simple word, but said gently and with a small
smile it conveyed so much more. But was that just wishful thinking on her part?

The butterflies in her stomach and her leaping heart
swooped together to form one mass of confusion in her
chest. She stumbled out a stunned, 'Hi...'

His smile slowly died and they stared at each other.
The air crackled with the tension of intense attraction
and hurt.

He rested his arms more heavily on his legs and leaned
towards her. 'How are you?'

She tried not to grimace and met his eyes. 'I'm okay.'

He studied her doubtfully and rolled his neck from
side to side, as though trying to rid it of tension. 'For the
past few days I've been trying to convince myself that
I was okay with you leaving. That you would never be
part of my life. But today I flew home to Kasas, after a
few days of business in Budapest, and realised just how
lonely the island was without you.'

Her heart leapt and hope fired through her. But then
reality jumped in and gave her a stern talking-to; he was
here because of the sexual attraction between them—
nothing more.

A slash of embarrassment coloured her cheeks. 'I'm not interested in a fling.'

His expression hardened. 'Neither am I.'

'So why are you here?'

He twisted around on the stairs and turned back to her holding the messiest bunch of hand-tied Coral Charm peonies she'd ever seen. He held them out to her.

She examined them dubiously. 'Where on earth did you get those from?' The florist who had put the bouquet together should hang her head in shame.

'I went to your floristry school. They told me you had already left. I wanted to bring you some flowers so I bought these there.'

'Somebody in the school created *that*?'

He looked indignant. 'No, *I* put it together—and I thought I did a pretty good job, considering.'

'Why?'

'Because I wanted to show you what you mean to me—if that means faffing around with flowers and embarrassing myself in front of a group of strangers who seemed to find it all very amusing, then so be it.'

Her head spun. This whole conversation was getting more unreal by the moment. 'How did you even know where I was? I didn't tell you the name of the school or what days I would be attending.'

'Sofia told me.'

He was the one who'd wanted to keep their relationship secret. Sofia would definitely suspect something now. 'Didn't she want to know why?'

'Yes, and I told her that I had messed up big-time and needed to find you to apologise.'

'But what about keeping our relationship private?'

'Finding you was more important.'

He spoke with such quiet intensity it left her unable

to draw breath, never mind find an adequate response. She took the bouquet from him and ran her finger and thumb along the fragile petals.

He gestured to the narrow confines of the stairs and the nearby bedroom doors. 'Can we talk somewhere more private? In your bedroom?'

Her budget had only allowed for a single room. Avoiding physical contact with him in such a small space would almost be impossible. She shuffled uncomfortably. 'It's a tiny room—nothing like the hotel rooms you would use. There isn't much space.'

His gaze narrowed. '*Aman!* Do you think I care about what size the room is when we have so much to talk about? Heaven help me, but if we have to have this conversation in a broom cupboard we will.'

Andreas stood and waited for Grace to pass him on the stairs. Beneath the top layer of the delicate fabric of her tea dress she wore a rose-pink slip, the borders covered in a deep pink lace... He was like a teenager around her—staring down her dress at the exposed slopes of her breasts, fantasising about undressing her.

With a tiny huff she flew past him. His hands itched to reach out and grab her. To feel her body against his again, to inhale her summertime scent, to feel her gentle breath on his skin.

She opened her hotel room door with an ancient key and went immediately to the balcony doors at the opposite side of the room and flung them open.

Yes, the room was small, but it was filled with her scent, and for a moment he couldn't move with the sensation that *this* was where he belonged. Surrounded by her scent, by the scattering of jewellery and make-up on the dressing table, the sight of her clothes in the wardrobe, her shoes below, a lone white and crimson bra hanging on a chair-back.

How was it possible that he adored every single item that belonged to her? Longed to hear when and why she had bought them? He wanted to bury himself in her, heart and soul. Know everything about her.

His head reeling, but more than ever determined to right the wrongs he had committed, he joined her out on the small balcony, which only had enough space for them both to stand.

'Great view.'

Beside him she leaned on the railing, her back arching. Her loose hair swung down to the sides of her face so that he was unable to see her. He longed to push it back, to be able to see those eyes, that full mouth again.

'You wanted to talk.'

Where would he start? His heart leapt wildly in his chest. Fear balled in his throat. He dragged in some air. Through the neighbouring rooftops the harbour was visible. His eyes ran along the harbour wall to the lighthouse at the end. His stomach rolled. He had to explain. But what if the damage he had done was irreparable?

'When my ex cheated on me it changed me.' He paused as humiliation raged through him.

Grace straightened beside him and studied him fleetingly. 'Because you loved her?'

Her quietly spoken question hit him hard in the gut. He gave an involuntary wince. 'The fact that you have to ask that question again tells me just how much I've messed up.'

She rested against the balcony railing and waited for him to continue, watching him warily.

'I wasn't in love with my ex. My feelings for her never came close to what I feel for you. The pain of my divorce was because of my pride. My father had warned me against marrying my ex and I ignored him.'

Unable to face her while saying what needed to be said, he turned and stared instead at the red clay rooftop of her hotel.

'A year later he was looking at photos of my wife, naked with another man. The paparazzi had sent the photos to him too, in a bid to blackmail him. It tore me apart to see his humiliation and disgust.' His stomach rolled again, and he clenched his hands into tight balls. 'We have our differences, but he didn't deserve that.'

On a soft exhalation, Grace said, 'How awful…' Her hand reached out for a moment to touch his arm, but then she pulled it back, crossing her arms on her chest instead. 'Did you talk about it?'

Boy, had they. He gave a bitter laugh. 'Well, he yelled at me non-stop for an hour, about the disgrace I'd brought to the family. And then all the old arguments resurfaced: how I had walked away from the family business, taken sides with my uncle.'

'But he couldn't blame you for your ex's behaviour?'

'He had warned me about her. After we argued my father and I didn't speak until Christos's engagement.'

'And that hurt you?'

More than he had ever imagined. 'Yes. He's stubborn and pig-headed, but in his own way he loves me. The day he passed that envelope of photos to me he seemed broken. Until he lashed out and spoke of the disgrace it had brought to the family name. My wife had cheated on me. So had a close friend. I felt like a failure. My pride had taken a huge dent. The only way I could cope was to throw myself into work and pretend that I didn't care.'

'What about your mum?'

'She was heartbroken and stuck in the middle, trying

to negotiate peace between us. Family is everything to her. She said nothing, but I could see with my own eyes her upset. I'd made it clear that I would never be in a relationship again. And of course that meant that I would never give her grandchildren.'

'Andreas, why are you telling me this?'

'My refusal to trust others again was because of shame and wounded pride. I refused point-blank to believe that I could ever trust in a woman again. I was convinced of it. It gave me safety and security, I would never be humiliated again. I would never endure the pain of being betrayed. And then *you* walked into my life. Loyal, generous, fun, giving. You. I hated how attracted I was to you. I tried to fight it. But I became more bewitched by you every time we were together.'

She stared at him, clearly confused, before walking back into the bedroom. There she sat on the side of the bed, its vibrant yellow bedspread a golden sun in the otherwise neutral bedroom with its white walls and recycled furniture painted in shades of white. She rubbed a hand along the nape of her neck, her head dipping so that he couldn't read her expression when he sat on the chair opposite.

She brought her hands together on her crossed knees and squeezed so tightly her unvarnished fingernails turned white. 'But you didn't trust me.'

'Before the wedding, as I got to know you, I *did*. It was the only reason I came to you on the eve of the wedding. I trusted in you. With me, with Sofia, with your family, you are supportive and strong. You don't play games. You don't try to manipulate others for your own ends. You're honest and loyal.'

Her hands flew up into the air. 'You didn't think that

on the day of the wedding. It was clear you didn't trust me then.'

He grimaced, but nodded his agreement. 'I'm not proud to admit that I panicked. Our night together, the morning after…it blew me away. It was different to anything I'd experienced before. I was falling for you and it scared me. You wanted love and romance. I couldn't give you either. At least I thought I couldn't.'

'I honestly didn't mention the wedding present deliberately. I'm so sorry that I did.'

'I know you didn't. You said the day after that I was looking for a reason to push you away. And you were right.'

Grace bowed her head and ran a hand over her face. Without seeing her expression, he knew he had hurt her again.

In a rush he continued. 'Not just because I saw that my mother suspected something was happening between us, but because the whole day was bringing back memories I had refused to think about since my divorce and I couldn't cope with them.'

'Why didn't you explain any of this to me?'

'Because I didn't even want to acknowledge it to myself. I just wanted my life to go back to the way it had been before. Comfortable and easy…never risking myself personally. I didn't want to fall in love and risk being hurt, being humiliated again, so I just jumped from date to date. And tried to convince myself that it was enough. But then I met you, and instantly I was falling for you, and it scared me to death.'

'Why were you so scared?'

'Because I once had a future mapped out for me. With a wife and children—my own family. And when that dream turned into a nightmare I decided that love and relationships were for fools. That it wasn't worth the risk of being humiliated, failing again.

'I thought I was against Christos marrying Sofia because they barely knew each other, but the reality was I hated having to face everything I'd lost—my dreams of having a loving marriage, children, a woman who would be my best friend.

'At the wedding Christos and Sofia's happiness mocked everything I had tried to convince myself didn't matter to me. And I was also trying to deal with the intensity of my feelings for you. I couldn't deal with how I was feeling: the pain of remembering a future that had been torn away from me, the memories of shame, my damn pride, and how I—a cynic—was falling in love with a woman who wanted to be swept off her feet.

'I just wanted it all to go away. It was all utter madness. I didn't know what to do, so I pushed you away. But for the past few days I've been the unhappiest I've ever been. You've changed me. You've made me look inside myself and realise just how lonely I was before you came along; how empty my life was with its endless work and partying. I'm tired of living a pretence.

'Seeing how courageous you are in helping your family, in what you said to me on Kasas before you left about not being honest with myself, I realised I needed to let go of my shame and humiliation. That I was letting my pride get in the way of ever loving a woman again.'

Though his stomach was churning, Andreas forced himself to admit it. 'The wedding was like an X-ray of everything that was wrong in my life, and because I didn't like what I saw I messed up. And I'm here to say I'm sorry.'

Andreas's apology had tumbled out in a rush of heartfelt words. It was going to be so hard to say no. Even now, with her heart shattering into smaller and smaller fragments of pain, because she knew the reality was that they could never be together, she wanted him with a desperate ache that was tearing her apart.

'You're not the only one who messed up on the wedding day. For the past few days I've been trying to understand why it hurt me so much that you were so distant, and I've realised it actually had very little to do with you.'

He leaned towards her, those broad shoulders tensing under the cotton of his shirt. 'What do you mean?'

She closed her eyes at the memory of her forehead resting on the solidity of his collarbone, the sensation of his chest rising and falling beneath her cheek. Regret and guilt washed over her.

'I was expecting too much from you. I should have seen that you were struggling and supported you, instead of constantly looking for signs that you were pushing me away. You had told me about the pain of your marriage, about your relationship with your father. I should have stepped back and given you the space you needed, but instead I was almost willing you to push me away because I knew it was inevitable. Deep down I wanted it to happen sooner rather than later... I was already in love with you, and I couldn't bear the thought of falling even more in love with you only for you to end it all.'

'Why was it inevitable?'

'Because you told me time and time again you didn't believe in love and relationships. And, let's face it, you aren't exactly the romance-loving guy I plan on marrying.'

'Maybe I could become a romantic?'

'I suppose miracles do happen.'

For a moment they shared a smile, and she wondered how she would manage to walk away from him.

'But there was another reason why I thought it was inevitable.' An awful, giddy light-headedness came over her and she had to pause to try and right the world, which had tilted for a moment. 'It happened with my mum.'

Her words came out in a bare whisper. It had taken every ounce of strength in her to force them out. It was as though her heart had been clinging to them, afraid it might shatter if she spoke them publically.

'And if she could do it so could you.'

Andreas moved forward in his seat so that their knees were touching. He laid a hand gently on her leg. Those green eyes held hers with a compassion so great she had to glance away in order to speak.

'All through my childhood it was me and my mum against my dad. To me, we were a team, protecting Matt and Lizzie against him. We never spoke about it, but we instinctively worked to take them out of his way when he was about to let loose about something. One year, when it was Lizzie's birthday, he came home at the end of her party and there was a huge argument about the house being a mess. What had been such a fun and happy summer's day instantly became dark and terrifying. He started shouting. He decided Lizzie should be taught a lesson for allowing her friends to mess up the house and lit a bonfire to throw her presents onto it. My mum rushed Lizzie and Matt upstairs, before they knew what was happening, and I hid as many presents as I could before locking myself in my room.'

'How old were you?'

'Eleven.'

'You were too young to be dealing with that.'

'Perhaps, but at the time it just felt like it was part of life—and I had my mum on my side. But then one day I came home from school and she had left us. I couldn't believe it. I was convinced my dad was lying. I thought he had hurt her. He wouldn't tell me where she had gone.

Eventually he told me out of spite, during an argument. She had moved home to Scotland. I spent a whole day travelling to see her. I wanted to make sure she was okay. Check when she was going to come home. But she wasn't ever going to come home. And when I begged her to allow Matt and Lizzie to come and live with her she said no.'

'Grace, I'm sorry.'

He edged a little closer and she took comfort from his nearness and the sincerity in his eyes.

'What did you do?'

'I buried my feelings and tried to forget everything about her—the relationship we'd had, that she even existed. I put all my time and energy into Matt and Lizzie. On the wedding day, because you were so distant, all the fear and pain of my mum walking out on me came rushing back and I couldn't cope. Added to that, I was missing Lizzie and Matt. And with Sofia getting married… I guess I just felt extra vulnerable because the people I love were moving on.'

She dragged in some air, tears of regret filming her eyes.

'I'm sorry I wasn't there for you more. I can understand now why you might have thought I was backing you into a corner.'

He came and sat beside her, his hand skimming against her cheek before tucking a strand of hair behind her ear. 'I promise I'll never leave you. *Ever.*'

What was the point in him saying that? They had no future.

'I want you in my life, Grace. I know I have been far from your ideal man, and that I haven't swept you off your feet, but I want to make up for that now. I want to take you on dates, visit Paris and Vienna with you, watch the Bolshoi Ballet, take you hiking in the Pindus Mountains.'

She could not help but smile. 'That sounds lovely, but I now know that I don't need any of that. Ever since my mum moved out I've built up this idea in my head that a great romance would fill the void she left. I thought that was what love was—grand declarations of love, the heady whirlwind of being swept off your feet, the surface romance that has no roots. Now I know it's something much more profound. It's trusting and respecting one another. It's about feeling secure and loved. In those hours before the wedding we *did* have that together, didn't we? In those hours I stopped feeling alone because of you. And that's all I want from love. Nothing else matters.'

For a moment he said nothing, but then a steely determination entered his eyes. 'Marry me.'

What? Where had that come from? He wasn't playing fair. This was close to torture.

'Marry you?'

'Why not? I don't want to lose you. And what better way can I prove to you that I trust you?'

How could he ask her to marry him when he didn't even love her?

'Andreas, I can't marry you just because you want children, a family of your own. I love you, but I'm not going to compromise. I want a man who's passionately in love with me.'

He regarded her with astonishment. 'Can't you see how in love I am with you?'

Her bottom lip wobbled. 'You *love* me?'

'Of *course* I do. I fell for you the moment Christos sent me that photo of you pulling a silly face. As crazy as it might sound, I looked into your eyes and fell in love with you even before I met you. I love everything about you. Your ambition…your loyalty. The fact that you love Kasas as much as I do. How kind-hearted you are. I've never been so attracted to a woman in my life. And it's killing me to think that I might spend the rest of my life without you, not able to see your smile, hear your voice, touch you. Make love to you. I need you in my life.'

Punch-drunk, she tried to buy time to let everything he said sink in by teasing him. 'Andreas Petrakis—is there a romantic soul lurking behind that tough armour you wear?'

'Yes, and if you agree to be with me I promise to show you every day of our lives how much I adore and cherish you.'

He was in love with her.

She tightened her fingers around his, her heart dancing in her chest. 'I'm sorry about not supporting you, doubting you. I love you so much, and I want to be with you for ever too, but for now I'd like us to spend time together, to have some fun without pressure or expectations. I want to have our first proper date, our first trip to the movies, our first summer together. To simply be girlfriend and boyfriend for a while. What do you think?'

With a single move he lifted her up and sat her on his lap. He began to nuzzle her neck and in an instant she was putty in his hands. Her eyes rolled as his lips moved along her skin, his mouth warm, his teeth playfully nipping.

In a low, sizzling voice he said beneath her ear, 'I'll go with it—for now. But I'm never going to let you go. I need you in my life.' And then, pulling back, those green eyes burning with love, he added, 'My helicopter is waiting at the airport; are you ready to come home to Kasas?'

She cradled his head in her arms and buried her nose in his hair, inhaling the lemon scent of his shampoo.

'What were the words you whispered to me when we made love?'

Love shone in his eyes when he lifted his head. '*Psi-himou*—my soul.' His hand cradled her cheek. 'Through your love and kindness you have freed me to believe in dreams again.'

Her mouth an endless smile, she kissed him.

EPILOGUE

THE PALE LATE-AFTERNOON winter sun warmed Grace as she sat on the step outside her hillside flower shop on Naxos, sketching in her notepad. A month after opening and she still got a thrill every morning when she arrived to open up. *Her shop.* She had done it. She was running her own wedding floral design business and florist. All financed by the money she had earned designing and supplying flowers for weddings throughout the islands during the past summer—thanks to the incredible publicity following Sofia's wedding.

In the large shop window she had placed an old bicycle, its yellow paint fading, the front wicker basket filled with an abundance of vivid orange and yellow gerberas. Overhead hung a mix of pale wooden hearts, crafted locally from driftwood. Behind the window display Grace had kept the shop simple: pale green walls, Andreas's uncle's ceramics positioned in the various nooks and crannies of what had once been a bakery, and simple teak wooden tables and counters for displaying the flowers... roses, calla and oriental lilies, alstroemerias, chrysanthemums, euphorbia, bear grass and bamboo spirals all sitting in a mismatch of flower containers.

The sound of footsteps on the cobblestones had her pausing as excitement tingled through her limbs.

It couldn't be. He wasn't supposed to be home until the end of the week.

She wanted to look up, but the fear of being disappointed had her instead staring blindly down at her sketches. But as the footsteps came nearer and nearer goosebumps erupted on her skin and she held her breath as a sixth sense battled with logic.

It's not him. It's only wishful thinking.

Polished black leather shoes came to a stop in front of her. *Andreas!* Her heart leapt into her throat.

'Yassou, psihimou.'

The widest, daftest grin broke on her mouth at the sound of his low greeting. Her eyes shot upwards, taking in the charcoal trousers, matching suit jacket and light grey shirt, open at the collar. A grin played on his lips, and his eyes held hers with a mischievous delight.

Pleasure and excitement sent waves of heat into her cheeks. 'You're home!'

'Yes, I'm home.'

Her heart tumbled. 'I thought you weren't coming until the end of the week?'

He sat beside her, and though her head spun at being so close to him, inhaling his distinctive addictive scent of spice and lemon, she forced herself not to touch him, enjoying these moments of teasing tension too much.

'I cut my visit to the Caribbean short.' With a playful frown he added, 'I had no choice but to do so as I missed you so much.'

She frowned too, pretending not to understand what he was talking about, when in truth the past five days without him had felt as though she had lost a part of herself. 'But we spoke at least three or four times a day.'

He shifted on the step, so that his knee touched against the cotton of her red trousers. He leaned in towards her.

'Yes, but I couldn't touch you, bury my mouth against your throat, run my hands over your body, make love to you.'

Her toes curled in pleasure at his low, sexy growl. For a moment she closed her eyes as the delicious desire which had been building inside her from the moment his helicopter had left Kasas last weekend almost made her fall apart there and then.

She cleared her throat. 'And I thought you were with me for my stimulating conversation…'

His hand enclosed her knee, and he gave it a squeeze before his thumb began to circle against the much too sensitive skin on the inside of her leg. She inhaled a ragged breath, and he gave a satisfied grin before he replied, 'I'm with you because every morning I wake smiling, knowing that you are in my life.'

Oh, God, she was about to cry.

'I missed you so much.'

'Not as much as I missed you.'

That wasn't possible.

She shook her head. 'I doubt that.'

His eyes challenged hers good-humouredly. 'Oh, really? I could barely concentrate in meetings… I lost my appetite. I couldn't stop talking to people about you or sleep at night, even though I slept with your nightdress.'

She tried not to giggle. 'You slept with my *nightdress*! Which one?'

'The dark raspberry one that drives me crazy every time you wear it.'

'The nightdress you bought for me in Vienna?'

'Yes. I stole it from the side of the bath before I left on Saturday morning.'

They both paused as they remembered how he had dragged a sleepy Grace into the shower with him that morning, peeling her nightdress from her body and tossing it away, and how quickly she had awoken to his touch.

She sat for a minute, drinking in the beauty of his face: the strength and pride of his high cheekbones and arrow-straight nose, that mouth that in an instant could make her forget everything but him, the wonder of his eyes that constantly held her in his grip.

'I love you so much, Andreas. It scares me a little. What if I ever lost you?'

He moved forward and his lips landed on her cheek. It was a light kiss, a tender one. And it was followed by a train of similar kisses of reassurance across her cheek to the shell of her ear. Grace arched her neck as her heart exploded and desire coiled in her belly. His breath was warm, his lips firm.

Against her ear, he whispered, 'I will always be at your side. I would lose everything I own, cut off my right arm, rather than ever be without you. You are part of me now. You give everything in my life meaning.'

She drew her head away and they stared into each other's eyes, making up for all those days apart, before she sought out his ear. She whispered with a smile, 'These past few months have been so magical... I never realised it would feel so incredible to be so loved, so supported, so encouraged. You give me a strength, a sense of security that allows me to take on the world with no fear.'

His arm circled her waist and they sat with her brow resting against his collarbone, neither talking, just drawing strength and pleasure from being together again, breathing as one.

Eventually he pulled back from her, a wariness growing in his eyes. 'I've invited my parents to stay with us for Christmas, along with Christos and Sofia.'

Amazed by the news of the invitation, Grace leaned even further back. 'You have?'

Andreas suddenly seemed nervous. He swallowed hard before he spoke. 'You have shown me the importance of family. And I want us to be surrounded by family. Our children will need their grandparents. Now that Christos and I have agreed to jointly take over the family firm it's time to build bridges for the future.'

Grace opened and closed her mouth a number of times as she tried to process everything he'd said. The invitation was a big step forward in Andreas's rebuilding of his relationship with his father. 'I'm so glad.'

'You must invite Matt and Lizzie to join us too.'

She couldn't think of anything better. 'That's a wonderful idea. Thank you.'

'It's your home too, Grace, there's no need to thank me. In fact I think we should make it official that it belongs to you.'

He moved off the step and knelt down before her. Grace gave a little gasp. His eyes met hers, gently teasing her with tender affection. From his trouser pocket he took out a navy velvet pouch. And from the pouch a solitaire diamond ring. He held it out to her. The huge stone sparkled brightly under the winter sun.

'The past six months have been incredible, but I want the whole world to know how much I love you. I want to introduce you to others as my wife. I want us to start a family. Will you marry me?'

Was this really happening? Was the man she loved with every cell of her body asking her to spend the rest of her life with him? *Did dreams like this actually come true?*

'Are you sure? Even after living with me for six months and knowing now how talkative I am?'

'I'm sure.'

'Even knowing how easily I cry?'

'It just makes me want to hold you in my arms all the more.'

'What about my addiction to the Bee Gees?'

He gave a sigh. 'You might have a point…there's only so much *Saturday Night Fever* a man can take.'

'And then there's my obsession with cheese and marmalade sandwiches.'

'Now, *that* could be a problem—and you haven't even mentioned how you like to steal my clothes.'

'Only a sweater every now and again—and anyway you can't talk…you stole my nightdress.'

He held his hands up and gave a guilty grin. 'True.'

Oh, Lord, when he smiled like that life just felt incredible.

His hand rested on her knee. 'I love you, Grace. I know I can be bad-humoured at times, when I'm under pressure, and that I prefer silence to music, that I'm not the best at talking about my feelings, and I've no interest in television programmes like you… But I'd happily sit and listen to you giggle at some sitcom for the rest of my life. Before you I had no future other than work and the endless pursuit of success. Now I can see a life of happiness and fulfilment with you, and hopefully with our own family.' With a playful wince he added, 'Now, can you please answer me before my knees give way?'

Grace sat dazed. In the past six months Andreas had proved time and time again what a passionate, tender and strong man he was. He supported her unconditionally in her business plans, told her endlessly how beautiful and clever she was. Looked at her as though she was the only woman in the world.

'Andreas Petrakis, I fell in love with you the moment

you passed me your jacket the first night we met. I knew that behind that scowl lay a man with a good heart. I love you so much. Of *course* I'll be your wife.'

Eyes aglow with happiness, Andreas stood and pulled her up and into his arms. First he placed the ring on her finger, and then he tilted her face up to him.

'I promise to honour and treasure you for ever.'

His kiss was deep and passionate, their bodies pressed hard together.

When he eventually pulled away, he tucked her loose hair behind her ear and said, 'Close the shop early tonight. We have a whole week of being apart to make up for.'

Grace nodded but, unable to bear the thought of being without him, dragged him into the shop with her. He held her close from behind, his hands wrapped around her waist, his mouth nuzzling her neck while she shut down the till. Together they pulled down the shutters, and in the near darkness, surrounded by the sweet, heavenly scent of flowers, they smiled into each other's eyes.

A single soul inhabiting two bodies.

* * * * *

MILLS & BOON

Cherish™

EXPERIENCE THE ULTIMATE RUSH OF FALLING IN LOVE

MILLS & BOON®

The Regency Collection – Part 1

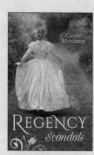
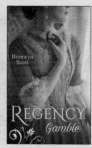

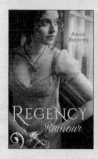
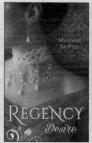

Let these roguish rakes sweep you off to the Regency period in part 1 of our collection!

Order yours at **www.millsandboon.co.uk/regency1**